I WITNESS

A MIKE PEABODY NOVEL

BY

PAT PATTERSON

I Witness, Pat Patterson
Published by P-Squared Press

ISBN: 9781965649152

Cover design by Pat Patterson
Interior design by atritex.com

Available in print from your local bookstore, online, or from the publisher.

Library of Congress Cataloging-in-Publication Data
Author's Last, First.
I Witness / Patterson, Pat 2nd ed.

Printed in the United States of America

PART I

CHAPTER ONE

Emergency Department
East Beach Regional Hospital
East Beach, North Carolina
Tuesday, January 23—01:58 AM (Eastern Standard Time—EST)

We have an old saying around here: Nothing good ever happens after 2:00 AM. When the rest of the world sleeps, madness creeps in, and the night people just seem to go crazy. Shootings, stabbings, wrecks, and explosions—I mean, if you can imagine it, we've probably seen it. For instance, just last week, some guy—strung out on crack—thought he could fly. He waited until the early morning hours and took a leap from his second-story balcony. Spoiler alert: He didn't make it.

Another guy, an addict named "Gas Can," drank a half gallon of 93 octane one night and came to us complaining of abdominal pain. We pumped his stomach and sent him home. An hour later, EMS brought him in with facial burns. Word was he went home and downed more gasoline. Only this time, someone struck a match, and flames shot out of his mouth. I mean, you see where this is going, right? Crazy.

I glanced at my watch—01:58 AM. Things were about to get interesting. But that's fine. I've been doing this job long enough to know how the night plays out. And, well, here's another old saying ...

Whatever.

The truth is, I take my job seriously—and I'm good at it. I've spent years honing my skills to become the best emergency physician I can be, and I believe I've reached that point. But at the end of the day, I'm still human—and humans get tired. I was running on empty, teetering on the edge of exhaustion, so I sat down at the nurse's station and let my eyes close for just a moment. Sleep swept over me almost instantly. I don't know how long I was out, but eventually, my head dropped, snapping me back awake.

I glanced around the emergency department (ED), hoping no one had noticed the drool dripping from the corner of my mouth. Someone had. My charge nurse, Mindy Collins, sat behind the counter laughing at me. "Peabody?" she teased. "You okay there, killer?"

I wanted to tell her to mind her own business, but I liked Mindy. There was something about her that put me at ease. She was fifty-something and aging, like me, and just a little too stout, but with the cute, freckled face of a girl half her age, and green eyes that sparkled like jewels. Her gray ponytail wagged when she moved, and she always smelled like a stick of fresh gum. I couldn't help but chuckle.

"I'm just tired," I said. "Long shift."

"This is the third shift in a row you've fallen asleep. What's going on?"

"I don't know, Mindy. I just can't seem to sleep anymore. Bad dreams."

"I'm sorry."

"I had a doozy last night. Found this trap door in the back of my gym, right?"

"A trap door?"

"Near that old meat locker where they used to store animal parts."

"Mike, I've never been to your gym, but it sounds pretty scary."

"Yeah, well, I opened it and looked in. Nothing down there. No doors, no windows, just this empty room."

Mindy cut me off with a raised hand. She answered a staff member's question about the patient in room fourteen and then nodded. "Sorry—go ahead."

"I climbed in, closed the hatch, and that's when it got weird. When I opened it again, everything was different."

"How's that?"

"I don't know, different. I was on top of a hill. The sky was black. There were no people around, no buildings or trees, just a bunch of rocks and a wooden pole sticking out of the ground."

"Weird. What'd you do?"

"Closed the hatch."

"That's it?"

"Well, I woke up."

Mindy chuckled, causing her bulbous chin to quiver. "Mike, have you ever heard of the butterfly effect?"

"No."

"I read a story in high school about a man who journeyed back in a time machine. He only had one rule—stay on the path, no matter what. Step off and the consequences could be catastrophic."

I nodded. "Science fiction."

"He tried to stay on the trail, but at some point, he stepped into the dirt, unknowingly crushing a caterpillar."

"A caterpillar?"

"A caterpillar that was meant to become a butterfly, which would have fed a small bird, which would have sustained a larger predator, and so on."

"It was just a dream, Mindy."

"Maybe. Just don't be surprised if things around you start to change."

I laughed. "Whatever."

"Anyway," she said, with a chuckle. "I think you should go back tonight for the surprise ending."

"I'm an ED doc. Nothing surprises me anymore."

My watch beeped twice—2:00 AM.

Here we go ...

I've been an emergency room physician for a long time, and at this point, not much rattles me. I figure I've seen just about everything. Like the time the kid swallowed the chemical lightstick, and we could see it glowing inside his stomach when we turned off the lights. Another guy wrecked his car about two blocks away and walked to us with a broken pelvis, broken leg, punctured lung, and closed head injury. He actually made it, too. I mean, you can't write this stuff. Violent trauma? Let's just say they don't call this place the knife-and-gun club for nothing. We had a stabbing victim last month, sitting up on the gurney talking to us, after having been stabbed thirty-four times. And don't even get me started on shootings. We see one just about every day, everything from BB-guns to 12-gauge shotguns.

So when the EMS radio crackled, and someone reported they were bringing in another gunshot wound, I didn't even blink. I've answered that call so many times I could do it in my sleep. Like I said, I've seen it all. So, again, I mean, *whatever.*

I drained my coffee cup and threw it into a bin. A quick self-assessment assured me I had everything I needed:

Stethoscope? Check.

Reflex hammer? Check.

Otoscope? Oops, just remembered, that needs batteries.

Cell phone, to text my wife for reassurance and a quick reality check, even at 2:00 in the morning? I patted my pants pocket. Check.

I walked up to the EMS console just as Mindy was grabbing the radio mic. She glanced sideways at me before keying it.

"Ready, Dr. Peabody?"

"Always ready, Mindy."

"Uh huh." Mindy keyed the mic. "Unit calling," she said, her voice calm and clear. "This is Regional. Please re-identify and go ahead."

"Okay, yeah, um, this is ... hang on, I'm, uh, sorry—"

Mindy glanced at me and frowned, her freckled face wrinkling. "Well, he sounds a little confused."

There was some muffled shouting over the radio before the caller came back. "Sorry, this is medic-seven."

Mindy and I know most of the paramedics and EMTs in East Beach, and we can usually recognize most of the voices over the radio, but neither of us knew this one. She looked at me and shrugged. I squinted and leaned a little closer to the console.

"Medic-seven," she said. "Go ahead."

"Our patient has been shot in the chest. Nine-millimeter, we think."

"We need a thoracic surgeon," Mindy announced to the room. "Someone, please call. Go ahead," she said, re-keying the mic.

"He's unconscious. They're working on him, um, hang on—" I heard the siren in the background change from *wail* to *yelp,* and then the radio went silent. When it returned, I heard the tail end of a deep-throated air horn blowing. "Sorry," the caller exclaimed. "Bad traffic tonight. Look, we, um, they ... they're working on him now."

"Who is this?" Mindy asked.

"Firefighter Davis, ma'am. East Beach Fire. I'm driving the ambulance in for Jim and Charlie."

"Okay, try to calm down. Give me what you know."

"Jim said to tell you, it's a red tag."

"Gender? Age?"

"Male. Twenty-three. One gunshot to the, uh, hang on—"

"Jeez," I murmured. "Somebody save me."

"Cut him some slack," Mindy said, scowling. "At least he's trying."

There was a brief pause, then the sound of muffled shouting—someone trying to pass along information from the back of the ambulance. The radio crackled again, and a new voice came through. This time, we recognized it.

"Sorry, Regional. This is Stockbridge—"

The sound of Jim's voice eased my worries, filling me with a renewed confidence in the patient's chances. Jim Stockbridge was one of the best paramedics I had ever worked with. He was also a friend.

"Adult male, unconscious, 9mm or .38, fifth intercostal space, left mid-clavicular, with no exit. He's shocky and pale with no radials, flat neck veins, breath sounds absent left. We decompressed with a ten-gauge dart. Intubating now."

Jim's report painted a clear mental image: a piece of lead embedded somewhere inside the victim. *Somewhere*—that was the problem. Bullets follow the path of least resistance, carving their own unpredictable route until they either exit the body or stop cold, having spent every last bit of energy. If it were me, I'd much rather the bullet kept moving—found an exit—and released that energy outside, not inside me.

"We're on University Drive," Jim continued. "E-T-A, three to four."

I've only been in the back of a moving ambulance once—a ride-along during med school with Pittsburgh EMS. One shift. That's all it took to know how brutal it can be. I still remember the chaos: the constant jolt of potholes, the way your body gets tossed around like cargo, and somehow, in the middle of all that, you're expected to perform delicate procedures, like starting intravenous lines (IVs), drawing up meds, and intubating difficult airways. It's like threading a needle during an earthquake.

If I closed my eyes, I think I could relive it now: The stench of diesel thick in the air, overhead lights flickering or burned out entirely. A medic strapped into the captain's chair, gripping a laryngoscope in one hand, an endotracheal tube in the other, fighting to intubate a dying patient as the rig bucks beneath him. I've intubated patients more times than I can count—but never while being flung around in the back of a moving truck. That takes a whole different level of skill.

Respect.

"Medic-seven," Mindy said. "We'll be waiting for you in resus one. Three minutes," she shouted, releasing the mic. "Has anyone called surgery yet?"

A bustle of activity broke out in the East Beach Regional Emergency Department. Nurses and techs ran about prepping for the incoming stretcher. I could see tension on their faces and a lot of weariness. It had been a long shift already, and they were tired.

So was I. I rubbed my eyes and glanced again at my watch—2:03.

See what I mean?

I figured I had about five minutes before the patient rolled in. EMS always underestimates their ETA. I headed down the hallway to the restroom—just enough time to regroup—a quick pit stop to use the facilities and splash some water on my face.

I caught a glimpse of myself in the mirror and instinctively recoiled. The man staring back looked worn thin. Bloodshot eyes, hair overdue for a buzz cut. He looked like someone running on caffeine and adrenaline—and he was. But I was the attending physician tonight, which meant the team would be looking at me. I had to look at least like I had it together.

I cupped my hands under the faucet, let the cold water shock me awake, and rubbed my eyes to shake off the fatigue. Checked my scrubs—clean enough. Tied my Reeboks a little tighter, like a runner at the starting block. Then I sat on the bench outside the trauma bay and mentally walked through my pre-game checklist:

Hemorrhage control, trauma triad (hypothermia, lactic acidosis, and coagulopathy), fluid ratios, etcetera, etcetera, etcetera. Check.

This is my routine. It grounds me—gets me in the right headspace for major trauma. I've done it the same way since Iraq. Running through the basics, step by step. It keeps me sharp. Focused. Helps me avoid missing something that could cost a life.

Like the time we almost lost a gunshot victim because no one noticed the .22 round that had entered through the corner of his eye. Tiny caliber, easy to miss. I might never have found it if the IV fluids hadn't started leaking out of his tear duct. That image never left me.

You learn fast in this job: The smallest detail can mean the difference between life and death. And the truth is, you never know what's about to come through that door.

My intern that night was a first-year resident on her very first shift, Dr. Jennifer Miller, a young woman with shoulder-length blonde hair, clear blue eyes, and a friendly demeanor. I'd hoped she'd be sharp, cool-headed, maybe even the kind who thrives under pressure. But after seven hours, she hadn't exactly inspired confidence. She seemed out of place in the emergency room. Eager, no doubt, and likely strong in the academic setting, but here, in the chaos and immediacy of real trauma care, she looked overwhelmed. Unsteady. Like someone still trying to find her footing in a world that doesn't wait for anyone to catch up.

At one point during the night, she stumbled out of a patient's room, hyperventilating, completely overtaken by panic. When she returned, her eyes were wide and unfocused, like she wasn't even sure where she was. I couldn't help but wonder why she'd chosen emergency medicine in the first place. It didn't make sense. Still, part of my job that night was clear: Help to shape her into a real emergency physician, whether I liked it or not.

And the truth is—I didn't. I hate teaching. I'm not good at it. I think I'd rather be locked in an UFC octagon with Bruce Lee than face another wide-eyed med-student who freezes at the sight of a bleeding patient and has no idea what to do next. And if I come across as an impatient physician with a god complex, it's because I probably am. But after everything I've seen and done, I think I've earned the right to be.

I sighed, crossed myself out of habit—something from my religious upbringing—and walked casually down the hall and into the trauma room, pleased to see that my entire team was assembled—four nurses, a respiratory therapist, my head nurse Mindy, and the new resident, Jennifer Miller.

Jennifer made eye contact with me and offered a sheepish smile. I winked at her and grunted. My eyes rolled. Like I said, I'm no teacher.

"Trauma surgeon, Mindy?"

Mindy nodded, causing her ponytail to wag. "He will be here ASAP."

"Get him here," I said. "And somebody get a number forty chest tube ready. If the paramedics are right, we'll need to drain his chest."

One of the nurses acknowledged.

I glanced at Jennifer and chuckled. I had to admit, she did look the part—spiffy white lab coat, new pair of Reeboks right out of the box, and she had all the right tools, too—stethoscope, reflex hammer, penlight, roll of tape. She even had a portable ultrasound unit sticking out of her jacket pocket.

Every good ED doc has their own favorite tools. I prefer to keep it simple—a Littmann Cardiology II stethoscope, a pair of trauma shears, and a roll of 2-inch medical tape. Mind you, I'm not a gear junkie, but truth be told, if I could, I would carry an X-ray machine in one pocket and a CT scanner in the other. I send out about three patients for pictures on an average night. But modern science has not progressed to the point of Star Trek medicine, yet, so I would just have to be satisfied with what I had. I patted my pockets.

Where's my reflex hammer?

Jennifer folded her arms tightly across her chest. I noticed her hands quivering, but that was nothing new. They'd been shaking for seven hours now. I walked across the room toward her, trying to display a bit of compassion, but I'm not quite sure she bought it. She glanced nervously at me, biting her lip.

"Dr. Miller," I said, smiling. "Are you ready?"

"I think so, sir. And remember, you can call me Jenny."

"This one's yours."

She nodded. She looked terrified.

"Jenny, it's just a trauma," I said. "You'll be all right."

"I know."

"Take a deep breath. I'll be right here if you need anything."

"Thank you."

So far, so good. My compassionate façade was working. I had already given up on her as an ED doc, but she didn't know that. She uncrossed her arms, took a deep breath, and then grabbed her reflex hammer and began to fiddle with it.

"And remember," I added. "You can call me Mike."

"Yes, sir."

I chuckled and sighed. *Dumb kid.*

I tried to remember what it was like to be brand new. Scared you might kill a patient, knowing everyone in the room was watching and judging your every move. Yeah, I remembered. *It's tough. Give it time.*

I heard the doors to the emergency department swing open down the hall. Muted voices filled the corridor. I stepped into position beside the trauma gurney and waited, picturing the scene outside the door, a scene I had witnessed a thousand times. There'd be three of them—someone pulling a bright yellow EMS stretcher with an IV hanging from a pole, another pushing the stretcher, sometimes doing the double-duty of squeezing an Ambu Bag to ventilate the patient, and another, a first responder—probably a firefighter—probably that scared young firefighter I had heard over the radio a few minutes before—walking alongside carrying heavy stuff like an oxygen cylinder and cardiac monitor. These were the guys and gals who did the heavy lifting, the hardest part of the job, bringing them to us, the ED docs, the more highly paid individuals who receive most of the credit for the lives saved.

I mean, I respect EMS. There have been many times I thought about dropping it all and joining them—getting out on the streets where the real action is, where you work alone in the dark and foul weather, dodging bullets, and watching your partner's back—but my mortgage payment always brought me back to reality. That and my new, canary yellow Dodge Challenger with the 6.2-liter high-output HEMI V8 parked outside in the physician's lot. That beast set me back a few paychecks.

Someone in the ED cleared her throat. I think it was Jenny. I came back to the present and glanced at her. A team of first responders was about to round the corner of Resus 1 with a red-tag trauma, her first trauma victim of the night—um, well, her career—a kid shot in the chest, one lung filling up with blood. Dr. Jennifer Miller was about to be tested.

CHAPTER TWO

Resuscitation Room-1
East Beach Regional ED
East Beach, North Carolina
Tuesday, January 23—03:21 AM (EST)

I've worked in emergency departments from Pittsburgh, PA, to Bagram Air Base in the Parwan Province of Afghanistan. Some of the places were quite pitiful, others state-of-the-art. There was this one makeshift clinic in a remote village, somewhere, that I wouldn't have taken my dog to. When I first arrived, they were reusing needles, they had no antiseptic supplies, and they were keeping their blood supply in unrefrigerated bins. On the other hand, there was a slick ED in San Diego with the best medical equipment available to man. That place even had artwork on the walls. I felt like I was working in a Beverly Hills mansion. Still, at the end of the day, I suppose, an ED's an ED, and it's only as good as the doctor who runs it.

We have a pretty simple setup here—fifteen bays for general emergency room patients, and the resuscitation bays for dealing specifically with trauma.

Trauma may be defined at the most basic level as any damage to human tissue. Even a splinter or a broken finger would qualify. But what I'm talking about here is major trauma, the life-threatening kinds of injuries where victims bleed out. Limbs are amputated. Bodies are burned. And chest cavities fill up with blood and air, preventing the lungs from expanding. You know, the kind of trauma that causes life to end.

We have three such resuscitation rooms here at Regional: Resus 1, Resus 2, and Resus 3.

These rooms are identical in size and shape, with a patient gurney in the middle of the room, and an abundance of stainless-steel cabinets, rolling carts, and poles for holding the various pieces of emergency equipment we use. A cardiac monitor-defibrillator stays atop a crash cart close to the gurney. The cart itself is filled with resuscitation meds and an assortment of IVs and equipment for airway management. Another cart contains various surgical and suturing supplies. A heated cabinet for IV fluids and blankets stands against one wall. A cooler for blood, plasma, and clotting factors stands against another.

Everything that might be needed for dealing with major traumatic injuries can be found in these rooms. I mean, they truly are state-of-the-art. But at the end of the day, my favorite feature of the resus rooms is their lighting. Lay a patient on the gurney, turn on the bank of overhead LED lights, and it's as if the sun were in the room. Bright, clean, crisp light floods my patients, but without overheating the room like the sauna back at Bagram.

I glanced around Resus 1 to make sure everyone was in place. They were. Mindy sat behind her laptop at the recorder's table, the other nurses stood around the gurney, and the respiratory therapist stood at the bed ready to take over the patient's airway. And of course, my new friend Dr. Miller was there. She still looked like a nervous schoolchild. I chuckled.

Whatever.

"Here we go," Mindy announced. "EMS is here."

Just then a large man in a yellow raincoat and a blue baseball cap entered the room, pulling a yellow stretcher heavy with patient and equipment. The word PARAMEDIC written across the back of his slicker gave away his identity as an East Beach medic, but his size and fruit-like shape (maybe pineapple) were new to me. As acting Medical Director for Carteret County, I tried my best to know all the personnel who worked under my license, but this one I did not know. I made a mental note to introduce myself.

A young firefighter squeezed through the door beside the stretcher next, wearing light brown turnout pants and a blue T-shirt advertising for the East Beach Fire Department. That T-shirt was soaked. His crew cut hair glistened under the harsh ED lights. He carried a cardiac monitor in one hand and an oxygen cylinder in the other. I chuckled at the eager expression on his face—a wide-eyed, deer-in-the-headlights, but I'm-going-to-get-this! kind of expression. I'd seen it many times before and knew from experience that he'd either get it fast or never at all. I was betting on him getting it fast. Most firefighters do.

Jim Stockbridge was the last team member to enter the room. He followed at the head of the stretcher, squeezing the football-shaped resuscitator bag attached to the plastic tube protruding from between the patient's teeth. I had always thought of Jim as a good-looking guy, the kind the ladies liked, with sharp hazel eyes and light brown hair, cut short but not too tight. He wore a navy-blue EMS uniform soaked by whatever rainstorm they had just endured, and a rolled-up towel around his neck to keep the rain from running down the back of his shirt.

Why Jim refused to wear a raincoat was a mystery to me. But then, Jim was like that—an enigma. Fearless and reckless, with the pragmatism of a NASA scientist and the adventurous spirit of a Navy SEAL. Jim's life had been hard and unkind, but he retained the kind of smile that puts people at ease. He's a man's kind of man, and I respected him for that. He winked at me. I winked back.

The tension on his face told me it had been a rough call. I'd pull him aside later to see how he was doing, but for now, his patient took priority. It was time to go to work.

The victim's eyes looked lifeless and dull. Not a good sign, for sure. An IV line dripped fluid into one arm, extending upward to a half-empty bag of saline. A white sheet covered his torso and legs, and a pair of brown feet protruded from beneath the fabric. A Vaseline-soaked bandage clung to the man's chest, indicating coverage of a sucking chest wound, the kind caused by a bullet to the ribcage. I had seen a dozen of those that month. Jenny Miller had not.

Time to teach.

"Dr. Peabody," Jim began, using my title as a show of professional respect. "This is the gunshot victim we called about. We found one entrance wound, nine-millimeter or thirty-eight, most likely. There's no breath sound at all down low, and lots of gurgling. I'm thinking hemo-pneumo."

A hemopneumothorax means the chest cavity is bleeding and the lung is collapsing. If Jim was right, we would need to insert a chest tube immediately.

"Very good," I said, turning to my new intern. "Jim Stockbridge, meet Jenny Miller. She'll be managing this patient. You can give her your report."

"Hi," Jim said with a smile. "This is my partner, Charlie."

Jenny nodded at Charlie and asked, "Where'd you find him?"

My head nodded. *Good question.*

Charlie nodded. "Strip club down on Angier Avenue. Some dude found him dancing with his girlfriend, left, and came back with a gun and shot him. We found him on the floor."

"Conscious or unconscious?"

Another good question.

"Fully alert on scene," Charlie responded. "Talking to me in full sentences, but he lost all that en route. Said he was having fun, dancing with a girl he'd just met when someone opened fire."

"Caliber?" Jenny continued.

He just told you, Dr. Miller. Listen.

"Nine-millimeter or thirty-eight," Charlie said, holding up his pinkie. I figured his finger was more representative of a .45 slug, but I got the point. "We just found one."

"How's compliance?"

Now, that was a good question. Good compliance means adequate chest rise without excessive effort when squeezing the bag-valve-mask device. Adequate oxygenation and ventilation of the lungs. And for me, just an overall feeling of success when you know that your technique is working, and well.

Jim squeezed the BVM (bag-valve-mask) and said, “Not good. It’s hard to bag.”

“We checked the tube just before rolling in,” Charlie added. “It’s still good.”

“Okay.” Jenny glanced at the tube. “What size is it? Eight-point-five?”

“Yep, and five cc in the cuff.”

Jenny glanced at the patient’s neck. “Trachea’s midline. Jugulars are flat. How much fluid has he had?”

Charlie tapped the IV bag and said, “Eight hundred. Still got no radials.”

Jenny nodded and tapped the drip chamber on the IV. “Wide open. Okay.” She pulled a black Littmann stethoscope from her pocket and said, “Let’s give him a listen.”

I nodded. My student, Jennifer Miller, MD (the anxious one who asked me to call her Jenny), seemed to be off to a good start this time. I felt proud, like a rooster must feel when its chicks first walk the barnyard. I couldn’t say the same about our patient, however. He looked like death. His skin had that sickly, pale tone that can only be seen in the presence of profound shock. He had lost a lot of blood, and if my suspicions were correct, most of it was inside his chest. Jenny placed her Littmann on the right side of the patient’s chest and said, “Go.”

Jim squeezed the bag.

Jenny nodded. “Not bad. Clear, if not a little heavy.” She moved her scope to the other side. “Again, please.”

Jim squeezed. This time, I saw Jenny wince. He squeezed it several more times before she glanced at me and said, “Heavy rhonchi on the left. No sound at all down low.”

It seemed like a good teaching moment. I nodded and said, “Why?”

“Massive hemothorax?”

“Are you asking me or telling me?”

"I'm telling you. Shot in the chest with flat neck veins, low blood pressure, and heavy rhonchi? That's a massive hemothorax."

"Good."

"Still, will you please check behind me?"

"Sure."

I placed my stethoscope on the patient's chest and moved it around to hear a more colorful version of what she had described. As advertised, our patient's left lung sounded messy. You could almost picture a bullet hole drilled straight through the middle of it, tearing tissues, lacerating bronchi and small arteries. Each squeeze of the ventilation bag produced a muffled, gurgling sound that can only be produced by a ruptured lung drowning in its own blood. I moved my stethoscope lower, only to hear silence. The victim's chest cavity was filling up with blood.

"Okay," I said, hanging my stethoscope around my neck and giving the medics a thumbs up. "The tube's in place. Nice work, guys. Jenny, hemothorax is right. Also, pneumo. What do you want to do?"

"Get him moved over?"

"Let's do it."

And with that, the trauma room erupted with activity. Charlie directed the move, as five pairs of hands grabbed the stretcher sheet and used it as a makeshift cot to slide the patient onto the ED bed.

Jenny looked confused. I leaned close to her and whispered, "Just try to remember your basics."

She nodded.

"And breathe."

Jenny inhaled deeply. "Yes, sir."

Jim's partner pulled the EMS stretcher out of the room. My respiratory therapist stepped to the patient's head and took over ventilation. Jim stepped aside and watched, waiting, as always, for an opportunity to assist.

Mindy issued a few commands, and people got busy. Someone spiked a second IV bag and hung it on the IV pole. Someone else attached a blood pressure cuff to the victim's arm and hit the start button. Another set of hands slapped a series of electrodes from the cardiac monitor on the patient's arms and legs. Jenny assessed breath sounds to ensure the endotracheal tube was still in place. She raised her thumb to indicate that it was. Then she began her trauma assessment, moving her gloved hands down the patient's body in a methodical way, searching for injuries, announcing her findings as she progressed.

"Scalp atraumatic. Face, eyes, ears, mouth ... clear and atraumatic. Neck—" she continued, moving down, and looking carefully at the patient's neck. "Trachea midline. Jugulars flat."

"Meaning?"

"Low blood pressure."

"Subcutaneous emphysema?"

"Oh—" Jenny gently walked her fingertips around the patient's neck to check for the Rice-Krispies-like sounds indicative of air beneath the skin. "Negative for emphysema."

"Good."

"Trachea intact," she said.

I watched intently, looking for reasons to take over, and finding none. *Good.*

In time, every ED doc develops a unique style of assessing trauma victims, using the basic skills learned in medical school and adapting them to suit their own purposes. And believe me, I've seen all kinds of approaches. The oddest I ever saw was a trauma surgeon who began at the feet using his hands, moving up to check the rectal tone next, and then continuing upward to sweep the entire body for signs of trauma. Most docs use a head-to-toe approach in the other direction—head, neck, chest, and abdomen, etcetera, until all vital areas are assessed. That's what Jenny did.

"So?" I said, when she had finished. "What's your conclusion?"

"No additional injuries. Limited reflexes. Hemorrhagic shock and hypoxia, secondary to hemopneumothorax."

"Textbook. Where's the bullet?

"No way of knowing without a scan."

"Correct. What would you like to do first?"

"Stabilize his pressure. Get some more fluids going."

"Which ones?"

"Um ..."

"Keep in mind, he's already had a liter of crystalloids."

"Whole blood?" Jenny said.

"Yes, and what else?"

Jenny hesitated. "Umm ..."

"How 'bout some plasma?"

"Oh, yeah. Plasma."

"Clotting factors? Come on, Jenny. Remember your damage control ratios."

"Uhm ..." The hand quivering resumed. She started to breathe rapidly, becoming disoriented and losing her concentration. "I, um, uhm," she stammered.

"Dr. Miller?"

"Umm ..."

"Dr. Miller," I repeated. "This is not rocket science. Take a deep breath and calm down."

Jenny turned and stared at me like a deer frozen in the headlights of an oncoming car.

I turned to Mindy and said, "Let's get one unit each of plasma, packed RBCs, and platelets. Where's the surgeon?"

"Prepping now," Mindy said.

"Also, let's get another liter of IV fluid going. Let's move, folks. I'd like to have him out of here and in surgery within ten minutes. Dr. Miller," I said, perturbed by her panicky, frightened demeanor. "He's filling up with blood. What would you like to do?"

"Perform a thoracostomy to remove the blood?"

"Are you asking me or telling me?"

"I'm telling you!" she barked. Then she winced and hung her head as if to apologize, and added. "I think."

"You think?"

"I know."

"What size?"

"What size tube?" Jenny frowned. I noticed tears forming in her eyes. It looked like she might fall apart at any moment. "I think it's, um, forty French?"

I realized we were out of time. Our patient was dying of hemorrhagic shock and hypoxia. He needed quick decisions and appropriate treatment, not an uncertain intern learning to practice medicine. It was time to take over, but I decided to offer her one last chance. "Listen, forty French is correct. Come up here. Let's do this tube together. We've got this."

Jenny shook her head and backed up a step. "I, I've never … I've never done this on a live patient."

"Then it's time you did one, right?"

"No—"

Now Jenny was wringing her quivering hands. She displayed a deep anxiety that removed any lingering confidence I might have had in her ability to perform under pressure.

"Dr. Peabody," she said, "if you don't mind, I'd really like to watch this one."

"You want to watch?"

"Yes, if you don't mind."

"Suit yourself." I was done with diplomacy. I glanced over my shoulder at Jim and said, "You want it?"

Jim's eyes widened. "Me?"

I shrugged. "Why not?"

"Sure!"

"Scrub up and grab a pair of sterile gloves."

Jim walked to the sink.

I glanced at Jenny and said, "Last chance."

Jenny looked around nervously and shook her head.

I sighed and pushed a button on my watch to activate the stopwatch feature. Then I opened the surgical kit on the stainless-steel tray beside the bed and withdrew a Betadine swab. I prepped the surgical insertion site just below the armpit, scrubbing it in widening concentric circles until an adequate sterile field had been formed, and then I took the scalpel and placed it against the skin.

The flesh spread apart like butter beneath a warm blade. A neat, ten-centimeter incision between the fifth and sixth ribs produced a hiss of bloody spray. I inserted two fingers to enlarge the hole and then withdrew them and said, "Okay, partner, she's all yours."

Without hesitation, Jim grabbed the 40-French chest tube from the stainless-steel cart beside the bed and pushed it inside the victim's chest cavity. I watched closely, verbally guiding his moves past the lung, until the tube had been inserted to the appropriate depth. "Okay," I said. "That's far enough. Now attach the other end of the tube to the Pleur-evac and turn it on."

Jim attached the distal end of the chest tube to the vacuum unit at the foot of the bed and pushed the ON switch. Physics did the rest. The machine sucked and slurped until 800 cc of bright red blood had flooded the reservoir. Jim's eyes widened. "Holy smokes," he murmured. "He was full."

I saw twice that much come out of a trauma patient's chest one time. That guy had been crushed by a horse during a rodeo event. I chuckled and glanced at my new toy, a Casio Tactical Rangeman G-Shock Solar Atomic watch. I pushed the stop button and announced, "Two minutes, forty-three seconds. Not bad."

"You timed that?" Jim exclaimed.

"Start to finish."

"Why?"

"I time everything. Didn't you see *The Equalizer?*"

Jim chuckled.

I checked the patient's radial pulse. This time, he had one. "How's compliance now?" I said, glancing at the respiratory therapist. She nodded and said, "Much better." I picked up a suturing needle and stitched the hose in place, closing the opening at the same time.

Jim pulled off his gloves and thanked me for allowing him to help. "Just don't let him die," he said, walking from the room.

"Not in my ER."

I glanced at my resident. Jenny looked stupefied. "You, you let that paramedic do the tube?"

"Why not? You wouldn't do it."

"But isn't that, um, against some hospital rule?"

"Probably."

"But you did it anyway?"

"Check his wrist. He's got a pulse now, doesn't he?"

Jenny touched the patient's wrist, looked at me, and nodded. "Is that good, or bad?"

"It means we restored his pressure."

"We?"

Jenny's eyes welled up. Then, without warning, she began to sob. And then to my utter amazement, she began to hyperventilate and ran from the room.

I glanced at Mindy and said, "Get this patient to surgery as soon as possible."

Mindy acknowledged with a curt, "Aye, sir!"

I walked out just in time to see Jenny round the corner down the hall. I decided it might be best to just leave her alone. I stuck my head back into the trauma room to make sure everything was set. Mindy assured me that the critical work was done and that they would take it from here, but she refused to make eye contact with me, and that concerned me.

"Mindy?"

"Yes? Doctor?"

Mindy rarely called me that. It was Mike, Dr. Peabody, or even, sometimes, Killer, but never Doctor. I approached her and saw her eyes roll. I sighed for the umpteenth time that night and said, "I did it again, didn't I?"

"You always do it again."

"Mindy, she refused to do that chest tube."

"Yeah? And then you gave it to your friend, Jim. You're supposed to be teaching interns, not paramedics. Have you forgotten this is a teaching hospital?"

"I tried my best to have her do it. She—"

"You embarrassed her, Mike. You embarrassed me. You embarrassed every woman in the room."

"I didn't mean—"

"Yes, you did. Look, I know you're in charge here, and I'm just one of your nurses, and I don't mean any disrespect, but someone needs to tell you how you can come across. Mike, you're arrogant. You think you're special. You may look like Denzel and be built like The Rock, but you're not a celebrity."

"Mindy."

"No, listen. You're a great doctor, and I believe you're a good man. But you are only that, a man. You are not God."

Mindy left me speechless and returned to her notes. The other nurses wouldn't look at me.

I walked out and down the hall to the physician's lounge, feeling somewhere just north of depressed. Not about patient care. I mean, I had just saved a trauma victim from drowning in his own blood, and that was good. He was on his way to surgery now and soon would be sitting up, watching TV, and eating hospital food. And there really was no rule about allowing a paramedic to perform a skill outside of his scope of practice, under my supervision, after all, I'm the medical director for the whole county, so I wasn't too concerned about breaking some silly hospital rule. But I was concerned about Mindy's comment. I mean, I know I'm not God.

But still, somebody's gotta be!

I felt the need to hit something. The sound of footsteps stopped me from punching a hole in the wall. A couple of nurses walked past me with raised eyebrows. I nodded at them and then waited until they had passed before whispering, "Peabody, are you insane? What is wrong with you?"

CHAPTER THREE

Emergency Department
East Beach Regional Hospital
East Beach, North Carolina
Tuesday, January 23—03:59 AM (EST)

I drink my coffee black, like me. Hot, strong, and black. I used to add one of those sweet and creamy dairy blends, but when my A1C numbers started rising, I figured it was time to stop adding sugary junk. It's also when I first realized how good coffee actually tastes. After that, there was no going back. So, my eighth cup of the night required no prep. I poured it into a cup and flopped my tired, frustrated frame into a chair at one of the round tables in the staff lounge, feeling like a zombie from The Walking Dead series. I glanced at my watch—3:59 AM. Three hours to go. I hoped those hours would be quiet.

I sipped my black coffee in silence, thinking of the near miss with our last patient. He could have easily died right there on the table from blood loss and asphyxiation, acidosis, hypothermia, and all the other things that routinely kill trauma victims. And running a code and watching my patient drift into the downward spiral of death was not my idea of a good Tuesday morning. But, we saved him. So there.

I closed my eyes and, for the next few moments, considered the sweetness of simply passing out and never waking up. After all, there were plenty of other ED docs at East Beach Regional who could take my place. I mean, for every Jennifer Miller out there who had little chance of becoming a successful physician, there were at least nine good residents ready to hit the rotation. So, the world could do without Michael J. Peabody, MD. Right?

No, this hospital needs you, I told myself. You're a good doctor. You've saved hundreds of lives. Who knows? Maybe thousands. So, arrogant? Well, why not? I think I've earned a little arrogance.

But, when you get right down to it, I couldn't help but wonder what good I'd really done in the world. I mean, I save lives. Big deal. Most of the people I've saved lately have been either drug dealers or gang members, so what's the use? I patch 'em up, and they go back out and poison or shoot someone else? I mean, if hell exists, and I really hope it doesn't, that's where most of them will end up, right?

And what about me? Where am I going? And if I hung up my stethoscope today, would anyone care? My patients? My colleagues? Doubtful. Most of them hate me. I don't know. But one thing I do know for certain is that an intern named Jenny Miller wouldn't miss me if I suddenly met my fate. I must have scared that poor girl to death.

Bored, I glanced at the magazines spread out across the table—Popular Mechanics, People, Guns & Ammo (good one, already read it). I tossed it aside and picked up a copy of Scientific American. The cover featured a close-up image of a butterfly. The title read: The Butterfly Effect, Small Change, and the Unpredictable Future. I chuckled at the title. Mindy and I had just discussed that. The first line of the article intrigued me, something about chaotic systems and small changes that cause dramatic, unpredictable shifts in future events.

"Good grief," I murmured. "What are the odds?"

I tossed the magazine aside and picked up the next one, a copy of National Geographic published in June 1980.

1980? Seriously?

In its day, Nat Geo was considered the finest photojournalism magazine in the world, a beautifully printed and written publication featuring stories that took the reader into the forests, jungles, and oceans of the Earth, and sometimes even deep into the imagination to places you didn't even know existed. I held a profound respect for the people and purposes that made that happen, and for the famous, yellow-bordered magazine that they produced. But 1980?

I picked up the decades-old magazine and stared at the cover, intrigued by the photograph of a one-year-old child captured on film with a brown orangutan hanging on his back. Neither creature looked particularly happy about the situation, but both looked to feel quite at home in the scene, as if kneeling together in a green bowl of soapy water was an everyday occurrence. Where was the photograph taken? I wondered. Africa? I scanned the article quickly and continued flipping through the pages, nonchalantly pausing to glance at the photographs, before stopping to stare at a strange image.

"What is that?" I murmured. "A face?"

The image revealed a rendering of what I assumed to be a human face constructed of carefully aligned cardboard pieces stacked one atop the other like a sort of vertical, 3-D puzzle. With a little imagination, I made out a nose, a chin, two eyes, cheeks, and a forehead. A face. But whose face? And why had someone chosen to produce a jagged, cardboard model of it? Curious, I glanced at the story title:

The mystery of the Shroud.
Written by: Kenneth Weaver, Senior Editor

The Shroud? The Shroud of Turin. I had heard of that. In fact, I recalled a documentary I had seen once explaining what the Shroud was, an ancient cloth believed to be the burial cloth of Jesus Christ. But, no, as I recalled, a carbon-14 dating test had determined the age of the cloth to be around five hundred years, not 2,000. So, they had deduced in that documentary that it was, in fact, a fake.

A fake. I stared at the image and laughed. *Just like God.*

"Religious people," I murmured. "Get real."

My staunch atheism reminded me that there is no God, and that to believe in him reveals weakness and blind acceptance. What kind of fool believes in something he can't see? Still, as I stared at the cardboard rendering, I couldn't help but wonder about it. I started reading. I mean, call me naïve, but if the senior editor of a highly respected magazine like National Geographic was writing a story about some piece of cloth, it must have some credibility. Right?

No way.

My antagonistic scientific mind began to whir as I read:

The Shroud is an ancient burial cloth, measuring 14' 3" long by 3' 7" wide, bearing the ghostly image of a man believed to be the crucified Jesus Christ.

Ghostly image? Of Jesus?

"Let's see."

I flipped the page and saw a photo of the face of the Shroud. The same face, I assumed, used to create the cardboard model that had first piqued my interest. It looked ghostly all right, and not at all what I would have expected Jesus to look like. I turned the page back and continued reading. The author spoke of details in the Shroud consistent with crucifixions performed in ancient Rome. Of eight-inch, iron spikes and Roman whips. Of a space-age computer, called a VP-8 Image Analyzer, used to detect 3-D qualities found in the Shroud, something never duplicated in another piece of artwork or two-dimensional graphics.

"Hmm, now that is interesting."

I had become so lost in the article that the sound of someone standing nearby clearing his throat almost didn't faze me. But when it sounded a second time, I looked up, surprised to see my friend Jim Stockbridge standing in the doorway.

"Hey," I said. "What's up?"

"Mike? Have you got a minute?"

Jim held a Panasonic Toughbook in one hand and a Styrofoam cup in the other. His stethoscope still hung around his neck as it had when he first arrived in Resus 1. I could tell he had taken the time to wash his face and hands and tuck in his shirt before calling back in-service.

"Of course. Come on in. I'm reading an interesting article." I put my finger between the pages and closed the magazine. "I'd like to get your take on it."

Jim walked in and sat down. "What's it about?"

"I don't know. Some piece of cloth. Oh, you did great on that last call, by the way. That guy could've died in your truck."

"Well, prayer works."

"That and a good chest decompression." I nodded at the coffee maker. "Want a refill?"

Jim tossed his cup in the trash. "I've only got a minute. What you did in there, I just wanted to say thanks."

"What, the chest tube? Forget it."

"No, most of those guys would never do anything like that."

"Most of them live in fear."

"That new doctor. What was her problem?"

"Jenny? She's scared. I don't have much hope for her."

Jim glanced at the magazine. "Can I see it?"

I handed it to him. "It's about something called the Shroud of Turin."

"Oh, the Shroud. Cool."

"You know about it?"

"Only that some think it's the burial cloth of Christ."

"You believe that?"

"Maybe, I don't know. But a lot of people think it is." Jim leafed through the magazine and stopped at a strange photo of a computer image. "Look at this. A 3-D computer image of the face. Cool."

I had to admit, I felt intrigued as I studied the image. I'd never seen anything like it. A series of green horizontal scans on an otherwise black screen produced an eerily accurate, if not noisy, rendering of a man's face in bas relief. The image appeared to rise out of the darkness of the screen like a phantom.

"Weird."

"They used this computer—" Jim tapped the screen. "It's called the VP-8 image analyzer. Designed by a guy for NASA to send back elevation images of the surface of Mars. So, apparently, this guy Weaver believes the Shroud contains three-dimensional information never found in any other piece of flat artwork. Huh."

"How's that possible?"

"I think that's the point. It's not. Here's more," he said, continuing to read. "The cloth bears the recognizable image of a man severely beaten and flogged, with wounds in the hands and feet suggestive of Roman crucifixion. It also says here they found human hemoglobin in the threads of the cloth."

I reached for the magazine. "Let me see that."

"Hang on." Jim unfolded a triple-paged photographic image in the middle of the article. What I saw mesmerized me. The cloth lay stretched out like a banner, bearing two separate images of the same man, one revealing his front side, the other his back, with his face and the back of his head in the center, as if the cloth had been folded over him as he lay upon it. "Check it out."

The cloth looked clean and well preserved, off-white in color, the image a subtle sepia. The victim, naked, with his hands folded over his groin, looked to have been brutally beaten and whipped. Blood flowed from what looked like small wounds in his wrists and feet, and there was a stab wound in his side. Upon closer inspection, I noticed the nose looked to have been broken. One cheek looked swollen. Some hair had been yanked from the beard.

I mean, I've seen my share of trauma, and the lengths to which men will go to punish one another, but I had difficulty wrapping my head around the degree of suffering that this man would have endured.

"You can almost see it," I whispered. "What they did to him." Jim handed me the magazine. I flipped the page and began to read aloud: "The scourge marks precisely match the size and outline of the one-and-one-half inch dumbbell-shaped lead balls discovered on a cat-of-nine-tails excavated at an archeological dig in Rome."

Jim's eyebrows rose. "They beat him to death. Then they crucified him."

"But why? I mean, what did he do to deserve that?"

"That's the whole point of the Gospels, Mike. Jesus claimed to be the son of God. They killed him for it. But he did it willingly. It was all part of God's plan to pay for our sins."

"You sound like you believe that."

"I do, Mike."

"Look. Not to trample on your religion, or anything, but I don't believe in some creator called God, and I definitely don't believe in sin."

"So, you're an atheist?"

"Well, I suppose. I believe there's some higher power out there, I just can't accept any form of organized religion. I mean, look at all the terrible atrocities performed in the name of religion. And I know there was a man named Jesus who lived a good life and healed people. And he may have had twelve disciples and even died on a cross. But, so what? From what I understand, lots of people died by crucifixion back then. But this idea that he died for my sins? That's where Christianity loses me. It's easier for me not to believe anything. But who knows? Tell you what, though," I said. "If you can show me the proof, maybe I'll believe."

"You want proof?"

Just then, Jim's radio chirped, and a dry-sounding voice came over the air. Jim adjusted the radio volume down slightly and listened to an EMS call dispatched to Medic-7. His unit. He wrote down the address on a small notepad, called en route, and then pointed at me and said, "To be continued. See you at the gym this morning?"

I shrugged. "It's my gym."

Jim walked out, leaving me alone with the magazine and my new curiosity about a piece of linen called the Shroud of Turin. I flipped to the last page of the article, where a photo of a large white chapel filled three-quarters of the page. Hundreds of people stood on the steps at the main entrance, as if waiting to enter. The caption beneath the photo read, *Cathedral of San Giovanni Battista—Home of the Shroud.* I tapped the photo with my finger. "The building where they keep it."

I thought about my upcoming trip to Florence, a trauma conference to coincide with Easter. I had read something about the keynote speaker's address having to do with, of all things, death by crucifixion. Would he be talking about the Shroud? What are the odds? Still, if Turin is close to Florence, maybe I should take a train and see it.

This is becoming weird.

I glanced one last time at the strange burial cloth and then flipped over the magazine to see if there was an address sticker affixed to it. There wasn't one. Who'd care if I borrowed it then, right?

I tucked the magazine under my arm and carried it down the hall to the men's locker room. After securing it in my locker with my day clothes, I went back to the emergency department and checked in at the nurses' station. Nothing brewing. Our gunshot victim had been transported to surgery, and all other patients were stable. I looked around and saw no sign of Jenny Miller. I glanced at my watch—4:28 AM. Two hours to go.

Awesome.

CHAPTER FOUR

Emergency Department
East Beach Regional Hospital
East Beach, North Carolina
Tuesday, January 23—07:12 AM (EST)

The rest of the shift proved to be tricky. I had to work solo since Dr. Miller had run out and never returned. I work better alone, though, so it worked out well because every case before 7:00 AM turned out to be a challenge.

My next patient came in with a blood pressure so high it could not be recorded. That meant over 300 mmHg systolic, which in most cases means a head bleed or an aortic aneurysm. That one was a real mess. Her chief complaint was a splitting headache, of course, but she also suffered from nausea, dizziness, and ringing in her ears. Bad symptoms, to say the least, but from my perspective, the worst indicator was the blood dripping from her tear ducts and streaming down her cheeks. That, and the bloody sweat oozing from pores all over her body.

I had read about hematohidrosis, but I had never seen it. It's a rare condition brought on by intense emotional or physical stress—a state where blood pressure spikes so violently that the delicate capillary networks surrounding the sweat glands rupture. It means, quite literally, sweating blood.

Mindy called Neuro-ICU to let them know we were sending up an 'exploder.' After that, she ordered a CT scan while I performed a quick stroke screen. I would've let Jenny do it, but she wasn't there. My team and I discussed vasodilators and decided on a loading dose of IV sodium nitroprusside. It worked, lowering her pressure to a more modest 220/112. Still not great, but blood had ceased to ooze from her pores, and that was a good thing. I watched her roll out, aware of the fact that I had just witnessed a rare medical phenomenon.

My next case was a 65-year-old gentleman brought in by EMS. His chief complaint was 10-out-of-10 chest pain radiating into his back. He said it felt like an elephant sitting on his chest. I hear that description all the time, and I always take it seriously. I mean, who can breathe with a pachyderm sitting on their sternum, right? The paramedics had already treated him with nitro and morphine, and yet, still, he looked like he was about to code. I don't think I've ever seen a paler, sweatier, sicker-looking guy.

"Doctor," he said, grabbing my hand. "Am I going to die?"

"No, sir. Not in my ER."

Dangerous promise, I know, but, hey, this is what I do, right? And I'm good at it. At least that's what everybody keeps telling me.

I took a quick look at his 12-lead ECG and knew right away the reason for his distress. The tall tombstone-like tracings on the paper revealed blockage of the anterior descending coronary artery—aka, the *Widowmaker*. Probably 100% blockage. Emergency angioplasty was not only indicated, but his survival would depend on it.

His pressure was stable, so I loaded him up with more opiates and sent him straight to the Cath-lab, proud that he had not coded in my ED.

My last major encounter of the night was with a 30-year-old who came to us after consuming a "magic mushroom" called psilocybin. At first, his friends and fellow consumers of the wildly hallucinogenic mushroom said it produced incredible psychedelic colors and sounds for them. But when their friend passed out and began to foam at the mouth, they decided to bring him to us.

I've seen a lot of organophosphate poisoning, but never one that bad. The poor guy was, quite literally, oozing out of himself, like a slug having just consumed Ortho Bug-Geta and turning to mush. He arrived at the ED drooling, with severe diarrhea, stomach cramps, and vomiting. And on top of that, he had a low heart rate and blood pressure, and asthmatic symptoms that almost shut down all breathing.

We had to work fast to reverse the cholinergic effects of the poison: IV fluids, high doses of atropine and pralidoxime, and a lot of clean up by the janitorial staff. I stabilized him and sent him to critical care as soon as possible. Frankly, I wasn't quite certain we would save that one, but, well, again, I am good.

We had a few more walk-ins before the end of the shift, but there were no critical cases, and I felt thankful for that. My relief arrived on time, and that was good, because by that point, I had had enough.

Normally, I would chat for a few moments with my intern before calling it a night, but Jennifer Miller was nowhere to be found. I shook my head and glanced at my watch—0712. I walked into the locker room, wondering if I would ever see Jenny again. I shrugged and murmured, "Whatever."

After washing up and changing into my gym clothes, I left through the back door of the emergency department, grateful to have another shift behind me. My thoughts turned to the gym and my upcoming fight with Rico. The bad news was I had just finished a 12-hour shift and had only one-fourth the energy I needed for a mixed martial arts sparring match. The good news was Rico had too. He headed up a special gang unit for East Beach PD and was also ending a twelve-hour shift. So, both fighters would be exhausted when the fight began. No heroes this morning.

I was just about to open my car door to head for the gym when a timid voice called from behind me. "Dr. Peabody?"

I turned to see a frightened Jenny Miller standing behind me, eyes wet, hands tight and shaky. "Jenny? Where'd you go? You missed some great cases."

"Can we talk for a moment, please?"

I threw my bag inside my car and said, "Well, I'm in kind of a hurry."

"This will only take a minute. I realized last night that I'm no doctor."

"Why would you say that?"

"You saw what happened."

"It was your first shift. We had some tough cases."

"I choked."

"It was stressful."

"Not for you. You controlled that room like a god."

"I've had years of practice."

"You were made for this. I wasn't."

"Jenny, it takes years to learn this business."

"I get that. But if last night was any indication, twenty years won't be enough for me. This is not going to work out. I just know it."

I had a strong suspicion she was right. I mean, she did show moments of brilliance in her assessments, her interaction with other staff was effective, and the way she dealt compassionately with the patients was admirable. Heck, she even prayed for that last gunshot victim, for whatever good that did. But it takes a lot more than a compassionate spirit to be an emergency physician. It takes mental toughness, grit, and strength … three qualities of which Jennifer Miller was sadly lacking.

"Dr. Mike, this is all I have ever wanted to do."

"Have you considered counseling?"

"Counseling? You mean getting it or being it?"

Jenny's face turned so red that for a moment I thought she might implode. She began to hyperventilate, and then, without further explanation, pulled her ID badge from her lapel, handed it to me, and then turned and ran back into the building. I thought about going after her, but decided to leave her alone. After all, why prolong her suffering?

I grunted and climbed into the Challenger. I was just about to close the door when I heard another female call my name.

Dang it! What now?

The person walking toward me had a demeanor much different than Jenny's. More like a statue or a robot terminator. I felt my heart rate increase. I climbed out of the vehicle to meet her.

"Ramona?"

Dr. Ramona Read (pronounced, "Red" or "Dread," as I sometimes called her, depending on her mood) stopped a few feet from me and crossed her arms.

I had always found Ramona quite beautiful. There was a graceful style about her—tall and lithe with smooth, light-brown skin characteristic of her Ethiopian heritage. But her glacial-colored blue eyes and hard cheeks barked of Northern European, making for a strong, intimidating-looking woman that I could picture one of two ways: a gorgeous Hollywood starlet or a fierce Roman soldier, depending on her mood.

The fact is, a pretty good person was standing before me, diplomatic and fair, a decent supervisor who took care of her subordinates and usually overlooked my egotistic behavior. But at that moment, she was the only person in the world I feared more than my third-grade teacher, a wicked old 4'10" lady, named Miss Prescott, who frightens me to this day. That one carried a wooden yardstick to smack the hands of naughty students. This one carried an air of dominance backed up by monthly evals and, when needed, disciplinary action forms. I figured I was about to be offered the latter. I took a deep breath and tried my best to stay relaxed. It didn't work. I folded my hands to prevent them from shaking.

"I'd like a word with you," she said, veins clearly visible on both temples.

"Okay," I said, closing the car door and folding my arms. "What is it?"

"What were you thinking last night? You scared that poor girl to death."

"Ramona, it wasn't me. She was completely out of her element, and—"

"Stop! Let me remind you that Dr. Miller is my number one student. Top of her class. I have high hopes for her, and I scheduled her with you because I thought you might want to teach her something."

"I tried to teach her something. She choked."

"But she could have succeeded, if you had helped her, Mike. I was in that trauma room when you had your paramedic friend insert the chest tube."

"I can explain that."

"Not now. It's bad enough that you would do that, but it enrages me that you gave it to him instead of having her do it."

"I tried to get her to do it."

"Not hard enough."

"But—"

"Mike, she needed a strong teacher last night, not a schoolyard bully."

I bit my lip.

"Dr. Peabody, listen to me. You are a fine physician, in my opinion, the best on our staff. Your medical knowledge, your skill level, and your decision-making abilities are second to none. But you are, without a doubt, the most egotistical, ostentatious, and genuinely arrogant doctor I have ever met. And believe me, I have known a few."

"That's not fair."

"You humiliated that girl, Mike. Drove her to tears. Now, I want you to apologize to Jenny Miller right away, and then I want you to invite her to assist you on your next shift."

"Do what?"

"That's an order."

"You want me to ask her to come back?"

"She deserves a second chance, and you will give it to her."

"I don't think so."

"Excuse me?"

"She's the one who ran out, Ramona. Not me."

"Then I'm afraid you leave me no choice. You just bought yourself a three-shift suspension."

"You're suspending me?"

"Mike, I like you. I always have. But you can be your own worst enemy. And you won't let me help you, because you are always fighting me. Now, you can continue hurting yourself if you'd like, but I will not allow you to hurt my students."

"So, you're a psychiatrist now, too?"

I watched the gap between her eyebrows narrow.

"You know," she said, her voice colder. "A wise man once said, 'Pride goeth before a fall.'"

"Yeah? Who said that?"

"A man named Solomon. He wrote the Book of Ecclesiastes."

"What's that?"

"It's a book in the Bible, Mike. Perhaps you should read it sometime."

CHAPTER FIVE

Big Mike's Slaughterhouse
105 South Main Street, East Beach, North Carolina
Tuesday, January 23—07:28 AM (EST)

Big Mike's Slaughterhouse is a fight club. A place for tough men, the kind of guys who don't mind bruises or the smell of their own sweat and blood. Twenty-four guys pay dues, share equal responsibilities for the day-to-day operations, and come here whenever possible to compete for a trophy that can't be seen or touched: Pride. No one person runs the place. We take turns holding various offices to satisfy the needs of an LLC, but since my name hangs above the front door, most folks just call it mine. I don't argue with them.

I found this place eight years ago when I first started looking for a venue. I told the realtor we wanted a warehouse space not easily found. The less visibility, the better. About 3,000 square feet would do, and we would need good plumbing and decent lighting. And a garage door in the back, if possible, for loading and unloading. He found a place that met every criterion except one—the garage door. But that's okay, because it turned out to be the perfect location for our club, the basement of an abandoned meat processing plant on East Main Street, a 3,200 sq. ft. warehouse with a locker room in back, a small office up front, and a commercial elevator for moving butchered meat. We've never used that.

I tried to research the original business, but I was unable to find much. Still, being located in one of the seedier parts of town, off a back alley and down a flight of stairs, we figured it would be the perfect place for our club, the last place the average person would go looking for Pilates or kickboxing.

I pulled into the gravel lot behind the building and sat for a moment thinking about the night shift, how I had mistreated Jenny Miller, and the disciplinary actions enacted by Dr. Dread. I mean, I could use a few days off, sure, but who was she to force it on me? "Go choke yourself, old battle-axe."

I climbed out of my car and slammed the door in a visceral show of anger that made me feel better somehow. After locking the car and setting the alarm, I walked across the parking lot and down the dark alley that led to the front door. I noticed a Chevy Camaro parked near the alley entrance and walked over. The guy behind the wheel looked suspicious to me, like he was looking for someone to assault, and I might be his next victim. He waved at me.

I ignored the gesture and descended the stairs to a heavy wooden door held together by turn-of-the-century iron bolts. The sign above the door was an antiquated reminder of the activities that used to happen inside. It originally read Little Joe's Slaughterhouse. I changed it to Big Mike's Slaughterhouse—my grim attempt at humor.

I unlocked the door and walked inside Big Mike's. As usual, the musty aromas of dried grease, body fluids, and wet towels filled my sinuses. I sniffed the air, savoring the primal odors, trying to imagine just what had happened in this basement to leave behind so many lingering smells. It made me feel like fighting, somehow, and fighting was why I had come.

I flipped a switch, and a bank of sodium vapor lights came to life down the hallway in the arena, the open section of the warehouse where we work out and fight. It would take a few minutes for the orange chemicals to reach full brightness. In the meantime, I would check emails and think. I walked into the office and was just about to sit down behind my desk when I heard the front door squeak open. The hallway brightened momentarily and then darkened again as the big door slammed shut.

Rico?

I glanced at my watch—7:28 AM. Right on time. I pictured my old friend walking down the hall in his uniform—blue jeans, white T-shirt, and brown cowboy boots. A gold shield would be hanging around his neck, and a Colt .45 M1911 would be holstered to his hip. After having finished the night shift, like me, he'd be dragging a little, but he'd be more than ready to jump into the octagon to exchange punches with me. It was our therapy. Our way of dealing with life.

"Puerto Rican gangster," I shouted. "Didn't think you'd show, mano."

I expected to hear one of Rico's standard announcements, like, "Mama Rivetti's #1 son is here," or "Peabody? Where's that oversized leatherneck?" Instead, silence.

I stepped into the hallway, surprised to find a young man with a pair of fighting gloves in one hand and a gym bag in the other. With the limited lighting provided by the bare 60-watt bulb on the wall by the door, I could make out the pale, freckled skin of an Irishman who could desperately use some sun. He looked like a fighter, though, with wide shoulders and Popeye arms tapered into heavy fists. And he stood with the kind of confidence only earned by repeated trips into the ring or battlefield. This guy was a fighter. I liked that. He reminded me of one of my favorite movie characters, Pete Dunham from Green Street Hooligans. But there was something about him that worried me, too, a strange air of weirdness.

"Can I help you?" I said, frowning.

"I'm sorry, sir, but the door was open. I was hoping to speak to the manager."

Polite.

"This is a private club," I said. "We don't allow visitors. Was that you I saw sitting in the Camaro outside?"

"Yes, sir."

"Those sparring gloves?"

He raised a pair of well-used Everlast gloves. "Yes, sir. Are you by any chance Mike Peabody?"

"Yeah. Who are you?"

"I'm Corbin Myers."

"Okay, so?"

"I'd like to find out about joining your club."

Corbin Myers was a foot shorter than I was, about five feet six, but he looked scrappy and tough, like a piece of chewy meat you can never quite swallow. His arms had been braised by the sun, as if toasted to match his red crew-cut hair and the three-day growth of beard that clung to his chin and upper lip. I looked him over, curiously. "How'd you find this place? We don't exactly advertise."

"My father. He said to ask for you."

"Who's your father?"

"Max Myers."

"Max?"

"You might know him as Maximillian Myers. He claims he once met you at Cherry Point Air Base. He was the base martial arts instructor."

"Max Myers?" The name sounded familiar. I rubbed my chin. "Max Myers, Max Myers, hey wait a minute. Tall, lanky guy? Irish-looking, like you, only taller?"

"That's him."

"Yeah, he had an Irish brogue, too. Thick accent. Didn't we call him something like, the Colonel? Or the Major?

"They call him the Sergeant."

"The Sergeant," I said, my head nodding. "That's right. I remember now. He was a civilian, but everyone called him The Sergeant. I fought him once, you know."

My mind returned to a difficult time when I was stationed at Camp LeJeune, North Carolina. I had just returned from Iraq, where I had done heavy urban field work as a Corpsman with 1st Battalion, 8th Marines. The Battle of Fallujah, they had named it, an all-out effort to take back the city from insurgents. A real mess. I saw more casualties that month than I have since becoming an

ED physician. And as a result, I battled depression, PTSD, and almost daily suicidal thoughts.

That's when my nightmares began. Sounds of explosions, images of wounded soldiers and Marines, visions of people dying in my hands.

I rotated back to the States after receiving a near-fatal gunshot wound to the chest. I never returned either. The guilt that followed was maddening. The fighting continued in Iraq, and I knew that they needed my help. I desperately wanted to be there, but going back was out of the question. And that was when I turned to fighting. It became a way for me to release my energies, to punch my way out of the madness, and to begin putting my life back together.

I did fill-in medical work at Cherry Point for a while. One of the other docs was into mixed martial arts, and one day after work, he took me to the base gymnasium to work out. He put me in the ring with this so-called Sergeant. Fight him, he said. And good luck.

Good luck? The Sergeant couldn't have weighed more than one-eighty wet. I was a solid two-seventy-five. I thought for sure I would kill him. Boy, was I wrong.

"Your dad was a tough cookie," I said, remembering his hard right hook. "Knocked me out cold that day."

"He said you fought pretty good for a spud."

"A spud?" I laughed at that. "Yeah, we only fought that once, though. How's he doing, by the way? Still instructing?"

"No, sir, he's in the clink."

"The what?"

"Prison. He's at Central Prison, in Raleigh. First-degree murder."

I felt stunned. I wanted to respond but didn't know how.

"So?" Corbin Myers said. "What about it, Guv? Can I join?"

"How'd your dad find out about this place?"

Myers shrugged.

My eyes had adjusted enough to the low light in the foyer so that I could detect moisture in the kid's bright green eyes. I felt a wave of compassion wash over me. It hit me all at once that Corbin Myers was a messed-up kid, a guy like me who needed help, not a ticket out. Despite his swagger, balled-up fists, and bulging arm veins, there was a weakness about him, as if he might somehow come apart right in front of me. In that way, he reminded me of another kid named Jenny Miller.

"I need to fight, sir. I just really need to fight."

I understood that. He just needed to fight. I needed to fight. There was something primal about fighting—it satisfied an inner need that some men feel to their bones. We had something in common, something solid, real, and tangible. I decided to offer him a chance.

"You know what? I think I can make an exception just this once, seeing how I knew your dad. Come into my office. You'll need to fill out some paperwork first, then I'll show you around."

"Guv!" he exclaimed, almost jumping. "Thank you."

"So, what else do you do, man? For a living, I mean."

"Me?" Myers followed me into my small office and took the chair in front of the desk. "I teach at Havelock High. Math and science. I also coach the baseball team."

"You coach baseball?"

"Yes, sir. Played third base in college, but only at the community college level."

"You must have an arm."

"Yes, sir."

"You still live in Havelock?"

"Yes, sir."

"That's not too far to drive. Do you have a fight resume?"

"A resume?"

"Yeah, you know, tournament wins, etcetera. Did you bring one with you?"

"No."

"Got a copy of one you can send me?"

"No. I don't have a fight resume."

"Have you been in any tournaments?"

"Twelve, and I won 'em all. But, frankly," he said, his face hardening with each syllable. "I don't see why my fight history is any of your business."

"It's required for membership."

"Who says?"

"I say."

"You make the rules here?"

"Hey," I said, put back by his response. "You want to fight here, or what?"

He looked at me quizzically. And then, as if a switch flipped in his brain, his eyes narrowed to thin slits. "Mind if I ask you a question?"

"Be careful."

"My dad told me you were a doc."

"That's right. I work in the emergency department at East Beach Regional."

"Kind of big for an ER doc, aren't you?"

"What did you say?"

"Your hands," he added. "They're massive."

"My hands?" I glanced at my hands. I had to admit they did resemble small hams. And there had been times when I had felt self-conscious about my weight, especially at medical conferences with the other physicians who were half my size. But I liked my physique, and I loved my hands. Balled into fists, they made for great weapons and had proven devastatingly helpful more than once in the ED. Belligerent crack heads and drunks and all. I held my hands out. "What's wrong with my hands?"

"Nothing, I just can't help but wonder how you do medical procedures that require dexterity in small places."

"I'm not a surgeon. I do just fine."

"You don't see too many African American ER docs, either."

"Excuse me?"

"Are you from those manky projects down the street?"

"Projects?" I stood up and stepped in front of him, my temples throbbing. "Mister, you are about three seconds from—"

"Look, no disrespect," he said, holding up his hands. "It's just, I saw that kip down the street on the way in, and, well, just put two and two together, you know. What are you?" he said, looking me up and down. "Two-fifty? Two sixty?"

Something was happening here, and I didn't like it. I was being baited. Set up for the kill. But how? And why? A chill ran down my back, the kind that makes your feet turn cold. "You know what?" I said. "Maybe this isn't such a good idea. I think you'd better leave."

"Oh, no, no, no! Wait!"

"There's the door," I said, pointing at the hall. "Beat it!"

"No! I mean, Mr. Mike, I'm sorry if I offended you. I really am. It's just, there's just something about fighting that changes me. I get aggressive. This place is for me, sir, I know it. I can smell it! I love the atmosphere here. Please, just give me a chance. I'll behave myself."

"Behave yourself? What are we, back in elementary school now?"

"I'm sorry, sir. Please give me a chance."

I had a strong suspicion I was about to make a mistake, but somewhere in my right cerebral cortex, I found a barrel full of compassion that weakened my constitution. Whatever switch had been flipped in his brain to produce that sudden outburst had been flipped back off, and he was acting like a gentleman again. I watched the kid for a few seconds and then shook my head, nodded, and said, "All right. All right, Mr. Myers, you caught me at the right time. Another member is coming in this morning. He's a paramedic just ending his night shift. He weighs about 210 pounds, and he's one of our best fighters, so I don't think you'll stand a chance. But if you want to give it a go, if you want to get your head busted in, I'll see if he's willing."

Myers jumped. "Where do I sign?"

"I mean it," I said. "You'll probably regret it."

"I've been beat before."

"All right, but you listen to me. Go off like you did a minute ago, and you're history. Got it?"

Myers nodded.

I had him sign the standard release form saying that if he died today, he wouldn't sue, and then I gave him a quick tour of the gym and turned him loose to work out. He was already wearing gym clothes—boxing trunks, sneakers, and a shamrock-colored T-shirt, which he quickly peeled off. He pulled on a pair of padded gloves and walked straight to the speed bags. "Let me know when that paramedic laddy gets here," he said. And within seconds, he was working on the speed bag. The rhythmic sound of it echoed across the gym.

"Yeah, right," I murmured, with a chuckle and a shake of my head. "Best of luck to you, Laddy."

The front hallway brightened again. The door crashed shut, and the hall returned to its normally darkened state. "Peabody!" a strong voice called. "Mama Rivetti's number one son is here!"

As predicted.

I walked into an empty front hall and peeked into my office, where I found my friend, Rico Rivetti, sitting with his back to the door, his dark, muscular frame nearly breaking the small wooden chair in front of my desk. He chuckled and said, "Look what the gym coughed up."

"7:35," I said, glancing at my watch. "You're late."

"What is it with you and time, anyway?" Rico said, swiveling around in his chair. "I've never known anyone who lives and dies by the clock the way you do."

"Time is everything."

I started to chuckle, but as the office light fell on him, my face tightened. He looked as pale as a sheet. He smiled at me, revealing a mouthful of clean white teeth, minus one, the result of a shovel to the face in a police incident several months before. But there was an unusual sadness in his normally bright eyes, as if he was dealing with something hard. A sickness in the family, perhaps, or the loss of a favorite pet. I couldn't help but wonder if he was spiking a fever.

"You don't look good, pal." I placed the back of my hand against his forehead. "You feel all right?"

Rico slapped it away. "Let's get in the ring, sport, and I'll show you how all right I am."

"You're an obstinate stump, brother."

"Rivetti means rivet, you know."

"In what language?"

"Italian."

"I thought you were Puerto Rican."

"My mama's Italian." Rico stood and slapped me on the back. I thought he looked unbalanced, as if he might fall. But even in his weakened state, he looked fierce and daunting. There was just something about this fire hydrant of a man that amazed me. He was in every way a specimen. "C'mon," he said. "It's time to fight."

"Take off that gun first."

Rico slapped me on the back and headed for the locker room.

CHAPTER SIX

Big Mike's Slaughterhouse
105 South Main Street, East Beach, North Carolina
Tuesday, January 23—07:40 AM (EST)

The arena floor at Big Mike's is bare and unforgiving—a cold, concrete slab stretching 3,000 square feet, divided into four distinct zones. A quarter of the space is dedicated to raw strength, featuring free weights and kettlebells—no frills, just the essentials for fast muscle gain. Another section is designed for building speed and power, with punching bags, speedbags, and a homemade power meter, a rough replica of the high-tech machine from *Rocky IV*. Rico Rivetti holds the record; he once hit it so hard the computerized display cracked. The rest of the floor is dominated by a broad sparring mat, with an octagon-shaped fighting ring in the center for mixed martial arts style fighting.

We have a full-sized locker room with showers, stalls, a row of metal lockers, and a washing machine-dryer combo for washing the multitude of towels we go through on an average day.

We follow modified UFC rules, which means we obey the Unified Rules of Mixed Martial Arts, a set of standards adopted by the NC Boxing Commission to ensure consistency of MMA events and to ensure fair play. MMA is a gritty fusion of fighting styles. It blends the striking of boxing and karate with the ground control of wrestling and jiu-jitsu, using every limb to break an opponent's defense and force a submission. The object is to win by decision (KO or TKO), or in our gym, by tap out, which is the fighter's way of saying, "You win!"

Rules are explained before each event, regardless of a fighter's level of experience, and each fight is carefully monitored by a referee responsible for enforcing those rules. The referee (Ref) is King. What he says goes. And he can end a fight at any time, no questions asked.

We run a practice facility, not for sanctioned events, so we have the liberty to modify the rules at our discretion. But for liability purposes, we pretty much toe the line, except when it comes to referees. We use general members in this role. No one has an official referee's license, and it has always worked.

The octagon was built to UFC standards, with an 8-sided floor exactly 30-feet in diameter, surrounded by a 6-foot chain-link fence to encage competing fighters. A swinging gate allows for entry and exit. A three-step staircase provides access.

After changing into my workout clothes, I climbed the stairs into the octagon. I felt surprisingly good, too, considering I had not slept in almost 72 hours, but I was well-fed and hydrated and could not help but believe that a win was in my future. The Marine in me possessed enough internal rage to take on the fiercest competitor. How could I lose?

My opponent followed close behind me, lumbering up the steps like a tired old bull. At 275, I easily outweighed Rico by 30 or 40 pounds. And at 6'5", I towered over his modest 5-foot something stature. But pound for pound, Rico Rivetti was the most powerful man I had ever met, a steel rivet of a man who, even in his presently diminished-looking state, was as formidable an opponent as I had ever met. He pulled the gate behind him and latched it.

"Prepare for a pounding," he said with a grin. "I feel like an animal today."

"You look like an animal."

I've known Rico Rivetti for close to forty years, and good-witted humor is a part of our day-to-day. We grew up together right here in East Beach, attended the same schools, and dated many of the same girls. We played football, baseball, and rugby together, sharing many broken bones. And after he married the love of his life, Mary, I married her best friend, Gloria. He joined the police department—I joined the Marine Corps. He runs an elite gang enforcement squad, I run an emergency department. And so, it goes.

To say that we are lifelong friends would be an understatement, because Rico and I are brothers in every sense of the word. My skin may be black, his, a light shade of brown, but our kinship is so tight that most people just assume we're cousins. But when we step into the octagon, any perceived bloodline is cut. Rico becomes my enemy, and I become his.

Our referee for the sparring session that morning was a fellow fighter, named Ray, an older gentleman, a little past his prime, who, anymore, serves primarily as janitor and guard. Ray explained the rules, had us display our mouthguards, and then led us to the center of the ring and had us bump fists. When we were ready, he turned us loose. Rico banged his gloves together and then, without another word, attacked.

We collided in the middle of the ring. I grappled for position and got so tangled up in his arms I thought I'd never break loose. Somehow, I managed to push free, but Rico made me pay with a roundhouse kick to my head. He followed with another that should have connected, but my peripheral mind responded in a microsecond, activating automatic muscle responses that pivoted my body beneath his hurling foot. Once clear, I retaliated with a snapping sidekick of my own. Rico dodged it, spun to one side, and counterattacked with a perfectly thrown punch that caught me square in the jaw.

Whoa!

I backed away and shook my head to clear the eruption of nebular gases in my brain. I could hear Rico laughing.

"Geez, Rivetti," I said, shaking my head to clear the stars. "What do you got in those gloves? Lead?"

Rico snorted and came back in, but this time I dodged his strikes and spun into a wicked back kick that would have leveled most horses. My left foot struck him in the temple and knocked him down. I wasted no time dropping on him. I locked an arm around his neck and then grabbed his closest arm and wrenched it backward. Then, for added measure, I wrapped a leg around his midsection and squeezed with all my might.

And that's how it goes … we fight until someone wins. We grunt and groan and kick and punch until someone's either knocked out or locked in an unbreakable position that forces him to tap the mat. That's where I thought I had Rico. His face bulged like a crimson balloon and his eyes looked about ready to pop from their sockets.

"Tap," I shouted.

Rico grappled and kicked. His face went from bright red to blue.

"You don't know when to quit," I said. "Tap the mat!"

But Rico showed no intention of quitting. A surge of new strength charged through my old friend. He clutched my forearm, broke my grip, and then twisted my arm backward as if snatching an oak branch from its trunk. Then, using one leg as a fulcrum, he broke free, pushed my eighth-ton body into the air, and rolled me onto my side.

I fell with a thud, shocked, and thoroughly surprised to find myself locked up tight with his leg wrapped mercilessly around my neck. Then came the death move. Rico grabbed his own ankle and pulled, flexing his muscular thigh as if closing a pair of giant pliers.

"Suck on that, Jarhead!"

Sucking was out of the question. I couldn't breathe.

Now, I'm a doctor, so usually I analyze everything related to the pathophysiology of the human body. And if I could have at that moment, the cloud of stars encircling my head would have made perfect sense. By temporarily compressing both of my carotid arteries at once, Rico had succeeded in shutting off all blood flow to my brain. And since brain cells can't survive without oxygen for more than ten seconds before cellular metabolism ceases, I was on the edge of going out.

Three seconds passed … four … five …

I threw one last burst of energy into breaking his hold, but it was no use. I was just about to succumb to the darkness when I heard an unexpected *crack!*

What followed next was the deepest animal-like groan I had ever heard, followed by hissing and loud cursing. The pressure eased around my throat, and fresh air flowed into my lungs. Blood returned to my head, and the stars subsided.

I lay on the mat, gasping. I could hear Rico cursing and Ray shouting, but all I could think of was breathing. I sat up and inhaled precious oxygen until my mind cleared and Ray's words sharpened.

"Someone call 911!" he shouted.

911?

I sat for a moment, just breathing, unable to focus on all that was going on until my vision cleared and I could see Rico sitting on the mat beside me, hissing and grinding his teeth, one arm pulled up tightly against his chest.

Before I could even ask if he was okay, he rolled over on the mat, heaved until his belly was empty, and then panted and tried to stand. "Ohhh," he moaned. "God, help me!"

"Rico?"

"Mama Mia," he said, dropping back to his knees. "Oh, mama, this one's bad."

"Call 911," I heard Ray repeat.

To my relief, the octagon gate flew open, and Jim Stockbridge bounded into the ring. If ever I was glad to see a paramedic, it was then. "Jim," I said. "Thank God you're here."

"Did you hear it snap?" he said. "It's definitely broken."

"Of course, it's broken," Rico spat. "Snapped it like a twig."

Jim reached down and helped me to my feet. I reached for Rico's arm to stabilize it and reduce the fracture.

"Forget the arm," Rico barked, recoiling. "I'm all right!"

"all right? Your forearm's busted," Jim yelled. "Let us help you."

Rico slapped Jim's hand away. "Touch me again, medico, and I'll break *your* arm."

"You stupid cop! Don't blame us if you end up losing it!"

CHAPTER SEVEN

Big Mike's Slaughterhouse
105 South Main Street, East Beach, North Carolina
Tuesday, January 23—07:58 AM (EST)

Good friends are hard to find. They can shout at you, beat you up, belittle you, defend you, and pretend not to appreciate or even care about you, but in the end, you know they will die for you. Rico, Jim, and I were like that. Good friends.

After Rico settled down, Jim and I helped him remove his sparring gloves and then made a futile attempt to assess him. I had my suspicions he was dealing with something more serious than a broken arm, and when he doubled over a second time and vomited all over the octagon, I knew I was right. A broken arm doesn't cause gut-wrenching spasms. And Rico's bones are not usually so fragile that one would just accidentally snap in the middle of a fighting position. My friend was in trouble. Bad trouble.

"Rico," I said. "What's going on with you, brother?"

"Forget it."

"You broke an arm. You're having abdominal pains and throwing up. Talk to me, pal. I'm a doctor."

Rico shook his head and started for the locker room. "Worry about yourself, flat nose."

Rico started to leave the ring, but then stopped and bent over again, gripping his belly as if trying to hold his guts in place. I watched him grimace and curse for about ten seconds and then straighten and walk out of the ring.

"Ray," I exclaimed. "Did you call 911?"

"On the way."

Rico disappeared into the locker room and then reappeared a moment later with his damaged wing tucked up tightly against his side. He apologized to us for being a jerk and then marched toward the front door as if on his way to a business meeting.

"Where are you going?" I exclaimed.

"To the hospital!"

"You're driving yourself? With a broken arm?"

The front door opened and closed again, and Rico was gone. I shook my head and turned to Jim. "What the heck was that?"

"You know Rico," Jim said with a shrug. "That man's as hard-headed as they come."

"Yeah, but the way his arm just snapped? And the way he was throwing up? Something's going on with him."

I suddenly felt as if I'd gone ten rounds with Hulk Hogan. I thought of heading for the locker room to throw some cold water on my face, but the rhythmic sound of an Everlast speed bag stopped me. I glanced across the gym at the wannabe member working it against the far wall. I had totally forgotten about him.

"Oh, hey," I said, finally feeling clear-headed enough to stand. "You see that dude over there at the bags?"

"The little guy in the green trunks?"

"Came off the street looking to fight. I volunteered you."

"Why'd you do that?"

"Because I knew you'd give him a fair fight. I want to check him out. I knew his father once and figured I'd do him a favor."

"Why don't *you* fight him?"

"I got nothing left. Besides, he's too small for me."

"He's too small for *me*, Mike. Look at him. What is he, 130? 140?"

I shrugged.

"Hey, I've got an idea," Jim said, motioning toward a big South Pacific-looking guy sitting in a chair next to the locker room entrance. "You remember my new partner, Charlie K?"

"Charlie Kay?"

"You met him last night at the ED."

"I did?"

"We brought in that gunshot wound, remember?"

"Oh, yeah. Big guy in the rain slicker."

Jim nodded. "I brought him here to show him around. He's a fighter, Mike. I think he might fit in."

Him? I studied the guy. He was a big one, about 6'3" and 260 pounds. But honestly, I thought, a little dumpy, like an oversized pineapple with short stumpy legs. I couldn't picture him doing anything more physical than serving rum drinks at a bar or playing a ukulele for a hula dance.

I shook my head. "Hey, Jim, no offense, brother, but that guy is no fighter."

"How do you know? Let's see what he's got."

I hesitated.

"C'mon," Jim said. "As a favor to me."

I hesitated and then nodded.

Jim waved him over.

Charlie K walked about like I had expected him to for a man his size and shape, sluggish and slow, with a short, lazy step. I chuckled to myself, but as he approached, I began to sense a certain style to his walk, a confidence that belied his fruity appearance. His deep brown eyes sharpened, piercing me with a gleam that filled me with a sense of respect.

"Charlie?" I said, stepping out of the octagon and extending my hand. "Mike Peabody."

"Yes, sir," Charlie said with a wide grin. "Charlie Kaihewalu."

"Ki-a-what?"

"Ki-ya-wa-lu. Most people call me Charlie K."

"Ki-ya-wa-lu. Where are you from?" I said. "Tahiti? Bora Bora?"

"No," he said, with an amused chuckle. "Oahu."

"Hawaii? So, you're a surfer?"

Charlie chuckled again. "Not exactly."

"I thought all Hawaiians surfed. What do you do? Sail? Paddle dugout canoes?"

"Just normal stuff. Football. Farming. Before I got into EMS, I worked on a banana plantation."

"Bananas?" I chuckled. "I would've guessed pineapples. So, Jim tells me you're a fighter?"

"Yes, sir."

"You can stop with the 'sir' business, okay? Just call me Mike."

"Yes, sir."

"So, what belt do you have? Black? Brown?"

"Sandan."

"San-what?"

"Third Dan. It means I'm a third-level black belt. I will gain instructor status soon."

"Which discipline? Most of the fighters here practice Brazilian Jiu-Jitsu and Karate."

"I practice an ancient art called Lua."

"Lu-wha?"

"Lu-wa. It's sort of a family tradition," Charlie said. "My ancestors developed it."

"No kidding? What's it about? Kicking and punching and ancient weapons and stuff?"

"Of course. We practice all the basic fighting techniques, but it's much more about, well, there's no delicate edge to this … breaking bones and dislocating joints."

"Say what?"

"Yes, sir. Finding an arm or leg bone, locking it in place, and then dislocating it to subdue the assailant."

"Yeah, well, if it's all the same with you, I'd rather not see any more broken bones today."

"Yes, sir, I saw what happened to your friend. No worries."

"Have you ever competed?"

"Yes, sir, but only as an amateur."

"We're all amateurs here. See that guy over there?" I tilted my head toward the stranger at the speedbag. "Name's Myers. He's looking for a sparring match. Interested?"

"Sure thing."

I glanced at Jim and shrugged. "Bring him over. I'll get Charlie signed in."

Charlie followed me to the front office. I asked him a few general questions to get an overall impression of his personality and quickly decided that Jim had chosen well. Charlie Kaihewalu seemed like a genuinely kind and polite individual, with a friendly demeanor and an excellent fighting resume. I hoped he would fit in. I explained that a license is required in the State of North Carolina for any sanctioned MMA event, but not for sparring in the gym. He said he understood. I had him sign the necessary paperwork and then led him back out to the octagon.

"I don't know anything about this guy you're about to fight," I explained. "Except that he's a lot smaller than you.

Charlie assured me he would go easy.

Myers was standing alone by the octagon when we returned, radiating the same intense energy, but with a sharper edge, like he'd just talked himself into believing he could take on the entire world and win. Charlie introduced himself.

Myers looked small beside him, standing easily six inches shorter and weighing a hundred pounds less than the big Hawaiian. But what he lacked in overall size, he made up for in stature.

"Jim?" I said, glancing around the gym. "Have you seen Ray?"

"I think he's mopping the locker room. It's okay. I'll ref."

Myers was the first one to enter the octagon. He did not dance around or jump in place like you see so many fighters do. He just stood there with his arms hanging by his sides, expressionless, as if entering a trance.

Charlie removed his shirt and climbed into the ring. He looked comfortable in the setting, loose and easy. He sported a massive chest with a tattoo of a pineapple on one pec, and his classic *life is good* smile on his big Hawaiian face. I should have felt confident that he could hold his own against Corbin Myers, maybe even crush him, but suddenly, I wasn't so sure. Myers' demeanor had changed. He looked malicious, even, to the point of being dangerous.

I got a strange feeling in my gut as Jim called the fighters to the center of the ring. Charlie grinned and lumbered in like a heavy mammal. Corbin moved in lightly, bobbing up and down as if he had springs in his shoes.

"Are both of you wearing mouth guards?" Jim said.

Charlie grinned to reveal a white rubber mouthpiece snugly concealing his upper teeth. Corbin did the same.

"Okay," Jim said. "I'm your referee. Keep it clean, boys."

Jim recited the basic rules, and then the two men touched gloves and backed away.

"Ready," Jim said, glancing at each fighter and then pointing at the center of the ring. "Let's fight!"

CHAPTER EIGHT

The Octagon
Big Mike's Slaughterhouse
105 South Main Street, East Beach, North Carolina
Tuesday, January 23—08:02 AM (EST)

The fight was over almost before it began. Corbin threw the first punch, but Charlie dodged it and threw a counter-punch that knocked Corbin back a few steps. While his opponent was reeling, he moved in, grabbed one of his arms, extended it to the limit of the elbow, and pulled him to the mat. Myers cried out, and for a few seconds, I thought his elbow might snap. This Lua fighting style seemed legit, and Charlie K seemed to know how to use it.

"Tap," Charlie shouted. "You're locked."

But Myers did not tap. In fact, in a slippery, eel-like move that defied my understanding of physics, the tenacious little Irishman twisted his body like a corkscrew and wriggled his way out of submission.

"Well," he said, flexing his arm, a mischievous grin on his face. "Fair play, Hawaii. I see you know some moves."

Myers sneered and jumped back in, seemingly unconcerned about the bigger man's weight and dexterity. But once again, Charlie knocked him back with a powerful punch and moved in for the kill. Within seconds, he had the smaller Myers locked up tight again, with one arm bent backwards, straining tendons and bending marrow.

"Tap," he shouted. "You're done this time!"

Myers ignored the order and threw a sharp elbow, striking his opponent in the face and knocking him backwards. Charlie grunted and fell, a deep gash on his cheek pouring blood onto the mat. Without slowing down, Myers dropped to his knees, driving his right knee hard against Charlie's temporal bone. Charlie went limp.

"Stop!" Jim shouted, rushing in between the fighters. "He's grounded! Get back! Get back!"

Myers ignored the command and punched Charlie hard in the face. Five times he hit him, six, before Jim was able to yank him away from the downed fighter.

"I said, get back!" Jim shouted. "What's wrong with you?"

Myers tried to rush again, but Jim grabbed him and held him at bay.

I had seen enough. I climbed into the cage, grabbed Myers, and threw him like a rag doll against the chain-link fence. "Are you out of your mind?" I shouted, pinning him against the cage. "What the hell is wrong with you? He was grounded!"

"I'm sorry," Myers stammered. "I don't know what I was thinking."

"Stay there," I shouted. "Don't you even think of moving!"

Myers nodded and held up his gloves in submission. "I'm sorry! I don't know why … Charlie, I'm sorry!"

I pushed the heel of my hand against the cut on Charlie's face, and shouted. "Ray! Get out here! We need help!"

A second later, the old man ran from the locker room.

"Get the first aid kit," I shouted. "And call 911!"

Jim knelt beside me and held pressure on the cut while I assessed Charlie's eyes. Ray bound into the cage and tossed Jim a roll of paper towels. "Here," he said. "Use this until I can find a proper dressing." Jim unrolled a wad of paper towels and crammed them into the laceration. The white fibers absorbed the blood like a sponge, turning a deep crimson before finally staunching the flow. Ray pulled a handful of 4x4 gauze pads from the kit and handed it to me. "Okay," I said to Jim. "Let's see it."

Jim removed the blood-saturated paper to reveal a deep laceration about three centimeters in length. I folded the dressings to cover the wound, and then wrapped Charlie's head with a roller bandage to secure the dressing.

"He needs stitches," Jim said. "You got your bag?"

"No. But he needs to go for a head scan anyway." It was one of those moments when I wished I had a portable CT scanner in my back pocket. But Charlie was breathing quietly and at a normal rate, and that was a good thing. I touched his wrist to check for a radial pulse and then turned and looked at Ray. "Did you call 911?"

"Yeah. They're on the way. Again."

I jostled Charlie. "Hey, wake up, big fella. Wake up."

To my astonishment, Charlie did wake up. His eyelids tightened, fluttered a few times, and then opened to reveal the confused expression of a man with a grade 2 concussion. But his eyes darted about a few times and then seemed to find a focal point and zeroed in on me. Both eyebrows rose simultaneously, and I realized he had made a connection.

"Jim?"

"No, Charlie, it's Mike. You okay, big fella?"

"Doc?"

"That's right. You know where you are?"

"Where … um … what happened? Where's Jim?"

"Right here."

"Oh, good. Man—" Charlie placed a hand to his cheek and groaned. "I feel like I got hit by a train."

I held two fingers in front of his face. "How many?"

"Four. Can I sit up?"

I chuckled. "Not yet."

Charlie sat up anyway, glanced around, and then spotted the blood on his torso and grimaced. "Is that mine?"

"Right here," I said, snapping my fingers. "Look at me. Where are you?"

"Sitting in a pool of my own blood in the octagon at Big Mike's Slaughterhouse." Charlie chuckled. "I think I just got slaughtered."

"Feel like you can stand up?"

"Of course."

Charlie stood. I examined his eyes again and felt satisfied there was no need for a scan. "Charlie, do you want to go to the hospital?"

"Not really."

I heard a siren in the distance and glanced at my buddy, Jim. "Medics? What do you think?"

"You're the doc."

"Yeah, and you're the paramedic. I trust your judgment."

"Well, I think that lac needs attention, but I'm not sure he needs to go by EMS." Jim glanced at Charlie, and said, "I can take you, man."

"No, thanks, partner. I can drive."

The front door of the building opened and slammed shut. I heard movement in the front hallway. A moment later two paramedics entered the arena carrying trauma bags and a cardiac monitor. "EMS," one of them shouted, his voice echoing across the arena. "You guys call us?"

"Yeah," Jim shouted. "Hang on." He looked at me and shrugged. "I'll go talk to them."

Jim left the octagon and walked across the padded floor. Charlie walked out and went to the locker room. I glanced at Myers and pointed a finger at him. "You stay put. I want to talk to you."

Myers nodded.

I followed Charlie to the locker room and waited while he collected his gear. "You sure you're okay to drive?"

"Yes, sir. Sorry for the blood on the mat."

I followed him back out and stood with Jim in silence as Charlie K lumbered down the hall and out of the building. Then we turned in unison and gazed at Myers.

"He was breaking my arm," Myers exclaimed. "What was I supposed to do, ask him to dance?"

Jim shook his head. "Throwing the elbow was bad enough—"

"There's nothing in the rules about elbows!"

"No," Jim continued, "but kneeing a grounded man in the head is. And when I ordered you to back off, you tried beating him to death."

"Pack your gear," I said. "I want you out of here."

"Seriously?"

"Get lost and never come back!"

"What kind of fight club is this?" he shouted. "I knock the guy out and you kick me out?"

"Now!"

"Hang on," Jim said, grabbing my arm. "Let me talk to you for a minute." He pulled me to one side and said, "Maybe he's got a point. You initially wanted me to fight him, right? Let me go."

"I think we've had enough excitement for one morning."

"Mike, somebody's gotta teach this punk a lesson."

"I can't have you killing him, Jim."

"I just want to send a strong message. You can stop it whenever you're ready."

I glanced at Myers. Perhaps it was the lighting, or maybe the sweat that covered his face, intensifying his features, but for the first time I noticed an awkward dent in the bridge of his nose that spoke of a history of brawling. He was missing a tooth, and he had a small scar beneath his right eye in the shape of a man's college ring. I mean, the guy was a fighter, the kind of fighter we usually looked for, except for one thing: he was beyond unpredictable. He switched on and off like a lightbulb. The word schizophrenic came to mind.

"I don't know. He seems unbalanced to me."

"Mike, I'm fighting this guy. Either in here or out on the street."

I wasn't too concerned about Jim taking care of himself. Frankly, I was wondering if he could hold himself together. He outweighed Myers, had a longer reach, and he had the home field advantage, too, as well as a 48-and-3 record fighting men in his own weight class. And justice was on his side. I had no doubt

Jim would beat him, but I was afraid he might not know when to stop. Still, in the ring, at least, I could control the fight. On the street, there was no saying what he might do. I decided to let it happen.

"So, what about it?" Myers said, stepping toward Jim and raising his hands. "We gonna fight, or not?"

CHAPTER NINE

The Octagon
Big Mike's Slaughterhouse
105 South Main Street, East Beach, North Carolina
Tuesday, January 23—08:25 AM (EST)

Jim walked from the locker room wearing his typical fight gear, which for Jim meant a pair of blue shorts, black Reeboks (no socks) and a pair of tattered red sparring gloves, the ones he had worn for every fight, every day since joining us. He also wore a relaxed looking grin on his face, a little too relaxed, I thought, for the situation. But that was Jim's style, ever confident. Always ready to fight. He possessed the nastiest front-kick-roundhouse combination I had ever seen, along with a wicked spinning back kick that has knocked me down more than once. I knew from experience that he could hold his own, and if I didn't outweigh him by over 80 pounds, I would probably never fight him again. Jim Stockbridge, Paramedic, was in every way an MMA fighter, and today he looked ready for war.

But Corbin Myers was beginning to scare me. My fear that Jim might badly overpower him was beginning to wane. He waited for Jim in the octagon, pacing back and forth like a caged animal. He had the same strange, trance-like appearance that I had seen before his fight with Charlie, only this time he looked almost possessed by Satan himself. I felt soft spasms surge through my belly. The physician in me saw red flags everywhere—spilt blood and broken bones about to happen—but the extreme fighter that existed in the frontal lobe of my mind saw another good matchup. A slugfest in the making. One thing was certain, whatever was about to happen, it would be a great fight.

I tipped my head toward the octagon, and said, "After you."

Jim's eyes burned with an intensity I had never seen as he climbed into the ring.

I stepped in behind him and moved to the center of the eight-sided mat. Myers stopped pacing and backed up against the far side of the cage, poised like a cornered wolf.

Jim tightened the straps on his gloves and then flexed and wriggled his fingers to increase their range of motion. He did some quick warm up stretches, shadowboxed himself for a moment, and then turned and gave me a wink. "Ready when you are, Ref."

I called both men to the center of the octagon.

"You two, listen to me," I started. "This is a sparring match, not a revenge match. I want a good, clean fight from both of you, unlike that last one." I looked at Jim. He nodded and said, "Of course." Then I turned to Myers. "Strict UFC rules. You got it?"

Myers nodded.

"No low blows, absolutely no head shots when a man is down, and when I say stop, I mean it! Let's make this a good clean sparring session or someone's going to jail. Now touch gloves."

The two men met and bumped gloves. I could feel the intensity in the ring. My guts were in knots.

"All right." I stepped between them and waved a hand. "Let's go to war!"

I backed away to give them room to fight, prepared to jump in at the first sign of trouble, but like the first fight, this one looked to be over almost before it even started.

Jim struck like a bolt of lightning, broadsiding his opponent with a hard punch that knocked the smaller man off his feet. It was a brilliant move. The perfect punch, so good I probably would've gone down.

Myers crashed onto all fours, momentarily dazed. He spat out a wad of something pink and frothy, then pushed himself up, turning back toward his opponent on unsteady legs. Guilt gnawed at me—why had I let this fight happen? "Hey!" I said, grabbing Myers by the shoulders and shaking him. "Open your eyes," I ordered. "Look at me!"

I had expected to see confusion, the dizzy sloppiness of a brain devoid of focus after having been pummeled with blunt force trauma, but there was no apparent dimming or disconnection in his eyes. He blinked a couple of times, shook his head, and then cursed under his breath and glared at his opponent.

"Are you all right?" I said. "Can you go on?"

Myers pushed me away and before I could blink, he was on Jim again. He threw a sharp front-kick that struck Jim in the chest. Jim coughed twice, took a deep breath, and then retaliated with one of his own.

It was on now, attack and counterattack, grappling and pushing away, but with an intensity I had rarely witnessed. Myers fired a flurry of stubby punches that seemed to confuse Jim at first, but Jim leaned away and countered with a sidekick that snapped out like a heavy piston on a steel rod. His foot connected in the center of Myers' chest with fight-ending power and precision.

A loud, winded grunt burst from Myers' throat. He fell to the mat in the fetal position and panted, struggling to catch his breath. Jim waited a moment, mercifully, giving him a few seconds to recover, and then jumped on top of him and wrapped one arm around his neck. With the other, he encircled his torso and bent him backwards as if to snap him in two. "Remember," Jim shouted. "You asked for this. Now tap!"

Myers was locked. He wriggled, kicked, and snorted, but Jim held tight. He had won. All he needed was the acknowledgement of the defeated fighter. Myers thrashed, attempting a desperate body roll, but Jim locked down tighter, cutting off any hope of escape. Myers' face turned a dark, angry red, veins bulging, eyes wild and straining. He gagged, spasmed once—then went limp like a puppet with its strings cut. His fight wasn't just over, it had been crushed out of him.

"Tap the mat," Jim said. "End it."

Myers closed his eyes as if to gather some hidden internal strength, and then, in what was without a doubt the slickest move I have ever seen, he threw back his right leg and drove his knee squarely into the side of Jim's head. Then, as Jim wavered, he flipped backward and rolled into an upright fighting position.

My eyes widened, so stunned I was by the man's tenacious, wolverine-like ability. I waved them back into action and the fight resumed.

Jim kicked, Myers punched … Myers rushed, Jim pushed him away. Then the two collided in the middle of the ring and fell to the mat, arms entangled, legs and feet battling for position. Jim managed to assume a firm Fujiwara hold, but Myers shifted his weight and quickly slipped away, rolling through to a 50:50 position, and then delivering his second elbow of the day, catching Jim square in the face.

Jim wavered and fell. Blood streamed from his nose.

"That's it," I shouted. "Fight's over!"

But Myers had no intention of stopping. He jumped on top of Jim and wrapped an arm around his neck.

Jim gasped for air. Blood poured from his face. I was jumping in to stop the fight when Jim grabbed Myers' arm at the wrist and twisted with such force that the other fighter had no power to resist. Myers' grip broke. Jim stood up panting, furious with rage. He tried to shout but his voice was a squeaky rasp. He grabbed the smaller Myers, picked him up, and flung him across the octagon into the fence.

A chain-rattling crash sounded. Myers fell to the deck. And then, like a seething wild animal, he jumped up, cursed, and ran out of the octagon and across the gym floor. Five seconds later he threw open the front door and disappeared. Three seconds later the heavy steel door slammed behind him. And for the first time in an hour a hush fell over the gym.

CHAPTER TEN

The Octagon
Big Mike's Slaughterhouse
105 South Main Street, East Beach, North Carolina
Tuesday, January 23—08:35 AM (EST)

I've seen some interesting fighters come and go over the years. There was this one guy from Raleigh, tall and skinny and about seven feet tall, with the longest legs I'd ever seen on a man. During his first workout he showed off by jumping up and kicking the net on the basketball hoop, 9 ½ feet off the floor. I mean, the guy could kick the moon, and I felt certain no one could beat him. But he lost in his first match to a kid half his size who punched him in the stomach and sent him out crying.

There was another guy from Korea with fists as fast as lightning. He had a sharp front kick, too, and a swinging roundhouse I saw him use to break three boards. Powerful. But when it came time for him to fight, he began to hyperventilate so much his opponent didn't know what to do. It was sad, really. It reminded me of a doctor I know, a young intern named Jenny Miller.

Yeah, lots of strange guys have come and gone over the years, but for my money, Corbin Myers wins the prize. He was a strong fighter, no question, with wicked hands and the most slippery moves I'd ever seen. And under normal circumstances, if I had to choose between him or Bruce Lee, I would have had to stop and think about it. But these were not normal circumstances. In fact, Myers was the weirdest kook who's ever stepped into our octagon. The way his personality flipped from normal to psychopathic in the blink of an eye, well, that was just bizarre. I couldn't tell if he was Mister Rogers, or the devil himself. In short, the guy scared me. And I felt a huge wave of relief wash over me when he ran down the hall and out the front door.

I waited until the door had slammed behind him and then turned and gazed at Jim. Like me, he seemed unable to speak.

Finally, he said, "Now that was weird."

"You think?"

"I sure hope we've seen the last of him." Jim snorted and pulled off his gloves. "I'm gonna go change, man. You feel like Sandy B's?"

"Of course."

It's a tradition. After the night shift, and a good fight or two, Jim and Rico and I usually go to our favorite diner, a place over in Beaufort, called Sandy B's. They know us there, serve us extra portions, and the food is outstanding. My "regular" fare is three eggs over easy, grits, bacon, hash browns, and white toast with extra butter and jelly. And if I'm really hungry, I'll order flapjacks on the side, smothered with butter and maple syrup. I mean, keep in mind, I'm a big guy, so for me, that almost does it. So why not?

"Maybe we should stop by Regional and check on the guys first," I said. "What do you think?"

"I feel certain Rico went, but I'm not sure about Charlie."

Jim walked into the locker room to change. I went up the hallway to my office and flopped into my leather chair. I had no intention of changing clothes. After grabbing a bite at Sandy B's, my next stop would be the walk-in tiled shower at 223 Swan Court. Then I'd be sliding between a pair of nice, clean sheets for a six-hour nap. Changing would be a waste of time. Instead, I spent the next few minutes thinking about all the strange things that had happened that morning: Jenny Miller falling apart and running out of the ED … Rico puking all over the cage … and that strange kid, Corbin Myers, almost choking the life out of Jim before turning and hightailing it from the gym. I mean, what a day already.

I opened my laptop to check emails. The first one was from Ramona Read, stating her intention to forgo my suspension if I would apologize to Dr. Miller. A second chance, she said. A pretty good deal. But I had already decided I could use a few days off, and there was no way in Hades I was apologizing to Jenny Miller. Never. No way. So, no deal.

I checked a few more emails and then closed the laptop and picked up the National Geographic magazine I had swiped from the physicians' lounge. I had earlier dog-eared the page that showed the full-length photo of my newest discovery, The Shroud. I turned to it and studied the image. The details seemed to pop off the page this time, as if somehow my eyes were opened to the possibility that it was authentic. I ran my fingers over the image and could almost feel the texture of the wounds. The blood flowing from the wrists and feet. The gaping wound in his side.

"Who are you?" I said, looking at his face. "What are you?"

Jim walked into the office wearing his EMS uniform, shirt untucked. Despite his casual appearance, he still looked impressive. He always did. There was just something about the guy, the way he carried himself—always proud, constantly eager for a challenge—and today he had an added snide look on his face as if to announce his latest victory to the world.

"Ready?" he said, nodding toward the exit door.

"Just about."

Jim noticed the Nat Geo, and said, "I see you're still reading that article."

"I'm intrigued by it."

"Are you a believer yet?"

"Haven't decided."

"Well, at least we're making progress. C'mon," Jim said. "Let's go eat."

"Give me a second. I'll be right out."

Jim left my office and walked out. The front door slammed behind him. I packed up my MacBook, grabbed some tax return paperwork from the file cabinet and then turned off the lights and glanced into the arena. I killed the sodium vapors and turned to walk out. Then it hit—a dull, heavy *thump, thump, thump* rattling right through the concrete wall. Like a sledgehammer hitting stone.

For a split second I felt confused, but I had heard that sound too many times at the range not to recognize it now. My eyes widened. I dropped my laptop and ran to the door. "Oh no, no, no, no, no!"

I ran out of the building and tore up the stairs. I smelled cordite, tasted pure panic. I ran down the alley a few yards and found Jim lying on the gravel, eyes wide and blank, jaw locked open, stuck on a final, choked surprise. A single, dime-sized hole punctured the center of his chest. Clean. No blood, no powder burns. Just a hole.

My heart pounded. My brain fought to comprehend the madness. I felt crazy, spastic in shock and rage. I dropped to my knees and was reaching to feel for a pulse, when I heard a demonic cackle behind me. A shiver shot through my body like electricity. I turned and felt my jaw drop, locked in disbelief, for there, standing in the thin column of sunlight shining into the alley stood a manic-looking Corbin Myers, his eyes wild, a chrome .38 caliber revolver in his hand.

"Not so bad now, are we, Guv?"

"Myers! What have you done?!"

"All I wanted to do was fight, but you and your cocky friend there . . . you had to make a fool of me, didn't you. You two despicable human beings. You're not God. But you *are* about to meet him."

Myers stared at me for the longest three seconds of my life, and then with mind-numbing silence, he sneered and raised the pistol to my forehead.

"See you soon," he said. "In hell."

They say the human eye cycles at a rate of 30 images per second, sending signals through the optic nerve to the brain just slightly faster than the conscious mind can assimilate. As a result, the world around us appears seamless, like a well-produced video rolling without interruption in the mind. A .38 Special bullet travels at a rate of seven hundred feet per second, not necessarily fast in terms of modern ballistics, but faster than the human mind can process, making it impossible to see in flight. But I swear to you, I saw a flash as that gun fired. A white-hot flash, speckled with orange and yellow sparks. And the bullet? I'll never know for sure if I saw that, because before I knew what was happening, my head whiplashed backwards—and everything went dark.

TWO MONTHS LATER

CHAPTER ELEVEN

Office of Nathaniel Newton, MD—Neurologist
Carteret Neurology Clinic—East Beach Medical Park
East Beach, North Carolina
Monday, March 31—10:15 AM (EST)

I know a nerd when I see one. Spending four years in medical school surrounded by them tends to sharpen your diagnostic skills. You know, the kind that can read a medical book in a single afternoon or take apart a computer and successfully reassemble it. Dr. Nathaniel Newton was like that. Poindexter to the core, much like the Screech character in Saved by the Bell, kind of jumpy and owlish with a brilliant mind but awkward social skills. He wore khaki pants, a white dress shirt and bowtie, and a plastic pocket protector filled with pens. The diplomas on the wall behind him painted a story of academic success: Undergraduate Degree from Columbia University. Medical School training—Harvard. Internship and residency in general surgery at Massachusetts General Hospital where he served as Chief Resident. Board certified by the American Board of Neurological Surgery, too. I mean, this guy was at the top. And all the nerds in my medical circle claimed he was the best neurosurgeon around. I hoped they were right.

"Hey, Doc," I said, hoping for a good sense of humor. "I've got a disease where I can't stop telling airport jokes. They say it's terminal."

I laughed. He didn't.

No sense of humor.

With fingers poised above the keyboard, as if awaiting the order to type, Newton raised an eyebrow and said, "Tell me how you are feeling, Dr. Peabody."

"Well—" I sat casually, trying my best to stay relaxed. "Okay, I guess. Pain's under control."

He continued to type without responding.

I sighed. "Headaches. I still have bad headaches."

His fingers hit the keys, creating a soft clicking sound. "Nausea?"

"Yes."

"Memory?"

"Yes."

He looked up without smiling.

"I still lose my memory at times, like you said I would. I got lost in the grocery store today for a minute. I had to stop and look at one of the signs to realize I was on the canned foods aisle at Food Lion. What a joke, huh?"

He frowned, typed some more, and then asked, "How about the hallucinations? Are those still coming and going?"

"I already told you, that's not what I would call them. They're more like dreams, you know? I mean, nothing like flashing colors, or psychedelic lights. Dreams."

"You're seeing things that aren't there, Dr. Peabody. We call those hallucinations."

"I know, I'm sorry, it's just that they seem so real."

Type … type.

"And the clouds? Still seeing those?"

"Yes."

"When?"

"Before and after the dreams. It's like I walk into a gray fog bank, experience a weird dream, and then walk back out to reality again."

Type … type.

"Do you ever taste metal or hear strange sounds?"

"Yes."

"Have you ever experienced incontinence?"

"Have you?"

He paused without looking up, and said, "Mike, has anyone ever told you you're arrogant?"

"Yes. And to answer your last question, I have never experienced urinary incontinence, and I never will."

"Okay, look—" Newton stopped what he was doing and made eye contact with me for the first time since I arrived. "I'm only doing my job. I'm not assuming anything today just because you're a fellow physician. And I would encourage you not to use the word, never. This *could* happen to you. You were shot in the head, Dr. Peabody, at pointblank range, with a .38 Special revolver. I performed emergency brain surgery on you two months ago, and you should not be alive. We still do not know the full extent of the damage, and one of my jobs is to make that determination. So, instead of attitude, I'd appreciate any help you could give me."

"I'm sorry, Doc. Just trying to have some fun. This has been a tough experience."

"I'm sure it has. So," he continued. "Any bowel incontinence?"

"No, sir."

"Just temporarily blinded by the light? That's what you once said."

"Yes, sir. Totally bizarre."

Type … type.

"And you still struggle to know what is real?"

"Hey," I said, irritated by his super-intelligent, mechanical, stenographic mode. "You do me a favor now, Doc. Put down that stupid laptop and talk to me."

Dr. Newton paused, sighed, and then closed the laptop and looked at me. His eyes burned into mine. I did not find it comforting.

"What have you been doing for fun?"

I shrugged. "Fun?"

"Yeah, you know. Movies? Books? Horseback riding?"

"Reading, mostly."

"I'm glad you are able to read. What have you been reading?"

"Well, um, mostly the Bible."

"The Bible?" I saw him smirk. "Have you read The Gospel of Matthew, chapter five, verse five?"

"I've read the whole thing."

"Then you know the part where Jesus said, 'Blessed are the meek, for they shall inherit the earth.'"

"I think I remember that."

"Meekness and humility, Mike. They go hand in hand."

I just stared at him. It felt like I'd just been body-slammed by some wiry little brainiac from Boston. Meekness is a virtue I'd always laughed at. But laughing was the last thing I wanted to do at that moment. I hung my head instead. "Point taken."

"So?" he said, reopening the laptop and continuing. "About that reality …"

"The reality is I struggle to know what is real."

"How's your overall vision?"

"Usually clear. Sometimes blurry."

He pulled his ophthalmoscope from a pocket and leaned in too close for my comfort. I smelled Listerine on his breath. I felt the inside of each eyeball light up as he examined my retinas. Apparently satisfied, he nodded and then returned to his typing.

Without glancing up from the keyboard, he said, "Your eyes look better. Retinal inflammation is down. How's Gloria taking all this?"

"Oh, geez, don't ask. Last week I forgot our anniversary. That didn't go over so well."

Type … type.

"But you know her, Doc. She's tough. Supportive. I catch her gazing at me at times, as if she's wondering what she can do to help me."

Dr. Newton grinned. "She must love you."

"Her patience is being tested."

Type … type.

"What else are you feeling?"

"Frustration. Anger. I'm not half the man I used to be. I can't fight or work out with weights. I can feel my muscles wasting."

"There are other forms of exercise, Dr. Peabody. You could swim. Ride a bike. Choose some kind of low-impact sport."

I didn't bother arguing with him. He would never understand. He was a slight man, narrow at the shoulders and shallow in the chest, and I doubt he'd ever pumped anything heavier than a bicycle pump. But I realized he was telling me the truth, too, and that he was trying to help me, so I decided to stop resisting him and start showing him the respect he deserved. After all, like I said, he's considered the best neurosurgeon around.

"Is this normal for TBI?" I asked.

"Well, that's a tough question, Mike. There's nothing normal about traumatic brain injury. Your MRIs reveal significant healing, but the symptoms concern me. It's just going to take time. Now, some people lose …"

The doctor's words trailed off as a dark gray cloud surrounded me …

I saw the orange flash … the bullet traveled at my face in slow motion, twisting on its axis, before a wispy trail of smoke …

> *The slug hit my forehead like a hammer, penetrating my frontal bone an inch above my eye. There was no sensation of pain, rather a deep penetrating punch followed by an explosion of colors. But the colors quickly melted and merged into an ugly gray mass of light followed by inky blackness. Darkness. A demonic darkness, with sharp fingers, grabbing at me and pulling me down ... but where? I remembered screaming. I remembered the intense heat. I remembered a feeling of utter, eternal hopelessness. And then the cloud dissipated, and I woke up in a sterile hospital room with no perception of lost time … and … and …*

"Mike? Can you hear me?"

The fog cleared and I opened my eyes to see Dr. Newton staring at me. "Mike?" he said, shaking me by the shoulders. "Are you with me?"

I shook my head and blinked a few times to clear my vision. "Doc? Did you see that?"

"See what?"

"The demons."

"Demons?"

"They came at me. They were pulling me, pulling me down. But, then, wait a minute, um—" Suddenly, I was wide awake again, and I realized it had all been just a dream, or a seizure, or something. "Sorry, I, I mean, it happens like that."

"Did you see the cloud this time?"

"Yeah."

"How long did it seem to last?"

"Minutes."

"It was actually about ten seconds. What did you see?"

"The bullet. Coming at me in slow motion."

"Was it lifelike?"

"Living color. It hit my forehead. Then, after the fireworks, everything went black, and then a bunch of demons surrounded me."

"Demons?"

"Yes, sir. Little, black, bat-like creatures with wings. They grabbed me, and pulled me down. It was like they were trying to pull me into the floor."

"Oh, my."

"Doc, it was terrible. It felt like, well, hell. What was that? Do you think it was some kind of premonition?"

"Mike, stop. Listen to me. Many victims of TBI deal with very strange symptoms, like these. Some for the rest of their lives. Others for a short time. It's just an unpredictable course. It cannot always be understood or charted. But no, this dream does not mean you're going to hell."

"Thank goodness."

"You should probably expect to see a lot of strange things over the next few months, though."

"Jeez, maybe I should write a novel."

For the first time I saw Nathan Newton crack a grin. He closed the laptop and clasped his hands together. "Do you have any questions for me?"

"Yeah, what do you suggest?"

"Well, that's up to you. But, I would recommend nothing stressful. No fighting or heavy weights. Light workouts, teaching, even some administrative duties if and when you feel up to it, but—"

"No emergency work?"

"No, sir. And no more driving."

"What?"

"Mike, listen to me. I saw what happened to you a moment ago. Do you understand how dangerous that could be if you were behind the wheel or in the emergency room? You could kill somebody."

The only person I wanted to kill at that moment was a guy named Corbin Myers, who, it turns out, had already done the job himself. They had found his body next to Jim's at the top of the staircase that led down to Big Mike's Slaughterhouse. Did himself in the head. Beat me to it.

"Okay," I said, with a sigh. "I understand. No driving or work."

"And, Dr. Peabody, I also believe we should start you on medication. These cloud episodes sound like complex partial seizures. You haven't described tonic-clonic activity, and I witnessed no convulsions. Why don't we try an anticonvulsant for a while, at least, until we get a better handle on it. Dilantin extended-release ought to do it."

I shook my head in disbelief. I was going to be taking Dilantin. I mean, I prescribe it for my patients all the time. I know almost everything about it—Generic name, phenytoin. Classified as an anticonvulsant. Blocks voltage-gated sodium channels in the brain, which prevents cerebral glutamate from rising to the high levels that stimulate excessive electrical activity. Etc., etc., yada, yada, yada—and it's one of the most often prescribed anticonvulsant medications for prevention of seizure activity. It's also the most common reason people have seizures—they forget to take it.

"A hundred milligrams ought to do it," he said.

"I get it."

I hated it, but I got it. I had never felt so impotent. Emasculated.

"I want to see you again one week from today," he added.

"Next week?"

"Just work with me, okay? If you're feeling better after a week on Dilantin, we'll consider pushing it out to every two weeks, but for now, I must stand by my decision."

I sighed. "Is there anything I can do that's fun?"

"Learn to ride a bike?"

"Guys like me don't ride bikes."

"Then write your book. I don't know. Just find something non-strenuous to do. Something easy to take your mind off things for a while."

I thought about my upcoming conference in Florence. "How 'bout Italy?"

"Are you serious? Not a chance."

"But I'm scheduled to go to a medical conference."

He just stared at me, as if expecting me to have another seizure.

"Doc, trust me," I said. "I'm okay."

Dr. Newton shook his head and muttered something unintelligible that sounded strangely like, "damned fool" and then shrugged and said, "Just promise me you'll be careful. Your brain is very vulnerable right now."

I stood and offered my hand. He shook it. To my surprise it was firm. I thanked him and started to leave. He stopped me.

"Mike, I know you already understand this, but once you start the Dilantin, you must remember to take it every day. It's quite possible that your next seizure will be a grand mal."

"I will."

I nodded. The last thing I wanted to happen was to drop to the deck and begin flopping like a fish. I thanked him again and walked out.

It was only a short walk from the medical park to East Beach Rehabilitation Center, Rico's latest address. He went there after an extended stay in the hospital for, what turned out to be, an aggressive form of prostate cancer. I couldn't help but laugh at the situation. I figured it was better than crying. I mean, check it out … my best friend—the hardest and toughest man I had ever met—a guy called Back Door by the gangsters in town, because they all knew he would be waiting for them at the back of the house when they ran out on a police raid—was fighting cancer.

And the updated version of the great Mike Peabody was a joke. I mean, there was a time I could run for miles wearing a pack and heavy boots. I've killed the enemy with my bare hands and rescued men from impossible situations most people could never dream of. Sewn up 10,000, treated 100,000 or more, and just two months ago, I fought Rico the Rivet in a final grudge match. Almost beat him, too. But today I couldn't walk five steps without a cane. "What's next," I muttered. "A walker?"

What a bummer.

I tried to push aside my bitterness, but as usual, I couldn't do it. I hated the cane, I hated the seizures, and most of all, I hated the man who had done it to me.

"Corbin Myers," I whispered. "Rot in hell."

Rico was asleep when I entered his room. I mean, what else would he be doing? He had stage 4 prostate cancer, and because of the intense damage already done to his liver, bones, and lungs, he and his family were already considering Hospice for end-of-life transition. So fast, it had all happened. So sad.

I almost cried when I saw him. He looked so small and eaten up with disease. It hurt me to see such a powerful man reduced to two-thirds his size, unable to piss without a tube, unable to stand or wipe his behind.

I sucked it up like a dutiful Marine and idled up next to his bed. I called out his name, not expecting a response, but to my surprise, he opened his eyes. He stared at me for a moment and then broke out in weak laughter. "Now this makes me laugh," he said, weakly. "Mike Peabody using a cane."

"Don't rub it in, fuzz."

Rico chuckled and then winced noticeably, gritting his teeth.

"You okay, brother?"

"Oh yeah," he said. "Just a little cramp."

"Are you due for meds?"

Rico glanced at his watch. "Yeah, probably. Forget about me, old man. What about you? How's the head?"

I touched the tender tissue just above my right eye where the bullet had entered my cranium. "I still get dizzy, especially when I lean forward to do something. But the nausea spells have decreased, so I suppose I'm improving."

Rico nodded. "Going back to work soon?"

"Doc won't allow it—nothing strenuous, no fighting, weightlifting, or driving. He's got me on anti-seizure meds, too. Can you believe that?"

"That sucks. Well, look at us. We're a sight, aren't we? Two old warriors reduced to this."

I shook my head. What could I say? I had just lost one of my best friends, and the other was lying on a bed dying of cancer. I wanted to cry.

"Oh, by the way," Rico said, "I heard they found the Myers kid with a bullet in his brain."

I let out a bitter sigh. "Chrome .38 Special. Two-inch barrel. Used it on himself—the slimy little punk. My only regret is I wasn't conscious to see it."

"Mike, that kid was messed up." Rico sighed and looked away. "Kind of makes you think, though, you know? About death, and all?"

I gulped. "C'mon."

"No, I think we should talk about it. I used to be scared to die. The unknown of it all. I've been listening to Mary rant on about her religious beliefs for a long time. I guess it just never took. But after all this? What she's been telling me is beginning to make sense. About salvation, and all."

Usually, I rolled my eyes when someone mentioned the word, salvation. But this time I thought of the demons in my last seizure. The darkness. I felt a chill run up my spine. I stared hard at Rico.

He reached out to me, as if to shake my hand one last time. I took his hand and clutched it, feeling little strength in his grip. The bull of a man I had always known as unbeatable—a modern-day Samson or Hercules—was gone. But I sensed a strong spirit about him all the same. Peace. Acceptance. A lump formed in my throat. The Marine in me tried to swallow it, but couldn't.

"Look," he said. "The doctor says it ain't good. Cancer has metastasized to my major organs, meaning I've only got a few weeks to live."

I swallowed something that tasted like bile. I had assumed as much, based on his appearance and the fact that they were already discussing Hospice. But the words hit me like a strong punch in my stomach. "How's Mary taking it?"

"Like a trooper. So, when are you leaving for Italy?"

I felt jolted by the sudden change of subject. "Are you kidding? Rico, I'm not going now."

"What do you mean, you're not going?"

"Doctor won't allow it. Besides, with you in this condition, there's no way."

Rico shook his head. "You *are* going. You've been jabbering about this shroud thing for two months. I'll be here when you get back. And I don't want you hanging around here, anyway, watching me wither away. When are you leaving?"

"I was s'posed to leave tomorrow, but—"

"Good! Go live your life, brother. I mean it! Take care of Gloria and grow old. And go to Italy and see the Shroud. Find out once and for all what you're looking for. Whatever it takes, man, find out."

"How? How am I supposed to do that?"

"Look at his face, Mike."

"What?"

"You know what I'm talking about. Just stare at it for a while. I think, then, you'll understand."

Rico grimaced as a strong wave of pain socked him in the abdomen. I started to push the nurses' call button, but I didn't need to. As if on cue, a scary-looking woman walked through the door with a 10 cc syringe in one hand. In another life, I figured, she could've been a Russian prison guard.

"Who are you?" she said, pointing the syringe at me.

"Relax, I'm his doctor. What have you got in that thing?"

"You're not his doctor," she responded.

"Nurse—" I felt like cursing. "No, but I am a doctor! I'm also practically family. Now, please, tell me what you're about to give him."

I saw her features soften. "Dilaudid, Phenergan, and Toradol," she replied. "This should make him feel better."

I nodded my approval. I knew from experience that it was an excellent cocktail for excruciating pain. I watched her attach the syringe to the IV port and push the contents into his vein. Rico inhaled deeply, as if he had received a loading dose of liquid ecstasy, and then he melted into the sheets like a lump of warm butter. Within a few seconds, he was snoring.

CHAPTER TWELVE

Somewhere over the Atlantic Ocean
Seat No. 12K
Delta Airlines—Flight #8417 RDU to CDG
Wednesday, April 1—11:24 PM (EST)

I've always hated flying. It's not so much that I'm afraid of being five miles above the earth, packed into a cylindrical tube with wings, or the idea that if we did go down in the Atlantic Ocean, there would be absolutely no chance of survival. I just don't like airplanes. And is it just me, or has legroom in these things decreased in recent years?

Last time I flew, I could stretch out a little, at least enough to partially straighten my legs. Not anymore. At that moment, I was in the middle of three seats on the right side of the plane with my knees pushed into the seatback in front of me. My shoulders spilled over into both of my neighbors' spaces, so basically, for everyone on my row, it was a bummer. Valium works well in situations like that, but I never used it. The only thing I hated worse than feeling miserable and not being in control of the airplane was being sedated and knowing that someone else was. Trust me, I'd rather be anxious. I held out my hands to see if they were still quivering. They were.

I closed my laptop and pulled out the ticket stubs for departure and arrival times.

"Okay," I murmured, glancing at my wristwatch. "It's Thursday night, 11:24 PM, and we're scheduled to arrive Friday at 12:22 PM. But that's Paris time—"

I suddenly remembered I was still on Eastern Standard Time. I reset my watch to Central European Time and continued.

“Current time in Paris, 5:24 AM—Central European Time (CET). We’re scheduled to arrive there at 12:22 PM, so that means we still have, what? Six hours and fifty-eight minutes? Or is it five hours and fifty-eight minutes? Or …” I couldn’t wrap my mind around the numbers.

Traumatic brain injury is so real. So frustrating. I tapped the wound on my forehead, two months old and healing. The soft, mushy feel of it reminded me that I hadn’t changed the bandage in a while. I’d take care of that at the airport in France. What was that place called? I couldn’t remember. I murmured a profanity and leaned my seat back. Maybe if I dozed off, we would be there sooner than later. I closed my eyes and started to nod off, but before I could even catch a wink of sleep—someone said, “You should use the flight tracker.”

At first, I thought I was dreaming, until I felt an elbow jab my right side. I glanced sideways at the guy sitting next to me. With a slim build, short silvery hair, and a pair of icy blue, scientific-looking eyes, he reminded me of a Norwegian IT tech or a Russian spy. He wore Levi’s jeans and a black T-shirt beneath a gray hoodie sweatshirt. Like me, he had a laptop on his meal tray. A white earbud protruded from his left ear.

“I’m sorry,” I said, “What?”

I half expected him to say something like, *“Do you realize you’re taking up half of my seat?”* Or *“Kindly move over, sir. You’re sitting in my Russian lap.”* But he said nothing of the sort. In fact, what he said surprised me. With a warm grin, he nodded at the seatback before me and asked, “Why don’t you just use the flight tracker?”

I frowned and said, “What’s that?”

“The flight tracker. You’re trying to figure out how long till we get there, right? Use the flight tracker. Let me show you.” He touched the screen on the seatback in front of me, and it lit up, displaying a cool menu that included everything from in-flight music and movies to a live flight tracker. He touched the screen again, and a map of the United States, the Atlantic Ocean, and Eastern Europe appeared. A small airplane at the top of the screen traced a thin line that arced all the way back to Dulles International.

"This is the flight tracker," he explained. "It displays our current position, updated every few minutes. And see here?" he continued, pointing at the data at the bottom of the screen. "Arrival time, remaining time, coordinates, everything."

I touched the icon displaying our position. "That's us?"

"That's us."

"But this shows us near the coast of Iceland. I thought we were going to France."

"We are," he said, with a chuckle. "Many North American flights crossing the Atlantic follow a northerly course to stay close to land, in the event of an emergency."

"Oh. I didn't know that."

I felt stupid. But I was right about the arrival time. We had six hours and fifty-eight minutes remaining.

He seemed to pick up on my embarrassment and said, "You must not fly much."

"Not overseas."

"I'm Will Hendricks. I'm from Ventura, California."

"Mike Peabody. East Beach, North Carolina."

"No kidding? I have an old friend who lives in Raleigh. We went to school together. If you don't mind my asking," he said, glancing at my bandaged head and then motioning to the cane tucked between our seats. "What happened?"

"I got shot by a madman."

"Oh. Well," he said, eyes widening. "I wasn't expecting that."

"No?" I chuckled, "Yeah, true story."

"Hmm. Where are you headed?"

"Florence. I'll be attending a medical conference there."

"So then, you're a doctor?"

"Emergency medicine."

"How'd you get shot? If you don't mind my asking."

"It's a long story."

I gave him a brief overview. At first, he seemed confused that I was an ED doc who owned a fight gym. But he soon accepted it with a shrug and said, “So, then, this conference? New emergency procedures? Something like that?”

“Yeah, but I’m going mainly to learn about crucifixion.”

“Did you say crucifixion?”

“It’s a trauma conference. This year, it coincides with Easter, so the topic is death by crucifixion. The speaker plans to use the Shroud of Turin to explain the pathophysiology. Have you heard of the Shroud?”

“Yes, I have. Hmm, interesting. That would explain the pictures on your laptop.”

“Oh, you saw those? Yeah, a little pre-conference homework. So, then, you do know about the Shroud.”

“A little. Are you planning to see it while you’re there?”

“See it?” How could I see it? The Shroud is rarely seen. It stays in a fireproof, climate-controlled vault in a dedicated section of the cathedral with around-the-clock guards. But the thought of seeing it in person sounded intriguing, so I decided to learn more. “I thought they kept it hidden from the public.”

“Historically, that has been the case. But in recent years, it has been brought out more frequently for exhibition. It’s considered a holy relic by many, and public demand is growing. It’s on display right now in the Turin Cathedral, you know.”

“Really? How far is that from Florence?”

“About four hours by super train. I’ve made the trip many times. When’s your conference?”

“Starts tomorrow and goes through Saturday.”

“Perfect. You could travel to Turin at the conclusion of your conference and see the Shroud on Sunday. That would be the perfect follow-up to the lectures.”

I squinted and studied the older man. “Will, what do you do?”

“I’m a photographer.”

“Landscapes and such?”

"Well, yes, of course. I spend a lot of time in Yosemite Valley with my four-by-five view camera, but that's only my hobby. My business is holographic imaging. I'm a scientific photographer."

"For real?"

"Open your laptop," he said. "I'll show you."

I opened my MacBook to the last page I had been reading, an article I had found online entitled, *Holographic Imaging—the Curious Face of the Shroud.*

"Scroll down," he said, tapping the screen.

I did.

"Stop there," he said, pointing at a bright blue image on the screen. It displayed an upright, transparent version of the 3-D rendering of the face that I had seen in Nat Geo, only more lifelike. "Move the cursor over that directional arrow beneath the image."

I did.

"Now, click on it," he said.

I clicked on it, and the image rotated clockwise. "Cool." I moved the cursor over the other arrow, and the image rotated the other way. "It's a hologram?"

He nodded. "I made that image."

"You?" I turned and gazed at him. "You made this?"

"We're taking the 3-D imaging of the Shroud to the next level in hopes of coming up with some more answers. I'm on my way over there now to do some more research."

"Who do you work for?"

"A research group, called Project-21."

"What's that?"

"Ever heard of STURP?"

"Shroud of Turin Research Project?"

"That's right, and Project-21 is the second-generation of STURP. You see, STURP was established in 1977 when modern research on the Shroud began. Only a few members of the original team are still living, and the others have all retired, except me. We revived the team with an updated name to indicate our presence in the 21st century. Thus, the name, Project-21."

"So, you've seen the Shroud firsthand?"

Will laughed. "Many times. I first saw it in 1977. I went over with the team and spent five days inspecting it. And then again in 2015, when we spent another three days with it."

"Incredible. How did you happen to get involved?"

"As a student at a school in California called Brooks Institute of Photography. One of my professors was the chief scientific photographer for STURP. He made most of the photos used for modern research. I served as his assistant. I also helped him with much of the art history research, the scorched-cloth theory, and the three-dimensional studies used to produce the images you have seen online."

"You made that 3-D image too? The green one I saw in Nat Geo?"

"Yes."

I sat for a moment without speaking. I mean, what are the odds? I had just recently become fascinated by a burial cloth that, until a month earlier, I had never even heard of, and now I'm sitting on a flight to Europe beside a photographer who had made the very image that had first lured me to it.

"Tell me this," I said. "Do you believe it's real?"

"The Shroud?" Will nodded. "Very real."

"No, I mean, do you believe it's Christ's burial cloth?"

"Without a doubt. There's too much evidence to dispute it."

"Hm." I found my head nodding. "So, other than your holograms, what kind of research is being done on it right now?"

"The research is multifaceted. We're still trying to get a sample of the original cloth for carbon-14 dating. And then there's the—"

"I thought they'd already done that."

"They did. And the results suggested with 95% confidence that the Shroud is between 635 and 765 years old, not nearly old enough to be the shroud that covered Jesus. But the samples used for that testing came from a section of the cloth where repairs were made over the years, new sections of cloth sewn in to replace frayed fibers. The first carbon dating tests were proven inaccurate. So, one of our objectives is to acquire a piece of the original Shroud from somewhere closer to the image. Of course, the Roman Catholic Church will not allow that."

"I wouldn't think so."

"Then there's the more recent wide-angle X-ray scattering analysis, new DNA studies, and blood serum analyses, all of which will help us to reevaluate the age and origin of the image. So, there's plenty of new research underway."

"Have you found any DNA on the cloth?"

"Plenty. Many people touched the Shroud over the years. But remember, DNA has a shelf life like everything else. In fact, the half-life of DNA is about 520 years, so every 1,000 years, 75% of the genetic information is lost."

"So, there's no way to prove whose it was, or who had touched it along the way."

"We need a method to look back in time at DNA … kind of like the way we look back in time with telescopes."

There was a pause in our conversation as the jet hit some turbulence and forced us both to hold tight.

"Say, Will," I said, genuinely intrigued by his explanations. "What do you think caused the image?"

"The original STURP team theorized that it was caused by direct contact with the body, and that the cloth fibers degraded over time, darkening, if you will, thereby leaving the image. But another, more popular theory involves the notion that, when Jesus rose from the dead, his body 'passed through' the cloth, in three dimensions. In other words, in every direction at once. The energy produced at the instant of resurrection left an unprecedented image restricted only to the outer fibrils of the linen. Something never found or reproduced before or since."

"How is that possible?"

"How is any of it possible? How's it possible for a man to be raised from the dead?"

He gazed at me with raised eyebrows.

I shook my head and shrugged. The only answer I could find was the simplest answer of all. "I suppose only God could do it."

He smiled and said, "Exactly. You see, Jesus is God. His birth gave us his life … his life gave us his death … his death gave us his resurrection … and his resurrection changed everything."

"And his resurrection gave us the Shroud."

Will nodded and leaned back in his seat. I leaned back in mine, overcome by the mystery of it all. Not only that Jesus had risen from the dead, but that he would have chosen to leave his image on his burial cloth. I shook my head in wonder and confusion. I saw the edge of the fog bank in the periphery of my vision. I shook my head, and it disappeared.

I turned to Will, and said, "They say the lines to see the Shroud are up to three or four hours long."

"That's true. Two million have seen it in the past two weeks."

"Two million?"

"You must see it, Mike."

I shook my head and explained my recent trauma, and propensity for seizures. "I'm not sure I'm up for that. Can't stand still that long."

"Not to worry," he said, with a grin and a wink. "I know the right people."

"What does that mean?"

"It means, I can get you in."

CHAPTER THIRTEEN

Charles De Gaulle International Airport
Paris, France
Thursday, April 2—12:57 PM (CET)

I said goodbye to Will Hendricks at the gate with the promise that I would think about his offer to see the Shroud. He said he could get me through security, under the guise of being his assistant, and after that, we would view the Shroud up close, and then I could watch him work his magic, whatever that means. I suppose making holographic images from a piece of flat cloth requires more than basic photography skills.

We had exchanged cell phone numbers, and I had promised to text him when I made up my mind, so I figured I would. He said I would be crazy to pass up such an opportunity, but I had just met this guy, and my reason for going to Italy in the first place was to attend a medical conference funded exclusively by my employer. So, a side-trip to Turin? Would that be okay?

I thought of all I had learned on the flight—some basic Shroud facts, like how they used to keep the cloth wrapped in gold foil for purity, further wrapped in soft red velvet for cushioning, and stored in a silver vault under the strictest of security measures, which included an air-conditioned, humidity-controlled, fireproof, sprinkler-system-protected vault, guarded 24 hours a day by specially selected and trained armed guards. But today it's stored flat in a specially made 15-foot framed case, protected by bulletproof glass, and climate-controlled to maintain a perfect oxygen-to-argon ratio. The case is displayed in front of the sanctuary for special expositions and returned to storage in a special chapel adjacent to the sanctuary. Guard numbers double during the exhibition, and local police are recruited for assistance.

Wow.

Will had also explained that, for public expositions, which have only happened eight times in the past 250 years, the cloth is exhibited at the front of the cathedral chapel. Guards remain onstage for the entirety of the event, then escort it to a special room in the basement for post-exhibit examination. Here, special scientific teams examine it under the strict eyes of specially selected nuns. In this case, the Project-21 team would be present, as well, with Will Hendricks serving as chief scientific photographer.

I made my way through the terminal, dodging other travelers and trying my best not to trip over my stupid cane. At one point, I became lightheaded and saw the edge of the fog bank coming toward me again, forcing me to stop in the middle of pedestrian traffic until it passed. One person pushed past me and uttered something impolite in French that might be interpreted as, "Get out of the way, dummy," or "Move, Yankee," which is exactly what I wanted to do. But I couldn't move. I couldn't even see straight.

When the fog cleared, I realized I had dropped to my knees. I stood up and tried to collect myself. I must've looked pathetic because an official-looking guy in a uniform pulled up beside me in a golf cart and asked if I needed a ride—at least I believe that was what he said. It was something like, "Monsieur, voulez-vous un tour?" Since he was heading in my direction and was pointing at the seat beside him, I figured that's what he meant. I politely refused, with a sad attempt at a French accent, saying, "Non, mare-cee bo-coop." He chuckled and departed to help another cripple.

I continued, regretting that I had not paid better attention in my high school French class. I spotted a café—that's one word that did make sense to me—and decided to take advantage of the opportunity to sit down. I also needed caffeine. I hobbled in and made my way to the counter, where I was greeted by a friendly-looking barista, who said, "Puis-je vous aider?"

"Say what?"

"Que désirez-vous?"

My head was beginning to hurt, and I quickly lost all interest in the French language or trying to be polite. "Coffee," I said. "I need coffee."

"Ah, café! Ah, oui. Noir, ou crème et sucre?"

"Look, Mac," I spat. "I can't understand anything you're saying. Just give me some black coffee."

The look on his face indicated that he understood the international language of a balled fist banged on a countertop. "Je suis desole," he said. "I'm sorry, sir."

"Forget about it."

Mac gave me the coffee in a paper cup with a lid. I paid for it with five dollars American and gave him back all the change he had handed me … one-and-a-half Euros, I think.

"Merci bien," he said. "Thank you."

I nodded. "De nada."

He frowned at me.

I found a small table to sit, sip my drink, and watch the silly French people go by. Mostly, I think, they were from somewhere else, though. I saw dark-skinned, light-skinned, pale-skinned, and tanned-skinned people of all ages and nationalities. People with hats, people without hats, and even two guys in what I assumed were berets, and they were not military. But that made sense, didn't it? This was an international airport, and just like in America, any fashion is acceptable these days. I even saw one woman, uh, person, I'm not sure, in a pink business suit wearing flip flops. "They" wore a glove on one hand and carried a green purse in the other.

Strange place, Paris.

I sipped my coffee and thought about my encounter with Will Hendricks, from Ventura, California. Now that is an interesting guy, I thought. Specializes in weird scientific photography. I mean, who would've thought a guy could make a living creating 3-D images that stand up and spin around? Odd. But then I specialize in patching up weirdos, so who's the nut?

Despite the heavy dose of caffeine I was drinking—and it *was* strong—my headache had not subsided. In fact, I felt certain it was getting worse. On top of that, I realized the fog was back, a thick, gray mist closing in on me from all sides.

"Oh, Lord," I cried. "Not now!"

I closed my eyes, and it disappeared. Reopened them, and it returned.

I don't think it was all the science talk that caused the fog to envelop me, or the idea still boggling my mind that Jesus had left his image impregnated in the fibers of an ancient linen cloth called the Shroud, or even the rush of the bold French coffee I was swilling. I think it was the Dilantin in my bloodstream, or, more likely, the lack of it. Had I forgotten to take it? Dr. Newton's words returned to me, a taunting echo bouncing inside my mind … *do not forget to take it.*

Oh, no!

The fog became so thick that I couldn't see. Then the colors arrived! All of them this time—reds, greens, blues … the colors of the rainbow, including viva magenta, Pantone color of the year— all flashing like strobe lights in my head …

And then it was as if I could hear the colors.

Now I'm hearing colors?

And tasting them, too. The reds tasted like copper. It was like sucking on dirty pennies.

I felt terrified.

What is happening to me?

I knew all too well what was happening to me: This is the 'aura.' The prodromal component of a tonic-clonic (grand mal) seizure that Dr. Newton and I had discussed, and that I had so flippantly dismissed as something that would never happen to me. But it *was* happening to me, and, because I knew too much for my own good, I knew what was coming next.

But the convulsion never came. The episode ended. And as always, the proverbial fog bank receded until everything had cleared, and I was still right where I had left myself, sitting at a little round table in a small café, in a huge airport in France, and I still had miles to go.

My left hand throbbed. I realized I'd burned it. The cup that once held steaming coffee was now a crushed, mangled ball of paper clenched in my fist. Black coffee was splattered everywhere, soaking my tickets and dripping off the edge of the table.

I stood up, swearing under my breath. The man at the next table stared at me, quizzically. He stood, walked over, and asked, "Monsieur? Vous allez bien?"

"No," I responded, "I think I had a seizure."

"Ca va?"

"Seizure."

"Monsieur?"

"Colors. Sounds."

He just stared at me.

I felt mortified. Confused. Scared.

For the first time in my life, I felt scared. I mean, look at me! Mike Peabody—Marine, MMA fighter, self-appointed savior of the medical world—a petrified little boy.

Other people ran up to help, and before I knew it, ten people were standing around me yelling at me in French. Then two guys in uniforms showed up, firing questions, grabbing my wrists to feel for a pulse. I jerked my hands away from them. One said something to me that indicated his level of annoyance, while the other grabbed my right arm and tried to attach a blood pressure cuff.

"Please!" I exclaimed. "I'm okay! Sah vah!"

"Ca va?"

"Dilantin. I need my Dilantin."

I rummaged through the front pocket of my pack and located the medication bottle. Without hesitation, I popped one of the pills and swallowed it dry, praying it would work. The seizures were getting worse, and the last thing I needed while traveling alone in Europe, in Charles de Gaulle airport terminal where nobody spoke English, was to find myself lying on the floor flopping like a fish out of water.

I'm not sure why, I mean, I don't exactly have an appreciation for prayer, but for some reason, even with all those well-meaning people crowding in around me, all I could think of to say was, "God, help me!"

CHAPTER FOURTEEN

Fiumicino—Leonardo da Vinci Airport
Rome, Italy
Thursday, April 2—4:44 PM (CET)

Maybe there is a God. I made my next flight and got out of France alive. I also completed the second leg of my journey without seeing the light or the fog. So, should I thank God? Jesus? I'm still trying to figure that out. The point is, I made it. "Thank heavens."

I spent a few minutes pondering my strange experience in Paris—seeing sounds and tasting colors. I know it sounds weird, but there's actually a name for that. It's known as synesthesia, a condition where sensory pathways overlap. So, based on what I just experienced, I suppose I qualify as a synesthete.

Terrific.

Someone once told me I know too much for my own good. They may have been right. But I enjoy having knowledge and applying it whenever possible. Anyway, back to that experience—to say I was frightened would be an understatement. I moved the medication bottle to my pants pocket. Dilantin wasn't intended for emergency use. It was developed as a preventative treatment, aimed at stabilizing neural activity to reduce the likelihood of seizures. Still, it made me feel better just to know it was there. Like I said before, it blocks sodium channels, and all.

The walk across Fiumicino (aka Leonardo da Vinci Airport) to the shuttle buses took me 25 minutes. It should've taken ten, but my legs felt like warm jelly. I had to stop several times along the way just to catch my breath. At one point, I got on the wrong shuttle train and had to take another one back again to start over. Ten minutes lost. I had never felt more confused. But somehow, mercifully, I ran into a couple of folks from America who had made the trip before. They escorted me to the depot and pointed out a bus with a sign that read, Roma Termini. I felt victorious.

I had done my homework well and knew that Termini was Rome's transportation mecca, with twenty-nine train platforms and daily service to cities all over Italy, as well as elsewhere in Europe. The name "Termini" (pronounced, *term-e-nee*) has something to do with the Roman god of boundaries, a dude named Terminus, or something, but other than the fact that it's where I wanted to be, that's about all I really cared about.

I jumped on the bus, found a seat, and tried to relax while we traveled the busy Roman avenues. At first, I watched the scenery with interest. It was just another big city, really, with office buildings, shops, delis, and streetlights like any other place, but there was a uniqueness about it that I found quite interesting. The occasional ancient stone building nestled in between rows of more modern architecture gave it the look and feel of, well, Rome. But after about ten blocks, the people and buildings began to merge, and I started thinking of home. I glanced at my watch—4:45 PM here. That meant 10:45 AM there. Gloria would be at work now, two hours into her day. I made a mental note to call her as soon as I arrived at my hotel. She needed to know I had safely arrived. I needed to hear her voice.

Next, my thoughts turned to Rico. Poor guy. I decided to call him, too. I murmured a quick prayer for him, but I had no idea who I was praying to. What is prayer, anyway? People say all the time, I'll pray for you, and all that, but what does that mean? Do they? I shook my head. I was looking for answers. I wondered where I would find them.

I let my eyelids close. Enough of Rome, already. I must have dozed off, because I don't remember anything else until the bus slowed and stopped, jerking me awake. I looked outside at a huge complex. The driver honked his horn and announced, "Termini!"

I thanked him in English. Like the Frenchman at the airport, he just frowned at me. *What is it with these Europeans?*

I climbed off with about twenty other people and made my way inside the vast architectural spread.

Termini is the main railway station of Rome, and to describe it as big would be an understatement. I could tee up a golf ball and hit it with my driver, and it would never get to the other end. Trains everywhere. People and luggage everywhere. Confusing, to a guy who had no idea where he was, or where he was going. But I will say this for Termini: she's beautiful, modern, and very well appointed with shops and amenities for the traveler. It reminded me of the massive indoor malls we used to have back home—before they bulldozed everything and turned it into those soulless outdoor shopping strips for the inside-the-beltline crowd.

It crossed my mind to stop and look around for a while, even spend a few Euros, but then, I had a train to catch. My travel agent had told me to catch the 5:35 to Firenze. I glanced at my watch—5:23. I needed to hurry.

I stopped at what looked like a ticket booth. That's where my plan took a dive. Every word on the kiosk was in Italian.

I fumbled around for a moment, looking for something that said Firenze (aka Florence). Nope. I felt a tap on the shoulder and turned. A nice-looking man with tanned skin and short black hair smiled up at me and said in convincing English, "Confusing, huh?"

I gave him a quick once-over. He wore blue jeans and a white T-shirt, tucked in neatly and held in place by a brown leather belt. A black, thigh-length leather jacket completed the ensemble. I looked for bulges on his hip that might indicate a gun or knife. Seeing none, I shook my head and pointed at the machine. "I have no idea what to do."

"Do you have an e-Ticket?"

"Huh?"

"Non importa," he said. "C'est facile. It's easy. Where are you going?"

"Florence."

"Firenze? Ahh, c'est facile!" He punched a few buttons, asked me to deposit the fare—19 dollars American—which I did. Then he waited until a ticket popped out and snatched it. "Here you go. It's there," he said, pointing across the terminal. "Frecciarossa 9400."

"Do what?"

"Firenze Express," he added. "Best hurry."

"Thanks."

"Grazie," he said, correcting me. "Here, we say, grazie."

"Grat-see."

Two months ago, I would not have accepted the word of a stranger and blindly climbed aboard a train called Frecciarossa 9400 bound for a place called Firenze, using terms like, *grazie* and *buongiorno*, but times change, and so do people. Besides, I had no idea where I was going, and he seemed to know.

Also, he didn't ask for it, but I gave him a tip, five Euros. He smiled, and then turned and hurried to another ticket booth, where yet another confused-looking traveler stood staring at her machine. He had quite a racket going, if you ask me, but then everyone's got to make a living. I hurried off to catch Frecciarossa.

When I arrived at what looked like the right platform, I double-checked my ticket (it matched), prayed it was the right one, and I wouldn't end up in Sicily, or worse, back in Paris. After standing on the platform in front of the train and staring up at the giant sloped nose for a moment, I walked around to the first car and boldly climbed aboard. A nice lady in blue slacks and a white blouse with a badge checked my ticket and pointed me toward the back of the train, saying, "Tre auto indietro!"

I shrugged.

"Three cars back," she said, in broken English.

"Grat-zee."

I found my seat "tre auto indietro" and flopped in it. After glancing around to see who else was traveling from Rome to Firenze—a whole lot of people, mostly dark-haired Europeans with thin bodies and good tans—I pulled out my laptop and fired it up. Within minutes, I had an internet connection with the onboard Wi-Fi.

I thought it might be a good idea to learn a little more about the subject of the conference before arriving in Florence, so I Googled the word, crucifixion. I found about a hundred articles. The trip was to take three hours and fifty minutes, so I figured I'd use the time wisely and read a couple of them. I zeroed in on one that discussed different theories on the general cause of death from crucifixion and pulled it up for a read. It proved to be quite interesting.

The article displayed a portrait of Jesus on the cross between two malefactors. Their positions on their crosses were quite different from his, one with his arms nailed in a bent position behind his head and the other with his arms stretched out too tight to allow for movement. In this painting, Jesus was positioned on his cross with a little slack in his arms to allow for movement, and his legs were bent at a ninety-degree angle to place him in a squatting position. The purpose behind that, the author explained, was to make it increasingly difficult for the victim to stand, forcing him to collapse with his full weight on his outstretched arms. Ultimately, this would make breathing impossible, causing asphyxiation.

Imagine standing with your back flat against the wall and bending your knees to a ninety-degree angle. Do that for a minute and then try to stand up. Your legs will burn. After a few attempts, you will not be able to stand. This was the very purpose behind his agonizing posture on the cross.

The author went on to explain that the most common cause of death by crucifixion was asphyxiation, the result of excessive pressure exerted on the heart when a body is hung in this position. "Two conditions are to blame," the writer contended. "Cardiac tamponade and pulmonary edema." I thought about that for a moment. I had seen plenty of both of those conditions, and his claim made perfect sense.

Cardiac tamponade is a condition produced by the buildup of fluid in the sac that surrounds the heart. It's a mechanical problem, much as if someone were squeezing the heart with their hands. The heart can't pump. Not only does blood pressure fall dramatically, but blood slowly backs up into the lungs. The lungs become saturated with bloody fluid, producing pulmonary edema.

Pulmonary edema gives the victim the sensation of drowning. It's typically caused by left ventricular failure due to myocardial infarction (or heart attack), but it can also be caused by mechanical issues like the one described above. The heart becomes unable to pump blood through, so it backs up into the lungs. The watery portion of the blood, under high pressure, seeps into the tissues of the lungs, causing edema. Gas exchange is hindered, causing oxygen levels to drop and carbon dioxide to rise. This is the definition of asphyxiation.

"Think of a sponge saturated with water," the author explained. "Then imagine trying to breathe through it. Do this, and you will have some idea just what Jesus would have experienced on that cross."

I wondered what might have caused the cardiac tamponade. Ventricular rupture? I mean, that often happens with an infarction, and rupture would allow blood to leak into the pericardium, producing the tamponade effect. But it could have been aortic dissection, too, a tear in the aorta from the high blood pressure he experienced in the garden.

I closed the MacBook and thought about it. Crucifixion must've been a horrible way to die. I paused and took a deep breath. It felt good. All I could think of to say was, "Jesus? Why?"

That made me think even more. Jesus. Who was he, really? And why, if he truly was the son of God, as Jim and Rico and so many other people claim, would he have put up with all that? I mean, if he were omnipotent, God, and all, he could've fought back. Why would he have allowed it?

I didn't get it. I just didn't get it.

All the thinking must've worn me out because somewhere during the trip from Rome to Florence, I fell into a deep sleep. I suppose my body just needed it. After the eight-hour transatlantic flight, the seizure at the Paris airport, and the death march across that never-ending Charles De Gaulle Airport terminal in Paris, my energy was spent. And I must have been down for the count, too, because I may not have ever awakened if a fellow passenger hadn't jostled me and kindly alerted me of our arrival in Florence.

"Sir," the young woman said. "Nous sommes arrivés. We are here."

"Here?"

"Firenze," she exclaimed. "Fi-ren-zaa."

"Florence?"

"Locals call it Firenze. You should do the same."

"I will."

I thanked her for the free Italian language lesson and sat there for a moment trying to remember why I was in Firenze, thankful too, that I wasn't waking up from a seizure-induced coma. This time it was from heavy-duty sleep. I grabbed my things and stepped off the train into a new world.

My lodging for the next few days was at a place called Hotel Boccaccio, just a short walk from Santa Maria Novella, the local train station. After grabbing my bag and walking three blocks to my hotel, I checked in at the front desk, and then, with the help of a kind bellhop, made my way upstairs to my room. The bellhop chatted in Italian the whole way, opened the door for me, and showed me the room. I tipped him and closed the door. I glanced at my watch—19:35—Italian time.

Home sweet home.

I glanced around the room. It was nice enough, quaint, with a double bed, a flat-screen TV—I knew how to use that—and a small bathroom with a porcelain toilet and, what I assumed to be, a bidet. It was an interesting-looking device. The shower looked inviting, one of those big walk-in deals with heavy tiles and thick white towels.

A double window with sheer white curtains opened onto the street. There was no screen on the window, so I was able to lean out for a 180-degree panoramic view. And it was a nice view, too. Picturesque, you might say, with a café called Marco's right across the street. The street boasted only light traffic, mostly small Citroens and Renaults, cars that you can park easily in a limited space. I saw no muscle cars or pickup trucks. Overall, the place had the expected feel and smell of Italy. I'm not exactly sure what Italy should smell like, but it did. It had a roasted coffee, baked bread, and vanilla kind of aroma, which I must admit, I found rather pleasant. I sensed the hint of black olives somewhere in there, as well, but I couldn't quite place it.

Instead of kicking back and catching a Zzz, I decided to leave my little room and venture across the street. I mean, why not? When in Rome, and all. Or in this case, Florence.

Marco's turned out to be a small affair with a pastry bar, a few small tables, and a veranda decorated with ivy. I walked up to the counter and ordered black coffee.

"Preferiresti un caffè o americano?"

The only word I understood in that question was Americano, so I repeated it.

The barista nodded and turned to fetch me a cup. He didn't seem to like me much. He kept scowling at me and glancing at my ball cap. I mean, I'm a Yankees fan, what can I say? Maybe he wasn't into baseball. Or Americans. Whatever—wasn't my problem. I could've whipped him with one hand, him and five of his surly mafia buddies. But he did serve my coffee hot and nodded when I asked if I could sit on the terrace, so I decided he was okay. I walked out there and found a small table overlooking the street. I sat down and sipped my drink.

I surfed the web on my phone and found the website for the medical conference. After confirming a 9:00 AM start, I checked in to see that I was properly registered and perused the itinerary. Lunch would be served at noon. Good. I like food. And that reminded me. Before calling Gloria, I Googled nearby restaurants and found a suitable place that served heavy Italian food. I could walk there in five minutes, eat well—lots of red sauce, hopefully—and then retire to my little room to sleep until the sun came around again. Boy, did I need that.

I closed Google Chrome and made a quick call to the states to check on Gloria. She didn't answer. Still at work, I figured. I left her a message, including *"I love you,"* and *"I miss you,"* and then hung up and dialed Rico. His wife answered on the third ring. I thought she sounded heavy.

"Mary," I said. "It's Mike! How's it going?"

"I thought you were in Italy."

"I am. I called to check on Rico."

"Um, well—" There was a short pause before she said, "Mike, Rico's not doing well."

I swallowed. "You know I'm afraid to ask."

"The doctor says it's days now, not weeks."

"Oh, Lord." I stood and paced the patio. "What are his symptoms?"

Mary chuckled. "No, sir. Stop being a doctor for a few minutes and just be his friend."

"Mary, I'm coming home. I'll be there by—"

"No! Michael, listen to me. Rico insisted that I tell you not to come home. He doesn't want you to have to … well, in his words … watch him die."

I sighed. "Pigheaded cop."

"He was adamant, Mike. I know you want to be here, but it's important to your friend that you stay there and experience this Shroud thing, whatever it is. He said to tell that stupid leatherneck not to change his plans."

I chuckled. "Rico the Rivet."

"He also said, 'Tell him, I love him.'"

Warm water flooded my eyes.

"One more thing, Mike. He said to tell you to look at the face. Study the face. Just look at it, and you'll understand. I assume he's talking about the Shroud."

Mary asked me to stay on the line while she prayed. It was not a simple prayer, but a strong one. There was power in her voice. In her words. It was almost as if she was talking to God. When she finished, she said, "We love you, Mike. Safe travels now, you hear?"

I told her I loved them, too, and added, "Tell that Puerto Rican tree stump, I said to quit faking and get up!"

After we had hung up, I sat for a moment thinking about the last time I had seen him, wasting away on the bed, slowly dying. "Cancer," I whispered, angrily. "Someone needs to find a cure."

CHAPTER FIFTEEN

Hotel Brunelleschi
Florence, Italy
Friday, April 3—7:38 AM (CET)

Google Maps indicated that the Hotel Brunelleschi was only about six blocks from Hotel Boccaccio. And just a quick side note here: it's very easy to become disoriented in Italy, since so many of the names of places sound so much alike, and so many of the people look so much the same, and, well, I think you get it. I'm just a dumb American, and after a while, all the words in Europe sound pretty much the same to me. And, well, like I said, you get it.

I hailed a cab and asked how long it would take to get there.

"Twenty minutes," he responded, waving his hand in the air. "Traffico."

Ah, traffico. Should've known. I felt rested enough and adventurous, so I decided to walk instead. And despite the use of my cane and the persistent limp in my left leg, I covered the distance in nineteen minutes. Success.

Located on Piazza Sant'Elisabetta, the Brunelleschi was a grand hotel, with white marble statues, slate floors, and a beautiful outdoor fountain with one of those obelisk things that looked like a miniature Washington Monument. I threw a quarter in the pool as I walked past, not so much for luck, I just wanted to get rid of it.

The hotel interior was spectacular. I pinched myself to make sure I wasn't dreaming. After all, when I travel, I tend to stay at Hampton Inn or Holiday Inn Express, not five-star international hotels, so this one overwhelmed me. I looked around for a few minutes, pretending like it was an everyday thing for me, and then limped down the hall to the auditorium.

That was far more spacious than I had expected, too, with comfortable chairs far enough apart that a big guy, like me, could relax. I took advantage of that and sat near the back of the room at the end of the row closest to the restrooms and coffee bar. Never hurts to be close to creature comforts. Not to mention my favorite stimulant—caffeine.

I had already had my usual limit of coffee, but I grabbed another cup anyway, knowing full well I'd be paying the price for it later. Small bladders and prostate issues always seem to cause that. I was perusing the program schedule and sipping at the cup when the presenter's bio caught my attention. Surprisingly, he was a career paramedic, not a doctor.

"Seriously?" I chuckled.

Apparently, he had studied photography under the STURP team's chief scientific photographer back in the 70's while in photography school. I read on: *After a 10-year career as a commercial photographer, Grady began a new career as a paramedic in Durham, North Carolina, where he served for twenty years. He now teaches medical classes and spends much of his spare time lecturing on the Shroud of Turin.*

Durham was close to home. That was cool. But a paramedic? I glanced at his name: Patrick Grady. This was supposed to be a medical conference for physicians. Why had they chosen a paramedic to deliver the keynote address? I pictured Jim Stockbridge up there and shrugged. *Well, let's see.*

The low rumble of casual conversation filled the room. Much of it was in English. The rest of it was, well? Something else. The presentation was to be delivered in English—since the presenter was American—and according to the program, interpreted into Italian. I figured that was good, since I don't speak Italian. Well, maybe a little now. After the airport, Termini, and the café, I knew to say "Buongiorno" instead of good morning, and "Grazie" instead of thanks. Also, "Vai a casa, Yankee," which means, "Go home, Yankee."

Out of curiosity, I glanced around the room at the other attendees, people mostly my age, middle-aged and younger. I estimated two hundred attendees or so, physicians or nurses, I assumed. But, again, who knew? After all, the speaker was to be a paramedic, and what kind of person attends a lecture about death by crucifixion anyway?

Most of the others were already seated, dressed casually like me, in business slacks and long-sleeved shirts. A couple of guys wore ties. The few women in attendance wore skirts and casual business clothes. One wore scrubs, as if she had just come from the hospital. I wondered if she was an ED doc. That, more than anything else I had seen since arriving here, made me feel just a little more at home. Medicine is medicine everywhere. So, I guess, are people.

A huge drop-down screen at the front of the auditorium displayed what I assumed was slide #1 of the PowerPoint presentation to follow. It was impressive, a black and white photo of the face of the Shroud above a title written in bold sepia lettering that read:

What Killed the Man in the Shroud of Turin?

Well, that was the question, wasn't it? But I had a pretty good idea I knew the answer—blood loss, heart failure, cardiac tamponade, and asphyxiation. Right? I mean, beat up a guy, scourge him with a cat of nine tails, and then hang him by his arms on a cross, and sooner or later, he'll die for a lot of reasons—suffocation, blood loss, acidosis, and heart failure. Not to mention the transected aorta he could've suffered from the ungodly hypertension he experienced in the Garden. I shook my head, truly humbled by the cascade of fatal symptoms.

"No man should have to die that way."

I bit my lip and began to wonder, who is this Jesus? I mean, really. And why did he leave his image on a cloth? Or did he? Is any of this real? I got the feeling there was a deeper, more emotional answer to this enigma I had yet to grasp, and that this paramedic was about to teach me something. That thought alone piqued my curiosity. I saw movement at the front of the auditorium and settled down in my seat. The program was about to begin.

A man with a medium build and thinning gray hair climbed the steps onto the stage. I noticed a slight limp to his walk, as if his hip bothered him, or maybe his back. He looked fit enough for a man of about thirty, probably a lifetime runner, maybe even a baseball player or golfer at some point in his life, but not a fighter.

Why do I judge people this way? I suppose it's innate. Just something I naturally do. I size up guys just in case things go sideways, and I'm forced to choose the ones to fight with, not against. But this guy? I didn't think I'd be selecting him to watch my back. He was of medium build, with a kind, almost youthful face. He wore gray slacks that matched his hair, a blue sport coat, and a white dress shirt, but no tie. He walked beneath the screen and stood for a moment, looking out at the audience without speaking. Then, like a magician performing an act, he held up his hand and the room fell silent. The lights dimmed. *Cool.*

He must have pushed a button on a remote, because the title slide faded and gave way to Slide #2, a beautifully enhanced color portrait of Jesus Christ, called Christ the Pantocrator. It lined up perfectly with the image of the Shroud it had replaced. That was cool too. A subtitle indicated that the portrait was produced in the 6th century, meaning somewhere between 500 and 600 A.D..

The portrait dissolved, giving way to the Shroud once more. It was a perfect overlay, revealing with haunting precision how every feature of the painting aligned with the ancient image. The point seemed to be that the artist had seen the Shroud and had made his painting of Jesus' face accordingly.

Fascinating.

"Wow," I murmured. "That is so cool." I felt convinced I was onto something big. Bigger than me. Perhaps, bigger than any of us.

I stared at the image. I had seen it so many times over the last two months that I felt I knew every detail by heart—the victim's drawn, tired expression, his nomadic hair and beard, the swollen cheek and broken features of his prominent, Semitic nose. But as I stared at the ghostly image on the screen, I felt a shiver run down my spine. I got a feeling deep inside my gut that I was actually staring at the face of Jesus Christ. I mean, could this be what he looked like?

"It's him," I whispered. "That's really Jesus."

"The Shroud of Turin—" the speaker began, his voice echoing mystically through the chamber, as if they had worked out a kind of amplified sound system that gave his voice more power. "An ancient cloth that bears the recognizable image of a man who was crucified and tortured in every way consistent with the gospel accounts of Jesus Christ. So realistic that the mind can almost see it come to life as one stares at it on the screen."

He was right. I felt as if I was looking at a person, alive even in death.

"But is this the face of Jesus Christ?"

I sat up a little higher.

"Did he leave his image on the threads of his burial cloth for us to marvel at and study today? Or could it be a clever forgery, as so many seem to believe?"

I had been juggling with that question for days.

"Maybe it's just a clever hoax," he said. "A painting. A forgery created by the brilliant mind of an artist like Michelangelo or Leonardo Da Vinci. Do we know? Will we ever know? Well, the answers to these questions remain a mystery. After more than four decades of research, we still don't."

A hoax? That was one theory I had never even considered. But it made perfect sense. I mean, some of the most brilliant artists of all time lived in the Renaissance period, so the idea that one of them had created a masterful painting of Jesus on a burial cloth seemed well within the realm of possibility.

"Many people have formed opinions," he explained, continuing. "But despite intense scrutiny, from microscopic studies to radiocarbon dating, and now even, holographic and radiation tests to determine if a body had simply passed through the cloth in every direction at once, somehow, magnificently burning the image into its threads, we, the scientific, medical, and religious communities, do not know for sure what caused this spectacular image. And we may never know. The image itself is, apparently, fading.

Fading?

"Who knows? In a hundred years or less, it may have completely vanished. Time, therefore, is of the essence."

I felt glued to my seat. I had never experienced such anticipation in a PowerPoint presentation, or what the speaker might say next. I shifted my weight to the edge of my seat and focused my attention on his voice, my eyes on the screen.

"But we will not be attempting to answer these questions today. Whether or not the Shroud of Turin is authentic, I will leave up to you. However, to use the passion and suffering of Jesus Christ in our studies is a must. The only record we have of a human being tortured in exactly the manner we see evidenced in the Shroud of Turin is the record of Jesus Christ that we find recorded in the pages of the Bible. So, I will be referring to scripture to make my points. I will not apologize."

I liked this guy. He *was* a fighter after all.

He continued.

"Historically, the Shroud dates to 1354, when it was first seen in the hands of the famed knight, Geoffroi de Charnay, of France. The apparent spoils of war, the Shroud was reportedly discovered folded up in the wall of the city gate of Constantinople, an ancient city in modern-day Turkey. It could have been folded up so that only the face was visible, and perhaps presented in a frame to resemble a portrait. It changed hands numerous times over the years, eventually becoming the property of the Roman Catholic Church. The church moved it to its current resting place in Turin, Italy, where it has been since 1578. Although it has only been shown to the general public on rare occasions, it just happens to be on exhibit right now in Turin at the cathedral where it resides, the Cathedral of San Giovanni Battista, or Saint John the Baptist."

I put my new conference pen to use and started scribbling notes on my new conference notepad. I could not write fast enough. There was just too much good information.

"In 1898," the speaker continued, "following one of these rare public expositions, the Shroud was photographed by Secundo Pia, a lawyer and amateur photographer. Up to that point, no modern photographs had been made, and no real studies had been performed, but Pia changed all that. You might say modern science entered the picture when Pia took his photos. Upon processing his images, he noticed that his negatives revealed positive images of the Shroud, with much greater definition than the image itself."

What?

"This meant that what he had photographed was, in fact, a negative, the concept of which was unheard of before the invention of photography in the early 1800's."

Grady paused, presumably to allow the audience the time to process that information.

I thought of the black and white negatives I had processed in my father's makeshift darkroom as a kid. I mean, you turn off the lights, unload the film in the pitch darkness, and then load it onto a processing reel. Once the reel is in the tank with the lid on tight, you turn on the lights and fill the tank with a sequence of chemicals: first, the developer, next, the acetic acid stop bath, and finally, the fixer, which hardens and "fixes" the film. Then, after the prescribed amount of time, you open the tank and wash the film with clean water. Finally, you unroll your processed film and look at it.

And interestingly, amazingly, for me anyway, it always seemed to work. Light values were rendered as density on the film, and dark values were rendered as clear. In short, everything was negative. The magic of photography.

Pia's jaw probably dropped when he lit his candles and realized he was looking at just the opposite—a positive. This meant that what he had photographed had been a negative. Revelation? The Shroud image was negative. Thus began a long trail of curious studies into the formation of the Shroud image and the possibility of its authenticity.

"So, here we are. And here's what we know: The victim depicted in the Shroud image was a man in his early thirties, five feet and ten inches tall, one hundred seventy pounds. He was strong across the shoulders and chest, with well-developed legs and arms, and an otherwise healthy-looking body. The body of a worker. A physical guy who worked with his hands. But make no mistake, that body was brutalized—beaten around the face and head, whipped relentlessly, and finally, nailed to something for a slow, excruciating death. A mean death brought on by vicious men."

The second slide faded and gave way to the third, a full-length image of the cloth spread out horizontally to display its every feature. I, of course, had seen this image too, first in National Geographic, and many times more online and in other magazines. But just as with the image of the face, the longer I stared at it, the more it was as if I were viewing it for the first time. I saw new depth. New details.

"This is the Shroud," he began. "Fourteen-feet three-inches long, by three-feet seven-inches wide. A fine, expensive linen cloth, spun in a sophisticated herringbone twill that would have been available only to the wealthiest people of that time. Keep in mind, if you will, that according to scriptures, Jesus was buried by a wealthy Jew, a man named Joseph of Arimathea. So it makes perfect sense that he would have used a fine linen cloth, such as we see here.

"Furthermore …" The speaker paused and advanced the slide to reveal a close-up image of one of the victim's eyes. "There is evidence that a Roman coin was placed over each eye during burial. But this was, of course, a pagan practice, so not all researchers accept the idea. Regardless, close-up imaging reveals details consistent with Roman coins, specifically, bronze *prutah* coins minted during the reign of Pontius Pilate, about 29 AD. Now, if you use a certain degree of imagination here, you might be able to make out a shepherd's staff, a sheaf of wheat, and various Latin letters."

I could not. But *prutah coins?* I made a mental note to Google that later.

Thankfully, the speaker stepped to one side of the stage to take a few sips from a bottle of water. I used the opportunity to close my eyes and think. I felt amazed, stupefied, small and uneducated, and incredibly blessed all at the same time. How did I get here? I wondered. Why am I here?

"Now, notice, if you will," he said, advancing the slide to reveal the full bodily image again. "The multitude of gashes that cover the entire body. Front and back. Arms and legs. Abdomen and buttocks and chest."

This was new for me. I had considered Christ's scourging, but I had never given it too much thought, choosing instead to focus on the signs of crucifixion.

"Almost every square inch of skin has been ripped to bloody shreds. This would indicate that the man in this burial cloth had been scourged over a hundred times, most likely from both sides, as if there had been, not one, but two offenders. See?" he said, using the laser to pinpoint two different angles of the markings. "You can tell by the opposing angles of the lacerations, that the whips came from different positions. And the gashes are about one and one-half inches long, which is consistent with archeological findings of Roman scourges from that time period.

The punishers would have used the then common, cat-of-nine-tails, a wooden handle with multiple leather thongs, each with a dumbbell-shaped lead weight attached to its end. Whipped hard against skin and flesh, the dumbbells would gouge and tear the flesh, pulverizing the underlying tissues to leave behind terrible bleeding and bruising. Devastating external and internal injuries. And the scriptures bear this out."

He advanced the slide and read it for us:

"Then Pilate took Jesus and had him flogged." (John 19:1)

And again:

" … *his appearance was so disfigured beyond that of any human being and his form marred beyond human likeness.*" (Isaiah 52:14)

"Let that sink in for a minute," he said, his voice almost a whisper. "Close your eyes. Can you see it? Can you picture this man being flogged, disfigured beyond that of a human?"

I tried.

"Probably not," he said. "Not realistically, anyway, because we no longer live in a time when public punishments, like floggings, are practiced. But in the first-century world, these tortures were common. The writer of the Gospel would have seen no need to explain in detail. So, bear with me as I try to paint a picture.

"Imagine if you will that they strip off your clothing. They tie your hands up over your head and bend you over a wooden post. Your backside is fully exposed, and any whip-end can wrap around your body to the other side to tear both front and back …"

I cringed.

"And then, two men, well trained at this form of torture, one on each side of you, take turns lashing you repeatedly across your back, your legs, your sides. And perhaps, at some point—" The presenter paused and sighed. "They turn you around and repeat the process across your front."

I felt almost sick. Even embarrassed. I saw wounded people almost every day, treated their wounds and sewed up their flesh, but I had never witnessed anything as brutal as this.

"Before I address the broken nose," he continued, "the swollen cheek, punctured scalp and facial trauma, not to mention the through-and-through penetrating wounds in both wrists and feet, let's discuss this point further. Even today," he explained, thrusting both hands out to emphasize the point, "if a patient arrived at your emergency department in a state of hypovolemic shock, bruised and bleeding, with hundreds of inch-long chunks of flesh ripped from his body, hypothermic, with his blood pressure dangling, he would have likely died. Would you not agree?"

The speaker waited for a response. The nods of approval around me confirmed a unanimous, "Yes" from the audience. The speaker continued.

"Now, I'm just a paramedic, but I've been around emergency rooms long enough to know that you guys would do everything in your power to stabilize this patient. Careful warming to battle hypothermia. Hemorrhage control. Airway management. IV fluids and blood transfusions. Antibiotics and wound care. Extended stay in a critical care unit would follow, of course, and yet even with all that, he might survive.

"Might! He would be at elevated risk for a systemic inflammatory response and sepsis, both of which can produce fatal hypotension. But remember, this man had no medical care at all. None. In fact, immediately after this scourging, he was forced to pick up a 90-pound beam and carry it up the hill to Golgotha. Keep in mind, too, that he began the night in the Garden of Gethsemane with a blood pressure off the charts high. So high, in fact, that he was sweating blood, which would increase bleeding from his initial wounds. Make no mistake, this man was in dire shape. Close to death."

I tried to map out the visuals, but the scene was a mess in my head. But I definitely got the main point: This Jesus had been punished mercilessly. I held my breath, waiting..

"Scriptures tell us Jesus picked up his cross and tried to walk, but he was so weak that he soon collapsed under the weight. So, yes, I believe the man in the Shroud of Turin was in shock, and he would have died from these injuries alone. But the worst was yet to come."

CHAPTER SIXTEEN

Hotel Brunelleschi
Florence, Italy
Saturday, April 4—8:38 AM (CET)

The worst was yet to come? I stared at the slide, wondering how that was even possible. Then, a sharp, burning reminder from my lower half reminded me that if I didn't move fast—things were about to get a lot worse, for me. I had consumed a lot of coffee, and my bladder had reached its breaking point. I bolted for the men's room, which turned out to be surprisingly elaborate. But rather than admiring the tiled urinals and gold fixtures, I used the momentary escape to process what I'd heard. The lecture had mesmerized me. It gave me that same rush I'd felt back in med school while studying major trauma, scribbling notes until my hand cramped. This paramedic from Durham was the real deal. I finished up, washed my hands, and hurried back just as the next slide clicked into place. It read:

ex / cruc / iating

"Excruciating," the speaker said, pointing his laser at the slide. "We know that to mean extremely intense, unbearable physical or mental suffering, often described as agonizing or torturous. It signifies the highest level of pain, going beyond severe to a point that is hard for a person to endure. Now, this common word is derived from the Latin term **cruc-**, which means *cross*, and the prefix, **ex-**, which means *out, out of, away from, forth*. Therefore, the term literally means *out of,* or *from the cross*. And that is exactly what the victim we see here experienced. Excruciating pain."

He advanced the slide and read it slowly for effect:

"Carrying his own cross he went to the
place of the Skull, called Golgotha.
There they crucified him." (John 19: 17-18)

"And there they cruc-i-fied him," he exclaimed, verbally dissecting the term. "Fixed him to a cross."

By this point in my career, I am numb to most descriptions of major trauma and pain. Not to mention medical term dissection. I can do that in my sleep. But when I heard him use the word crucify, it had a particularly strong effect on me.

I shivered as he described the 9-inch spikes used by the Roman soldiers, and how, if you look at close-up images of the hands, no thumbs are visible. I wondered why, until he explained that the executioners were knowledgeable and clever in their methods designed to produce maximum pain. It has been proven that a nail driven through the wrist at just the right place between the medial carpal bones—called the Space of Destot—not only produces the excruciating, hot-electrical shooting pain of crucifixion, but it causes the thumbs to flex, drawing them inward.

"See?" he said, pointing his red laser at the wrists. "No thumbs."

Hmm, now that is interesting.

He explained the position in which they had hammered him to the cross. How breathing would've been impossible without a continuous back-and-forth effort of standing on his impaled feet, to hanging from the nails in his wrists, the rough wood tearing at the fresh wounds on his back and shoulders. The effect was maximum torture. Pain and suffocation. Finally, he explained, death would have come from asphyxiation—the lethal combination of excessive carbon dioxide (hypercapnia) and insufficient oxygen (hypoxia). And every physician knows this produces a state of acidosis and extreme anaerobic metabolism, the combination of which is lethal.

"After hours of hanging on a cross like this, unable to properly ventilate the lungs and lower the pressure building up within the chest cavity, the heart, under too much pressure, slowly begins to fail, and the result is agonizing. The lungs fill with fluid—of course, you know this as pulmonary edema—and myocardial infarction is underway. Death is imminent now. It's only a matter of time."

I wanted to disappear. I felt guilty, inexperienced, and naïve. How had I, a veteran combat physician with years and years of experience dealing with trauma, never heard any of this?

"I'll leave you with this, then," the speaker said, as he concluded his 90-minute talk. "We may never know if the Shroud of Turin was the burial cloth of Jesus Christ. But one thing is certain: the man wrapped in that cloth suffered unimaginable pain, and then he died from asphyxiation and heart failure. A crushed and broken heart."

The lecture ended. The crowd stood. The applause was resounding.

I stood and did my best to maintain equilibrium. I saw the cloud approaching and had to sit back down. The aura lasted for a minute or two, but I somehow willed it away. My vision cleared, and I could see people milling about again. Some were hurrying up front to speak to the presenter. Others were engaged in discussion. I? I felt as if I'd been hit by a truck. I also felt exhilarated, astonished, and fully convinced that everything he had said was true. Whoever Jesus was, and whether or not the Shroud really was his burial cloth, he had suffered unimaginable torment. But why? I wondered. Why?

I walked up to the stage and waited until the crowd settled down. I could tell by his appearance that the speaker was of Anglo-Saxon descent. Irish, maybe, or even German. I waited for the right moment and approached him. "Mr. Grady," I said. "I'm Mike Peabody."

"Hello," he said, gasping, as he looked up and saw my bandages. "My, what happened to you?"

"I was shot."

"Oh, my."

"I'm okay. I'm recovering. I just wanted to tell you how much I enjoyed your lecture. I'm a new student of The Shroud, and you have enlightened me."

"I am so glad to hear that. Have you seen it yet? It's on display right now in Turin, you know."

"Actually, I had heard it was there. I was thinking about traveling up to Turin tomorrow. I'd like to see it in person."

I thanked Grady again, and then went outside to be alone for a while. I wanted to think about our conversation and the many details he had provided in his lecture. I felt more convinced than ever that I needed to see it. I had no idea why, I just knew I had to see it. I composed a text message to Will Hendricks and pushed SEND. Then I sat down on a brick wall next to a small fountain and planned my next move. I would need to purchase a ticket for the super train. Where would I get that? Will's response came within a minute, and I could almost hear the excitement in his text:

Oh wow! So glad to hear it, Dr. Peabody! Stand by for info ...

I decided to sit by for that info. My leg hurt, my head ached, and my memory was all over the place. I didn't have to wait long before a second text dinged my phone:

Walk to the train station: Santa Maria Novella.
Buy a ticket for the Red Bullet train #9904,
07:25 AM. 3h 5m ride.

Disembark Porta Nuova, Torino. Catch a cab or walk to the cathedral, not far …

He ended the dialogue with the following text:

See you tomorrow 12:00 PM, statue of Julius Caesar, plaza beside cathedral. Come expectantly. You're going to LOVE this! –Will

CHAPTER SEVENTEEN

Santa Maria Novella
Red Bullet train #9904
Florence, Italy
Sunday, April 5—7:25 AM (Central European Standard Time—CEST)

The express train from Firenze to Torino was ultracool. Like the first one, the one I rode from Rome to Florence, it was another one of those Trenitalia Frecciarossa jobs, categorized as a "Red Arrow," which means it's one of the fastest trains in Italy. Red Arrows reach speeds of 300 km/h, or in American parlance, 190 mph. Fast in anybody's language. I had a window seat this time, and a trip that wound through some of the prettiest scenery in all of Italy, so I decided to sit back and enjoy the ride. No magazine articles, no internet, just the ride.

The train departed at precisely 7:25 AM and accelerated into the Italian landscape. We quickly hit top speed, and the landscape blurred into motion—fields of green, clusters of trees, and glimpses of villages and towns flashing by.

There wasn't much to look at, really, just incredibly beautiful countryside, so after a while I found myself daydreaming, wishing I could stop the train and just start walking. I'd end up where I ended up. I mean, it looked about as peaceful a place as I'd ever seen. You could almost smell it—the red wine and cheese. Black olives and bread. And I'd fit in, right? After all, every small village in the world needs a good doctor, and I was a good doctor. But was I? Whether or not I could even operate with the specter of an impending seizure leaning over me was yet to be determined. But somebody out there needed me. I could feel it.

The trip lasted, as advertised—three hours and fifty minutes. The train slowed to the hissing sound of air brakes and eased to a stop. After a few seconds, the doors slid open. I stepped off feeling like an old pro. I had logged over 400 miles on high-speed trains, so my confidence was high. I double-checked the signage to make sure I was at the right stop—Torino Porta Nuova—yep—and then stepped off the train and opened Google Maps, which I had already programmed to point me to the cathedral.

I had only taken a few steps to the northeast when I noticed a large white sign featuring a picture of the face of the Shroud of Turin. Beneath the picture were some words written in bold black font:

Solenne ostensione della sindone

Sindone means *shroud*, I think. I typed the words into the new Italian-to-English translation app I had downloaded onto my phone and quickly received the interpretation:

Solemn Exposition of the Shroud

I wanted to say something, like, "*Well … cosa sai? … What do you know?*" but the only word that came from my mouth was the somber word, "Solemn." I felt humbled. Like I was on a pilgrimage to see an astounding religious artifact that was far too important for words, and I had just discovered it. A large black arrow at the bottom of the sign pointed up the street in the direction I was already headed. So, for the second time in as many days, I felt successful. I had made it from a platform in a train station in Firenze, Italy, to another station in a city called Torino, 250 miles north. Let's keep moving.

It took me forty-five minutes to complete the trek. I stopped at an outdoor market along the way and bought a juicy, blood orange, which turned out to be the tastiest thing I've ever put in my mouth. I also stopped to view an Italian ambulance I saw parked on a side street. Neat. With a sloped-back, aerodynamic nose, it looked a little like the bullet train I had just ridden. But it had a Star of Life emblem on the hood, just like back home. And signal lights front and back, and a bright color scheme featuring white, orange, and lime green. In many ways, it looked like any ambulance I might see pull into the dock at East Beach Regional, but with the word *Ambulanza* written across the hood, it would have been difficult to mistake its true nationality.

I clicked a few photos of the truck. The two paramedics—a male and a female—sitting in the cab didn't seem to mind. They wore black ball caps, bright orange polo shirts—as orange as the one I had just eaten—and curious expressions on their faces. I gave them a wave and walked on. A moment later, I heard a siren and watched the same truck rush by. Some things are the same everywhere.

Eventually, the sidewalks of Torino gave way to a cobblestone sidewalk that led to the front steps of the Turin Cathedral—Saint John the Baptist Cathedral (San Giovanni Battista). The church didn't look special, I mean, it was pretty cool and all, but it reminded me of most of the other big buildings I had seen along the way, old and bold and white, with ten-foot doors, and a grand staircase that swept across the front of the building. In a way, it reminded me of The Alamo in San Antonio, Texas, where Davy Crockett and his boys took a stand. A concrete bell tower stood to the left. A tiny cross stood at the apex of the chapel, fifty feet above the street.

I watched people meander up and down the steps, some entering, some exiting, giving the building a more lived-in appearance. Interestingly, everyone seemed to have the same kind of astonished-looking expression on their face, as if they had just seen God.

Me? I still wasn't sure what I was doing there, but, as I said earlier, somewhere deep inside I just knew I had to see the thing.

I glanced around for someone looking like Julius Caesar and spotted him across the street amongst some interesting-looking reddish structures. I walked over, stopped at the base of the statue, and looked up at him. Old Julius stood there in a toga, all green and weathered looking, his head about sixteen feet above the ground, and his right arm raised into the air, as if saluting his beloved Rome.

I chuckled. The poor guy had no idea what was coming: a gruesome assassination at the hands of his friends.

I was taking a selfie with Julius, when I heard my name called. Startled, I glanced in the direction of the voice and saw an exhilarated-looking Will Hendricks coming my way—Will, the scientific photographer, the man I had just met the day before on a plane ride from the U.S. The man who had promised this would be a day I would never forget. He was dressed in khaki pants and a dark blue polo shirt with a tie—just like me, except for the tie. He had a mischievous grin on his face. His hair blew in the breeze. He hurried across the plaza in my direction. I raised my chin to greet him. He raised his hand like Caesar's, as if pointing at the clouds.

"Mike!" he shouted. "You made it!"

I glanced at my watch—12:01. Right on time. "You said noon."

"I wasn't sure you would come. You seemed so skeptical. The Shroud, man! It's right over there. Ready to go see it?"

"That's why I'm here."

"I'm so glad. C'mon," he said. "We need to hurry. I want you to see it before the end of the exposition."

I followed Will across the street and down a steep stone staircase on the side of the building. In many ways, it reminded me of the staircase where Jim and I had been shot. We entered through a heavy wooden door on big iron hinges. A sign above the door read, *Ingresso vietato.* No admittance.

I felt my stomach churn. Two officials on the inside of the door checked Will's credentials, questioned him, and then frisked me and waved us through. After passing through a metal detector machine, at which point the fusion plates in my lower back were discovered, they ran a wand over me, frisked me again, and then sent us on our way. Will led me into a shadowy stone corridor that stretched beneath the chapel's foundations. The air turned chilly and damp. I saw water droplets seeping from the walls. "The cathedral is over six hundred years old," Will explained. "Over the past two weeks, two million people have stood in line, right here, to see the Shroud."

"Two million?"

"People enter in groups of twelve and have three minutes to look at it before exiting to make room for the next group. I'm part of the research team. We will have no time limit." Will went on to explain that security would be high. "An Italian guard will be standing at attention on each side of the display. But a small army will be nearby, so be on your best behavior," he said, with a laugh. "Also, a Catholic nun will be addressing the group. You won't understand a word she says, but that's okay. Just seeing it will be enough."

I could feel my stomach tighten as we ascended another steep staircase and slipped through a set of double doors that led inside.

The interior of the cathedral was dim. And quiet. Almost dead quiet, except for an occasional whisper, a cough, or the shuffling of feet as visitors moved through the line. Every pew was filled, but no one seemed to move. I remembered the word *solemn* I had seen on the poster at the station. It now seemed more appropriate than ever.

A woman began to speak in front of the church, in Latin or Italian or some other language I could not understand, as Will had warned. Her words sounded eloquent and romantic. I couldn't see her because of the huge column blocking my view. A line of people wound all the way around the back of the church to a side door. As I was watching, the guards closed the entrance, marking the end of the exhibition.

"That's it," Will said, nudging me. "It's over. C'mon."

C'mon where? I followed him a few steps to the end of one of the pews. And that's when I first saw it.

Right there—displayed horizontally at the front of the church, in a heavy wooden frame and behind, what I assumed to be bulletproof glass—was the Shroud of Turin. A guard stood on either side of the display wearing an ornate black uniform and a red helmet with colorful plumage. An elderly woman in a white robe stood to one side, addressing the crowd. Her voice sounded weary, as if she had been speaking for days, but her eyes appeared vibrant, as if beaming with pride. I recognized the word, *Sindone.* Shroud. It was the only word I comprehended.

I felt mesmerized. It wasn't a picture in a magazine this time, an online image, or a cardboard rendering, but the actual Shroud of Turin, a holy relic believed by many to be the burial cloth of Jesus Christ.

"Wheeew," I whispered, exhaling quietly. "My God, there it is."

"Pretty cool," Will whispered. "Right?"

I could not help but marvel at the image of the body, sepia in color, bold against the lighter background, but strangely muted. I also could not help but notice that, even from a distance, details were hard to distinguish. I spotted the blood stains marking the nail holes in the victim's hands and feet. The scourge marks scattered over the torso and legs. The lance wound on one side. But what amazed me most was the long, drawn expression on the victim's face.

Just look at it, then you will understand.

The word epiphany is overused, but for me, this was truly an epiphany. I was looking at Jesus. The one many call, Christ. I had no doubt. Rico had been right. Just look at him, Rico had said. Then you will understand. Suddenly, I understood.

Will leaned over, close enough for me to smell the mint on his breath. "Pretty amazing, huh?"

I couldn't speak. I heard him chuckle.

He nudged me and walked down the aisle to the first pew. I took a seat beside him, and together we sat and stared at it for another sixty minutes, or so, as the line wound down. Then the last of the faithful pilgrims heard the Nun's soliloquy and were ushered from the church. I watched with genuine interest as the room emptied. The doors were locked, the nun disappeared, and an army of workers and guards appeared.

"Geez," I said. "Where'd they come from?"

"Out of the walls," Will said with a chuckle. "C'mon," he said. "The exposition is officially over. Let's go downstairs and get ready."

"For what?"

"The best part. C'mon, you'll see. Follow me."

CHAPTER EIGHTEEN

Shroud of Turin Exposition
Cathedral of San Giovanni Battista
Torino, Italy
Sunday, April 5—12:50 PM Local Time (CEST)

Will's words reminded me of a scene in the Bible where Jesus saw Peter and Andrew fishing and called out to them, saying, "Follow me." They did follow him. For the next three years. They heard him preach, cast out demons, heal people, and perform many other magnificent deeds, but ultimately, they also saw him suffer. They saw him beaten, scourged, and nailed to a wooden cross outside the city. He died, and they buried him, but three days later he arose. And after that, things would never be the same.

Follow me.

What kind of man drops what he's doing and follows a stranger?

I followed Will to a quick dinner in downtown Turin. I had something that resembled lasagna. He had a salad and Italian bread dipped in olive oil. Afterwards, we walked back to the cathedral through the same metal detector. I followed Will down a hallway behind the chancel to a steep staircase that led to the basement. On the way down, he explained that the Shroud lives in the same bulletproof encasement in which I had seen it displayed. "It's rarely opened. But our team has been granted a three-hour window for close-up studies. And after that, some X-ray studies will be performed. The crew will unlock it, the nuns will examine it, and then we will be given the green light. I'll set up first and produce the holographic images. After that, I'll have a few more tests to complete."

"What happens to it after that?"

"The case will be vacuum sealed again, the proper gases pumped in, and the crew will move it to its home in the chapel, where they store it under lock and key. Actually, it's protected by a state-of-the-art alarm and fire system that rivals the security vault of any Las Vegas casino. It will be locked away there until the next showing."

"When will that be?"

"No one knows. Maybe never. Believe me, they spare no expense to protect the Shroud. They consider it holy, Mike. Priceless beyond words."

I followed Will into a modern, sterile-looking lab with LED lighting. I noticed cabinets on every wall. Clean countertops and a big sink. A long, flat, stainless-steel table sat in the center of the room, glistening, awaiting the arrival of the priceless artifact.

"Is this where they will lay it?" I asked.

"No, they use this table whenever it's removed from the case. It won't be removed today. It's in the next room," he said, pointing at a heavy door.

I felt my stomach turn again. How did I get here?

Will shared more of the Shroud's history with me while we waited. Where it had traveled, how it had gotten to Turin, and how it had survived two fires, leaving burn marks and water stains that are still visible today. "So, the patches you'll see were sewn in by nuns following the 1532 chapel fire in Chambery, France. We're lucky to even have it. The fire might've destroyed it."

He had just started to explain the presence of blood in the fibers of the cloth when the door opened, and a friendly-looking man of about seventy walked into the lab wearing a business suit and blue latex gloves. Short, round, and baldheaded, with wire rim spectacles on the bridge of his nose, he reminded me of Winston Churchill, only without the scowl and stubby cigar. He greeted Will by name, introduced himself to me as Dr. Francesco Gallo, curator of the Shroud, and then asked us to step back. In fact, he shoved us back.

Just then, two nuns in white robes and red silk scarves entered the lab, followed closely by the same two guards who had been standing at attention next to the Shroud exhibit. Their uniforms looked even more exquisite up close, with white epaulets and brass buttons. A red stripe ran down each leg. The two men proceeded to the door, unlocked it, and rolled it up. The lights inside the chamber lit up automatically. The guards stepped inside, followed closely by the two nuns.

"This way," Dr. Gallo said, taking me by the arm.

I took a deep breath and stepped inside the room, amazed at the reverence I felt. Before me in the center of the room, beneath a high ceiling embedded with lights and a cable system, the framed encasement sat like a long coffee table covered with red silk. The nuns lifted the silk sheet and carefully folded it. The guards unlocked the case and attached six silver cables hanging down from the ceiling. Then, with the push of a button, the cables tightened and slowly lifted the heavy sheet glass to the ceiling.

The Shroud lay before us, all fourteen feet of it, pristine beneath the balanced white lights. The curator heard me gasp and sidled up next to me. "Beautiful, isn't it?"

All I could manage to say was, "Unbelievable."

The nuns approached the table and lowered their heads. I saw their lips move, but heard no words. Then they ran their gloved hands gently over the surface in unison, smoothing out any wrinkles and assessing it for imperfections. I felt impressed by their delicate movements as they stroked and pressed the ancient fabric. One of the old women glanced at me and winked. "È il Signore," she whispered, a reverent tone to her voice.

I glanced at Dr. Gallo. His face seemed to glow. He leaned over and quietly translated. "It is the Lord."

"Yes," I whispered. "I believe it is."

Will Hendricks patted my shoulder and said, "I'll be right back. I'm going to grab my equipment."

"Can I help?"

"No, no. Stay and enjoy this."

Will left the room. The curator stepped up to the table and, along with the nuns, began inspecting the cloth, as if looking for the tiniest flaw. The guards stood at attention. I wondered if they ever breathed. They did not seem to be armed, but I knew they had a dozen brethren in the wings wearing Army fatigues and toting Beretta submachine guns, ready to jump at the first sign of trouble. But that made sense, didn't it? This holy relic would never be more vulnerable, and they were sworn to protect it.

I shifted my attention back to the Shroud, knowing that I would never again have this opportunity.

I could feel my knees trembling as I studied the details of the cloth, impressed by the difficulty of making out an identifiable form. The image appeared as nothing more than blurry shades of sepia extending from one end of the cloth to the other. I stared at it curiously, fascinated by the lack of clarity at such proximity.

"An artist could not have done this."

Dr. Gallo must have heard me mumbling to myself, because he stepped away from the table and said, "A penny for your thoughts, Dr. Peabody?"

"This is not a painting."

"Tell me why you say that."

"Because the details are indistinguishable up close. You can only see it clearly from a distance. So how could an artist—Da Vinci or Michelangelo—have painted something so accurate, so anatomically correct while standing at arm's length? I mean, it just doesn't seem possible."

"You are absolutely correct, sir." Dr. Gallo grinned widely, displaying a set of uneven teeth. "This is not a painting, and there is much more evidence to prove that. Would you like to touch it?"

"Touch it? Me?"

"Will tells me you are quite a student of the Shroud."

I couldn't speak.

"Come up here then. It's all right."

I stepped up to the table beside Dr. Gallo. He handed me a pair of exam gloves, which I quickly donned.

"When you're ready," he said, "you may touch the edge. Gently."

I hesitated and touched the cloth. I'm not sure what I expected to feel when I touched it, but no electric shock or power emanated from the fibers. Just a feeling of confirmation that I was touching the very cloth that had been used to bury Jesus.

"The son of God," I whispered.

Dr. Gallo leaned close to me. "You are an eyewitness now."

"I'm speechless now."

"The Shroud has this effect on people."

I had already determined that Dr. Gallo was a godly man. Faith seemed to emanate from his being, as if he were filled with something special that spoke of his confidence and strength. Usually, I would feel threatened by someone like this, but instead, I felt drawn to him.

"Look at the nail holes," he said, pointing out the blood stain on the victim's right arm. "Note the location. The wound is not in the hand, as depicted in many paintings of the crucifixion, but rather, in the wrists."

I thought about that. From my studies of human anatomy, I had already deduced that a large spike driven through the flesh between the bones of the hand—called metacarpals—would not stay in place under the weight of a human. There are no tightly connected bony structures there to hold the bones together, just soft tissue, so there would be nothing to prevent a spike from ripping out when put under weight. However, since the eight bones of the wrist—carpals—are held tightly together by connective ligaments, they could easily support the weight.

Dr. Gallo walked to the end of the frame. "Look at the feet," he said. "See the way one foot was placed atop the other?"

I inspected the blood stains there. I could see where blood had flowed, not from one, but from two separate wounds in the center of the top foot.

"So," I said, remembering the lecture the day before. "If Jesus was nailed to the cross with his legs bent at a ninety-degree angle, as I have heard he was, then he would've had to stand on those nails to breathe. Right?"

"Yes, that is correct."

"Then the pain must've been—"

"Excruciating?"

"Exactly."

"Go look at that face again," he said. "Let all of the details burn into your mind."

I made a mental recording of the details as I studied the nose and eyes.

"Now, close your eyes," he said. He waited until I had complied and then continued. "Try to imagine that you are a citizen of ancient Jerusalem. For the last three years, a man named Jesus has walked the streets preaching to the people, amazing them with his remarkable powers, healing and teaching them, and claiming to be the Son of the living God."

I had no reference for this. I had read each of the Gospel accounts of Christ several times by that point, but only the parts dealing with his passion and crucifixion. I knew nothing about his prior life or ministry. I suddenly regretted my ignorance.

"Crowds followed him everywhere," Dr. Gallo continued. "His followers loved him. But the authorities grew to resent and hate him."

I thought of the many different reactions I had seen in my lifetime at the very mention of the name, Jesus. Some people smiled, some recoiled, and others shrugged with indifference. What was it about this man, I wondered, that gave him the power to provoke so many different responses? I nodded slowly, and he continued.

"Now, picture this. It's Thursday night, the day before Passover preparation. You follow Jesus to a garden just outside of town. He drops to his knees and begins to pray. Soon, blood pours like sweat from his brow. Then an armed guard arrives and arrests him. They lead him to the Governor's palace, where they beat and scourge him. He is sentenced to die. And then the next morning, about 9:00 AM, they lead him out of the city gates and nail him to a wooden cross.

"You follow him, Michael. You witness it. You watch him die a horrifying, excruciating death. But before he dies, he looks up just long enough to make eye contact with you. You, Mike Peabody! And then he cries out, 'Father, forgive them.' After that, he gives up his spirit. You have been blessed. Simply being here today, seeing this cloth with your own eyes, touching it. You have been given a priceless gift, Dr. Peabody. Do you understand?"

I did understand. I felt a sense of unexplainable awe. Fear. Sorrow. Remorse. Wonder.

Dr. Gallo continued to speak to me, but his words faded as the cloud of brain activity washed over me in a palette of harmonies and liquid hues. I tasted odd sounds, saw copper flavors in my mouth, heard reds and greens. The synesthete was back, and that could only mean one thing:

Oh no!

Uncontrolled electrical impulses began to light up my brain, stimulating a wave of ionic flux to sweep across my cerebral hemispheres, causing intense muscular contractions and uncontrolled bodily functions. I fell to the concrete floor, striking my head on the table and landing on one arm. My arms pulled inward, and my legs stiffened and straightened into wooden planks. My entire body became locked in spasm, tightening my chest wall and preventing all movement. I couldn't breathe. I felt terrified. Death was coming, and it was not okay.

But in the next few milliseconds, I learned that, at death, the spirit simply pulls away. Pain had vanished, fear had fallen away. Time no longer mattered. Space had no meaning. I was being lifted by invisible hands, carried weightlessly over the room. I looked down on the Shroud. I looked down on *me!*

I could see my body convulsing, saliva spewing like foam from between my teeth. Blood flowed from cuts on my arm and cheek.

Like a physician watching his patient give in to the calming effects of an IV drug, I watched the convulsions ease off and then cease. Dr. Gallo shook me and shouted. I waited to see if I would respond or even breathe again, but all I did was just lie there, motionless. I heard new voices and became aware of more people in the room. Then two people in orange shirts rushed in and leaned over me, one with an Ambu-bag over my face, another compressing my chest. "Uno, due, tre …" Another attached defibrillator pads to my chest, and the cardiac monitor began to whine, like a strobe unit charging to a crescendo. Someone announced, "State alla larga!"

Stand clear!

A jolt of electricity passed through me, stiffening my entire body in synchronized spasms that lifted me off the floor and dropped me again, transforming the multicolored cloud into inky blackness. It surrounded me like a murderous phagocyte, digesting me and biting into my flesh to inject me with fire and pain. Then it swallowed me completely and dropped me into a deep, horrifying darkness. I heard laughter. I felt fear and unimaginable sorrow.

"Hell! I'm in hell!"

PART 2

CHAPTER NINETEEN

Golgotha—The Place of the Skull
Outside the City Gates of Jerusalem, Israel
Thursday—2:25 PM Local Time

The electric current delivered through my upper body by the defibrillator had jolted me off the floor and vaulted me into a strange unknown. I felt petrified to learn whether I was alive or dead. It was not a peaceful walk into a brilliant, beckoning light that I had heard so much talk about, but rather a frightening crawl into a dark and hopeless dungeon. A hot, thirsty, painful place, devoid of goodness or any semblance of hope. Demonic laughter wracked my brain. I screamed. I felt mad. I wanted to go back, to figure out where I had gone wrong and make amends. One more chance was all I wanted, and I would avoid this darkness forever.

"Please, God," I cried. "Help me!"

Mercifully, I woke up.

I discovered myself lying flat on my back in a blur of blue overhead light, liquid cyan far better than the hellish blackness I had just experienced. My eyes stung. I could smell burnt flesh. Sharp rocks dug into my back. I tried but couldn't sit up.

I rubbed the cold sweat from my eyes and performed a self-assessment. My ribs ached. I glanced at my bare chest and saw an oval burn mark in the shape of a defib pad. I touched my collarbone and winced. My arm was wrapped in white gauze saturated with blood.

To say that I felt discombobulated, confused, disoriented, and afraid would have been an understatement, but one thing was certain—I wasn't dead. Or at least, the dying process had ended, and I was on the other side, wherever that was.

"God," I whispered. "Where am I?"

I wiggled my toes and fingers. Everything moved. I could feel my heart beating. I tasted blood. I could hear the familiar tinny sound that had buzzed steadily in my ears since boot camp on Parris Island many years before. Where am I? I reached up to grab something, but found nothing solid to grasp.

"Hello?" I whispered. "Will? Dr. Gallo? Is anyone there?"

I sniffed the air and detected a sweet, earthy aroma. A foreign smell, much different than the architectural odors in the halls of the Turin Cathedral.

I felt myself jump involuntarily. Once. Twice. Some kind of strange creatures were swooping down on me, fluttering past my face. I swatted at them, hitting nothing but air. Where am I? I wondered. Where's the Shroud? Why am I lying on the ground with these unseen things attacking me? "What is this?"

My vision slowly cleared to reveal a blue sky with a single puffy, white cumulus cloud floating through it. I saw no birds or insects. Maybe I was dreaming again. But I had only to wait for a moment before the fluttering sound returned, and something black swooped past my face in a zig-zag pattern.

"What are you?" I shouted, swatting at the unknown.

Whatever it was, it gave me the creeps. A bat? A bird? I didn't know, but it did not feel right. I felt a sudden chill in my spine.

I needed to get out of there, and fast. I stood on shaky legs and glanced around me. I was standing atop a hill devoid of growth, and with no structures, but for a few sharp boulders and a wooden post about eight or nine feet tall. I spotted a cliff's edge about twenty yards away and walked carefully toward the edge. My jaw dropped.

The scene below me took my breath away. A large city of stone, surrounded by a tremendous wall that stretched into the distance. A sea of rooftops—house after house—blended with rectangular buildings of every dimension filled the interior. I was not high enough to see the streets inside, but people moved around outside the gates, hundreds, if not thousands of people coming and going, into and out of the city.

I scratched my head. "Where the heck am I?"

The wooden post seemed out of place atop the hill. Square, rather than round, and about eight inches per side, cut from rough, aged hardwood—something that had stood the test of time. I approached and examined a heavy iron spike jutting from its base about three feet off the ground—a massive nail encrusted with a thick, deep-brown crust.

"Is that blood?"

The post topped out about four feet above my head, carved into a square peg at its peak, as if to receive a cross-member of the same diameter. I glanced around and noticed other holes in the ground, as if pre-dug in preparation to receive similar posts.

Bile rose in my throat. I spat it out and panted for a few seconds before looking up again at the post. An icy fingertip slithered down my spine. I sensed a dark presence and felt my skin turn cold. I turned around to see a dark shadow flit past me and disappear. Then another. And another. I heard laughter and braced myself as a flock of leather-winged creatures flew in and encircled my head. I swung and punched at the air. It was as if I had been thrown into the octagon to fight an invisible monster.

"Go away!" I shouted. "Why are you doing this?"

The creatures pushed me backwards, causing me to trip and fall just before reaching the cliff's edge. I peered at the ground a hundred feet below, and, to my astonishment, I saw a pile of bones. Bleached skeletons, laughing and beckoning me. I stood up, frantically searching for escape, and ran down the backside of the haunted hill, stumbling, and falling face-first onto a dusty road. Then, once again, I saw darkness.

A sharp sting jolted me awake. My ears rang with a deafening hum, and every muscle groaned in protest. I was suspended somewhere between reality and a strange, celestial haze—until a second crack slapped against my cheek, shocking my clearing head and pushing it ever closer to the present. "Hello," a voice called from the haze. "Wake up."

I swung at the air, trying desperately to fight away the apparitions attacking me. "Leave me alone! I didn't do anything!"

"Sir, wake up. I'm here to help."

A shape slowly materialized out of the haze, hardening into the distinct form of a man and then fading again into an indistinct silhouette. I gazed at it, trying to untangle the twisted neurons in my brain, not sure if I should submit to his command to wake up, or fight. I tightened both of my fists and prepared to strike. "Who are you? What do you want?"

"Brother, I am here to help you," the shadow said, and once again I felt the sharp sting of an open palm against my cheek. "Wake up."

I swung my fist in the direction of the shadow and felt it connect.

"Uggh!" The shadow grunted and retreated slightly. "Please, sir. No. Do not hit me again. I am your friend. You are okay now. Do not hit me!"

"Who are you?" I repeated. "Where am I?"

"You are safe now. Just breathe."

"But, I don't know where—"

"Breeeathe!"

I took a deep breath. My ribcage hurt. I felt woozy and confused. I felt a wet cloth rubbing coarsely against my cheek and slapped it away.

"You cut your cheek. Let me wash it."

My senses sharpened, bringing into focus the strange shadow leaning over me, a small-framed African male with a curly beard streaked with grey. His brown skin was as dark as my own, wrapped in a brown robe and covered by a dirty white tunic. His eyes, deep sunk and black as coal, bore into mine with a gaze of curiosity mixed with sincere concern.

"What happened? Where am I?"

"You ran down the hill and fell. You cut your face." He held up a white linen cloth covered with blood and red dirt. "See?"

I touched my cheek. He pushed away my hand.

"Leave it," he said. "Please allow it to dry."

"I fell?"

"Down the hill. You were running like a man possessed, screaming the whole way. Then you fell face-first onto the road and began to shake like a demon."

"So, then, I … wait a minute. I'm alive?"

He looked confused. "Beelzebub seized you."

"Be-el-za … ?"

"The devil. Brother, relax. You are alive. The evil spirit has left you. What were you doing up there? That is not a good place."

"I have no idea. I woke up and I was there."

The good Samaritan eyed me curiously. I had regained enough of my senses by that point to understand that I was in the postictal state that follows a grand mal seizure, when the mind is confused by a mixture of body chemicals and the delirious effects of hypoxia.

"I had a seizure?" I glanced at my surroundings. "Where am I?"

"We are just outside the Sheep Gate."

"The sheep's gate?"

"Sheep Gate."

I scratched my head. Why was I sitting on a dirt road at the base of a hill a quarter mile from a tall stone wall? I turned around and looked behind me. The road wound into distant hills. People walked past us carrying small animals toward the gate. A boy led a donkey pulling a wooden cart loaded with sheep. The odor of animal dung became stronger. I glanced at the dirt and noticed I was lying in a pile of animal poop.

"This isn't Turin," I said, brushing away the dung.

"Too-reen? Sir, Turin is thousands of kilometers away."

"But how can that be? I was there just a minute ago. What day is it anyway? Sunday?"

"It is Thursday."

"Thursday? No, that's not right! And why are all these people carrying sheep?" A strange discomfort in my mouth caught my attention. I tried to swallow, but my throat refused. My tongue felt parched and rough, coated in a sticky dryness that made me crave something wet. "You know what? Never mind. You got any water?"

"Water, I've got." The man produced a leather bota bag and held it to my lips. "Drink."

I frowned. "Is that some kind of canteen?"

"Drink!"

He lifted the bottle. I drank. The water tasted wonderfully cool, coppery until I had taken a few swigs, then wet, marvelous, and familiar. I drank until the bottle was empty and then handed it back to him and glanced back over my shoulder at the stone wall beside me, a monstrous barrier that stretched into the distance and wrapped around the town within.

"What city is that?"

"That is Jerusalem."

"Jerusalem? You mean, as in Israel?"

All I knew of Jerusalem was what I had learned on CNN and Fox. It's the capital city of Israel, and one of the oldest cities in the world. Located close to the Mediterranean Sea, and considered a holy city by Christianity, Islam, and Judaism, it has been a focal point of world political tensions for many years. From my vantage point on the street, it looked like a busy place, but nowhere as large as the city of one million described on Fox. I wondered.

"And that hill up there?" I pointed at the rocky precipice from which I had just run. From street level, it looked about 90 to 100 feet high. "What is that?"

"That is Golgotha."

"I'm sorry?"

"Golgotha. It's where they crucify. There is much death up there. You must never go up there again."

"That's the Golgotha where Jesus was crucified? So, I wasn't dreaming."

"Yeshua?" Simon shook his head, as if confused. "Crucified?"

"It was evil up there. I thought it was hell!"

"Much evil. Now, my brother, forgive me, but I must ask—" He squinted, curiously, and nodded at my mid-section. "Where is your tunic?"

"My tunic?" I glanced down and for the first time realized that I was naked. I wore my watch on one arm, a bandage on the other, and a pair of wool socks. Nothing else. "Good grief, where are my clothes?"

I covered myself with my hands. He removed the jacket he was wearing and handed it to me. "Cover yourself with my tunic," he said. "You must allow no one else to see you like this. If they believe you are possessed by a devil, they will not allow you entrance."

My new friend held out his hand. I reached up and accepted it. He pulled me to my feet and helped me don the tunic.

I felt foolish. I mean, two months ago, before being shot in the head, if you had told me—Mike Peabody: U.S. Marine Corps Corpsman First Class, emergency physician, and MMA fighter—they'd find me half-naked and postictal in a foreign country, in a different time, being tended to by a stranger wearing a tunic and a funny little hat, I would have beat you up. On top of that I was wearing a robe about three sizes too small for me. I mean, I felt downright ridiculous. But then, everything about this situation was ridiculous. I sighed and cinched the belt around my waist.

"Thank you," I said. "What's your name?"

"I am Simon. I come from Cyrene. What is that thing on your wrist?"

I glanced at my wrist. "My watch? It's a Casio G-Shock."

"Cas-ee-oo."

"Solar charging, atomic."

"A-tom-ic? What does it do?"

"Tells time. Plus, I use the stopwatch a lot."

Simon frowned as he studied the watch. He seemed confused by it. "Take it off. Make sure no one else sees that. They might mistake you for a magician or warlock."

Simon was not a large man, but he carried himself with the confidence of a heavy fighter. He smelled like sweat and sawdust and reeked of hard work and discipline. His face looked chiseled and hard, belying his kind, humble demeanor. His hands looked muscular and calloused. He wore a dagger on one hip and a small leather pouch that jingled when he walked. I removed the Casio from my wrist and shoved it into the pocket of the tunic.

"I don't understand," I said. "This is Jerusalem?"

He shrugged. "Yes."

"And you live here?"

"No, I live in Bethlehem."

"Bethlehem? Isn't that where Jesus was born? What are you, like, a slave?"

"No, I am a tekton. An artisan of wood and stone. I work for the government."

A small donkey stood nearby, its smooth gray coat and black mane contrasted by a colorful blanket draped across its back. A white star marked its muzzle. Despite its quiet stance, its ears pricked forward with an alert, restless energy—as if it were just waiting for the signal to move.

"That your donkey?"

"No, she does not belong to me. I was taking her back to the stables in Bethlehem when I found you."

"Bethlehem. Man, this is nuts. Look, Simon, is it? I don't know what to do. I'm lost, and I have no idea how I got here. Can you help me get back to Turin?"

"No, but I know a man who might be able to help you. Let's get you cleaned up and dressed, and then we will search for him. Come. The donkey will carry you."

"That little thing can't carry me!"

"Oh, you are wrong. God has blessed her with incredible strength."

I had my doubts. The poor little animal didn't look big enough to carry a 50-pound sack of grain, much less a 270-pound man.

"You will see. Climb on her back."

Reluctantly, I submitted. Simon helped me swing a leg up over her back and then boosted me aboard. To my amazement, her legs didn't buckle. She protested with a soft bray and then lurched forward with a strong gait.

"Amazing," I murmured. "Unbelievable."

"Back inside," Simon said, as he grabbed her rein and turned her around. "Your work is not yet finished."

"What's her name?" I asked.

"Her name is Baruch Aton."

"Bar-ook a-taan? What kind of name is that?"

"It is Hebrew. It means, blessed donkey."

The donkey trudged along happily under my significant weight, filling me with respect, and a much greater appreciation for the term, beast of burden. But blessed? I couldn't see that.

"This poor little girl," I said, my head bouncing in beat with her strides. "I'm sure she doesn't feel very lucky right now."

"Oh, she is happy, I assure you. She knows she has been blessed."

"Blessed, how?"

"Do you not know what happened this week?"

"I just got here, remember?"

"This little aton had the privilege of carrying the Messiah into the city."

"The Messiah?"

"The Teacher, Jesus of Nazareth."

For about the tenth time in as many minutes, I felt my head spin. I remembered reading about the day that Jesus rode into Jerusalem on a donkey.

"Wait a minute," I said, struggling to assemble the pieces to this odd puzzle. "You're telling me this is the donkey that carried Jesus Christ into Jerusalem?"

"Some think he is the Christ. Most call him Yeshua, or Teacher. He entered the city on this donkey four days ago. People laid down palm leaves to honor him."

"Palm Sunday. That means this Sunday is Easter. The first Easter."

Simon shrugged. "East-errr?"

My head began to pound, my ears to ring. "Oh, Lord!" I let go of the donkey's mane and clutched my head between my hands. After rubbing my eyes and shaking my head forcefully, I swore and shook my fist at the sky. "This can't be real!"

"Brother," Simon said. "Calm down."

"Calm down? Mister, don't tell me to calm down! I'm either in the most vivid nightmare ever, or I've gone back in time! Two thousand years!"

"Brother?"

"I don't know what's happening. What is happening to me?!"

"Keep your voice low," he demanded, grabbing the donkey's reins and leading her off the road. "You have attracted enough attention already."

"Look," I shouted. "Help me! I don't know why, or what for, but I am not making this up. I was in the cathedral lab with Dr. Gallo, and I died, and—"

"Brother!"

"The paramedics shocked me. I felt a cold shadow come over me. It was as dark as night. I heard terrible laughter. Bats appeared and pushed me toward the cliff. Claws grabbed me and dug into my skin, pulling me down. I saw skeletons. I ran for my life and fell. I remember screaming, and—"

"Stop!" Simon shouted.

"It was hell! It had to be hell! Please, God," I shouted. "Not hell!"

Simon yanked me from the donkey's back. I fell to the ground, and he dropped onto me, pinning my shoulders. "Stop it," he whispered. "You must be quiet!"

I tried to fight back until I realized that a dozen bystanders had gathered in a loose circle around us, eyes wide as they watched me grovel in the dirt. Simon waved them off with a sharp gesture. "He's all right, friends. He hurt his head."

The crowd murmured and shifted. Hot embarrassment flared through the cold terror still gripping my chest.

"Listen, brother," Simon whispered. "You are not in hell. This is Jerusalem. It's okay. It's okay now, relax. Breathe."

"But—"

"Breathe," he repeated. "Just breathe."

I took a deep breath … a second, a third.

"Breathe."

My hysteria slowly passed, and the crowd departed. Simon released me and leaned back on his knees. "Are you okay now?"

I could see the strength of three men in his gaze, tempered by the quiet compassion of a shepherd watching over a lost sheep. Looking up at him, my terror faded—I knew I could trust him. "I'm sorry," I said, reaching up with my hand.

"No, I am sorry," Simon said, grabbing my hand and helping me to a sitting position. "But you left me no choice. You were losing your mind."

"It was so real." I stood and brushed the dust from my tunic. "I thought I had died, and wherever I was going wasn't good."

"Look at me," Simon said, shaking me. "You are safe now. Do you understand?"

I glanced around at my strange surroundings, slowly nodding. "If you say so."

"Okay, but you must not act that way inside the city walls," he continued. "Demoniacs are not allowed in the city. If you lose yourself in there, the soldiers will arrest you."

"You think I'm possessed by a demon?"

"No, but I believe you were under attack. You were talking out of your mind. Look," he said, turning me around and pointing at the cliff from which I had almost fallen a few minutes before. "Do you see it?"

My eyes fell on a massive, pitted boulder bulging from the cliff-face like the brow of a weathered cranium. Two dark caves hollowed out the rock beneath it, perfect eye sockets, with a jagged fissure between them for a nose. Lower down, a shelf of fractured stone jutted out into sharp cheekbones. The pieces snapped together into a horrifying whole.

I gasped. "It's a skull."

"Yes," he said. "It is Golgotha. The place of the skull. It is the face of evil etched in stone. It has infected your mind. You must never, never go up there again!"

"Don't worry," I said, with a shiver. "I don't intend to."

"Why were you up there in the first place?"

"I don't know," I whispered, shaking my head. "Like I said, I woke up there."

"Woke up?" His eyes narrowed as he studied me, trying to piece it together. "Were you alone?"

"Yes."

"Are you in some kind of trouble?"

"No."

"What were you running from?"

"The Devil! Look, I need to get home! What am I going to do?"

"Calm down. I will help you, but, first, we must tend to your wounds. Then, we will find the one called Peter. He will know what to do."

CHAPTER TWENTY

The Sheep Gate
Jerusalem, Israel, the Year 33 A.D.
Thursday—2:50 PM Local Time

If Golgotha is the face of evil etched in stone, then the wall that encircled Jerusalem was the stone fortress built to keep that evil out. It reminded me of the wall around an English castle, only without the moat and wooden drawbridge. Sandstone walls glistened in the afternoon sun, with colors ranging from pinkish white to gold, and with rook-like castles and notched parapets through which archers could shoot their bows. The gate was wide enough for five people to pass through at the same time, and high enough to accommodate a short giraffe. It had an ornate façade higher than the general opening, with an arched header fifteen feet above the ground. I watched many people pass through, most heading into the city, and most with a lamb or a goat under one arm.

Simon led Baruch Aton to a wooden trough close to the gate. She lapped up a half-gallon of water before lifting her head, only to let it hang again as she closed her eyes. She looked at peace. Her relaxed disposition made me feel better, somehow, as if I had received a low dose of a sedative. And a sedative I could use. I felt as if I had experienced a bizarre time warp. I mean, I was supposedly in Jerusalem on the day before Jesus Christ was to be crucified. Seriously? I pushed the ideas to the back of my mind and decided to lay them to rest. No good could come from wondering. It certainly would not help get me home.

"So, what's with all these sheep?" I said.

"Ah, the sheep. Yes, this is the Sheep Gate," he explained. "It is through this gate that most of the sacrificial lambs are carried."

“Why?”

“Because it is the closest gate to the temple.”

“No, I mean, why all the lambs?”

“These are Passover lambs that will be sacrificed at the temple.” Simon seemed to notice my confusion, and continued. “The Jews offer a sacrifice once a year to celebrate their escape from slavery in Egypt. It is a tradition that began during their time of captivity when the angel of death moved through the land killing every firstborn son.”

I shook my head. “Sounds like a bad day.”

“The last of the Egyptian plagues. They say it was a frightening night. But the main point is that to avoid the angel’s punishment, each household selected its most perfect lamb, a year-old male without blemish. The household would butcher their lamb, spread its blood over the lintel and doorposts of the home, and then lock themselves inside to dine on the sacrificed meat. The angel of death, upon seeing the animal’s blood on the doorpost, would pass over that home and spare the oldest son, or sons, inside.”

“I get it. Pass over. Passover. But what if they had no lamb?”

“Like that man?” Simon replied, pointing at a citizen walking through the gate with a juvenile goat. “He has no lamb, so he will offer a goat instead. Many will purchase a lamb at the temple today. It is a huge money-making machine for the Jewish leaders. There are many rules. Too many for you right now. But, regardless, the sacrifice is to be made on Preparation Day, on the evening before Passover. Passover begins tomorrow afternoon.” Simon glanced at the sun. “The killing will begin soon.”

The killing will begin soon. He sounded so nonchalant, like we were talking about mowing the grass.

“You see that pool over there?” Simon pointed at a small stone pond just on the other side of the gate. “It’s called the Pool of Bethesda. It is known for its healing properties, but during Passover, it serves as a place to wash the sacrificial animals.”

Nearby, about two dozen people stood in the murky water, scrubbing small sheep and goats. They hummed a melody together as they worked, a happy, ritualistic sound that echoed off the stone walls.

"Those people," Simon explained, gesturing toward the crowd, "live outside the city and have come for the celebration. A million will come in total."

My jaw dropped. "A million?"

"Yes. It is an important celebration for all Jews. We will travel from all over the region. These are arriving late. They are cleaning their animals in preparation for slaughter. Like I said, each animal must be a male, one year or less, clean, and without blemish to be considered an acceptable sacrifice."

"Where's yours?"

"I delivered my lamb yesterday. She was washed in this same pool and will be butchered tonight, along with all the others."

I shook my head. "Sounds crazy."

"Look, I understand that our culture confuses you. Much of what you see today will appear strange. Try to just watch and learn."

I watched a man climb out of the pool, a huge swimming pool even by today's standards, 200 to 300 feet long, equipped with stone staircases on each end and separated in the middle by a crossover island. He hurried toward the gate with his lamb, only to stumble and drop the poor thing into the dirt. He scooped it up, jumped back into the pool and proceeded to wash it again. I had never seen anything so ritualistic, and yet, so seemingly important.

"This place," I whispered, too low for him to hear. "Unreal."

"Now, you listen to me," Simon said. "We are about to enter Jerusalem, the Jewish Holy City. I will take you to the doctor there. He is a good man. You will encounter many people, as well as many Roman soldiers. You may be questioned. If you are, if we are stopped, let me do the talking. And if someone forces you to answer, tell them you were assaulted on the road from Turin, and you do not know by whom. You also cannot remember what happened or how you got that bandage on your arm. Do not mention seizures, bats, hell, or any of that. Do you understand?"

"Yes, but I was not assaulted. That would be lying."

"Do you wish to live?"

I nodded.

"Okay then. And make absolutely no mention of time travel or crucifixion," he added. "Do not show anyone that thing you had about your wrist. If you do, they may take you for a magician and crucify you. Only approved magicians and sorcerers can practice dark arts. Now, in case they ask, what is your name?"

"Mike Peabody."

"Pee-bah-dee?"

"Call me, Mike."

"Mike?" He scratched his chin and said, "I will call you Michael. It is an accepted, angelic name. And you, too, are African, Michael? A slave?"

"No, I'm American. A physician."

"I do not know American. Today, you are an African slave. There will be less to explain. But, if you are a physician, as you say, you will have much to discuss with the man you are about to meet. Dr. Loukas is our local physician. A respected man."

I followed my new friend through the Sheep Gate to enter a scene that could've passed for a Hollywood movie set. Curved streets of dirt and cobblestone, filled with masses of people, led between houses and buildings of sandstone and stucco. Some structures had curved archways, others square. Vines and plants grew everywhere, making everything appear seamlessly connected, as if for a part of the greater good. It was like the city was a giant creature made of sandstone, the plants its connective tissue, and the people and animals its blood. People, donkeys, goats, bulls, and dogs moved through the streets around a tall rectangular building with a grand staircase that led up to a large wooden door. In front of the door stood three soldiers in colorful uniforms with brass helmets and chest armor. Each carried a sword on his belt. One held a lance.

"Who are they?"

"Roman soldiers. And that is the temple where the animals will be slain," Simon explained.

I swallowed hard, looking toward the distant temple courts. "When does it begin?"

"In a few minutes," Simon said, his voice flat, almost clinical. "We cannot get any closer, but if you would like, we can wait here. When it begins you will hear it—the gurgling screams of the dying. An undeniably terrifying sound."

A cold knot tightened in my stomach. I took a step back, shaking my head. "No thanks!"

"The priests will butcher many thousands before the day is over—two hundred thousand or more. The screaming will continue into the night. Do you see?" he said, pointing at a deep, stone-lined ditch running parallel to the street. "Drainage for all the blood that will be spilled. The canal will carry it outside the city walls."

I shivered. "It sounds horrible."

"It is."

As I stared at Simon, trying to understand the significance of the blood, an image flashed through my mind—a picture of a young man on an altar, his father with a sharp knife in hand about to plunge it into his heart. I could see it and almost hear it—the glistening of the blade, the cries of the boy as he awaited his violent death, and the shout of a glowing angel commanding the father to stop.

An angel?

I inhaled deeply and held my breath. Somewhere in my deep subconscious, the facts were emerging—the purpose of the blood, and the need for a brutal sacrifice. I was on the verge of remembering. But how? Had I read about this somewhere in the past few months since my injury? Had I studied it? I couldn't place it.

My temples began to throb. I exhaled loudly, and exclaimed, "Simon, I still don't understand. Why all the blood?"

"The blood serves as payment for the sins of the people. It is a Jewish law that comes from the hand of Moses, written in Hebrew, for Hebrews."

"Wait a minute. The Torah?"

"Yes."

"And you are a Jew?"

"I am."

"Then you must know the Torah."

"Of course. My family has always strictly followed the Torah."

"You know, this is coming back to me."

Somehow, that made sense to my otherwise confused mind. I suddenly remembered a world religion elective I had taken during my pre-med years—a deep dive into the Torah, the first five books of the Bible. I remembered learning that the shift in terminology from Hebrew to Jew was actually quite fascinating, occurring sometime after the Babylonian exile. So by the 1st Century (which is now), a Roman, or let's say a Cyrenian—I glanced at Simon—or a modern time traveler like me, would absolutely use the term "Jew."

"Simon, I remember now. I studied this in college."

As he had done so many times that day, Simon just looked at me with intense curiosity, as if trying to understand the futuristic nature of my comments.

"Wow—" I turned my attention from the drainage ditch and glanced around at the bustling streets, absorbing the overwhelming sights and smells of the 1st century world. "So this is Jerusalem."

"Yes," Simon said, looking proudly at the passing crowds. "In all its glory, on one of the busiest days of the year."

The distant sound of clashing cymbals and tambourines suddenly made me jump. Then pipes and horns began blasting out a tune, as if to announce the beginning of a celebration. Soon, the melodious sound of harps, singing, and chanting joined in to create a primitive orchestra. I found it loud and unpleasant, but I could imagine its significance by the smiling faces of the people passing by.

"What is that?" I said. "Some kind of celebration?"

"Yes," Simon said. "It is beginning."

Just then, I heard men shouting, followed by a muffled screech that pierced the temple walls. My body lurched backward instinctively, recoiling from the sound.

"What was that?"

Then came another screech. And another. Within seconds, a horrific chorus of gurgling cries flooded the streets, thick and wet—the helpless bleating of small animals submitting to the blade.

"The sheep?" I cried, my fingers digging into Simon's arm. "Is that the sheep?"

"Yes," Simon responded. "The killing has begun."

My knees felt weak as we stood, listened, and watched. I could only imagine the grisly scene inside the temple where the priests did their work—grabbing animals and slitting their throats ... laying one down to grab another. I felt a horror I had never known. Who are these people? What kind of culture is this? I noticed a small splash of crimson in the corner of my eye and turned to see the beginning of a tiny rivulet of dark red fluid trickle out of the temple wall. The drainage ditch began to redden as the thick fluid flowed. My eyes widened as I watched it grow. The screams continued, and the ditch began to fill.

I felt like crying.

"I can't take this anymore," I said, grabbing Simon by the arm. "Get me out of here!"

"I'm sorry," Simon said. "You weren't ready for that. Come quickly. I want you to meet Dr. Loukas."

I followed Simon into the streets, walking in silence for the next few moments, happy to be leaving behind the pitiful cries of the doomed. My heart felt heavy as stone. The idea that God required such a heavy price for sin. I felt a lump form in my throat.

Simon seemed to sense my pain, and said, “Are you all right, my friend?”

“I don’t know,” I said with a sigh. “I’ve witnessed a lot of death in my life, but never anything like that.”

Nobody seemed to notice me as we walked. Most of the people looked in a hurry to get somewhere else. And most were dressed the same as Simon, wearing tunics, hooded robes and leather foot coverings much like the loop sandals worn by hippies in the 1970s. I glanced down at my bare feet wishing I had a pair.

I felt totally out of place in this new environment, maybe even a little scared. But why did it matter? If anyone did notice me, they’d just think me a slave. And what choice did I have, anyway? Where else could I go? I needed someone to trust, and Simon seemed like the right man to help me get home.

“Uh-oh,” he said, slowing his pace and lowering his head. “Trouble.”

I figured he was referring to the two Roman soldiers approaching on horseback. Both were physical specimens, both appeared dressed for battle, and they looked to be zeroed in on us.

“Legionnaires,” Simon whispered. “Let me do the talking.”

“Slaves,” the older of the soldiers shouted, yanking his horse’s reins. “Stop right there.”

Simon grabbed my arm. “That is Crudelis. He is Centurion. Very cruel. Do exactly what he says.”

It was plain to see that the two men before us were warriors. And honestly, I thought they looked spectacular. Wearing matching red tunics, sturdy silver breastplates, shoulder pads, and helmets of bronze or gold, they reminded me of Roman Legionnaires from movies like Gladiator and Spartacus. Heavy swords hung from their waists. One carried a stout spear about seven feet in length. Both were well-built men, much like the fighters at my gym. I hoped we would not have to tangle.

"What's going on here?" Crudelis exclaimed, dismounting. His silver-colored hair contrasted sharply with the shiny gold color of his helmet. His eyes burned into mine like sapphires pulled from a blacksmith's forge. "Where did you get that donkey?"

The other soldier dismounted and grabbed Baruch's rein. "I know this animal. See the star on its muzzle? This is the one that carried the king."

"The king? Ha!" Crudelis scoffed. "He is no king! He is a carpenter from Nazareth. And these two slaves have stolen this donkey."

"We're not slaves," I said. "And nobody stole her."

The Centurion swung and backhanded me across the face. I fell to the ground, dazed, aroused by the taste of my own blood. My heart raced and my fists tightened.

"Did I ask you to speak?" he shouted. "Who do you think you are?"

I tightened up and was about to rush the Centurion when Simon stood in front of me and pushed me back. "No!" he shouted. "Don't!"

I had never felt more intense anger. I am not the kind of man who backs down from a challenge, and this was, without a doubt, a challenge. I stood and assumed a fighting position. Simon stood in front of me and begged me. "Please," he whispered. "Let it go. Do not provoke him. Do you understand? He will kill us!"

I glared at Crudelis, seething, memorizing his features and silently praying that we might meet again in a dark alley. Crudelis scoffed and looked away, unimpressed by my defiance.

"The donkey is with me," Simon said. "My friend is innocent. But I did not steal the donkey, Dominus. The Teacher's Disciples hired me to carry this animal back to Bethlehem."

"Then why are you here, instead of on the road south. I do not believe you. Which disciple?"

"The one they call Petrus."

"I know this man. He, too, is a troublemaker. I should hamstring you both."

"No, please, Dominus. It is true. He paid me three denarii. See?" Simon opened the small leather pouch on his belt and produced three coins. "Here," he said, offering the Centurion his money. "It is yours."

"Keep the money," Crudelis grunted. "You will need it to pay the toll on the way back to Bethlehem. And you, African?" he said, turning to me. "I give you permission to speak. What is your story?"

I started to answer, to risk another beat down and tell him I was neither African, nor a slave, but a hard-working physician with the most powerful military in the world behind me, including the US Marine Corps, but Simon hurriedly explained that he had found me unconscious on the road outside the Sheep Gate. "He injured his head and needs medical attention."

"Is that right?" Crudelis asked me, poking his finger at me. "Speak up!"

I nodded and said, "That is correct."

He asked about the wound on my forehead. I lied and told him I'd been kicked by a horse.

"And this?" he exclaimed, twisting my arm to expose the bandaged wound. "What happened here?"

How could I explain what had really happened? That I had suffered a seizure in the Turin Cathedral and had cut my arm on the Shroud examination table? I made up a story about how I cut myself during a fall onto sharp rocks. My answer appeased him. He looked me over carefully, sneered, and then waved his hand, as if at a pair of pack animals. "Move on," he said. "I do not want to see you two again."

Crudelis climbed back upon his mount and rode away, laughing. The other soldier held up a hand to silence us until his commander was out of ear shot. Once we were alone, he leaned close to Simon, and said, "I am Cornelius. I have seen you with his disciple, Petrus. I, too, am a follower of the Teacher, but secretly. If you see him, tell him to be careful. There is big trouble coming. It comes tonight."

"What is coming?" Simon asked.

Cornelius led his horse away and left us standing in the street.

"That was strange," Simon said, watching the soldiers depart. "What do you think he meant by that?"

"Exactly what he said. He will be arrested tonight."

"Who, Petrus?"

"No, Jesus."

"The Teacher? How do you know this?"

"I've read the story, Simon. I told you. I'm not from here."

"I do not understand."

"You will. Who is Petrus?"

"Petrus is my friend. He risked his life once to protect me from the soldiers, otherwise, I would have been thrown into prison. I have sworn to serve him. I would have gladly taken the donkey home for nothing. His payment was an act of kindness."

"That's an odd name, Petrus."

"It is Latin. Most call him Peter. He is a disciple of the Teacher. A leader. A close follower. He gave up everything to follow him, as did all the Disciples. Peter, Andrew, James, and John were fishermen. Matthew, a tax collector. I'm not sure about all the others, but the twelve he selected have given up almost everything. Their livelihoods. Their homes. They have followed him everywhere for the past three years."

"And they will soon give up their lives."

Simon just stared at me. Of course, he could not have known that they would all be martyred for their faith, all, that is, but the one named John.

I realized I had a tactical advantage over Simon. I had read about the twelve Disciples. They would be there with him until the last few hours, the one named Judas would betray him, and most, out of sheer fear, would run away and would not be present for his crucifixion. But most would later become leaders in the early church and ultimately die for their faith. Peter would become the first Pope of the Roman Catholic Church, but ultimately he would die on his own cross. Upside down. I liked Peter. He was a fighter.

"I would like to meet this Peter," I said.

"You will. But first, we must care for your wounds. I am hoping Dr. Loukas is home."

We continued down the city streets. The road narrowed to the point where it was just wide enough for a donkey to pass, and then it widened again into a circular area of dwellings with a community well in the center. I caught people staring at us as we walked down the lane. Perhaps it was the bloody cut on my face, rendered by the backhand of Crudelis, or perhaps the limp in my step. Whatever the reason, I felt out of place there, a little scared, and yet, at the same time, remarkably excited.

"There," Simon said, pointing at a stucco covered structure about a hundred yards in the distance. Like the other houses it seemed like a continuation of the last rather than a standalone dwelling. "That is the physician's home."

Simon led the donkey to a hitching post in front of the dwelling and tied her up there. The aromas of fresh bread, stew, and spices filled my nostrils. Charcoal and incense wafted from within, along with soft candlelight, casting a warm, welcoming glow.

"Wait here," Simon said. "I will see if Loukas is in."

Simon returned a moment later and invited me inside. He showed me to a couch, a futon of sorts that was surprisingly comfortable. From my vantage point I could see a kitchen, a bedroom, and what I assumed was the doctor's examination and treatment room. Each room glowed under the warmth of candles and oil lanterns attached to the walls. I felt relieved to be sitting, happy to be warm, and oddly safe. Simon sat down opposite me on a wooden bench.

"Loukas is with a patient," he explained. "He will check your wounds when he is finished."

"Thank you."

"Now," Simon said, clutching his hands and leaning forward. "Michael, I think you understand that I am risking my life to help you. Here, they think of us as slaves. Some think of us as less than human. I am willing to go out on a limb for a fellow human being, but in return I need you to be completely honest with me. You did not just travel through time and appear atop Golgotha. Who are you, really? Why are you here?"

"Simon," I said, leaning toward him. "I am telling you the truth."

"No," he responded. "There must be something you're not telling me."

"There's not. I'm a doctor from a country called America, a place that does not yet exist."

Simon sneered and shook his head. "Not yet exist. What do you mean?"

"I live in a society much different from yours," I said. "In a time that I can only figure to be about two thousand years in the future. I do not know why I'm here, or how I got here. I died in the basement of the Turin Cathedral and woke up here. That's all I know. Everything I told you is the truth. Honestly, I'm just as confused as you are."

Simon sighed. "Well, what happened to your head?"

I touched the scar on my forehead. The flesh was still tender but no longer raw. "We have advanced weapons you have yet to see, called guns."

"Guns?"

"Yes. Guns shoot projectiles at high rates of speed."

"As fast as an arrow from a bow?"

I chuckled. "Ten times faster. I was hit by a bullet from a type of gun called a pistol. An insane man with a pistol wanted me dead."

"A pis-tol." His face screwed up tightly and then loosened again. "And this man? He tried to kill you?"

"Yes."

"When you were having your fit at Golgotha, you mentioned something about a burial cloth. Why is that significant?"

"The Shroud of Turin is believed by many to be the burial cloth of Jesus Christ, your Teacher. Believe it or not, it bears an image of a man scourged and crucified somewhere around 33 A.D.."

"I do not understand A-D."

"It stands for anno domini. Latin for—"

"Year of the Lord."

"Yes. The calendar we follow in my time is based on the Roman calendar that began when Jesus was born. I have yet to see him, but, based on the measurements on the Shroud of Turin, he should be about five-feet, ten-inches tall, and about 170 pounds. Long hair and beard. Long Jewish nose."

Simon nodded. "That fits the Teacher's description. And you say the image on this cloth indicates the victim was crucified?"

"Beaten, scourged, and crucified. And if I'm correct, and this is indeed 33 AD, and this Sunday is Easter Sunday, it will begin here. Tonight."

CHAPTER TWENTY-ONE

The Medical Office of Loukas, MD
Jerusalem, Israel, the Year 33 A.D.
Thursday—3:24 PM Local Time

We did not have to wait long for the door to the back room to swing open. A humble-looking man of about 40 years of age appeared, drying his hands with a towel and wiping his forehead of sweat. His unusually thick, flat nose gave the impression of a boxer, but his fingers were that of a surgeon. Like many others I had seen that day, he had dark hair, olive-brown skin, and expressive dark eyes capable of intense passion. He carried himself with confidence but appeared as tired as an ED doc on a 48-hour rotation. "I am so sorry," he said. "I am dealing with a difficult case. What can I do for you gentlemen?"

"Dr. Loukas," Simon said, standing. "I am Simon of Cyrene. We met in Bethlehem recently. You were treating a woman with a bleeding issue, and I was fetching a—"

"A donkey! Oh yes," Loukas said, shaking Simon's hand. "Of course. Simon the African. You were fetching a donkey with Petrus. For the Messiah to ride, yes?"

"Yes, I am taking her back. She is tied up out front now."

"Well, please," he said. "Come in. And call me Loukas. No title is needed here. How can I help you?"

"Well, sir," he said, turning to me. "My friend needs medical attention."

"So, I see," Loukas said, walking over and gently probing my cheek wound. "What happened here?"

I spoke up. "A big dude named Crudelis."

“The Centurion? Oh, my. Yes, he is a very cruel man. This is deep enough to require sutures. And here?” he said, examining the head wound. “What caused this?”

“It’s a long story.”

I watched his eyebrows rise. I proceeded with the story, knowing he would most likely not understand. “A high-speed projectile, fired from a pistol.”

“A pis-tool?”

“A pistol is a firearm. A fighting weapon that, well—” I paused and glanced at Simon . He shrugged. “Let’s just say it has not yet been invented.”

Loukas stared at me for a moment and then burst into laughter. “I’m sorry I asked. What is your name?”

“Michael.”

Loukas chuckled, causing his oversized ears to wiggle. He was not a physically impressive man, but rather slight, with a small chest and arms and oily looking black hair. He had a soft way about him, a gentle touch, and I thought he smelled like garlic. But what he lacked in physical prowess, I noticed, he more than made up for in his eagerness to serve. He examined my injured arm, then led me back to the couch and said, “Sit tight, Mr. Michael. I’ll be right back.”

I nodded and took a seat, eager to sink once again into the padded cushions. I could not remember a time when I had felt so physically exhausted, even after my last slugfest with Rico. My head hurt, my legs felt like lead weights, and my arms were too heavy to lift. Thankfully, the cloud was nowhere in sight. I leaned back on the sofa and nodded off.

Loukas hurried back into the room, startling me awake. He carried a tray of supplies and a steaming wooden cup. “Drink this. I think it will help.”

“What is it?”

“A mixture of ground coffee beans, rosemary, and fresh leaves of catha edulis.”

“Catha edulis?”

"Khat. It should give you energy."

"I should think." I had read about khat, the highly addictive stimulant used by many western Asians for the feeling of euphoria and supernatural strength it produces. I figured a bit of euphoria would be good. I smelled the brew and sipped it. It tasted bitter, like burnt coffee. I turned my nose up and drank it, anyway, feeling an almost immediate rush. "Wow! This concoction really works."

"I thought it might give you a boost. Now, before I suture that arm wound, suppose I perform a quick exam?"

"Thank you."

"But before I do," he said, pulling up a stool and sitting on it. He looked at me and raised an eyebrow. Like Simon, he looked suspicious of me. "Suppose you tell me who you are and where you are from."

"Sir?"

"Your accent—" He paused and glanced at my clothing. "That is not your tunic. And these wounds. What am I dealing with here?"

I glanced at Simon. He shrugged and muttered something that I assumed meant, "Whatever." I explained the situation about the shooting, the seizures, the cardiac arrest in the Turin Cathedral, and about my strange trip back in time. At first, like Simon, he just stared at me in disbelief. I thought he might kick me out of his house, but instead, as if blessed with wisdom and understanding beyond his years, he nodded and said, "You say you were shot? What does that mean?"

I explained modern ballistics to him, right down to caliber, muzzle velocity, and the effect that penetrating wounds can have on the human brain. Ten long seconds passed before an electronic beeping sound began to emanate from my pocket. "Oops." I reached into the pocket, pulled out the Casio, and canceled the alarm I had set three days ago. "Forgot about that," I said, sheepishly. "Sorry." I glanced at Loukas to catch his response. What he said surprised me.

“You are from a different time and place.”

I nodded and shrugged.

“May I see that?” he said.

I handed him the watch. He studied it intently. “What does this do?”

“It tells time.”

“This tells time?”

“Yes. Well, and lots of other things.”

“Fascinating. And these numbers? 1-5-2-4?

“Current time.”

He seemed to ponder that for a moment. “Fascinating,” he repeated. I could see the gears whirring in his mind. “I wonder,” he muttered. “Hmm—”

His voice trailed off. He handed me the watch. I attached it to my wrist and decided to risk leaving it there.

Loukas placed his hands on my head. I felt surprised to learn that basic assessment techniques had changed little over the centuries. He worked his way down, from my head to my toes, much as I would, stopping at all the major points of anatomy to assess for abnormalities. After palpating my chest wall a second time, he ordered me to lie down.

Curious, I complied and assumed a supine position.

Loukas leaned over me, placed his ear directly on my chest, and closed his eyes. “Take deep breaths.”

“Don’t you have a stethoscope?”

“Sshhh. Breathe, please.”

I complied.

“Breathe normally now,” he said, moving his ear directly over my heart. Apparently satisfied, he looked up and said, “Sit up, please.”

He moved his hands to my abdomen and was about to palpate the area for masses when I stopped him. “Hey, I’ve got an idea. Do you have a horn or something?”

“A horn?”

“You know, a trumpet, or bugle, or something like that?”

Loukas left the room and returned a moment later with a crescent shaped horn about 18" in length. I noticed it had four small holes drilled on one side. "Will this work?" he said. "It's an ox horn."

"Perfectly. Here," I said, placing the broad end of the horn over my chest and covering the holes with my fingers. "Put your ear on the pointed end and listen."

Loukas did as suggested. I took a deep breath and watched him pull back in amazement. "It's so loud," he exclaimed, eyes wide with excitement. "It's amazing!" He moved the horn over my heart and asked me to breathe normally. His face lit up. "I can hear the heart valves opening and closing! It's as if I were inside your chest! This is an outstanding assessment device. What did you call it?"

"Ours are a little more modern, but we call that a stethoscope."

"A steth-o-scope. Interesting." Loukas scribbled a few notes on a piece of papyrus and then proceeded with his assessment, performing a full cranial nerve exam first, beginning with the optic nerve and proceeding through to vagus and spinal accessory. After that, he checked my pulses, my extremities for range of motion, and then he pulled out a crude reflex hammer and tapped each leg beneath the kneecap. My legs responded with reflex jerks.

"Stand," he said.

I stood for a balance check and walked a straight line for him, impressed by his assessment technique and his apparent understanding of the human body. I could see he possessed knowledge that almost equaled my own.

"So," I said with a feeling of genuine respect. "What's the verdict? Did I pass?"

"Your pupillary response is sluggish. And you have decreased reflexes on one side, which might be consistent with a lingering brain injury caused by this so-called ballistic trauma. This could be the cause of the seizures you have been experiencing. I have seen convulsions following major head injury."

"Yeah, I'm supposed to take Dilantin once a day, but I lost it somewhere along the way."

"Di-lan-ten?"

I sensed his confusion and said, "I don't suppose that's been invented yet, either. Among other things, it's an anticonvulsant. Works by blocking sodium channels in the brain."

"I see."

Did he see? I didn't think so. He stared at me as if trying to comprehend. He was a doctor, so I felt certain he had the capacity to understand ion channels and stuff—diffusion and active transport, depolarization, all that. But these concepts were so far outside of his field of learning that broaching the subject would be unfair. I had hoped we might find time to discuss it in detail later, but the pharmacology lesson would have to wait.

"Finish that drink," he said. "It is good for you."

I wasn't so sure the khat was good for me, but I had to admit, it did make me feel better. I downed the rest of it and paused to check my radial pulse. It was fast.

But that makes sense, doesn't it?

The doctor in me began to think.

Khat speeds up the heart much like amphetamines, by triggering the release and blocking the reuptake of key neurotransmitters, like dopamine and norepinephrine. The resulting increase in bodily functions produces high blood-pressure, elevated mood, and a sense of invincibility. Man, no wonder I feel like flying.

"Hey, Doc," I said, finally summoning the courage to ask. "Are you the Dr. Luke from the Bible?"

Loukas frowned and poured a cup of red wine over the cut on my arm. I figured it was the modern way of cleansing wounds. I didn't ask.

"You have once again spoken of things I do not understand," he said. "What is, Bible?"

I thought about that. I seemed to remember reading somewhere that the Gospel of Luke was written in 85 AD … 52 years into the future. Boy, I thought, this is getting weird. So, of course, Dr. Loukas would have no idea that he would someday write a good portion of the New Testament—the Gospel of Luke and the Book of Acts. In fact—I did a little quick math—52 years from now, he would be about 90-years-old. So how, I wondered, would that even be possible? "Wait a minute," I murmured, considering another possibility. "Doc, do you have a son?"

"Yes, I do. Why?"

"What do you call him?"

"We call him Luke. It is a nickname, of course. His real name is Luka, a variation of my own."

"Interesting. Look, Doc, I'd really like to meet your son."

"You will meet him in a few minutes."

"He's here?"

"Of course." Loukas seemed to pick up on my interest. "Luka is a Greek word, you know. It means, 'bringer of light.' The formal variation is Loukas, which is what I am called. Most people call him by his formal name, as well, but we call him Luke."

Loukas brought an ancient looking needle to my arm, and said, "This will hurt a little. The khat will help numb the pain."

"How long have you been here?" I asked.

"Oh, many years. I moved here after medical school and started my practice."

"Then perhaps you've met the—ouch!" I winced as the slightly rusty-looking needle entered the flesh of my arm. But I had to admit, the khat did help. A local anesthetic would have been better, but this method was acceptable. "Have you met Jesus?" I said. "The one they call the Teacher?"

Loukas chuckled and pulled the thread tight. Then he jabbed the needle into my flesh again. "No, but I have seen him many times. I saw him yesterday on the street in front of the temple. He was preaching boldly about the kingdom of God. He said something that resonated with me. He said, 'believe in the light while you have the light, so that you may become children of light.' Something like that. There is much darkness here. I sense it almost daily. I like the idea of walking in the light instead of in darkness."

"You believe what he says?"

He shook his head. "I am intrigued. But I am also a doctor. I have little time for religion."

I could relate to that. To me, religion has always been for weaklings and old people. But I was beginning to have second thoughts about that, especially when I considered Rico's sudden conversion. And that soldier who warned us? Cornelius? He was no pansy. I mean, I call myself a warrior, but he really is. And he claimed to be a follower of Jesus.

What am I missing here?

"I guess I'll have to see it to believe it."

"See what?" Loukas said.

"Nothing, just thinking out loud. Look, this suturing material you're using?" I said, watching the doctor weave the needle back and forth across my arm in a continuous zig-zag pattern. "What is it?"

"Silk. Some prefer catgut—animal viscera twisted into a threadlike string—but I like silk because it does not stretch as much, nor does it dry out as fast."

"Dr. Loukas, where did you receive your medical training?"

"Cnidus, under the Great Asclepiades."

"My professors called Cnidus the birthplace of medicine."

He nodded. "I suppose that's right. Do you have medical training, Michael?"

"I do. Eight years, post-grad."

"And all this time I just assumed you were a slave."

"I'm getting a lot of that. Hey, Doc, can I make a suggestion?"

"Please."

"Well, where I work, we use a different suturing method. Can I show you?"

He agreed, and I walked him through the procedure, having him perform a series of simple interrupted sutures in succession without cutting the thread. "Now," I said, as he completed the last loop. "Tie that last one and cut the thread."

Loukas did as directed and then leaned back to examine his work. "Incredible," he said. "Each suture becomes its own knot. If one breaks—"

"The others will still hold."

"I like it." He smiled, revealing a mouthful of teeth, browning at the roots. "Why did no one teach us this at University?"

"I'm sure they did not know. Maybe you should teach them."

Loukas stared at me for a few seconds, scribbled a few more notes, and then moved his attention to my cheek wound. I sat still and watched him, fascinated by his demeanor. He had a soft, gentle style about him, but he hesitated not at all in assessing and treating his patients. He also took to the new suturing method quickly, performing a perfect series of interrupted sutures across my cheek, before clipping off the remaining silk thread.

"There," he said. "Done. Be sure to keep these clean. They say cleanliness is next to godliness."

"You're a fast learner, Doc. I believe you have a bright future."

It astonished me to think that the vast knowledge my medical colleagues and I possessed began with wise men at seats of learning, like Cnidas, where Loukas received his education. Guys like Plato and Hippocrates, and Alcmaeon of Croton, the Greek philosopher and writer who first identified the brain as the seat of understanding. It all began there, with them, some 400-500 years ago.

During that time, medicine was nothing more than an idea. A philosophy shared by and argued over by brilliant men like these, skilled in the art of speech and writing. They studied the anatomy of the human body, much as a modern geneticist might study a strand of DNA, to establish the foundation of everything we know today about disease and trauma. It was all very raw then, exploratory, and fresh. But by the time of Christ—right now, as fate would have it—medicine had evolved. Natural medications had been discovered, and treatment regimens had become common. Doctors focused primarily on concepts of cleanliness and righteousness as a means of preventing disease, along with treatments of skin diseases and bleeding issues. Sickness was a way of life … and death. Doctors aimed to make their patients comfortable and sometimes even exiled them, until given to the throes of death. It was during this time that my new friend Loukas had completed his studies, and from what I could tell, he was doing well, but his understanding was archaic at best.

He tore a piece of clean linen from a roll and wrapped it snuggly about my arm. After tying the loose ends, he said, "This should help to keep it clean. Is it too tight?"

I made a fist. "No, it's perfect. Thanks."

Loukas sat down and stared at me for a moment before saying, "Michael, the way you talk. Your vast medical knowledge. That thing on your wrist that tells you time and beeps. I realize you are from a different time and place. That is okay with me, and I will tell no one. But if you go out there on the street and interact with the wrong people, especially the Roman guards, they may mistake you for a warlock or a magician and have you burned at the stake. Perhaps even crucified."

"As I said, we already met Crudelis and one of his soldiers, Cornelius."

"I hear good things about Cornelius. He is a follower of the Teacher. But you must avoid Crudelis. He is an evil man who would like nothing more than to beat you and throw you into prison. Now, listen to me. I have no idea who you are or where you're from, and I don't want to know. But if you truly are a physician, then perhaps you can help me. I have a patient in the back room who is dying."

CHAPTER TWENTY-TWO

The Medical Office of Loukas, MD
Jerusalem, Israel, the Year 33 A.D.
Thursday—4:43 PM Local Time

I feel quite certain that this is a first. Someone from the 21st century being here, in Jerusalem, the day before Jesus Christ is to be crucified ... well, like I said, I think it's a first. I don't know if I'm lost, dead, or the most alive I've ever been. I guess I should just go with it. After all, something big is happening here. Maybe in some strange way, it's all for my good.

Loukas led me to a small room, a crude version of my own emergency rooms, only, with a fireplace in one corner providing heat and some much-needed lighting. A noxious, sweet incense emanated from a smoking pot on the floor in one corner, barely masking the odor of feces. The room looked well supplied, with surgical instruments of the time hanging on the wall: probes, scalpels, scissors, knives, forceps, a saw, a bone chisel, and a hammer. I recognized what looked like a traction hook, and even a crude-looking catheter designed to go up the rectum into the body. *Hooo-weee.* A water pitcher, a large clay bowl, and a stack of blankets lay on the shelf beneath the surgical instruments, adding a touch of softness to the otherwise sadistic looking setting.

A wooden exam table stood in the center of the room, holding a middle-aged male in extreme distress. By the looks of his pale skin and decreased mental status, I could only assume he was close to death. I touched his arm. It felt cool and clammy. His forehead felt hot and sweaty. Breathing came in wheezing gasps, and heavy drool gurgled from his mouth and nose. I noticed that he had soiled himself. A young male of about fourteen or fifteen years of age scrubbed the floor with a wet sponge, doing his best to clean up the mess. He glanced at me and smiled, without speaking.

"My son," Loukas said. "Luke."

"Luke," I said. "It is so nice to meet you."

"Thank you, sir," Luke responded, bowing his head. "And you."

Loukas beamed with pride. "He plans to follow in my footsteps, you know."

"Yes," I said, the realization hitting me that I was looking at the young boy who would one day write two books of the Bible. "I do know."

As I watched Luke labor with the sponge, it occurred to me that this teenager was destined for more than to be a servant of the medical profession. This was Luke, the doctor to be. A follower of Jesus Christ who would one day write the Gospel of Luke, the third book in the New Testament, along with another book called The Acts of the Apostles. I whispered to myself, "Dr. Luke! Amazing!"

"Son," Loukas said. "Go fetch a clean cloth. Wash your hands in the barrel out back. Remember, cleanliness is next to godliness."

Luke ran from the room.

I stepped up to the patient. "What'd he eat?" I said, touching his wrist and feeling no pulse. "This looks muscarinic."

Loukas shrugged. "He stumbled in here a few minutes before you arrived, complaining of abdominal pain and nausea. Diarrhea and vomiting. He claims to have eaten mushrooms."

"Well, that would explain it."

"So, you have an idea?"

"I'm thinking he ingested a source of pure muscarine. Do you have any poisonous mushrooms around here?"

"Yes," he said. "I believe we do."

"I'm thinking either the Inocybe or Clitocybe families."

"I'm afraid I don't—"

"Have you heard of inosperma erubescens?"

"What's that?"

"Um, you might call it the deadly fibercap mushroom. It is a highly poisonous hallucinogen, and I know for a fact that it grows in this part of the world. I heard a lecture about it just last month."

Loukas shrugged.

"Let's see."

I touched the patient's neck and located a low carotid pulse. Slow and weak. I had dealt with plenty of mushroom poisonings over the years, including some more advanced than this one, but never outside of the confines of my emergency department. The solution could be simple, depending on the substance consumed, but without proper airway management tools, IV supplies, and anticholinergic medications to reverse the muscarinic effects of the mushroom, it would be difficult, if not impossible to manage.

"What have you done for him?"

Loukas shook his head. "What can we do? He is unrighteous. He was seeking devils through the hallucinogen."

"Maybe. Or perhaps he just ate too much of the wrong mushroom. Why don't we start by giving him some charcoal to bind whatever's left in his stomach."

"Charcoal?"

"Where I'm from, we use activated charcoal to treat ingested poisons. The massive surface area and adsorptive properties of charcoal tend to bind other compounds, thereby rendering them unabsorbable by the GI tract. Does that make sense?"

"Kind of."

"Isn't that charcoal in the fireplace, there?"

"Yes."

"See if you can get this poor guy to vomit again, and I'll crush some charcoal and put it into solution."

"Will that work?"

I shrugged. "We need to start somewhere."

Loukas spoke to his patient in Hebrew. The man stuck his finger into his mouth and heaved into a bowl.

I grabbed a handful of raw charcoal, a wooden bowl and spoon, and, in mortar-and-pestle fashion, crushed the charcoal into a fine powder. "Now," I whispered. "I need a solvent." I glanced around the room and located a bottle of bicarbonate. "This should work." I poured some of the powder into a flask, added a small amount of water, and stirred it to create a thin slurry. After that I poured in the ground charcoal and stirred it. "This should help," I said, handing it to Loukas. "Have him drink this."

Loukas asked no questions, just trustingly nodded and encouraged his patient to sip the thick, black solution.

I turned my attention to the next part of my homemade treatment regimen. I needed atropine, a drug that was not isolated until 1833. I rubbed my hands together. "What to do? Hey," I said. "Does belladonna grow around here?"

"Belladonna?"

"Atropa?"

Young Luke grabbed his father's arm. "He means, Deadly Nightshade, papa."

"Oh, yes," Loukas added. "Deadly Nightshade. The magicians use it to produce deep hallucinations."

"Well," I said, chuckling. "We could use some on this guy. In low doses it's a profound muscarinic antagonist. Got any?"

"No, but I know some people who might. Luke," he said, taking his son by the arm. "Go ask Myron the Necromancer for some nightshade. I will seek it from the priests. Now go!"

The two ran out, leaving me alone with the patient. I walked into the front room to check on Simon. He stood and asked, excitedly. "Where'd they go?"

"I sent them on an errand. Look, my friend, I know you're a praying man. This might be a good time to say one. That patient has almost no chance of making it."

I walked back into the treatment room and looked around for the materials needed to create an IV setup. Of course, I came up empty. There wasn't much plastic tubing around the place. What I did find, however, gave me an idea for an alternate administration route—the rectum. I used to use it a lot as a drug administration route when we couldn't gain IV access, especially in small children. It's a highly vascular region, which provides rapid absorption of many liquid drugs. I had used it many times in my ED, so I figured it would work here.

I picked up a three-foot wooden reed I saw standing in the corner and bent it a few degrees. It flexed nicely without crimping. "Perfect." Whatever Luke might have used it for I didn't know, but I felt certain he had never used it for the purpose I had in mind.

Without waiting for permission, I bent the reed until it snapped in half, producing a 16-inch tube. Then I grabbed the ox horn we had used earlier as a stethoscope, and, using a little MacGyver ingenuity, attached it to the reed to fashion a makeshift catheter.

"Hey," I murmured, eyeing my invention with pride. "This could work."

About the time I was finishing the world's first rectal catheter, young Dr. Luke ran back in with a burlap bag in hand. "Mr. Mike," he said, handing me the bag. "Deadly Nightshade."

"Good, Luke. Where's your father?"

Loukas ran back into the room short of breath and said, "What next?"

"Help me with this mixture," I said. "How much chemistry training did you get in school?"

"You mean alchemy? Air and water? Fire and earth?"

"No, I mean hydrochloric acid and sodium chloride."

Loukas shrugged.

"Okay," I said. "I earned my undergraduate degree in chemistry, which is the science of the substances of which matter is composed and how they interact. What I am about to do is based, loosely, on good science." I realized Loukas wouldn't have any hydrochloric acid, since it wasn't invented until the 1900s, but he would have some other acids around that could do the trick. I mean, red wine is acidic. So is vinegar, and it's much stronger. "If we add some vinegar to these crushed belladonna leaves, we might be able to make an antidote similar to a drug we call atropine hydrochloride. It could help reverse this patient's symptoms. Does that make sense?"

Loukas shook his head. I realized I was on my own.

"Let's see," I said. "If I remember my basic chemistry, vinegar is CH3COOH. If we use the acetic acid in the vinegar—" I paused to do some mental calisthenics, "we can extract the alkaloids from the leaves into a crude tincture that acts just like a primitive atropine solution. Yeah, that might just do it."

"Do what?" Loukas said.

"I need some vinegar. Got any?"

"Plenty. Luke, go get the apple vinegar out of the kitchen."

My chemistry experiment worked. So did my rectal catheter. It proved to be a little messy, and a painfully slow way to administer drugs, but within thirty minutes of receiving his last dose of my homemade atropine mixture, the patient's symptoms subsided. He sat up, told me his name, and even stood on command. He vomited once, eliminating a large amount of black charcoal and bile, which meant all the remaining mushroom particles had been successfully removed from his stomach.

I checked his wrist—his pulse was still weak, but his skin felt warm and dry. All oozing from the various parts of his body had finally ceased, and he no longer looked like he was slipping away from this life. I wished I had some IV fluids to properly restore his blood pressure, but, overall, I felt pleased. Against all odds, the crude extraction had worked.

The patient bowed and thanked me. "God bless you, sir. God bless you."

"Thank Loukas and Luke," I said, patting young Dr. Luke on the back. "They're the heroes."

I thanked Dr. Loukas, as well, regretting that I had no way to repay him. "I'm sorry," I said. "I am penniless."

"You have already paid me," he responded. "A charcoal drink to absorb poisons? Deadly Nightshade as an antidote for hallucinogenic mushrooms? A device for—" He held up my bugle-shaped MacGyver contraption, and said, "—rectal administration of medication? Before you depart," he said, "Please explain to me the drug you take for prevention of seizures. You called it, I think, di-lan-ten. How does it work?"

I had no idea that he could possibly understand what I was about to explain to him, but I proceeded anyway. He sat quietly and listened as I explained the mechanism of action of Dilantin and other sodium channel blockers, stopping me only once with a question about the cell. I described the membrane as a flexible, thin, semi-permeable boundary composed of a phospholipid bilayer, proteins, and carbohydrates.

"Many of these proteins," I further explained, "are there to serve as channels and gates, to control what goes in and out of the cell."

Loukas nodded. He did understand.

"These gates stay closed when membrane voltage is achieved, opening only when depolarization occurs, to allow sodium to enter. But when the membrane becomes unstable, from, say, toxic mushroom ingestion—" I used my hands to illustrate two doors opening. "These gates open prematurely."

"Yes!" he exclaimed.

"Sodium rushes in early, and bad things happen. Kind of like opening the gate at a crowded rock concert. People get trampled."

The last statement made him frown.

"Anyway, Dilantin stabilizes the cell membranes, maintaining voltage, and making them less apt to depolarize unexpectedly."

"Thus preventing seizures. Amazing!" Loukas stared at me as if I were a god. "How do you know these things?"

"Common knowledge."

"Well, you have taught me so much today. So very much."

“Glad to help. Oh, and hey,” I said, kneeling and facing young Luke. The boy stared at me, longingly, like a dry sponge seeking water. “Are you a writer, son?”

“Why, yes sir, I am. I have written many papers on the future of medicine. I hope to write one soon on the treatment of mushroom toxicity.”

I glanced at Loukas with an expression revealing my amazement. “Seriously?”

“He’s well advanced for his age.”

“He’s gonna make a great doctor.”

I turned back to Luke, remembering his soon-to-be-written gospel account of Jesus’ passion.

“I’ve got an idea for another paper, if you’re interested. You might want to take a closer look at this man they call the Teacher.”

“Why?” Luke asked, quizzically.

“I have a feeling he’s about to make history.”

I turned to leave. Loukas stopped me. “Michael,” he said, “be careful out there brother. Remember, the Roman patrols are not your friends.”

CHAPTER TWENTY-THREE

Jerusalem Stable
City of Jerusalem, Israel, the Year 33 A.D.
Thursday—7:08 PM Local Time

I stepped into the street to wait for Simon, my sensors up, and my ears still ringing with the fading echoes of Dr. Loukas' warning to be careful. The last thing I wanted was to be burned at the stake or crucified. That thought brought a shiver. I forced my brain out of clinical tracking and snapped it right back into infantry mode, sweeping the immediate perimeter to scan for threats—no guards, no horses, no Centurion. Clean for now.

I could feel my hands quivering. I balled them into fists and then slowly opened them again. I stared at them for a moment, trying to reconcile 21st-century emergency medicine with the ancient dirt beneath my fingernails. The sheer adrenaline of my patient encounter in Loukas' office was beginning to fade, leaving behind a profound, clinical fascination with what I had just pulled off against all historical odds. But as I shifted my gaze back to the gathering gloom of the Jerusalem streets, my wonder quickly curdled again into a cold, heavy knot of anxiety. I had survived the uncertainty of treating a poisoning patient with homemade drugs and tools, but the city around me was a powder keg, and the fuse was already lit. Tomorrow was Friday. If my memory of the timeline served, the real danger hadn't even begun.

Stay frosty, Marine …

I took a deep breath to steady my nerves, extended my arm, and placed the width of my four fingers horizontally against the horizon. The sun sat right on top of my index finger, which meant it was about fifteen degrees up. With my limited astronomical understanding, I knew that meant we had one hour till sunset. Simon must have been thinking the same thing because he pointed at the sun and said, "The day of preparation begins soon. We must find Peter quickly."

"Which way?"

"That way," he said, pointing deeper into the city. "We must drop off Baruch at the stable. There's a man there I need to see. He takes care of all livestock and knows just about everything that happens."

"Sounds good. But let's be careful," I said. "Things are about to get dicey around here."

I followed Simon to a remote corner of the city that possessed an atmosphere all its own, with a cacophony of sounds, and a variety of odors from burning coal to animal feed. At one point, we passed a leather tanner's shop displaying various hides and leather accessories. The manly smell of fresh belts and oils filled my nostrils as we passed by. Another court featured a red-hot furnace with a bellows-type blower for heating up the coals. An artisan pounded on a strip of metal. Another worker in the same yard sharpened a blade on a stone wheel, pumping it with his foot and grinding the metal to produce a shower of sparks. At the end of the street, we entered a corral of sorts where donkeys, horses, sheep, and goats grazed on yellow wheat straw and grain.

Simon tied Baruch Aton to a hitching post inside the fence and patted her on the neck. "Wait here," he said to me. "I should not be long."

I patted Baruch on her head. We had shared a dangerous journey, and I felt I owed her my thanks. I talked to her like a family pet, thanking her for bearing my considerable weight, apologizing to her for turning her around on her journey home, and then I fed her a bundle of straw, which she gladly accepted.

I wasn't trying to eavesdrop, but when the conversation inside the barn rose above a whisper, I overheard Simon say something about "Petrus," something else about "the other Disciples," and a deeper voice saying something like, "I think you will find them there." And, "Be careful. The Sanhedrin are watching."

A moment later a tall, muscular man walked out of the barn and unhitched Baruch. He looked more German to me than Italian, with light hair and skin, and the strong chiseled face of a statue. His right hand was missing a finger, and he moved with a noticeable limp. "Hello," he said, looking me up and down. His bluish-gray eyes intrigued me. His voice made me shiver. "My name is Claudius."

"Michael."

"You are a fighter, Michael? Yes?"

It sounded more like a statement than a question.

"Does it show?"

"I know a warrior when I see one. I was once a fighter myself." He paused and stared into the distance, as if picturing a faraway place. "I was one of the lucky ones. I earned my freedom." That's when I noticed the scars on his arms, and another across one cheek. "You two men be careful tonight," he said, turning to Simon. "I sense danger. You may stay in the stable if you'd like."

"Thank you," Simon said. "But we must find Petrus tonight."

"Please be careful, my friends. Avoid the Roman soldiers at all costs. I have heard talk. I have many friends in high places."

Claudius placed one hand on Simon's shoulder, the other on mine, and then, to my amazement, this brute of a man proceeded to pray over us, for our protection, for our mission, and for safe passage home. "God be praised," he said. "Amen." Then he nodded at me, and said, "God will lead you home, my brother." With that, he took Baruch's leash and led her inside the barn.

"Let's go," Simon said. "We have a kilometer to walk."

"Who was that guy?" I asked.

"Claudius is the stablemaster. He was once a Roman gladiator."

"A gladiator?"

"Yes, he fought in Circus Maximus, one of the great arenas of Rome. His former name was Claudius the Great. He was the champion. I once saw him fight."

"Man, I would hate to get on his wrong side. He must be a devout man, though, the way he prayed over us."

"Like Cornelius, he is a follower of the Teacher. I have deep respect for him."

I glanced at the sky as we exited yet another gate. It felt odd to be leaving the bright, noisy streets of Jerusalem and re-entering the cold, outer district of the slopes of Mt. Zion. I noticed that my leg no longer hurt, which I found curious, and I felt strong again, too, uninhibited by the fear of seizures or the chronic anxiety that had accompanied me for the last two months. Excitement? Lingering khat in my system? I didn't know, but I relished the feeling. I was in another world now, but as tangible and even more authentic somehow than the one I had recently left.

I followed Simon along a trail that paralleled the city wall, glancing up at the parapets that resembled the upside-down dental molding on a giant colonial home. Just overhead I saw two guards standing watch with bows in hand.

The sun, having just dipped below the horizon, produced a deep orange glow above the mountains that reflected off the wall in golden hues. The sky transitioned to a warm liquid blue overhead, and then to dark gray as it merged with the opposite horizon, creating a perfect backdrop for the heavenly orbs just beginning to glow. Venus and Jupiter stood out with a brilliance I had never seen. The red planet, Mars, followed well behind in the east, before a mostly full moon that would soon fill the night with light.

I had never seen the sky so brilliantly displayed. I wasn't sure what I was feeling, but in a way, I felt strangely blessed, as if the Creator had anointed me. I felt happy to be alive, ecstatic to be here now, and amazed to be on a mission in Jerusalem, not in a dream but for real. It was an electric feeling, and in my heart, I felt as if something big was happening to me. Something more important than finding my way home.

"I'm sorry for the secrecy," Simon finally said, "but Claudius was nervous. He is frightened that arrests will come tonight. He fears we could be arrested, too. He asked where we were going and warned me against it."

"I can take care of both of us."

"No," Simon said, wincing. "I do not believe you understand the fierceness of these men. The Roman soldiers can be ruthless. You met Crudelis, and you saw the wooden post atop Golgotha. You know what they do to criminals."

"Claudius mentioned the Sanhedrin. Who are they?"

"The Sanhedrin are the Jewish elders, the ruling council in Jerusalem, composed of the Pharisees and Sadducees. They are the judges."

"Religious guys?"

"Yes, but self-righteous. They rule with an iron fist. They answer only to Pontius Pilate, Governor of Judea. He has the power over life and death, but I have also heard that he is weak and tends to give in to the demands of the Sanhedrin. If they demand it, he may throw the Teacher into prison, or worse. They hate everything about him."

"Why do they hate him so much?"

"Oh, so many reasons. He threatens their religious authority. Challenges their traditions and Sabbath laws. And most of all, he claims to be the son of God."

"Is he? The son of God?"

"I do not know. But I do know this … the Sanhedrin are evil, and they will eliminate any person they see as a threat."

"Then we should warn him. Where is he?"

"Right up there." Simon pointed at the small mountain in front of us. "The building you see with the two lamps out front sits above the sacred tomb of King David. Claudius believes the Teacher is there with Peter and the other Disciples right now, preparing the Passover meal."

"Then, let's go."

"Oh, no, we must wait. It would be inappropriate to interrupt them. We will wait until they have finished. Come."

I followed Simon into a grove of trees. We spotted a campfire and sneaked toward it, concealing ourselves in the foliage in the event we encountered soldiers, or bandits. To our amazement, the camp was unattended. The flames of the fire were low, but there were enough branches and twigs on the ground to build it back up and keep it going through the night. "Praise Elohim," Simon said, tossing a handful of sticks onto the coals. "He has provided."

"Simon?" I said, fanning the fire. The sticks burst into flames, filling the woods with hot, gray smoke. "What do you believe? I heard you mention Elohim."

"I am a Jew. My father was a Jew. His father was a Jew."

"But what about the Teacher? Who is he, to you?"

"He is a prophet. A good man."

"But not the son of God?"

"I do not believe so. But, Michael, what matters right now is what *you* believe."

"I think we're just here. Part of some massive creation, maybe. I don't know. I guess I believe that when we die, the lights go out and it's just, you know, over."

"No God?"

I shrugged. "I've never given it much thought."

Simon shook his head. "I am so sorry. To believe in a higher power is the essence of life. It gives us meaning. Purpose."

"I've always believed in things I could see and touch. Science. Medicine. Nature. Things I could evaluate and explain mathematically."

"Tell me something," he said. "Are you married?"

I studied his face. The orange glow of the flames danced across his features, casting eerie shadows from below, yet there was an undeniable warmth and contentment in his eyes that assured me I could trust him.

"I am," I responded. "Why?"

"Do you love her?"

"My wife? Yes, of course."

"Explain that mathematically."

I chuckled. "Point taken. I guess what I'm trying to say is I'm just not sure what I believe anymore. A lot of very strange things have happened to me. It must mean something." I threw a large branch onto the flames and watched it ignite. "I don't know," I said, in a low voice. "All this talk about God, and all. I just don't know."

"This man they call the Teacher," Simon said. "I have watched him. Like Claudius, I heard him preach yesterday. There was something about the way he spoke, and the aura around him. He possessed love, and yet incredible charisma and power. And he spoke with such authority. He claims he came to save us. To give us eternal life."

"And do you believe that?"

"With all of my heart. He is the Messiah. I pray I may one day serve him."

CHAPTER TWENTY-FOUR

Garden of Gethsemane
Outside of Jerusalem, Israel, the Year 33 A.D.
Passover Friday—1:56 AM Local Time

I once read of a man who stayed awake for 264.4 hours as part of an experiment to determine the effects of sleep deprivation on the brain. After three days he experienced hallucinations and confusion, and by the tenth day he could not perform simple math. Eleven days without sleep. Is that even possible? Maybe for him, but not for me.

Once during med school, I stayed awake three nights in a row to finish my final project. Unfortunately, on the third night, somewhere around 3:00 AM, I fell asleep and woke up too late to finish the project. Fortunately, I still earned an A, but more importantly, I learned a valuable lesson:

The human body will, eventually, sleep …

At some point during the night my body proved that point. I fell asleep and was dreaming of flying bats and dark creeping shadows when something woke me. At first, I lay there confused, half awake, rubbing my eyes to clear the cobwebs clinging to the corners of my dreaming brain. I spotted Simon lying nearby with his head on a stone, snoring quietly. Our campfire had burned out. Hours had passed.

A man's voice turned my head toward a distant corner of the grove. I followed the sound to a small clearing, a lush garden of sorts, with decorative rock formations and plants. On the far side I could see a man kneeling on the ground before a bench, his hands clenched together, his face raised as if he were speaking to heaven. I saw a faint glow of light emanating from him, an aura, as if he possessed unseen powers, unexplainable in human terms.

I have always fought my own battles, refusing to bow to any man. It is my badge of honor—my creed. Yet, as I sat there, witnessing that awe-inspiring fusion of agony and strength, watching blood seep from his skin like beads of sweat, I suddenly understood I was in the Garden of Gethsemane, and before me knelt the Teacher:

"Jesus."

A wave of overwhelming awe and humility washed over me, stealing the strength from my legs. "It's him," I whispered, dropping to my knees. "My Lord, it's really him."

Witnessing a moment so sacred and private made me feel utterly out of place, an intruder on a divine struggle. But as I watched him pray, and saw the blood dripping from his face and arms, I realized he was in deep trouble. I had never seen true hematidrosis outside of textbooks—the systemic capillary breakdown under sheer, unfathomable stress. He was bleeding from the inside out before they even touched him. How, I wondered, would he possibly survive the night?

Suddenly, my watch beeped, piercing the somber silence of the garden. I ducked low and glanced at my wrist—2:00 AM. Then a terrible thought struck me, an ominous reminder:

Nothing good ever happens after 2:00 AM.

As if on cue, demonic, blood-curdling laughter filled the garden, the same wicked laughter I had heard atop Golgotha. Something unearthly and evil. My skin crawled. My stomach turned.

I waited and watched, wondering if I might see a band of demons appear. But it wasn't a demon that walked out of the fog and up to the Teacher. It was a man. He came with a large mob, a band of soldiers, and a group of white-robed, official-looking men I figured to be Sanhedrin.

"Master," he said, kissing Jesus on the cheek. "My master."

"He's the one," a guard shouted. "Seize him!"

A team of guards grabbed him. Then a large soldier rushed in, pushing the others aside. I recognized him immediately as the Centurion, Crudelis. "Get out of my way," he demanded, throwing one of the guards to the ground. "You say you're the son of God," he spat, slapping Jesus with the back of his hand. "Let's see you get out of these shackles!"

Before the guards could affix the iron cuffs, a burly man plowed into the fray, swinging his sword in a wide, lethal arc. The blade caught a man in the mob, slicing his ear away in a spray of dark blood.

At the sight of the gruesome injury, the crowd broke, gripped by sudden panic.

I lost my mind and charged, zeroed in on the monster, Crudelis. Reaching him before he could react, I tackled him and went for a quick choke hold. But Crudelis was slick. He pulled free and countered with a snapping backfist, tearing the skin of my cheek with the metal rivets of his wrist-guard.

"So," he sneered, grunting and rubbing his throat. "The slave knows how to fight!"

I threw two quick punches at his face, breaking his nose and tearing his lip. The infuriated Crudelis reeled but would not go down. He sprang with catlike speed that belied his awesome bulk, throwing a powerful right hook, knocking me off my feet.

I went down hard. Stars exploded inside my skull. My head became heavy and dull. Crudelis dived into my guard, pinning his weight on my chest as his hands closed around my throat.

I had no intention of allowing him to crush my trachea. I raised my right leg, slipping it over his shoulder and wrapping it tight around his neck. Then using my considerable weight, I pulled down with all my might. The big man rolled over backwards and fell, but one second later he was back on me, pounding my face with both fists.

Perhaps I had been weakened by the seizures and near-death experience, or he was simply a superior fighter, or it really was nothing more than a bad dream, and I would soon awaken. All I really knew for sure was he intended to kill me. I was finished, powerless, with blood spewing from my cheek, and unconsciousness closing in. Crudelis had me, and I believe I would have died, if not for the mountainous man who appeared out of the riot.

Like a charging bear, Claudius the Great lunged forward, tearing the Centurion off of me and throwing him to the ground. I watched through a dim fog as he beat Crudelis without mercy. He was on the verge of snapping the man's neck with his bare hands when, without warning, an unseen force blasted him, and everyone else, backward.

"Peace!" a voice rang out.

The mob fell to the ground. I lay there panting, unable to move. Then I watched with astonishment as the only man standing—Jesus—picked up the severed ear and gently replaced it on the side of the injured man's head. He glanced toward heaven, as if in prayer, and then removed his hand. I saw no sign of injury or blood.

"My God," I murmured. "What did he do?"

Jesus looked over the crowd, scanning us slowly, and then walked over to where the sword-wielding attacker lay on the ground. "Peter," he said, calmly and quietly. "Put away your sword. Shall I not drink the cup the Father has given me?"

I had never witnessed such a show of awesome power. The garden had been transformed from a wild melee to a scene of unanimous obedience. I sat in silence as the one called Peter stood and sheathed his sword. Minutes passed before anyone else spoke or moved. Then, slowly, the guards began to rise and approach Jesus. Quietly they attached the shackles to his hands and feet and led him away, without a word.

Others began to stand and move about, speaking quietly amongst themselves as they exited the garden. Crudelis stood and wiped the blood from his battered face. Without a word, he glared at Claudius and then walked away to join his guard.

I was wiping blood from my nose when Claudius approached and offered me his hand. He pulled me to my feet, and said, "Are you okay?"

"Yeah, thanks. Looks like you made an enemy."

"Who, Crudelis?" Claudius grunted. "We've been enemies for a long time. He, too, was a gladiator, you know. Like me, he won his freedom. But Crudelis went to the dark side and became a Legionnaire. He quickly rose to power. He is not a good man."

"I noticed. You'd better watch your back, huh?"

Claudius shook his head. "I'm not afraid to die. But I am afraid for *your* life. What were you thinking, attacking him?"

"I wasn't thinking, I was trying to kill him. I'm just glad you showed up."

"I'm glad the Teacher intervened."

"What just happened, anyway? When he spoke it was like a shockwave from a high-explosive blast."

"He is the son of the living God. He has all power. Mark my words—one day every knee will bow before him."

Just then a small band of guards came back into the garden and surrounded Claudius, swords drawn. Two men approached him with shackles.

"What is this?" Claudius roared.

"You are under arrest for assaulting a Roman official," one guard said. "You will stand before Pilate for sentencing."

Claudius did not resist as they bound his hands and feet.

"Pray for me, brother," he said, glancing my way.

"Move!" the lead guard shouted, jabbing him with his sword.

Claudius winked at me, turned, and followed the soldiers from the garden.

"What do we do?" I shouted.

"Pray for him," Simon said. "There is nothing else you *can* do. Do not make another scene. We are fortunate they did not arrest *you*. Now, come," he said, clutching my arm and pulling me. "I want you to meet someone."

I looked back and watched Claudius the Great as he disappeared from the garden into the trees. "Lord," I quietly prayed. "Protect our friend."

I followed Simon through the crowd to a man I recognized as the one who had cut off the other's ear. He was a large man, my size but a few years younger, with a heavy build and a thick black beard. Like mine, his clothes were splattered with someone else's blood. And like me, he seemed stunned, as if he could hardly believe what had just happened. He looked up when Simon spoke to him and for a moment did not seem to recognize him. Then his face grew into a wide smile, and he reached out and hugged the smaller man.

"Simon of Cyrene! Brother, you are here!"

"Your brother and servant for life."

"You should hide," Peter said, turning serious. "They have arrested the Teacher, and Claudius, as well. We must go!"

"Before you go, please take a moment to help my new friend."

Peter turned to face me. It wasn't his stature that commanded attention—it was his eyes. They burned with a startling intensity, a hidden fire that seemed to radiate from somewhere deep within. "You're bleeding," he said, pressing his palm against my cheek. He closed his eyes, murmured quietly, and then said, "Amen" and removed his hand. "What is your name?"

"Michael."

"Michael," he said. "I am Peter."

I touched my cheek and nose, and realized I felt no pain. No blood stained my hands. My eyes widened. "What did you just do?"

"I prayed for you, my friend."

"You healed me? Peter? You really are, you're Peter?"

Peter chuckled. "You've heard of me?"

"Everyone has heard of you. You're the fisherman. Jesus called you and you followed him. I've read both of your epistles."

"Sir, I have authored no epistles. I am a simple man. Just a fisherman. But you are correct in saying I am a follower of Jesus.

I will never forsake him! We have given our lives to our master, and we must follow him. I must go. Hurry. Tell me how I can help you."

"I need to find my way home. I don't know what to do. I don't even know how I got here."

Peter stared at me for a moment as if analyzing my situation. Then without hesitation he laid a hand on my shoulder and prayed for me again, thanking God first for the blessing of life, and then for a quick resolution to my problem. "Help my new friend find his way," he prayed. "Help him to learn to trust you. Make his path straight, and if it be thy will, take him home."

Peter locked eyes with me for a moment, offered an encouraging nod, and then turned to the man standing behind him. "John?" he said. "Where have they taken him, brother?"

"The western gate," John said. "I heard one of the guards mention the Praetorium."

I looked back and forth between Peter and John, astonished to realize I was looking at the two Disciples I had read so much about in the Gospels. The men who would establish the first church and write much of the New Testament. They fit the mental images I had drawn up for each of them, too: Jewish, with long noses and olive skin. Peter looked muscular and tough, with oily black hair and a thick beard. John was taller and leaner, dressed in a maroon-colored robe, with a soft complexion but equally strong-looking hands. But, except for Peter's prayers and the miraculous healing of my injured cheek and nose, neither man impressed me in the way that I had expected them to. They didn't come across as powerful and charismatic, ready to set the world ablaze with a new religion, but as ordinary men. Peter even smelled like fish.

"The Praetorium?" Peter said. "Why?"

John shook his head. "I think they are taking him to Pilate."

"Oh my."

"What should we do?" one of the other Disciples said.

"We follow him," Peter responded. "Where he goes, we go. Remember?"

Peter pushed past the other men and trotted off in the direction of a gate in the city wall, 200 yards away. John hurried after him. The others stood for a moment speaking quietly amongst themselves, before turning to follow.

I remembered hearing a sermon on the radio a few weeks back about the Apostle Peter, his death by crucifixion, and how he had told his executioners to crucify him upside down. How he did not feel worthy of execution in the same manner as his master. I remember feeling a pit in my stomach then, wondering about the commitment of a man who would submit to such punishment. I respected him then, and I respect him even more now.

"Something big is happening here, Simon, and I'm not about to miss it. I'm going after them!"

Simon nodded. "Me, too. Where you go, I go. Remember?"

CHAPTER TWENTY-FIVE

Courtyard of the Praetorium
Palace of Pontius Pilate, Governor of Judea
Jerusalem, Israel, the Year 33 A.D.
Passover Friday—5:16 AM Local Time

The night—long, cold, and frightening—had been filled with conflict. First there was the fight in the olive grove when Crudelis almost choked me out. Then the arrest when the soldiers beat up the Teacher and took him away in chains. And then an uprising on the trail leading up to the palace involving an unruly crowd of townspeople. Simon and I narrowly avoided being arrested along with about a dozen others who were caught trying to sneak into the Praetorium to watch, well, whatever was happening. I remembered that Jesus was to be scourged at some point after the arrest, but I couldn't remember all the details. I suddenly wished I had read the accounts of his passion more carefully.

Simon and I ran up a dark alley and hid until the streets had cleared of guards, and then we made our way around the building to a courtyard with a large fire pit. A crowd stood around the fire warming themselves, a gathering that included four Roman guards and a couple of fancy looking Jewish men dressed in fine linen robes.

I felt myself shiver. The fire looked inviting. I nudged Simon. "What do you think, man? Join them?"

Simon shook his head. "Those are Sanhedrin."

"Yeah, I see 'em."

I recognized their type from around town, and a few had been right there in the garden, nodding their consent when Jesus was arrested. They stood out instantly in their regal robes, formal turbans, and heavy prayer shawls with long, twisted fringes knotted at the corners. They carried themselves with a cold contempt for the commoners around them, an arrogance so thick it hung in the air like smoke. They made no effort to hide their disdain for the Teacher, either. One spat the word *heretic*. The other muttered a blasphemy so vile I didn't care to repeat it.

I hated them instantly. If I'd had them in the ring, I would have beaten them both to a pulp. But to tell you the truth, I felt intimidated by those two devils. Their council ruled the courts in Jerusalem, and from what Simon had told me, they had sentenced many to die. Crucifixion had become a common practice in Jerusalem, and I had seen firsthand the evil of Golgotha. I wanted nothing to do with it, or those men. Still, that fire sure looked good.

We hid in the shadows for a few minutes and had almost decided not to enter the courtyard, when I noticed a familiar face in the crowd.

"Hey," I whispered, nudging Simon. "Isn't that Peter?"

Peter had his hood pulled over his head and his bearded chin low, but there was no mistaking the shape of his bulky frame. A tall, slender man stood beside him wearing a maroon-colored robe. I recognized him from the garden as the disciple named John. Both stood close to the flames. Neither seemed eager to socialize with the others standing close by. I waved my hand to catch their attention. John glanced our way, and then motioned with his hand for us to join them.

I nudged Simon. "What do you say, brother? Cold?"

"Freezing."

Simon and I stepped from the shadows and walked across the lane into the courtyard, approaching cautiously, until we realized that no one cared. People stood together in small groups, engaged in quiet conversation. The orange-tipped flames slowly warmed my body, causing a dreamy weariness to flood over me. I found myself thinking of my wife, how much I missed her, and desperately wanted to hold her. I felt as if I was dreaming, until a sharp commanding voice broke my reverie.

"You!" One of the guards spat, pulling his sword and pointing it at Peter.

Peter stepped back and raised his hands. "Me?"

"I thought I recognized you. You were there. In the garden. I saw you with that teacher!"

"No," Peter exclaimed. "I don't know the man."

"I saw you with him, too," one of the Sanhedrin agreed. He stepped forward and pointed a gnarly finger at Peter. "You pulled your sword and cut off the servant's ear."

"Sir!" Peter cried. "You're mistaking me for someone else!"

"We should add you to the executioner's list," the Sanhedrin spat.

"Which is growing by the minute," the other elder said, with a laugh.

The crowd stirred.

I felt as if I were watching a Broadway play I'd already seen, knowing exactly what the next scene held before the current one even ended. Then it occurred to me why: I had already read this story. All four Gospels—Matthew, Mark, Luke, and John—recount the moment Peter denies Jesus three times before the rooster crows. In the end, he flees into the night, crushed by the bitter shame of betraying his closest friend.

Almost as if coming from backstage on a cue, a teenaged girl called out from the other side of the fire. "He's lying," she announced, pushing through the crowd and grabbing Peter's sleeve. "You were with him." She turned and gestured toward the elders. "That teacher was on the street preaching. This man was standing right beside him."

"No!" Peter shouted. "I have already told you, I do not know the man!"

Just then I heard the sharp and strident crow of a rooster, a distinct "cock-a doodle-do" somewhere in the distance.

Peter dropped to his knees and began to weep. "Teacher," he cried. "I have denied you. My Lord and my God, please forgive me."

Those standing close to Peter backed away. The Sanhedrin moved in, scoffing him and calling him names. "Lord your God? You have blasphemed the name of God!"

Peter stood and ran from the courtyard.

"Peter!" John called, running after him. "Wait!"

The crowd laughed. The guards mocked. The Sanhedrin cursed him as a fool.

Anger flared hot in my chest, threatening to boil over. Simon caught the shift in my posture and instantly gripped my arm. "Calm down," he murmured, his voice barely a breath. "Be still. They have not yet recognized us."

I nodded and lowered my head.

The small talk around us resumed. Then the same guard called out, "You!" I glanced up. This time the guard was pointing at *me*. "You were there, too," he shouted. "In the garden. With the Teacher!"

"Yeah?" I responded, tired of the accusations and bullying. "I was there. So what?"

"He's the one that attacked Crudelis!"

It had been a long night. I was tired, I was hungry, and my head still hurt from battling the Centurion. But I could not stand it any longer. Someone had to stop the cruelty and put these vicious Romans in their place. I stepped forward, fists tight.

I realized that what I was contemplating was suicide. I was about to take on a man with a sword. A Roman Legionnaire, skilled at high-intensity, close-quarters combat. There was no way I could win. We were in *his* octagon this time, and he had an entire army on his side. But I was out of my head with anger. A cold surge of adrenalin hit me. I raised my fists and steeled myself for battle.

The guard drew his sword and stepped toward me. I braced myself for the impalement sure to end me, but instead of thrusting his sword into my belly, the man's face broke into laughter. "Well done, slave," he bellowed. "I hate that man!"

"We all do," another guard chimed in, laughing out loud. "Crudelis is a swine. I wish you had choked him to death!"

The Legionnaire patted me on the back and rejoined his friends. The crowd emitted a deep sigh and murmured amongst themselves. I nodded and moved back to the fire, unsure how to respond, afraid to speak. I could feel my heart doing flip-flops inside my chest. Simon placed his hand on my shoulder. "Breathe, brother. Just breathe."

"Sheesh," I whispered. "I thought it was curtains for me."

"What will happen to the Teacher?" someone in the crowd asked. "Who cares?" the guard responded, sheathing his sword. "Prison? Death? It's up to Pilate now."

The guard's comment left me pondering what was next for the Teacher. I mean, I remembered something about a scourging, a crown of thorns, and a purple robe, but the details remained a blur. "He mentioned, Pilate," I whispered to Simon, leaning close so only he could hear. "What did he mean by that?"

"Pilate is Governor of Judea. He will determine the teacher's fate."

We stood by the fire, soaking in the warmth for what seemed like hours, waiting with the others as the tension mounted. We received multiple reports of Jesus' movement as he was bounced between various officials—Caiaphas, Pontius Pilate, and Herod Antipas—for preliminary hearings. Finally, we heard the shouts of angry men echo from within the Praetorium, a few yards away. I knew in an instant that he was back. I felt myself cringe with the knowledge of what was coming.

"Pray for him," I murmured.

The whip cracked, followed instantly by a scream—sharp, jagged, and full of anguish. A leaden silence settled upon us, thick and suffocating, as the weight of what was happening took hold. I even noticed the guards and Sanhedrin wince at the distinctive cracking sounds of leather whips biting flesh. Cries echoed across the courtyard again, and again, and again.

Crack … scream. Crack … scream.

The crowd within the praetorium began to cheer with a contagious madness that swept out into the courtyard, until everyone around us cheered.

I could almost picture the whip-ends tearing the Teacher's back to shreds.

Crack-crack … scream.

Cheering and shouting.

The agony of the punishment seemed unreal. I had never felt such shame. But what could I do? How could I help him now?

Crack … crack.

By this point, the roar of the crowd inside and out had reached a feverish pitch. The Sanhedrin seemed to revel in the madness. One of them sneered and pointed at the doorway leading to the inner courtyard of the Praetorium. "That Teacher," he shouted above the din, his face mad with delight. "He is finally getting what he deserves!"

That sadistic comment did it. A white-hot surge of fury blinded me. Any trace of fear was gone, replaced by a rage so violent it felt like my skull could not contain it.

Crack-crack … scream.

"I can't stand this anymore," I said, grabbing Simon's arm. "Come with me! We've got to help him!"

We ran through the doorway to enter a large inner courtyard filled with hundreds of shouting people. I pushed through the crowd until it was impossible to get any closer to the front of the auditorium. I stood on my toes for a clear view, and what I saw took my breath away.

Jesus leaned over a wooden lectern, his feet shackled with iron chains, his hands bound by thick rope and stretched out wide. A torturer stood on either side of him, each with a wicked looking instrument in his hands—a cat-of-nine-tails, a wooden handled device with multiple leather strips, each with a small metal dumbbell tied to its end. The two men took turns whipping his back, his legs and buttocks, his arms and shoulders. The thongs whistled through the air striking his raw flesh and wrapping around him to catch the tender parts of his chest and abdomen. They stopped only to catch their breath and to laugh at the bloody mess they were making, finally ending their sadistic work when he was no longer able to stand.

"He's had enough," one of the guards shouted. "Stop."

"Not yet," the other torturer spat, striking him one last time. A chunk of bloody flesh sailed through the air and landed on my cheek. I wiped it away and glanced at my hand. Blood.

I was numb. They had torn him to shreds, leaving behind a mess of exposed tissue and bone. Almost against my will, my mind shifted into physician's mode. The empathy retracted, replaced by a cold diagnostic clarity.

Major trauma. Systemic inflammatory response, and the body's physiological response to critical wounds …

His body, in a frantic effort to stop the bleeding, would have already launched an inflammatory response—not just at the injury sites, either, but throughout his entire system. Platelets were turning sticky, trying to form clots at the site of every leak, but in healthy tissues as well. This would lead to organ damage in otherwise healthy systems.

Meanwhile, tiny surface blood vessels would dilate to increase blood flow to the wounds, and plasma would seep into the skin to flush out toxins and ease the trauma. These are normal, protective responses. But in his case, they'd have a dangerous downside: the cumulative effect would drop his blood pressure significantly, lowering him into shock.

Shock is a well-understood physiological response to significant blood loss. Simply put, it's a state of inadequate tissue perfusion—where there isn't enough circulating blood volume to deliver oxygen to the body's tissues. In response, the body quickly releases key catecholamines, such as adrenaline, which constrict blood vessels to raise blood pressure and preserve vital organ function. But if the trauma isn't addressed, the situation rapidly deteriorates, progressing into decompensated shock, disseminated intravascular coagulation, organ failure, and eventually death.

The point is, Jesus was in trouble.

His sobs—raw and desperate—were all but drowned out by the savage roar of the crowd. They circled him like predators, eyes wild, voices rising in a frenzied chant: "Kill him! Kill him!" The sound was deafening, merciless.

Then a voice from above shouted, "Silence!" A hush fell over the crowd.

I looked up and saw a man standing on a balcony above the whipping post, dressed in regal fashion—a red tunic, a skirt of heavy leather strips, and a thick brown vest guarding his chest. In his hand, he raised a wooden rod, wielding it like a scepter. "People," he shouted. "Listen to me!"

"That's Pontius Pilate," Simon said, leaning close. "Prefect of Judea."

"Prefect?"

"Governor."

Pilate motioned to Jesus with his scepter and said to the crowd, "Behold, your king!"

"No!" they shouted. "He is not our king! Kill him!"

Pilate pleaded with them, trying to reason, but the crowd wouldn't be swayed. Their voices surged into a single, furious roar, drowning out everything else. "Take him away!" they screamed. "Crucify him! Crucify him!"

CHAPTER TWENTY-SIX

Pathway to Golgotha
Outside the City of Jerusalem, Israel, the Year 33 A.D.
Passover Friday—8:36 AM Local Time

Jim Stockbridge once told me about a wreck he responded to on a highway near East Beach. He found six people trapped in a collapsed van, all broken and pinned in place by the folded steel of crumpled seats and door posts. One of the victims, a thirty-something-year-old female, looked him in the eyes and, with a sad expression, asked, "Am I going to die?" Jim was not about to lie to her. Besides, she knew the truth. She knew she was dying. "Ma'am," he responded, "I'm sorry, we will not be able to save you. But please know we are going to do everything possible to save the rest of your family." And with that, she smiled weakly, thanked him, and drew her last breath.

We all die—our final breath is coming. It's what we do with that last breath that matters …

At the conclusion of the mock trial, the soldiers draped a purple robe over the Teacher's shoulders and pressed a crown of twisted thorns onto his head, pounding it into his scalp with wooden clubs. The thorns were horrifying—not just for their length, but for their cruel precision. Three to four inches long and needle-thin, they were driven deep, one pressed so perilously close to his eye it seemed a miracle it hadn't punctured the globe. He wept, silent tears carving clean tracks down his dust-stained cheeks.

"Hail," one of the guards sneered, dropping to one knee and bowing his head in sardonic reverence. "Behold, the King of the Jews."

The guard's mockery sparked the crowd. Laughter morphed into a savage roar. Soon, the entire volatile mob was pressing in—spitting, jeering, and hurling venomous curses through the heavy air.

"Get going you!" the guard shouted, rising and shoving him forward. "Move!"

The furious roar of the crowd followed him out of the inner courtyard, echoing off the high stone walls of the Praetorium like fading thunder. The judgment had been passed, the political theater was over, and the grim reality of Roman execution was settling into place. As the guards aggressively cleared a path through the swelling mob, the humid morning air outside felt thick and suffocating, charged with a collective, manic bloodlust. Simon and I fell into step among the onlookers, our movements rigid, driven entirely by a cold, heavy dread. The wooden crossbeam was brought out, and as the morning sun began to bake the dusty streets of Jerusalem, the countdown to the final hill officially began.

We followed him through the Garden Gate with a large crowd of over a thousand. "Guilty, guilty," the mob shouted, following behind him, the closest spitting on him as he trudged along. "Crucify! Crucify!"

I struggled to stay close, desperate to keep him in sight. His broken body, bloodied and bloated, sagged beneath the crushing weight of the beam. His face was bruised and raw, nearly unrecognizable. He staggered beneath the load strapped across his shoulders, legs buckling until he collapsed—first to his knees, then fully down, his face slamming into the dirt. Blood burst from his nose on impact.

I'm an emergency room physician, which means I see more trauma in one week than most people see in a lifetime. I knew without doubt that with all the bleeding and beatings and scourging this man had endured, he was close to the end. Systemic inflammation, massive hemorrhage, dehydration, pain, and simple exhaustion had taken such a toll, that without surgery, volume replacement, and a healthy dose of antibiotics and pain killers, he would most certainly die. So why crucify him? I wondered.

I was so busy pondering the pathophysiology of his impending death that I never noticed Crudelis and his band of soldiers approaching me. Startled, I held up my hands. Not much else to do when six soldiers surround you, one pressing the tip of a spear into your gut.

The crowd backed away with a collective groan.

"Seize him," Crudelis shouted, pointing at me. "That's the one!"

A guard stepped forward and punched me in the belly, knocking the wind from my lungs and making me puke. As I bent over, gasping for air, another slapped shackles on my wrists. A third wrapped a thick, leather strap around my neck like a choke collar on a dog.

"You're coming with us," Crudelis sneered, his face swollen and bruised from a recent fistfight. "You will soon learn the fate of those foolish enough to assault a Roman official. And you, little African," he said, shoving Simon to the ground. "Pick up that crossbeam. You will carry it for this—" Crudelis turned and spat on Jesus. "This king!"

Simon glanced at me with terror in his eyes. I nodded and mouthed, silently, "Stay strong."

Simon hoisted the six-foot beam onto one shoulder. Then standing, he turned and waited for Jesus before taking a step, despite the whips of another guard ordering him to move.

Jesus struggled to find his footing, collapsing back to the earth. He knelt for a moment, chest heaving as he fought to catch his breath. A guard seized a handful of his hair and violently yanked him back to his feet. "Move, you! You have an appointment with destiny." Jesus looked like he was on the verge of collapse, but somehow, he managed to stand and continue up the steep path. He never spoke a word.

I felt the leash tighten around my neck. "You too, slave," the guard shouted. "Move!"

The man in me—the cage fighter, the Marine, the killer—was dying to break the chains and attack. To destroy the evil men around me and rescue Jesus from his enemies. But deep inside, in the heart of my soul and the pit of my stomach, I knew that to fight back now would be to violate everything that he stood for. He was the real man here, a strong, powerful fighter, and yet with more love and patience and deep conviction than I had ever seen. That love seemed more powerful than a cageful of MMA fighters, or a legion of Roman soldiers. I knew, then, in my heart, that I could follow this man anywhere.

I took a deep breath, knowing it would be one of my last, swallowed my pride, and submitted to the guard's command.

The death march continued until I heard a mix of cries and groans and raucous laughter ahead. The crowd slowed and stopped for a moment before continuing. I didn't have to wait long to understand the reason for the commotion, for as we progressed another thirty yards, I realized terror I had never known.

Simon paused and pointed overhead. "Up there," he said, his face darkened by fear. "Elohim, have mercy."

I looked up. There, dangling twelve feet above us, Claudius the Great hung suspended beneath the massive archway, his hands pierced by jagged spikes. He had been crucified, left to hang by his helpless arms until death swallowed him whole. The savage price he paid for daring to attack the Centurion, Crudelis. The cost of being a man.

He called out to Jesus as he passed under him. "My Lord," he said, through clenched teeth. "I honor you. My King!"

I wanted to scream. To fight. I wanted to climb the pillars to the center of the great arch and free my fellow warrior from his terrible spikes of death. But there was nothing at all I could do. "Claudius," I shouted. "I'm sorry, brother. I'm so sorry."

Claudius gazed down at me and shook his head. "Fear not, my brother. Just follow him. Follow, and we will meet again!"

I had no time to grieve over the old gladiator. My guard yanked the leash, choking me, forcing me to follow the slow march up that terrible hill. I trudged along with the angry mob, grieving for Claudius, fearing for my own life, and frightened for the man I knew as the Teacher. I had seen the post atop Golgotha. I knew the horrors that lay ahead for him.

"Crucify him," the crowd chanted. "Crucify him."

A premature dusk settled over Golgotha as we reached the summit. The air grew cool and thin. Then came the laughter—mocking, cold, and unmistakably satanic—drowning out the cries of the mob. A bat darted past my face, a jagged blur in the darkness. I squeezed my eyes shut. "Oh, God, no," I whispered. "Not again."

The same wooden post I had seen earlier stood empty in the center of the hill, only a few yards from the cliff's edge, and with the same bloodstained spike sticking out of its base. This time, however, on either side stood another cross shaped like a giant wooden T, each occupying a condemned man hanging by his hands and feet. One, I noticed, had been tied to his cross with rope, the other had been nailed. Both men appeared to be in great agony. Both were clearly dying.

"Have you come to torture us?" one of the victims cried, pushing up on his feet to breathe. "Kill us now or leave us in peace. Please, have mercy."

"Shut your mouth," Crudelis demanded, "or I'll break your skinny legs."

Painful grunts drew my attention, and I turned to watch Simon crest the hill, the massive timber crushing down on his back. With a guttural groan, he dropped the beam and immediately lunged back to assist Jesus. A guard intercepted him, swinging a club straight into the side of his head. The impact was sickening—enough to fracture a man's skull.

"Unless you want to be nailed to your own cross," the guard bellowed, "back off and let him be!"

But my resilient African friend dragged himself up on trembling legs. Ignoring the guards' jeers, he took Jesus by the arm and assisted him forward another step. A soldier kicked him squarely in the ribs, sending him sprawling into the dirt. Yet again, Simon found his footing, stood tall, and refused to back down.

"Leave him be," Crudelis spat. "Someone needs to help this skinny Jew."

Jesus reached the top of the hill and fell to his knees, gasping for air. I could tell by his demeanor, his skin color, and the utter weariness on his face that he was done. Traumatic shock had taken its full effect, and he was bound to die.

But the executioners wasted no time in furthering his punishment. They threw him onto the beam and stretched his arms out wide. One soldier knelt on each of his forearms, while two more pinned his legs to the ground. A fifth took an iron spike and placed its tip at the precise spot in the wrist to support his weight and render maximum pain. Then he raised his hammer into the air and brought it down with a loud *clang!*

Jesus screamed. Many people cried. Many in the mob cheered.

The hammer fell again: *Clang! Clang! Clang!*

"I thought you were God," one of the Sanhedrin shouted. "Why don't you free yourself?"

"Shut up," Crudelis spat. "Or you, sir, will be next!"

The councilman turned and slinked away, his wicked face etched with fear.

The executioners moved to the other arm and repeated the process, impaling his other hand to the beam. Then a team of soldiers, using ladders, lifted the beam off the ground with Jesus hanging from it, his legs flailing, his chest heaving. Once above the post, they dropped it onto a notch, locking the timber to the post to create a T-shaped cross. Jesus groaned, and for a moment I thought he had passed out. They waited, joking and mocking, until he was fully alert again before proceeding. Then they bent his legs to a 90-degree angle and nailed his feet to the post, one foot atop the other. Two horrid spikes. Blood-curdling screams echoed across the plateau.

The Teacher, Jesus, was affixed to his cross. Crucified.

I have witnessed a lot of serious pain in my career, but at that moment, as I gazed at his tortured body, I developed a deeper understanding of the word, excruciating. His was the kind of pain that squeezes tears from your eyes and animal groans from deep within your chest. The kind that makes you wish for death, or at least a numbing agent to soothe the excruciation.

They offered him a sponge soaked in myrrh, a known anesthetic, but he refused it.

He struggled to stand on his nail-pierced feet, only to collapse again to hang by his hands for rest. Spasms gripped his chest. I imagined searing pain shooting up his spine into his brain, and yet, he still found the courage to look down on his executioners and cry, "Father, forgive them, for they know not what they do."

I couldn't watch, but I had to watch. I had to see it. I had to witness it to fully understand. They say he did this for all of us. For me.

As I stared at his face—pale, battered and bruised, one eye swollen shut, the cartilage in his nose deformed and bent—I couldn't help but wonder what was keeping him alive. Blood covered his entire body. Almost every square inch of naked skin was torn and raw, seeping blood and plasma. And yet, as he hung there looking down at the mob, his legs and arms quivering, his chest heaving, he noticed some loved ones and offered them words of encouragement. How, I wondered, did he make it this far?

"What kind of man is this?" I murmured. "How is he still alive?"

"I do not know," my guard murmured. "I have witnessed many crucifixions, but never one so vicious as this."

"He must be special," I responded. "Some say he is the son of God." I turned to the guard and studied his empty eyes, hoping to see a spark of life. What I saw made me pause. "What do you believe?"

"I do not believe anything," he said, his eyes cold and uncaring. "There is life, then we die, and then there is death."

I thought about his response. I thought about Simon's trust in Elohim. I thought of Claudius the Great, who believed in the Teacher even as he hung in the air. And about Jim and Rico and Gloria, and even Ramona Read. She believed. So many who do believe, and yet, so many others, like the wicked Crudelis, who do not.

Who's right? What is the truth? How can we know for sure?

My guard stood stiff and tall with a calloused expression on his face. I saw myself in him. I felt sorry for him. Deeply compassionate. I had never seen a man more lost and emotionless. Or had I? I couldn't shake the memory of the darkness that overtook Corbin Myers just before he pulled the trigger, determined to end my life. It seemed so long ago now, in another life, or perhaps, even, in another realm.

"Father," I whispered. "Forgive Corbin Myers. He did not know what *he* was doing."

We were standing in a crowd about fifteen feet from where Jesus was hanging, close enough to hear his whispers and his conversations with the other victims. I felt amazed at how low they were to the ground, not high and lifted up, as I had seen in portraits of Christ's crucifixion, but so low that a tall man could almost look them in the eyes.

By this point, the hilltop was crowded with curious onlookers who had climbed the hill to watch the condemned men die. Some of the people laughed and mocked, some cried. A woman knelt at the foot of Jesus' cross and wept. I spotted the disciple John standing to the side with two women. Peter and the other Disciples, I noticed, were nowhere to be seen. Simon limped over and stood by my side. "This is madness," he said, shaking his head. "So sad."

I opened my mouth to respond, but the words died in my throat. I stood with Simon, chained to my guard, watching and waiting as three agonizing hours bled away. The minutes trickled past like grains of sand through an hourglass, each one heavier than the last. Witnessing the slow unraveling of the condemned men was soul-crushing. Above us, they groaned and shifted against the wood, fighting for every ragged breath and desperate for even a moment's reprieve from their agony.

At noon, the sky suddenly died. It wasn't the predictable shadow of a total solar eclipse, where the moon blocks the sun and leaves a deep, reddish horizon framed by twinkling stars. This was an unnatural, suffocating black—a sky turned dark as pitch. The moment the light vanished, pandemonium tore through the crowd. I watched and waited with my guard. The darkness continued to deepen until becoming so complete and oppressive that I could feel its weight on my shoulders. So black I could not see my hand. I could hear the criminals crying for help, shifting restlessly on their crosses. Jesus remained silent.

The darkness continued for three more hours, looming like a shroud cast over the entire hill. It wasn't just a lack of light, it felt physical, a crushing pressure that threatened to squeeze the very breath from my lungs. And endless. It seemed it would last forever.

Finally, the sky brightened, the sun began to burn, and I had to shield my eyes from the intensity. I looked up at Jesus and saw him struggling to breathe. He appeared to be close to death. I prayed he would look at me. Just look down and make eye contact with me one time. I wanted to tell him I was sorry, that I had nothing to do with this. But in my soul, I knew the truth. He was doing this for me. He was doing this because of me.

I heard him speak to one of the women, calling her mother. Then he looked at his close friend, John, the disciple, and asked him to look after her. He looked out over the crowd. Some jeered, some cried, and some cursed and spat on his wounds. I noticed flies buzzing around his head. A dog licked the blood from his feet. One of the criminals crucified by his side cursed him. The other begged for forgiveness. Finally, he did what I had hoped and looked down at me. Our eyes met. It was only for a second, but it seemed like an eternity. I felt as if he was gazing into my soul, filling me with hope as he died. His love burned into my heart in a way I will never forget.

Jesus had hung on the cross for nearly six hours when I saw him draw one final, deep breath and whisper, "It is finished." Then, his body went entirely limp. The remaining air escaped his lungs like a slow hiss from a punctured bellows, leaving behind an awful, sudden silence.

Those around me whispered and murmured in confusion. Even the Sanhedrin seemed bewildered. "We must get the corpses down soon," one of them exclaimed. "We must not violate the Sabbath. Kill them!"

After some coarse talk and shouting, one of the Roman soldiers laughed out loud, and said, "All right, all right. Hold your horses, little man." He picked up a wooden club and swiftly broke the legs of the two criminals. The poor men cried and groaned as they fell with their full weight on their outstretched arms. "There," he said, turning to the elders. "Will that do?"

"No," the Sanhedrin elder said, pointing a bent finger at Jesus. "Him, too."

"I think he's already gone. What's the use?"

"Let's make sure he's really dead," another soldier spat, approaching the center cross with a spear. With a swift thrust, he drove the lance into Jesus' side and backed away as water and blood gushed from the wound. "Oh, he's dead," the guard cried, laughing. "I think you can take him down now!"

I saw tears well up in Simon's eyes. Without a word, he stepped forward to the foot of the cross and sank to his knees. "The Lamb of God," he whispered. "Slain for the sins of many."

To my amazement, the shackles suddenly snapped and fell from my wrists. The earth beneath my feet buckled and quaked. Shouting in terror, my guard fled into the gloom, leaving me entirely exposed to a raging cyclone that whipped across the hilltop. Leathery black bats swarmed the air, encircling my head in a frantic blur as a chorus of satanic laughter echoed from the dark. My mind reeled with sheer, maddening confusion. People around me scattered and fell. I panicked, and like others around me, almost ran away. But I decided that, if I was going to die, I would die like a man. I would die by his side.

When the wind died down, an unearthly silence fell over the land, as if all of nature had stopped in reverence to watch. Perfect silence. No wind, no birds chirping, no roosters crowing. Just quiet. His body hung motionless, limp in death.

Finally, a familiar voice rang out. The deep, throaty voice of the mighty Crudelis. He had not run away, like so many others. He stayed until the end. But he was not the proud, cursing man I had encountered before. He looked humble and defeated.

I watched the old warrior drop to his knees beside Simon, tears flowing down his hardened Roman cheeks. He hung his head and cried. "Truly," he said, his words broken by spasmodic sobs. "This was the Son of God."

CHAPTER TWENTY-SEVEN

The Garden Tomb of Joseph of Arimathea
Outside the City of Jerusalem, Israel, the Year 33 A.D.
Passover Friday—5:42 PM Local Time

It's a brutal, awkward task to lower a corpse from a ten-foot cross, especially when heavy iron spikes have anchored the flesh to the wood. The two spikes driven through the Teacher's feet proved to be devastatingly tenacious, requiring a heavy iron tool to bend and pry them from the wood. When a frustrated guard barked an order to just smash the bones and yank his legs free, my stomach turned. But before the soldier could move, Crudelis stepped forward, his deep voice cutting through the tension.

"Back off!" the Centurion growled, glaring at his own men. "We will do it their way. Get back!"

The soldiers slunk away into the shadows. Crudelis turned, his bruised face hardening into tight, grim respect as he nodded to a wealthy Jewish elder waiting anxiously to one side.

"You may proceed, sir."

With quiet urgency, a member of the Sanhedrin named Joseph of Arimathea stepped up with a small group of disciples to remove the spikes. After many minutes of agonizing work the last spike came free. Then he nodded at me, as if to ask for my help. I motioned for Simon and joined in. Using ladders and linen sheets to support his weight, we carefully lowered the Teacher's limp, cold frame from the beam and laid it on a long linen cloth at the base of the cross. His shroud—the incredible piece of cloth that would one day become the Shroud of Turin.

I had never felt more ashamed—at the utter depths that people are willing to go to make others suffer. But, at the same time, I felt honored to be playing a part in such a crucial historical event. I mean, think about it—they were asking me to help lower Jesus' body from the cross and onto his shroud.

How did I get here? Lord, why me?

Joseph used a clean rag to wipe the heavy deposits of blood from the front of the body and then folded the cloth over it. As a team, we lifted the shrouded man and began the heavy march down Golgotha to a waiting tomb.

I had been told the tomb was the resting place intended for the man in charge—Joseph of Arimathea, a man of high standing in the Sanhedrin who had traded his silence for this one final act of devotion. At first I was confused to learn that he was Sanhedrin, but I could tell by the love and concern on his face that he, too, was a true believer. A genuine follower of Christ.

There was a heavy, sacred silence as we reached the tomb and carried the body inside. It smelled of fresh-cut stone and the sharp, floral scent of expensive spices meant to serve as burial ointments. Joseph removed the cloth and positioned the body supine, legs straight with one foot atop the other, and arms folded reverently across the lower body. He was about to lay a white linen napkin over the face, when a Roman guard shoved him aside and pressed two bronze coins over the Teacher's eyes with a cruel sneer. "A toll for the ferryman," the guard mocked. "Let's see if your king can cross the Styx."

"No!" Joseph exclaimed. "That is blasphemy!"

"What I have done, I have done," the guard shouted. "Leave it!"

The moment the soldiers stepped back out of the tomb, Joseph defiantly plucked the pagan bronze pieces from the Teacher's eyes and cast them onto the stone bench in disgust. He then covered the face with the napkin. After hurriedly packing a few pounds of expensive burial ointment beside the body, he folded the burial cloth over him, and saw everyone out of the tomb. The guards rolled an 8-foot stone in place to seal the entrance. Two Roman guards were ordered to stand watch.

"Passover is upon us," Joseph said. "We must leave now. We will return on Yom Rishon, the first day of the week. It is then that we will complete the burial process."

"The two coins," I said, walking beside the Jewish elder. "He did that out of mockery, right?"

"Yes. Mythology suggests it was needed to pay a toll to Charon, the ferryman of the underworld, to ensure safe passage of the soul across the River Styx."

"The river Styx? Isn't that in hell?"

Joseph nodded. "It is only a myth. He meant total disrespect."

"Man, I'm sorry. And the napkin you placed over his face? A true show of respect?"

"Yes. It is a symbol of purity, and a way of demonstrating honor."

Simon and I followed John and the others to a hidden room deep in the city. Joseph went with us, doing his best to avoid any religious leaders or guards from the palace. It was unheard of for the Sanhedrin to associate with followers of Christ, and he had already risked so much by asking Pilate for permission to bury the body. I, too, felt somewhat frightened, but I felt honored to be in their presence—John, Phillip, the other Disciples, and so many other of Jesus' followers. I felt so unworthy, and yet so blessed. I also felt as if I was receiving a crash course in the New Testament, living out the events of the four Gospels as they happened, in real time. God had chosen me to experience this for some reason. But why me? I couldn't help but wonder.

Why in the world, me?

Simon and I hid with the Disciples throughout Passover. They offered us sanctuary, meals, and fellowship for the next two nights, telling us many stories about Jesus and all he had taught them. Ten Disciples were there. Many of his other followers were there, as well, but Judas Iscariot was dead. Someone had found him hanging from a tree limb by a piece of rope. And Peter? The bold, brash Peter who had drawn his sword in the garden? He was nowhere to be seen.

"Where's Peter?" someone asked.

"He ran away," John explained. "We were with him—" John paused and glanced at me. "Michael, Simon, and I, in the courtyard when he denied the Teacher three times."

"Then a rooster crowed," I added. "Just as predicted."

"Pray for him," John said. "Everyone, pray for our brother, Peter."

"John," someone said. "We will pray for Peter, of course. But explain to us, please. What has happened to our Lord? Why did he have to die?"

"He had to die," John explained. "To become our living sacrifice. The blood he shed on the cross now covers our sins, so that we, too, might be found perfect in the eyes of our heavenly father."

"Just like the Passover lambs," I murmured. "He was sacrificed to pay for our sin."

John glanced at me and nodded. "No lambs need ever again be slaughtered on our behalf. His blood is our atonement. You see, our heavenly father loves us so much that he gave his only son to die in our place, so that we would never have to."

"So we could have eternal life," I said.

"Yes. So that whosoever believes in him might never perish."

John raised his hands to Heaven and offered a corporate prayer for Peter, for direction, for protection from our enemies—the Roman soldiers and the Sanhedrin—and for the new church they would soon form. There was much weeping, and a lot of discussion, and I heard them make the decision to one day begin a church and call it, "The Way." They would preach, John said, they would pray for others, and they would lay hands on the sick and heal them. "But first," John said, "we must wait for our helper to come."

"Our helper?" someone asked.

"He said he would send us a helper. The Holy Spirit. Until then, we wait."

"What then, John? What will we do after the helper comes to us?"

"We will go out and tell the world."

The next two nights were a blur. I had grown so close to that small group of believers that I forgot all about trying to get home. I had long conversations with John, who, it turns out, was Jesus' closest friend. He seemed to understand everything—who Jesus was, and why he had come. He explained to me the history of the Hebrew people, and the nature of God.

"John," I said, pulling him aside as others rested. "I'm still struggling with something you said. I mean, if he was the Son of God, why did he have to suffer so much? He could've come down from that cross at any time, right? Couldn't he have found a better way?"

"His violent death is an illustration for us as to the intense cost of our sin. His, could not have been an easy death. Sin requires the ultimate price. And he paid it for us."

"What about this spirit thing? I can't wrap my head around that. Who exactly is the Holy Spirit?"

"Michael, it is crucial that you understand this point: God has always existed in three persons, from the beginning of time. The Father, the Son, and the Holy Spirit are one."

"How can that be?"

"It is. Jesus was with God in the beginning. All things were created by him. And the scriptures tell us that before creation began, the Spirit of God hovered over the waters. You see?"

"Kind of."

"God created man in his image on the sixth day of creation. And he loved us. But God is holy, and when sin entered the world, it became necessary for him to turn his back on us. But in his divine plan, he came to earth in the form of a man."

"Jesus."

"Yes. To live a perfect life, which made him the ideal—"

"Sacrifice."

"Correct."

"Hmm."

"He became the sacrifice for our sins. I mean, you saw the slaughter, Michael. Thousands upon thousands of lambs, sacrificed at the temple, for the forgiveness of sin."

"Yeah, it was a blood bath."

"Right, and so was the cross. You saw how he died. It was horrible."

"It was excruciating."

"Michael, that is what this is all about. The cross was necessary. Death is the price of sin. Eternal separation from our heavenly father. But Jesus became the ultimate sacrifice for us to bring us back into God's presence, as he first designed it."

"Sin is heavy."

"It is deadly."

"So, no more lambs?"

"Animal sacrifice is no longer necessary. He paid the price, once and for all. And he will come back for his people, Michael. That he promised. To take us to where he is going. But remember what I told the others? He promised to send us a helper in the meantime."

"The Holy Spirit."

"Yes. Our helper will be the third member of the Trinity. That same spirit that hovered over the waters of creation will give us power to do his work until he returns."

John shared many other truths with us as we hid in that cold upper room. He preached morning and night, and led us in prayer. We could hear the muffled roar echoing through the city streets, a rising tide of unrest that felt like it was closing in on us. Most stayed pinned in the shadows, terrified that the world outside was finally coming for us, too. But I felt a strange peace. Something powerful had washed over me like a flood. Something calming that anchored my spirit. And for the first time in my life, I felt, somehow, as if I had been freed. I guess you could say, I was saved.

Early Sunday morning, before the first hues of dawn brightened the horizon, a frantic pounding sound echoed through the upper room, awakening everyone. We scrambled from our corners, the sound cutting through our shallow sleep like a blade. No one spoke, we didn't have to. Every eye went to the door, and every hand reached for a heavy piece of furniture or a hidden blade, convinced the Temple guards had finally found our sanctuary.

I balled up my fists and waited as James boldly moved to the door and drew the bolt. The heavy door groaned against its hinges as he slowly pulled it open.

I was ready to attack whoever or whatever entered, but instead of a rush of guards, Peter stumbled across the threshold. The room gasped as he fell into the light.

"Peter!" James exclaimed, catching him. "Are you hurt?"

I ran to the door and bolted it.

Peter was a sight, his sweaty skin a sickly, pale grey in the flickering torchlight. He looked to be utterly spent—eyes wide with a raw, primal fear that suggested he was still running from something we couldn't see.

The others closed in on him, a tight circle of desperate faces, everyone leaning in to catch even the faintest word. The air in the room grew heavy and hot as we crowded around, our own fears momentarily forgotten in the hunger for news.

After catching his breath and drinking a cup of water, Peter exclaimed, "Friends! Do not leave this place! Not for anything. The soldiers are questioning anyone they find on the street. They're going door to door. They're arresting anyone who followed the Teacher. Even the Centurion, Crudelis, has been arrested."

"Crudelis?" I exclaimed. "They arrested Crudelis?"

"He is before Pilate now. They found him hiding in the barn of Claudius, the animal tender. I hear he may be executed."

"Executed? Why?"

"They are arresting anyone who bowed to him on Golgotha or called him Lord. They chased me across town, you know. I was almost caught."

"Where have you been?" someone asked. "Why did you leave us, Peter?"

"I've been hiding. I was ashamed. I did not know what to do, so I ran. John was with me, he saw what I did."

"Peter—"

"No John! I was wrong. I denied the Teacher in front of all those people, just as he predicted. I turned my back on him. I was so ashamed, I almost fell on my own sword. I wasn't there when he died either. My Lord," Peter cried. "Forgive me. I failed you!"

"It's not safe for us," someone said.

"What do we do?" another exclaimed.

"We wait, brothers and sisters," John said. "We calm down, we trust the Lord, and we wait. Our God is with us. He would not want us to panic. Do not forget that."

"I'm sorry," Peter said. "I'm so sorry."

Peter's brothers gathered around him: James, John, the ones called Matthew, Nathaniel and Phillip. They laid their hands on him and prayed. Peter cried like a baby. I felt so sorry for him that I almost cried. I stood back with Simon and watched, amazed by the brotherhood of these men, this small band of men who had given up their lives to follow their master. When they had finished praying, John said, "Come, let us break bread together. He would not want us to worry."

Just then we heard another knock on the door, much lighter than the last. Someone unbolted it and two women entered, panting, struggling to catch their breath. I recognized them as two of the women at the cross.

"He is gone!" one of them cried. "They have taken him away!"

"Slow down," Peter said. "Who?"

The older woman, the one I recognized as Mary, the mother of Jesus, replied, "The tomb is empty."

Peter pushed past us, lunging out the door into the thick darkness.

"No, Peter," John shouted. "It is not safe!"

John glanced at his friends and then ran out after him, followed closely by the women and the rest of the Disciples. Simon nudged me. "Brother," he said. "I no longer care for my own life. I need to see this!"

"Me too," I said. "Let's go."

The sky was just beginning to brighten into the pale grey of dawn when we reached the tomb. We had to play a dangerous game of shadows to get there, ducking behind stone walls to avoid patrols of Roman soldiers and the watchful eyes of the temple guards. The stone used to seal the entrance had been rolled aside. I knew the tomb would be empty; I knew the resurrection was a fact of history. Yet, seeing the dark, vacant mouth of the cave with my own eyes was a different kind of truth. Real. Undeniable.

"He has risen," I whispered. "Just as he said."

The Disciples stood beside the cave entrance peering in. Simon and I joined them. "What's happening?" Simon said. "Where are Peter and John?"

"Inside the tomb," one of the Disciples responded. "They told us to wait out here."

The men spoke quietly amongst themselves. I saw fear in their eyes. Deep concern on their faces. "Where could he be?" one of them whispered. "Who took him?" asked another. After a moment John walked out of the tomb holding a folded cloth the size of a table napkin. "I found this on the bench. It is the cloth that covered his face."

"Glory!" one of the women shouted. "He is coming back! See how it is folded?"

"What do you mean by that?" I said. "The fact that it is folded?"

"When a folded napkin is placed on a tabletop during a meal," John explained, "it means to the server that the diner who sat there will soon return. He had not yet finished his meal."

"That is true," Peter said, stepping out of the tomb behind John. "It was his way of saying, I will return. I also found this. It is the same cloth we used to wrap his body."

The Shroud.

I could feel my heart racing as Peter showed us the wadded-up piece of linen he had found inside the tomb, the same piece of cloth I saw in the Turin Cathedral 2,000 years ago. I mean, 2,000 years from now. I mean …

"Oh, mercy. Look, you there. What's your name? Phillip?"

The young man standing beside Peter—another of the Disciples, strong and lean and eager to serve—raised his hand. "Me?"

"Yes. Help Peter unfold the cloth."

"Why?" Peter said.

"Just pull it apart," I said, seizing one end and thrusting it toward Phillip. "Stretch it out! I think he left something on it for us."

Peter's brow furrowed.

"Just do it! Please."

Peter shot a skeptical glance at the younger Phillip. The two men slowly grabbed the cloth by the corners and backed away from one another, stretching the fabric between them. I watched, my chest tight with excitement, as they pulled it taut to reveal a fourteen-foot length of fresh linen. A distinct pattern of blood stains mapped the cloth—but there was no image.

"Oh—" My chin dropped. "Man, I was so sure."

Peter shook his head. "What were you expecting to see?"

"Wait a minute," I said. "It's on the other side. Flip it over!"

"Huh?" Peter grunted. "Michael, what are you—"

"Flip it over! Turn it around!"

Peter and Phillip shrugged at each other and then slowly flipped over the cloth. As they pulled it tight, my knees almost buckled. What I saw took my breath away. The cloth bore the sepia-colored image of a man scourged and crucified, a photographic negative as precise as any ever made by a Nikon camera.

"The Shroud!" I gasped.

The cloth was clean of water stains, crease marks, and scorched areas. It was brand new, not yet affected by the two-thousand years that had passed by the time I first saw it. But I could easily discern the victim's entire body—front and back—scourge wounds—distinct blood stains at the wrists and feet, his posture frozen in time, in the position I had watched the Disciples lay him in the tomb. I felt overwhelmed by the staggering weight of the details—but it was his countenance that truly drew me in. I stared at the long, drawn features of his face. An image of pure suffering—a man beaten, torn, bloodied, and swollen, who had just borne the devastating weight of the entire world on his shoulders.

"Rico," I whispered. "You were right. I understand now."

"Understand what?" Peter said. "Michael, what do you see?"

I hesitated a moment and then waved him over. Two other Disciples took a turn holding up the cloth while Peter, John, and Phillip stepped away about fifteen feet to join me. All three gasped in unison as they turned.

"Look!" Peter exclaimed.

"My Lord," Phillip whispered, his youthful face radiant with awe. "It's Him!"

"Will you look at that?" John said. "You can see his face. His hands. His feet. It's the Teacher!"

"Yes!" I exclaimed. "It's him. I know for sure now. Jesus is the man in the Shroud."

"But how did he leave that image?" Peter asked. "And what does this mean?"

"It doesn't matter," John declared. "All that matters is he did it. He lived, he died, and he rose again, just as he said he would.

And he left us an image of his passion to remind us just how much he suffered."

"Yes," I said, with a nod. "For us. For all of us."

I finally understood the purpose of the Passover lamb in Hebrew tradition. Each man's lamb was slain to serve as a payment for his sin. But by the shedding of his blood, Jesus became the Passover lamb for all of us. A living sacrifice to pay for our sins, once, and for all.

And for the first time since having heard of the Shroud of Turin, having studied it, seen it, worried over it, pondered its authenticity, and finally touching it with my own hands, I understood that it was only a cloth, not to be idolized or worshipped. It's his burial cloth, for sure, but the Shroud doesn't bring us closer to God. Only Jesus does that.

"Come," Peter said, directing the other Disciples in the proper folding of the cloth. "Don't let it touch the ground. Fold it so that only his face will show."

"That's right," I said, leaping with excitement. "If we put it in a frame, like a portrait, no one will suspect it to be anything other than a painting. We will hide it in plain sight."

John looked at me and nodded. "Great idea."

"Everyone," Phillip whispered, glancing around to make sure we were not being watched. "We should tell no one of this. He left us this cloth for a reason. We should protect it at all costs. For all time."

John nodded. "I agree with Phillip. No one else should know."

"What will we do with it?" Peter asked.

No one had an answer.

The Disciples worked together to fold the cloth, as instructed, into a 20 x 24-inch rectangle where only the face showed. John carefully shoved it into a leather sack he carried over his shoulder. And then, with the two women who were there, the small band of Disciples circled up and began to pray. Simon and I held back, feeling somewhat like outsiders, until Peter asked us to join them.

I felt a strange connection to these people, these original Christians. A new fraternity. A family. We took turns praying, thanking God for what we had just witnessed, for what his son had just accomplished for us, and for the future, which lay ahead. I prayed aloud for the first time in my life, in front of other men and women I hardly even knew. But it felt natural. It felt right. I felt no sense of shame.

As the one they called James was praying, a band of soldiers appeared, armor clanking, swords rattling. "Who is in charge here?" one of them shouted.

Peter stepped forward with a confidence that seemed to physically push the soldiers back. "I am in charge," he barked. "What do you want?"

"I know you! You are one of his followers!"

"Yes," Peter exclaimed, stepping even closer to the men. "I am!"

The soldier appeared confused by Peter's sudden show of confidence. "I saw you in the garden last night, didn't I? And by the fireside in the courtyard?"

"You did," Peter replied. "And you saw me run away scared, too. But you will not see me run again. Do what you came for."

"What have you done with the body?" another soldier asked. "Who rolled back the stone?"

"We have done nothing with the body," Peter assured him. "This is how we found the tomb. Open and empty."

"He is risen," I said, moving forward to stand beside Peter. "The Son of God, Jesus Christ, has risen."

I watched in disbelief as the soldiers retreated, turning and walking away in absolute confusion. For a long moment, the crowd stood frozen. Then, Peter drew a deep breath and began to preach. While the others gathered on the dirt at his feet, I found a secluded spot to sit down. My mind was reeling. I desperately needed to be alone.

More people arrived, taking turns to peer into the empty tomb, and then sitting down to listen to Peter's sermon. I noticed

Dr. Loukas standing to one side with his son, Luke. I was about to go speak with them, but before I could, a large man dressed in armor walked up and gazed down at me. He wore a sword, and looked, as always, ready for battle.

"Crudelis?"

I slowly stood to face the Centurion. My first thought was to brace myself for a blow, but when I detected the sadness in his eyes, I realized he was not there for trouble, or to arrest me. I sensed genuine humility, and a spirit of gentleness and conviction.

Crudelis hung his head, and sighed. "I do not know what to say."

I tilted my head, curiously. "I heard you were arrested."

"I was," Crudelis said, his deep voice softer than I had remembered. "But by Pilate's order, I have been set free. Thank the living God I did not end up like Claudius."

I pictured the proud ex-gladiator hanging by pierced hands from the stone archway. "Claudius was a man."

"Claudius was a true warrior. He is gone now, but I believe his spirit lives on." Before I could respond, Crudelis extended his hand, and said, "I was wrong. To you, and to so many others. Please, sir, I beg your forgiveness."

I shook my head, then his hand, and then placed my other one on his shoulder. "We've all wronged each other in one way or another. I ask the same of you. Please forgive me."

"I believe we just witnessed something that will change the world."

"I believe that, too."

We stood silently for a few moments, staring at the scene, and then, as if preparing for battle in the octagon, we squared up and gazed into each other's eyes. Pound for pound, we were equals, one warrior as fierce as the other. One man as broken as the other. I saw his eyes fill with tears. I wiped away my own.

"I hope I never have to fight you again," I said.

"Me too, my brother."

The mighty Crudelis saluted me and walked away. I never saw him again.

After Crudelis had departed, I looked for Loukas and Luke. Sadly, they were nowhere to be found. I had hoped to share my thoughts with them, to hear their stories, and to learn just what they had witnessed. I figured young Luke would be taking notes for his next paper, and perhaps, for the gospel he would one day write. Sadly, they were not to be found. I was about to walk back up to the tomb with Simon for another peek inside, when I heard Peter calling us.

"Men," he shouted, waving his hand. "Over here."

Simon followed me to a small grove of trees near the tomb. Peter smiled as we approached. His eyes looked raw and bloodshot, his cheeks still mapped with the tear-stains of an impossible night, but his face beamed with joy.

"I have something for each of you," he said, reaching inside his tunic. He removed his hand and opened it to reveal a pair of bronze coins. "One of the guards placed these over his eyes—"

"In the tomb," I exclaimed. "We were there. Joseph threw them aside after the guards left."

"Yeah, John told me. I found them on the bench. Take them," he said, handing one to each of us.

"I thought they were considered pagan."

"The coins aren't pagan—the people who killed the Teacher were." Peter closed my hand around the crudely minted coin. "Let it serve as a reminder of the evil you witnessed here this week."

I felt too stunned to speak. I opened my hand and studied the coin that had once covered the Teacher's eye. A curved shepherd's crook stood in relief in the center, bordered by a series of letters that were hard to read. I flipped it over to see what looked to represent a stalk of wheat on the other side, and then I closed my fist.

"Thank you," I whispered, my voice hard to find. "I will always treasure this."

"Don't lose it," Peter said, glancing at Simon and winking. "There's only one other like it in the whole world."

I rolled the coin over in my hand several times, looking at both sides intently, doing my best to comprehend the fact that it had been touching Jesus just a few hours before. Perhaps even minutes. I mean, does anyone know when Jesus rose from the tomb? I tucked the coin into the bandage around my arm for safekeeping and glanced at Peter.

"Where do you think he is now? Heaven?"

Peter nodded. "He told us he would go to the one who sent him."

"He is in paradise," John said. "I heard him tell the thief on the cross beside him, 'Today you will be with me in Paradise.'"

"Listen to me," Peter said, grabbing me, his eyes boring into mine. "Our Teacher, Jesus Christ, this man we've been following for the last three years, he rose from the dead. Don't you ever forget this! He is the Son of God. He lived among us. He healed people. He bled, he cried, and he died. And we buried him. But he rose again. We saw it with our own eyes. You saw it. He is alive. And he's coming back!"

Perhaps my Dilantin levels had dropped too low again, or maybe it was all a dream and I was about to wake up, but for some reason, my cloud was back.

I braced myself for the impending seizure, but this time, instead of the ugly gray cloud I had grown accustomed to, followed by the mean spasmodic jerking of a full-blown convulsion, I found myself enveloped by a clean, white mist—a cool flood of joy that calmed my being and gently lifted me off the ground. I felt no pain, confusion, or fear. Instead, I felt refreshed and renewed, filled with a calm assurance that everything was all right.

As the mist began to part, a figure emerged. His features sharpened as he approached, taking on the familiar appearance of a man—the man I had just seen crucified and buried. The risen Teacher stood before me with his arms extended. I noticed the nail wounds on his wrists. His face was bright and reassuring. I felt shocked and emotionally overwhelmed, yet filled with a sense of peace and joy more intense than I had ever known. I wanted to touch him, to see if he was real. I reached out my hand.

"No," he said. "I am not finished with you yet."

Then, just like that, he was gone.

PART 3

CHAPTER TWENTY-EIGHT

Chapel of The Holy Shroud
Cathedral of San Giovanni Battista
Turin, Italy
Sunday, April 5—2:16 PM Local Time (CEST)

I'm no scientist, mathematician, or astrophysicist, so how could I be expected to grasp the spacetime continuum? I mean, honestly, who truly does? They say it's a fabric where length, width, and height are woven inextricably with time—a single, four-dimensional tapestry that defines our reality. What is that? I don't know. I have no clue. But whatever it is, at that moment I felt as if I had just passed through it. It was a jarring, impossible displacement. I was here, then I was there, and now I'm … well, where am I, anyway? That cool, comforting mist was still with me, but the peace I had felt just moments before was being replaced by the frantic energy of people in a hurry. Two figures leaned over me, wearing orange shirts and black caps. I knew that color combination—I had just seen it recently, but, in my current state, I could not remember where. The figures looked like aliens from another dimension.

"We got him!" someone exclaimed.

Got him? Got who?

I squinted, craning my neck in a desperate attempt to bring the blurred figures into focus. A pair of faces began to emerge, hovering above me—distorted and unfamiliar.

"Si," the other one said. "There he is!"

There who is? Are they talking about me?

"Ciao," the male voice said. "Bentornato."

"Huh?" I reached out to grab him. "Jesus? Is that you?"

"No sir," the man responded, pushing away my hands. "I am not Jesus."

"Where is he?" I exclaimed. "Where did he go?"

"I do not know where Jesus went, sir. I am Enzo." It was a stranger's voice, thick with a heavy Italian accent, vibrating with a professional calm that felt strangely out of place in the middle of my disorientation. "I am your emergency paramedic. Welcome back."

"Paramedic? Wh-where's Simon? Where's the—" I reached to my side, expecting to feel a donkey's leg, a stone, wooden post, or anything ancient. Instead, I felt a cold metal pole. I grabbed hold of it and squeezed. "What is this? Where am I?"

"You are in the Shroud exam room, sir."

"Ex-am … "

"In the Chapel of San Giovanni Battista. You were examining The Holy Shroud when you collapsed."

"Collapsed? The Shroud is here?"

"Sir, wake up," he said, gently slapping my cheek. "Come back to us. We are in the Turin Cathedral."

"Turin?" I shook my head, squeezed my eyes shut, and then reopened them to a somewhat clearer scene. Enzo's sharp green eyes searched mine with a clinical, knowing intensity, as if he were gazing down at a confused drunk he'd pulled off the sidewalk. "Simon?" I slurred. "Is that you, buddy?"

Enzo chuckled. "Check his blood sugar."

"On it," a female voice responded. I felt a prick in my index finger. After a few seconds I heard a beep. "Eighty-two," she said. "It's good."

"Who, who are y'all?"

"Sir," Enzo said. "We are ALS providers. We saw you earlier, you know. You took a picture of our ambulance."

"I did?"

"Yes sir. Now, listen carefully. You have been resuscitated. My partner and I will take you to the hospital now."

"No," I said, trying to sit up. "Wait a minute. Who are you again?"

I felt Enzo's hand pushing me to the floor. "We are prehospital providers, sir. Paramedics, with Croce Rossa Italiana."

"Cro-che … "

"Please, sir. Be still."

I lay back, too exhausted to argue, half awake and half in a drug-induced coma, my mind operating at about 50%. I had an IV in my arm, dripping clear fluid from a bag suspended in the air above me. Something tickled my nose. I reached up and pulled away a thin plastic cannula blowing air into my nostrils.

"Please leave that," the paramedic said, fitting the air tubing back into my nostrils. "It's oxygen. You need it."

"Why?"

"You've experienced a cardiac arrest, but everything is okay now."

Cardiac arrest?

I watched the female paramedic attach a syringe to the IV port and slowly inject a clear liquid. "You experienced cardiac arrest, sir. I'm giving you a drug called amiodarone to keep your heart rhythm stable."

"I know amiodarone," I slurred, shifting automatically into clinical tracking as I struggled to sit up. Enzo's hand instantly clamped onto my shoulder, shoving me back down. I fought against his grip, grabbing his forearm with a surge of panicked adrenaline. "Let me up! I need to get up!"

"He's fighting us," Enzo barked, leaning his weight into me. "Give him two milligrams of midazolam to take the edge off."

"Midazolam?" I argued, my mind wildly spinning to keep up with the threat. "No—that's a benzodiazepine. Sedative. Anticonvulsant—"

"Don't forget anti-combative," Enzo added dryly.

"I don't need it! Look," I snapped, desperately trying to find my authority. "I'm a doctor!"

Enzo managed a tight, unbelieving chuckle. "Is that so? Because the ID we pulled from your wallet says you're a paramedic. Just like us."

"Paramedic? What? No, I'm a … how long was I out?"

"Fifteen minutes, maybe."

"But how can that be? I was in Jerusalem for five days."

Enzo chuckled. "Sir, I assure you, you've been here the entire time."

"Wait a minute," I said, still confused. "Who'd you say you are?"

He laughed. "Sir, my name is Enzo. I am a paramedic with Croce Rossa. This is Emma."

"Emma?"

I glanced at Emma, a cute girl with black hair, equally black eyes, and a 3 milliliter syringe in one hand. She adjusted the IV flow with her thumb and then pushed a small amount of medication into my vein. I felt my head begin to swim. It was not a bad feeling.

"Tell us where you are," she said, taking my hand and feeling my wrist.

"Um—" I glanced around the room, a little less anxious, I noticed, than I had been the moment before. "Turin?"

"That's right."

"This is the cathedral for, um, for the um … the Shroud of Turin, right?"

"Yes, and what is your name?"

"Mike Peabody."

"Who are you, Mike? What do you do?"

"ED doc."

Emma glanced at Dr. Gallo. "He is a paramedic, right?"

Gallo nodded. "I think he's just confused."

"But I *am* a doctor," I argued, slurring my words. "Board certified."

Enzo chuckled. "What year is it?"

I chuckled. "Not thirty-three AD, that's for sure."

Emma laughed. "I think he's okay now."

"Where's Dr. Gallo?" I said, craning my neck to look for my friends. "And Will?"

"Right here," Will Hendricks said, peering from behind the Shroud table, his classic California smile slightly blurred. "You gave us quite a scare, man."

"And here," another voice exclaimed. I glanced to my right and saw a bespectacled, bulbous man in a white lab coat come into focus. His face and ears appeared to glow with excitement. "Where have you been, young man?"

"Dr. Gallo? Oh," I said, closing my eyes and flirting with the desire to doze. "Would you believe, Jerusalem?"

The entire room laughed.

"I saw Jesus … Peter … the cross … I was there when they found the Shroud."

The people around me laughed again, only more quietly. Then Enzo began barking orders, and I felt myself lifted by the group onto a yellow stretcher. They buckled me in, hung the IV on a pole, grabbed the cardiac monitor and oxygen cylinder, and then, with the help of the guards, rolled me from the room. The last thing I saw before passing through the doorway to exit the cathedral was my two friends standing there waving at me—Will Hendricks and Dr. Gallo. Oh, and a fourteen-foot piece of linen stretched out behind a bulletproof glass—The Shroud of Turin. A holy piece of cloth that God had used to change my life.

CHAPTER TWENTY-NINE

Room Number 13
Humanitas Gradenigo Hospital
Turin, Italy
Sunday, April 5—10:16 PM Local Time (CEST)

I can't remember anything after they rolled me out of the cathedral on that stretcher. Whatever drug Emma had given me must've worked, because the next thing I knew, I was lying in a crisp hospital bed with a cardiac monitor beeping behind me. I glanced down at my chest and saw a single wire leading up to the monitor, instead of the standard three or four. Something Italian, I figured.

Interesting.

An IV dripped a saline solution into my right arm, and, embarrassingly, a clear plastic tube extended from beneath the blanket to a bag on the bed rail. It contained yellow fluid. I glanced at my wrist and realized my watch was missing. My beloved Casio. A fresh bandage encircled my bicep, and I wore a light blue hospital gown—the kind that ties in the back.

Seriously?

I glanced around the room, somewhat confused by the curtained cage that surrounded me on three sides. I saw nothing much of interest—a stainless-steel cabinet, an air and oxygen port on the wall, and the other typical diagnostic monitors found in most EDs. I heard someone coughing in the distance and people talking nearby. The pitch of their voices changed as they walked past my chamber.

"Hello?" I called out. "Is somebody there?"

A second later, the curtain slid back and a middle-aged man with black hair and wire-rimmed glasses entered the room. Tall and thin, wearing a white lab jacket with pens in the pockets—typical—he reminded me of my hawkish doctor back home, but with a row of clean white teeth and a sparkle in his eyes that radiated genuine kindness. His black sneakers looked too young for his age, his casual limp too old. He could've been a physician in any emergency department anywhere, making his rounds and moving quickly from patient to patient, except I saw no stethoscope or reflex hammer. No hurry in his step. He also looked oddly familiar, as if we had just spoken yesterday. I felt an instant connection to him. How could that possibly be?

"Ah, Michael," he said, his voice European. "Welcome back, old friend."

Old friend?

I tilted my head, my eyes narrowing as I tried to place the accent and the sudden warmth in his greeting.

"Michael," the man responded, with a chuckle. "It's me, Greco."

"Greco?"

"Ah, of course." The doctor nodded, understandingly. "You just woke up. Allow me to introduce myself then, sir. I am Greco. Attending Physician, Emergency Department, Humanitas Gradenigo Hospital."

He extended his hand and I shook it. I smelled Listerine on his breath.

"Mike Peabody," I responded. "Attending Physician, Emergency Department, East Beach Regional Hospital."

Greco laughed out loud. I had no idea why.

"So, Dr. Greco?"

"Just Greco," he said. "You know that."

He chuckled, as if hiding a secret, and then sat down and glanced at a piece of rectangular plate glass in his lap. About one-half inch thick, with a greenish tone, it looked like a window pane with smoothly routed edges. He placed his fingers over the bottom third of the glass and began to tap against the surface, as if upon an invisible keyboard. A row of green letters appeared as he typed.

My stomach let out a low, insistent growl that made us both pause. Greco glanced at my belly. "Sorry," I said. "I can't remember the last time I ate."

"Well, let's fix that. A-bot?" he said, turning his head and murmuring briefly. He waited a moment, and then nodded, and said, "Grazie." Then he turned his attention back to me and said, "Dinner will be delivered shortly. They served sausage and pepperoni pizza tonight. I hope that will be all right."

"What did you just do?"

"Ordered your dinner."

Greco noticed my confusion, and said, "I used A-bot. I'll explain that later."

"A-bot? And that thing you're tapping on?" I said. "It looks like a window pane."

"This?" He held up a sheet of glass roughly the size of a standard clipboard. "It's called a Screen."

"Screen? Can I see it?"

"Of course."

Greco handed me the Screen. I felt intrigued. It looked like it was forged from clear glass, yet it felt as light as a feather. Some kind of plastic or plexiglass? The surface displayed sharp green text, in what looked to be Times New Roman, above the image of a standard computer keyboard, with a few symbols I did not recognize. In the upper corner, a high-resolution color photo of my own face stared back at me. I flipped it over and realized the data was suspended inside the screen—the text and image were perfectly legible from both sides, hovering in the transparency.

"Man," I said. "This is cool. What is it, like a souped-up iPad, or something?"

He chuckled. "Or something. This is about ten generations past the old iPad. I haven't used one of those since college."

"For real?"

"This one seamlessly connects to the holder's A-bot chip for integrated communication with others via satellite, or device-to-device. It even utilizes the new AI-dB technology, which makes my job ten times easier."

I just stared at him.

Greco chuckled again. "I can access any medical database with this thing. Any encyclopedia, dictionary, publication, or drug database in the world. Also email messages, voice communications … you name it. This can do it."

"Holy smokes," I said. "You Italians are way ahead of us in technology."

"Actually, you are correct. We did develop the first model, but it was you Americans who perfected it."

He pulled another device from his pocket and placed it against my forehead. I started to ask about it, but he shushed me. The machine began to hum and click quietly. He slowly circumnavigated my head with the thing, and then set it down and glanced at the Screen. A series of small color images appeared. I looked closer and realized it was a brain.

"What the heck? CT scans of my brain?"

"Indeed."

I picked up the smooth white, palm-sized device. "This is a CT scanner? How can I get one?"

"Oh no," Greco said, with a chuckle. "Far too expensive. I don't know of any EMS systems using them yet."

Huh?

My brain registered his comment in the category of 'something is amiss' and then moved on. I was far too fascinated by the pocket-sized CT scanner to consider another anomaly. "This is all so unbelievable," I said. "It's like medicine changed overnight. How long have I been gone, anyway?"

Greco frowned. "I don't know. You have been with us since mid-afternoon, but before that?" Greco shrugged. "Anyway," he said, turning his attention back to the Screen. "Your brain certainly looks no worse for the wear. Just minimal edema. Do you have a headache?"

"I do. A pretty good one."

"That's to be expected. I'll get you something for that." Greco studied the screen. "These images look good overall. Your brain appears to be structurally sound. You have a small arteriovenous malformation behind your right eye, but that's no cause for concern. I do see evidence of an old injury—" He tapped the screen and studied the new notes that appeared. "Says here, while fighting. Are you a fighter?"

"Yeah, MMA. But what about the gunshot wound, Doc? Don't you see that?"

"Gunshot wound?"

"It happened several months ago. The kid shot me with a .38. Frontal lobe to temporal. You must see that."

Greco adjusted his glasses and gazed at the Screen. He finally looked up, his expression one of genuine confusion. "Michael, I don't see any evidence of a gunshot wound."

"But what about this?" I said, touching my forehead and feeling clean, undamaged skin. "Wait a minute," I said. "Where's the wound? It went in right here!"

Greco just stared at me.

I could feel the cold prickle of sweat on my neck. The memory of the impact was so vivid I could almost smell the metallic tang of blood and the sharp scent of gunpowder. "Are you telling me that never happened?"

Greco shook his head and sighed. He set the Screen down on the bedside table. "Michael, let's take a step back. Shall we? I've looked at every slice of this scan. There's no sign of fracture, no scarring, and certainly no evidence of a projectile pathway through your cerebral tissues. Except for some mild edema following the temporary lack of blood flow during cardiac arrest, your brain is perfectly healthy."

I stared at him, my mind spinning. "Then, the last several months—the shooting, the rehab, the pain, the struggle to remember. Was that all a dream?"

Greco shook his head. "I'm sorry, Michael. I don't know."

I gulped. Just then, an orderly walked in with a steaming cardboard box that smelled of Italian sausage and pepperoni. The mouth-watering aroma reminded me of an Italian Pizzeria on Long Island, called Marco's. I suddenly pictured red-and-white checkered tablecloths, orange candles, and bottles of Chianti. I felt my stomach growl, again.

"Smells incredible, but shouldn't I be on a liquid diet or something? I mean, didn't I just die?"

Greco chuckled. "I can order that if you would like."

I opened the pizza box. My mouth began to water.

"No, this will do."

"Tell you what," Greco said, patting me on the shoulder. "You eat, and then rest. I'll be back a little later to talk."

Greco returned about two hours later, waking me from a dream about wooden poles and bats. It had become a common theme for my nightmares, so to be awakened felt more like a blessing than an annoyance. I sat up and rubbed my eyes, thankful to lose the bats.

"Hello," he said, sitting down on a chair beside the bed.

"What's up, Doc?"

"How was your pizza?"

I glanced at the empty box on the floor. "Better than Papa John's."

"Papa ..." Greco shrugged and shook his head. "How are you feeling?"

"Like I just died and woke up. What time is it?"

Greco glanced at his wrist—he was not wearing a watch. "It is just after midnight."

"How long did you say I've been here?"

"You arrived at our facility at about 2:45 PM yesterday. So, about ten hours."

"And, was I dreaming, or did you really scan my head with a portable CT device?"

"I did. Is your head still hurting?"

"Not as bad." The pain had dropped from a throbbing six-out-of-ten, to a dull ache. "I think the food helped."

"Any nausea?"

"No." I shrugged one shoulder. "This hurts a little, though. Ribs, too."

"That's to be expected after receiving CPR. Do you remember anything about the event?"

"So, I really did arrest? For real, I mean?"

"Oh, yes. The paramedics resuscitated you in the Shroud exam room. Frankly, I'm surprised to find you sitting up in bed."

"Where am I now?"

"This is Humanitas Gradenigo Hospital. We are located directly across the plaza from the cathedral where you arrested."

"In Jerusalem?"

"No," he said, with a chuckle. "Torino. Michael. You are in Turin, Italy. You were examining the Shroud when you collapsed. You were in the …"

The doctor's voice trailed off and gave way to a vivid scene, a color video projected onto a white cloud in my mind:

An electric shock … a current coursing through my body and lifting me off the floor … a wooden pole … bats …

Far in the distance, I could hear my name being called. "Michael? Michael?"

… a tomb, linen burial cloth …

… a bronze coin bearing the image of a shepherd's staff …

Even farther, almost too distant to hear, "Michael? Mike, come back!" The cloud faded and Greco's voice returned with its previous volume and clarity. "Mr. Peabody?" he exclaimed, leaning over me, slapping my cheek. "Come out of it."

"Wait," I said, trying to find my bearings. "Wait. Give me a minute, please." I could smell the pleasant aroma of warm food—pizza? I inhaled deeply and tasted the savory weight of garlic on the back of my tongue. I glanced around the room—a stainless-steel cart, a cardiac monitor beeping, a thin European man leaning over me with the smell of Listerine on his breath—and slowly remembered. "Greco?"

"Yes," he said, calmly, his hand resting reassuringly on my shoulder. "Welcome back, my friend. I think I just witnessed one of your seizures. Where did you go?"

"Jerusalem. But why am I still having seizures, if I wasn't shot?"

Greco shrugged. "It happens sometimes, after cardiac arrest. They won't last long."

"I was seeing things. It was so clear."

"What kind of things?"

I scratched my head. "Bats."

"Bats?"

"The tomb. Coins. Wait a minute," I exclaimed. "The coin! Where is it?"

"What coin?"

"My coin," I replied, suddenly remembering I had placed it in the arm bandage for safekeeping. I patted my arm, hoping to feel the hard shape of an ancient coin minted during the reign of Governor Pontius Pilate. I felt nothing but the sore, sutured tissue of my arm wound tightly by cotton bandaging. "It's not there!" In a panic, I unwound the dressing, but nothing fell out. "Oh, no."

"Michael," Greco said. "What are you doing?"

"Was there a bandage on my arm when I got here?"

"What?"

"A bandage? A bloody bandage?"

"No," Greco said. "No bandage that I recall. Just a fresh wound. My nurse applied this one to cover it." Greco rewrapped the bandage and tucked the loose end under. "Michael, what is it?"

"I can't believe I lost it," I whispered, my voice sounding thin and hollow in the sterile room.

Greco's brow furrowed. "What did you lose?"

I sighed and stared at the doctor, hoping for an answer in his dark, thoughtful eyes.

"Peter gave me a coin. One of the two placed over Jesus' eyes during burial. Priceless," I whispered. "Utterly priceless."

Greco was silent for a long moment, his medical composure teetering on the edge of fracture. He stared at me—really looked at me—the way a doctor studies a patient who is physically fine but psychologically failing. "Michael, you were brought in with a laceration on your arm and another on your cheek. Both had already been, well, let's just say, very oddly sutured. We ran a full neurological workup because you were disoriented. But there was no bandage or coin. There was no gunshot wound. And there was no Jesus."

The clinical finality of his words hit me like a physical blow. I looked down at the fresh white bandage on my arm. Underneath it was a simple laceration—not the entry point of a miracle, and not the coin of a past I thought I remembered.

I clutched my head with both hands. "Oh, what has happened to me?"

"Look at me. Are you okay?" he asked, eyes boring into mine. "Are you with me now?"

"Yeah, I think so."

"Can you go on?"

"Go on?" I shook my head and sighed. "What choice do I have?"

Greco shrugged.

I mean, what else could I do? I was at the mercy of, well, everything and everybody. I felt pain, confusion, and not just a little sadness. I had no idea whether whatever I thought had just happened to me had really happened, and less of an idea what to do next. But I realized I was not alone. I saw deep compassion and understanding in Greco's eyes. He reminded me of another doctor named Loukas, whom I had met somewhere back in my dream. I felt I could trust him. I needed to trust him.

"Let's go on," I said. "Maybe you can help me figure this out."

"Where was I?" Greco sat down and returned to his Screen. "Oh, yes. As I was saying, you were working with the Shroud of Turin when you collapsed. The ambulance brought you to us. Do you remember that?"

"I remember black pants and orange shirts."

"Yes, those are the colors of EMS."

"And baseball caps. There were two of them, weren't there? A guy and a girl?"

"That is correct. I know them well. Enzo and Emma. What else do you recall?"

"Not much. The girl, Emma, injected something into my IV, and then it got blurry."

"She administered midazolam. You were becoming agitated."

"Sorry 'bout that."

"I examined you early on and ran some tests. Seems you are in fine shape, considering. Your EKG was normal, your vitals stable, and your bloodwork is nearly perfect. I did find something very interesting, though. It seems your lacerations have been sutured, and not with nylon or synthetic material, either, but with a silk-like thread. I haven't seen anything like that since …"

Greco's voice faded as the cloud swept over me again with intense sensory stimulation … the acrid smells of rich black coffee and incense … the red hues of slow-burning charcoal … the stinging sensation of a sharp needle jabbing into my cheek …

"… but that type of suturing has not been in common use for over a hundred years. My family's research in electrocauterization has changed injury closure methods dramatically …

A wooden post … a bloody spike … a cliff with the face of a skull clearly visible on it …

"Michael … Michael … Nurse," I heard Greco shout. "Bring some more midazolam, please."

"No," I said, shaking my head and squeezing my fists to force my brain into submission. The cloud dissipated. "I'm okay, now. I'm okay. I'm just—"

"Just what?"

"Remembering."

A nurse hurried into the room, dressed in blue scrubs and holding a small syringe. She looked strangely like my charge nurse back home, with graying hair pulled back into a ponytail, and breath smelling like a stick of cinnamon gum. I felt my jaw drop.

"Give him five milligrams of that," Greco said.

"Wait," I demanded, pushing away the syringe. "Mindy?"

The nurse pulled back, and said, "Yes? Sir?"

"Mindy? It's me, Mike."

Nurse Mindy squinted and frowned curiously. "Yes sir," she said, glancing sideways at Greco. "I'm sorry, but I—"

"That'll be all, Mindy," Greco said. Mindy cleared her throat and walked from the room.

"Greco, was that—"

"Listen to me, Michael. I understand that many things appear confusing to you right now, and certain abnormalities, even delusions are possible."

"But—"

"You must give it time. You were in cardiac arrest for ten minutes, and even the best chest compressions are only sixty-percent effective. Your cerebral cortex was deprived of oxygenated blood for at least ten minutes. Thus, the seizure activity and dream-like memories. It will take some time for your brain to return to normal."

"Yeah, but that was Mindy, my charge nurse."

Greco hesitated and responded, "Michael, Mindy is my charge nurse. You do not have a charge nurse."

"But I do! I mean, I think I do. I mean, oh, good grief." I rubbed my eyes and fell back against my pillow. "Everything has changed. What is happening? I don't know what's real and what's not."

Greco sighed. "Please," he said. "Take your time and tell me everything you remember."

I talked for the next ten moments, without interruption, explaining everything I could remember—from the medical conference in Rome to the cathedral in Turin. From seeing the Shroud for the first time and then collapsing on the floor of the exam room. From waking up atop Golgotha, to meeting Simon. Greco typed notes as I spoke, pausing only to wait for me as I recalled my crazy journey. His expression shifted from curiosity, to total amazement, to deep concern, to wild-eyed imagination, and back again. "Wow," I heard him murmur. "Unbelievable."

"It was so real. I mean, I saw Jesus crucified. I was there when they found the empty tomb."

Greco grimaced. "Dreams can sometimes be quite vivid."

"But it wasn't a dream, Doc. I'm telling you, it was real! Or at least, I think it was. I don't know. If I only had the coin to show you."

"Yes."

"Either way, though, things are different now. I've changed. Everything has changed."

"Fascinating. And when did this journey begin, Michael?"

"The instant they defibrillated me. I floated up into the air and looked down on the room. I could see myself convulsing."

"An out of body experience?"

"Maybe. I mean, I saw the first responders arrive. I watched them shock me, push drugs, perform CPR, everything."

"Slow down."

I couldn't slow down. I had to get it out.

"Everything around me went black. Total fear."

I closed my eyes and saw the video running in my brain, as clear as crystal, as frightening as your worst nightmare.

"I tried to run back to the light—I was very aware of the light—but these creatures. These horrible creatures. They pulled me back, and down into the floor! Death! Fire! Greco, it was maddening! But then it brightened again!"

I opened my eyes and stared at the ceiling.

"Everything cleared up, and I realized I wasn't in the cathedral—I was on top of a hill. It was as if I had entered a different realm. At first I thought it was hell, but then I saw Simon leaning over me."

"Simon?"

"A little African man. A good man. He helped me, took me inside the city, and showed me around. We walked the streets and saw the temple. I mean, I saw it all. I met his Disciples. I witnessed everything. I met a doctor there, too. He looked like you. He was the one that stitched up my cheek and arm."

Greco nodded slowly. "Very interesting. What was this doctor's name?"

"Loukas."

With that, Greco froze, his entire posture stiffening as he gazed at me with rapt attention. The air in the room seemed to still, the previous ease of our conversation vanishing in an instant. His expression shifted rapidly—a flash of total amazement giving way to deep curiosity, then to a wild-eyed, imaginative spark, before finally settling into a mask of profound concern. "What did you say?"

"Loukas. He said he was from Athens, Greece."

Greco rubbed his chin and turned his attention to something in the distance, as if picturing a far away scene. "You know," he said, his voice almost a whisper. "My family is from Greece. My parents and siblings still live in Athens."

"Yeah?"

"I come from a long line of doctors. My family tree can be traced back to the mid-1500's, where my forefathers worked in medicine, and in, of all places, Jerusalem." After a moment, he seemed to reorient himself and turned his eyes back on me. "Would you believe that my grandfather's name was Loukas? And his before that? And his before that?"

"Loukas? Really?"

"Yes, Michael. Loukas is my name, too."

CHAPTER THIRTY

Room Number 13
Humanitas Gradenigo Hospital
Turin, Italy
Sunday, April 5—00:32 AM Local Time (CEST)

The sedative Greco administered proved to be remarkably effective. I drifted off almost instantly and slept with a heavy, dreamless intensity I haven't known in years. I woke feeling truly rested, the kind of deep restoration that usually feels out of reach. Outside my window, a single bird was singing a clear, rhythmic melody that seemed to cut through the morning stillness.

The sky was a brilliant, cloudless blue, flooded with early light that felt almost too bright for my eyes. As the fog of sleep cleared, my mind immediately circled back to my conversation with Greco the night before. I found myself staring at the dust motes dancing in a shaft of sunlight, wondering how many small, unseen choices had shifted to lead me exactly to this moment.

I was surprised when Greco entered my room, fully alert and apparently well rested.

"Geez," I said. "Don't you ever sleep?"

Greco laughed and returned to his familiar position on the chair beside my bed, Screen in hand. "I do not require much sleep."

"So I see. Look," I said, picking up our conversation where we left off the night before. "Do you think … I mean, Doc, is it even remotely possible that I met one of your ancestors? Dr. Loukas?"

"Michael—"

"Am I going crazy here, or did I go back in time?"

Greco hesitated momentarily, and then nodded, and said, "Yes. I believe it is possible."

"So, I'm not crazy?"

"No, I don't think you're crazy. At first, I'll admit I did. But your story is incredibly convincing. And if it's true—if you really did go back in time—then you may have already altered the course of history."

"Right. I mean, look at it. You say there's no evidence whatsoever of a gunshot wound, but I swear to you, I was shot in the head by a madman named Corbin Myers just a few months ago. Before that, I was a successful ED doc in North Carolina. You laughed when I told you that."

Greco listened to me, this time, without chuckling.

"I had a charge nurse named Mindy, who looked exactly like your charge nurse, Mindy. And now, you throw all of this new technology at me, too, like a pocket-sized CT scanner? And this new space age iPad thing, called a Screen? Something called A-bot living inside your head? You can talk to her and she does things for you? I mean, call me crazy, my friend, but this is like a new world for me where everything has suddenly changed."

"I agree. And consider this ... you claim to have just learned of the Shroud of Turin, when in fact, you are a leading expert in the study of Shroud formation."

"I am?"

"You and my son. You have worked for the American chapter of the Shroud of Turin Research Project, Project 21, for years."

"Your son? I'm sorry, what?"

"It is true. You collaborated with your professor, Milner, Chief Scientific Photographer for STURP, before he died. You helped him work through his photographs. As a young student at the photography school where Milner was a professor, you printed many of his images. You took the image of the face of the Shroud off the 3-D computer and assisted him with his research into the art history behind the Shroud."

"But, no, Will Hendricks produced the 3-D image."

"No. I saw you take it with your own Nikon camera. We were at the Jackson home in Colorado Springs. In his basement. You do not remember?"

"So, you're saying I was a photographer?"

"Before turning to EMS."

"EMS? I'm a doctor."

"No, but hold on, there's more. Shall I go on?"

I wasn't sure I could process any more changes, but the sheer fascination of it all sparked such a deep curiosity that I urged him to go on. To hear more would only solidify my conviction that something truly remarkable had happened to me. I nodded. "Please do."

"I discovered sutures on your face and arm that haven't been commonly used by physicians in this century. And you claim the ambulance crew shocked you out of ventricular fibrillation, but their report indicates you had already shocked yourself by the time they arrived."

"What do you mean, I shocked myself?"

"Michael, ALS providers seldom defibrillate V-Fib and V-Tach anymore, not in civilized countries, at least. The defibrillator app built into the CHIP makes external defibrillation obsolete."

"What chip?"

"The CHIP. The computerized history and information processor." Greco grabbed my wrist and turned over my arm to reveal a one-inch scar about ⅓ up my forearm. "Your membership CHIP. Your ID."

I stared at the scar on my forearm. Touched it. Pushed on it. "There's something in there?"

"Your CHIP. It replaced cash and credit cards a long time ago. Then, as technology advanced, it became a seamless connection between you and the internet. You can control it, much like the old iPhones people used to use. Go ahead, ask A-bot to tell you the time."

"So, I've got an A-bot?"

"No, you've got a CHIP. A-bot is like the old Siri. Just ask her."

"A-bot," I said. "What time is it?"

A rectangular screen lit up on my wrist, displaying the time in bright green letters—22:26 CEST. I jumped, almost out of my skin, when I heard the same information in my mind, spoken by a polite female, as if I were wearing headphones. "Man, did you hear that?!"

"That's A-bot."

"Where is she?" I said, looking around, as if to find the source.

"She's in your mind, Michael. Her power comes from the CHIP. It's all there. Everything that used to be on your iPhone."

"You've got to be kidding me. Where did I get this? And where's my watch?"

"You got it a few years ago, after the COVID virus ran its course. Everyone has a CHIP now. No one wears a watch anymore." He showed me the one-inch scar on his own wrist. "It keeps your vital information handy—Name, address, social security, birthdate, medical history and medications, even your doctor's name. You have uninterrupted instant access to the internet. And you can send messages to loved ones just by thinking. Go ahead, try it. Just think of a message, and it's sent. Send a message to Ramona. Tell her you're okay."

"Ramona?"

"She already knows, of course, because I contacted her."

"Ramona Read?"

He nodded. I stared at him for a moment, waiting for the punchline. There wasn't one.

"Why the heck would I contact Ramona Read?"

"Michael, Ramona is your wife."

I mouthed the words, "My what?"

Greco nodded.

"My wife's name is Gloria."

"No," he said, shaking his head. "Michael, Gloria died years ago."

"What?"

"I'm sorry. It's true."

Trembling, I felt my throat tighten into a suffocating knot. Tears welled in my eyes, spilling over as I managed a single, broken word. "Died?"

"It's been twenty-five years since her accident. She died on your first anniversary. You don't remember?"

"Twenty-five years?" I swallowed hard against the thick lump rising in my throat. "What, what happened?"

"She was killed in an automobile accident. Another robocar malfunctioned and struck her head-on. Her surround-a-bag system operated properly, but it could not protect her from a piece of cold steel. She died of penetrating chest trauma."

A wave of cold numbness washed over me, leaving me momentarily paralyzed. The room seemed to tilt on its axis, and for a few seconds, the air in my lungs felt like lead—impossible to exhale. I could see Greco's lips moving, but his voice had retreated into a dull, distant hum, as if I were underwater. My mind, usually so sharp and analytical, could only loop around that single, impossible reality, unable to find a foothold in this new world.

"I can't believe it."

"Michael," Greco said. "I'm very sorry. Gloria is gone. But you have been happily married to Ramona for twenty-two years. She's a beautiful, smart, loving woman. And a wonderful mother."

"Mother?" I whispered. "Are you telling me I have kids?"

Greco received a call and excused himself. I lay in my bed for the next ten minutes trying to picture Gloria's face. My memory conjured up an image of us together at one of our happiest moments on a riverside in Alaska, after having finished a rafting trip on a roiling, glacier-fed river. She was ecstatic, wet hair and all, laughing out loud and hugging me. I could not imagine her gone. Tears flooded my eyes.

And Ramona? That, I could not understand. We had dated briefly in the early days, a few flickering moments of connection, but that felt like a lifetime ago. The version of Ramona etched in my mind was the one who emerged after she climbed the ranks to department head—a woman who had traded warmth for efficiency, becoming so cold and unyielding that I eventually found her impossible to be around. Now, I was expected to believe she was the center of my world?

No way!

But still, I needed to know. I decided to take Greco's advice and send her a message. I whispered to myself, "A-bot, send a message."

To whom? The robotic voice responded.

Incredulous, I thought of her name, "Ramona."

What would you like to say to Ramona?

"Holy cow, it really works! Um, hi, Ramona, it's Mike. How are you doing?"

Ten seconds later, I heard a quiet beep between my ears followed by the voice of my old boss, Ramona Read:

Oh, Michael! Praise the Lord! Oh, we can't talk now. They're switching off all electronic connections until after takeoff. Can't wait to see you in the morning. We love you!

"We?"

Simon's with me. He sends his love. Gotta go …

I felt overwhelmed on so many levels that I could not contain myself. "Simon?" I exclaimed, breathing deeply, the pressure in my chest making it hard to breathe. "Who is Simon?"

Greco parted the curtains and walked back in. "Sorry," he said. "I had to take care of a fracture."

"Greco, who's Simon?"

"Simon is your son."

I gasped. "I have a son? How old is he?"

"I believe he is twenty-one."

"Doc, you're telling me I have a twenty-one-year-old son?"

"Michael—" Greco sighed and sat down. "You have no idea, do you? You really don't remember."

I shook my head, my tongue glued to the roof of my mouth as if I'd forgotten how to form the simplest sounds. I tried to swallow, to find some moisture, but my throat felt as though it had been lined with sandpaper, leaving me staring at Greco in a silent, wide-eyed plea for clarity.

"I've been giving this a lot of thought," Greco said. "Michael, have you ever heard of the butterfly effect?"

The butterfly effect …

I leaned back, the hospital pillow crunching like dry leaves beneath my head. I closed my eyes, trying to block out the sterile hum of the room, and thought of Mindy. She'd once told me about a traveler who stepped off a path in the past, only to return to a world he didn't recognize. She called it the butterfly effect. I'd brushed it off as a campfire story then, but now, the air felt thin, like I was the one who had stepped off the path. I opened my eyes, gave a stiff nod, and answered his question. "The butterfly effect is when you go back in time and interact with people and things, and as a result, everything changes."

"That's correct. I believe you have somehow experienced the butterfly effect. Now tell me, did you interact with others while you were in Jerusalem? Did you touch anything?"

"Are you kidding? I interacted with many people. Touched everything. I got into a fistfight with a Roman soldier and even saved a guy's life. Does that count?"

"Oh, mercy."

"I worked with the doctor I told you about. Your ancestor, maybe? Loukas. He had an OD patient who overdosed on mushrooms. I made some atropine out of belladonna leaves, and a charcoal slurry for toxin binding."

"My stars," he whispered. "Michael, you did this?"

"Yeah, I showed him how to make a stethoscope, too—wait a second!" The realization hit me like a bolt of lightning. "Greco, are you thinking what I'm thinking?"

Greco's eyes glossed over with wild imagination. "Michael, if what we believe happened truly happened, then your being there—interacting with others, sharing knowledge— may have changed medical history."

"Holy smokes!"

"Technology too."

"Like the Screen," I exclaimed, so excited that my voice began to tremble. "That portable CT scanner, and maybe even the CHIP? All those things are new to me. So, I guess that means the butterfly effect is real!"

Greco looked stunned. For the first time since we had met, the man was genuinely speechless. His mouth hung open slightly, his eyes wide as they searched mine, trying to reconcile the impossibility of what I'd just described with the calm reality of the room. It was as if he were watching the foundations of his own understanding crumble and reshape themselves in real-time.

But me? I felt energized! About ready to explode with excitement.

"I mean, look at it, Doc! I remember a world with watches. And iPads instead of Screens. And iPhones instead of CHIPs. You know what? I just thought of something else. Dr. Loukas seemed particularly interested in my watch. A Casio tactical. Do you think that his—"

Greco regained his footing and jumped in, finishing my sentence. "—that his early interest led to the changes in electronics we have today? Yes. I think it's possible." Greco muttered to himself and typed a few notes onto his Screen. "Wow!" he said, shuddering. "Something else just occurred to me. You say you produced atropine from crushed belladonna leaves?"

"And charcoal, yeah. What about it?"

"I'm just going out on a limb here, but have you ever heard of a drug called Belladil? Anti-seizure medication?"

"Never heard of it. Most of my patients take 300-milligrams of Dilantin a day. Phenytoin," I added, using the generic name.

"Phenytoin is used exclusively for cardiac arrhythmias, not seizures. Belladil is the standard."

"It must be new. What is it?"

"It's been around since the 1950's, Michael. Belladil, generically known as belladolantin, is a mixture of belladonna extract, activated charcoal, and VX-548."

"Dude, I have no idea what you're talking about."

"VX-548. Suzetrigine. A sodium channel blocker used for pain."

"Greco—" I rubbed my chin, turning his words over in my mind as the pieces began to click into place. "I think I know where you're going with this—I explained calcium and sodium channels to Loukas. He had never heard of them. I made atropine from belladonna and activated charcoal from cooking charcoal. I'm wondering if maybe he did the early research on all this and that led to the development of Bellado, do …"

"Belladolantin." Greco rubbed his eyes. "This is beginning to blow my mind."

I heard Greco's nurse, Mindy—my nurse Mindy—calling for him over the intercom. "Be right back," he said, hurrying from the room.

I felt numb with new knowledge, as if I had traveled forward in time, instead of backwards. The urge to yell tore at my throat, but I locked it away, tightening my grip until my knuckles went white. I thought back on my time with Dr. Loukas to compare it with these new findings. “Loukas,” I whispered. “You genius. You did it, didn’t you? You really did it!”

They moved me to the intensive care unit sometime during the night, a cold, sterile wing of the hospital with much less human interaction than the emergency department. In fact, at some point during the night, I was awakened by a sharp stinging sensation in my arm. I bolted upright when I realized it was a machine—a robot—injecting me with a syringe of clear fluid. After finishing, he, she, it dropped the syringe into a trap door on its leg and rolled out of the room. Another robot delivered my breakfast. It set down the tray, said something in a tinny Italian voice, and then rolled out. “Thanks,” I said, thoroughly amused.

“Prego,” the machine responded. “Gustare.”

I shook my head. “Whatever.”

I noticed a beeping sound behind me and turned to see a nice, normal sinus rhythm marching reassuringly across the cardiac monitor screen. At least that made sense. My breakfast smelled pretty good, too. I was just about to dig into it—croissant, jam, hard-boiled egg and coffee—when a thin, scary-looking human entered my room with a boxy-looking device in one hand—kind of an iPhone on steroids. She shook the device to awaken it and placed it against my bare chest.

“What the heck is that?” I chuckled. “Looks like a Star Trek medical scanner.”

“Muta,” she said, shushing me. “Quiet!”

I grimaced. She reminded me of a witch I’d once seen in a movie—the one that hung out with the scarecrow and lion—only not quite as friendly. She had black hair, a pointy nose, and long fingers that I could easily imagine being green. I had a sudden flashback to a scene with a broom and a flock of flying monkeys. The image made me grin.

“What’s your name?” I asked, trying to lighten the air.

"Martina," she said, placing a strong accent on the third syllable.

Martina adjusted the box slightly, positioning it at about the 3rd intercostal space just right of my sternum. She pushed a button and, instantly, the room filled with the sound of mild thumping and clicking heart valves, delivered with the precision and clarity of a Littmann Cardiology II stethoscope.

"What the—" I about jumped off the bed. "Where'd you get that thing?"

Martina frowned and rolled her eyes, as if dealing with uneducated Americans bored her to tears. "È uno stetoscopio digitale," she said, pausing and placing the device higher on my chest.

"I've got a digital stethoscope. Doesn't look anything like that. Let me see it."

"Smettila," she demanded, slapping my hand. "Respirare!"

"Look," I said, my blood pressure rising. "Enough with the Italian. I don't understand your language."

"Breathe!"

That, I understood. I did as ordered and listened with amazement as audible breath sounds emanated from the advanced speaker system, the clearest vesicular breath sounds I had ever heard. I waited patiently, obeying her commands as she moved the device across my chest, to my back, and then to my neck, where I heard the familiar swooshing of carotid artery blood flow, only with a slight adventitious murmur.

"Hmm, sounds like there might be a carotid artery test in your near future."

"So, you do speak English. Let me see that thing," I said, grabbing the device from her. "This is amazing."

I looked the device over, and then placed it on my abdomen. I was rewarded with the gurgling sounds of digestion.

Martina grinned, warming her otherwise chilly face about fifty-degrees. "Pretty cool, huh?"

"Amazing," I said, glancing at her. "I want one."

"Eat your breakfast," she said. "It's getting cold."

I threw the egg in my mouth and devoured it.

"Have you met Loukas Greco yet?" she said.

"The doctor? Sure," I said. "I spent the night in his ER."

"Yes, well, his father's company developed that device, you know."

"Greco's father did this?"

"Yes, it's true," she said, taking the stethoscope from me and slipping it into a pocket. His father is legendary in the medical industry. His company designed the Screen, the rectal extravenous administration catheter, or REAC, and this thing. And his cousin, a chemist working for one of the big pharma companies, developed the drug, Belladil."

"The anticonvulsant med."

"Yes." She glanced at one of my IVs. "You're receiving some now."

"No kidding?"

"They are a very successful family. And very well respected, too. Everyone here loves Dr. Greco."

My mind drifted back to Loukas. He had been so hungry for new ideas, so ready to research things that shouldn't have existed for another millennium. A cold realization settled in my chest—had I inadvertently handed him the keys to the future? If my time with him had triggered advancements ahead of schedule, then the world I returned to wouldn't be the one I left. It was the butterfly effect, and I was the one who had stepped off the path.

I buried my face in my hands, too excited to speak.

"Martina, Greco mentioned a son. Does he have any kids?"

"Oh, yes," she said. "He has a son."

"And what is his name?"

"His name is Luke Greco. I believe he lives somewhere in the U.S.A."

CHAPTER THIRTY-ONE

Intensive Care Unit
Humanitas Gradenigo Hospital
Turin, Italy
Monday, April 6—9:00 AM Local Time (CEST)

It's difficult waking up to a new life. I mean, mine had changed in so many ways, I could hardly believe it. I thought of Gloria and started to cry. I would miss her so much, and yet, according to Greco, she had already been gone for many years. And on top of that, I just learned that I'm now married to my old boss, Ramona Read, who, it turns out, isn't my boss at all, because I'm not a doctor anymore. And, I have a twenty-one-year-old son, named Simon. "God," I whispered. "I'm going to need your help with all of this."

I glanced at my arm, amazed to think there was a 'CHIP' implanted four inches above my wrist. I knew it was in there, because A-bot talked to me almost constantly. She woke me up about twelve times during the night to answer thoughts that I must've had while dreaming. At one point, she said something about Jesus' cross being hewn from the wood of an olive tree. I'm not sure where that came from.

To tell the truth, the CHIP kind of scared me. I mean, it just kind of seemed like a step in the wrong direction for me, I suppose. Shoot, for mankind. But it did offer advantages. I had ordered breakfast that morning by simply thinking about it. I had also read an article about the Los Angeles Dodgers and their newest pitching prospect from Japan. Apparently, he can throw the ball 110 mph. Something about a bionic arm? I picked up the croissant—pronounced 'cornetto' in Italian … I'm learning—and put it in my mouth. It tasted wonderful. Thank God, I thought, some things never change. A-bot answered without delay:

Michael, change is an inevitable part of life. It's a constant occurrence, whether we like it or not, and can be both positive and negative. Embracing change and adapting to it is a key aspect of personal and professional growth. Here's why change is—

"A-bot," I said. "Shut up."

The robotic voice ended. Greco had told me there's a way to adjust the settings on A-bot so she's not quite so twitchy, but that will have to wait. I shook my head and took another bite of jam slathered croissant. Not bad.

I thought about my discussion with Greco about the butterfly effect. I understand now that it's real. That everything we do in life, whether in the past or present, will have an effect on the world and the future. Everything. Everything we do, everything we say, touch, eat, create, destroy … everything! It causes change. It affects people. What a responsibility we humans have. I would try to learn to control myself better. I chuckled at that. Self-control.

I finished my breakfast and leaned back for a short nap. I mean, what else was I going to do? I was lying in a bed in the intensive care unit of a hospital in Italy. I had tubes, wires, and catheters attached to my body, and there was no one around to talk to except for a couple of robots and a nurse named Martina who enjoyed sticking me with needles. I felt drowsy, so I closed my eyes. I was teetering on the edge of light sleep when I sensed someone standing beside the bed. I glanced up and saw that it was a woman. About five feet-six inches tall, with a feminine build and glacial-colored blue eyes. She wasn't dressed in hospital scrubs or a lab coat, but in civilian clothes—sharp and elegant, as if on her way to a party. "Mike?" she said. "Sweetheart?"

"Who is it?"

"Sweetheart, it's me," she responded. "Rome."

"Rome?"

"Ramona."

"Ramona!" I bolted upright.

The first thoughts that crossed my mind were of fear and a primal, urgent impulse to defend myself. But then the fog lifted, my head cleared, and I sensed a quiet peacefulness about her spirit—strong but humble, decent and kind. She carried a sweet smile and rosy cheeks that seemed to glow from within, a startling contrast to the cold memory I held of her.

Ramona walked up to me, took my hand, and then leaned down and gently kissed me. It felt wonderful. Then she pulled away and gazed into my eyes. It was like a warm salve, that same cold, Icelandic blue, but with a touch of liquid silver that made them almost electric. I felt something as she gazed at me, an emotion I knew I would never forget … love. This woman I had once craved, and then had learned to hate, I could tell she loved me. She squeezed my hand and released it.

"Dr. Greco told me about your time-travel experience."

"Ramona? I, I don't know what to say, this is—"

"I know."

"But, I mean, I just learned that you, that we're, you know—"

"Married? Mike, sweetheart, you've been through a lot. It's going to take you some time to understand all this. Fortunately, we've got plenty of time."

"Ramona Read."

"Ramona Peabody," she said, correcting me. Then she kissed me again, and said, "There's someone here with me who is dying to see you."

Just then, a young man a foot taller than Ramona stepped into the room. His skin was deep-toned like mine, his physique a mirror of my own—broad and powerful. He moved with a quiet confidence that spoke of intelligence, yet his expression held a striking, familiar kindness. He approached the bed, and said, "What's up, dad?"

“Simon?” My eyes exploded with tears. I could no longer hold back my emotions. All of the fear, pain, amazement, joy, utter astonishment I had experienced, it all surfaced at once. I sobbed like a baby on his birthday, filled with pride and newfound love, and unspeakable joy for the discovery of my new life. “You’re Simon?”

“Yes,” he said, rolling his eyes. “Still Simon.”

“I’m sorry, son. Please forgive me, but this is the first time I’ve seen you.”

“Dr. Greco told us about your experience—something about a butterfly effect?”

“Yeah—” I shifted to the edge of the bed and stood for the first time since arriving. “And believe me when I tell you it’s real.” I wrapped my arms around Simon. It was like clutching a bull. I pushed him away and studied his features. I hoped I would never have to fight him.

Oh, you will, Michael, A-bot’s voice chimed inside my head. He’s an MMA fighter, like you.

I shook my head. “How old are you, son?”

“Twenty-one.”

I hugged him again, and then Ramona joined us, and we shared a group hug that went on for minutes. My wooziness took over again and I was forced to sit down.

“Well,” Ramona said, sitting on the bed beside me. “We’ve got a lot of catching up to do, huh?”

I nodded. “More than you know. They say I’ll be here for at least another week. That’ll give us plenty of time to talk.”

“Dad,” Simon said, walking to the window and pointing at the stone cathedral across the plaza. “That’s where they keep the Shroud, right? Think maybe we can see it before we leave?”

I chuckled and nodded. “I think I might know someone who could arrange that.”

CHAPTER THIRTY-TWO

Somewhere over the Atlantic Ocean
1,000 miles from the coast of North Carolina, USA
Delta Supersonic Streak Transport (SST) Flight #2001
Sunday, April 19—06:06 AM (EST)

The Supersonic Streak Transport was a true marvel of aviation—and, to date, the most staggering change in this new world I was still trying to wrap my head around. It reminded me of a ship out of Star Wars, sort of an elongated space shuttle with a needle-sharp nose and massive delta wings. During takeoff, the invisible hand of acceleration pins you deep into your seat, turning simple actions—like reaching for a drink or turning the page of a book—into a conscious, muscular effort. Capable of reaching speeds as high as Mach 2.5, which is a little over 1,900 mph, it could bridge the 4,600-mile expanse between Rome and Raleigh-Durham in a little under two and a half hours. I mean, I had already accepted the fact that I was a modern-day Christopher Columbus, or something, but I still had trouble accepting the incredible changes I had witnessed.

I glanced at Ramona Read Peabody—my wife. I realized I hardly knew her, the real her, anyway, but I was looking forward to finding out more. She seemed accustomed to all the changes around me. But of course, she would be, right? She had lived in this new world her entire life.

I felt a sudden pressure in my midsection and realized I needed to find a latrine. Usually, I dread airplane restrooms, but this time was different. Walking down the aisle, standing steady, and returning to my seat—all without a flicker of pain or the need of a cane—felt nothing short of exhilarating. I sat back down in my seat beside my beautiful wife and buckled back in, thanking my lucky stars for a second chance at life.

Ramona read a book most of the way across the Atlantic, while the rest of the plane snored, including Simon. I didn't feel like sleeping, so I spent much of my time playing with A-bot, asking her questions and seeing how quickly she could respond. Just for kicks, I changed her name to Martina, and made some other adjustments to her settings so that I could better control her responses. I had also learned that by simply thinking the words, I could open Google— actually, they now call it Google Master— and access anything on the internet, including photographs and videos.

Out of sheer habit, I glanced at my bare wrist before remembering I no longer had my watch. I asked Martina for the current time, and a cold shudder ran down my spine as the digits bled through my skin, flashing on my forearm in bright green letters like an organic neon sign. I rubbed at the flesh, half-expecting it to feel like plastic, before pulling myself together. "Eastern Standard Time," I said, chastising her. New numbers flashed up—06:06 EST.

Can I do anything else for you, Michael?

"Yes," I whispered, trying to remember the name of the conference speaker in Florence. Grady, was it? Patrick Grady? *Yes, that's it.*

"A-bot, look up the name Patrick Grady and reference it to the Shroud of Turin."

There was no response. I repeated the request, once again without effect. I was about to ask for the third time when a playful female voice whispered,

You changed my name, Michael. Don't you remember?
This is Martina, not A-bot.

"Martina," I said, with a grin. "See if you can find out anything about Mr. Grady—where I might contact him, etc. Then repost those images of the Shroud. The eyes, specifically. I'd like to look at the prutah coins again."

Martina posted an article about the late Patrick Grady, member of the STURP team that had investigated the Shroud in 1977. Unfortunately, the article explained, Grady died in a train crash in 1978, while traveling between Bologna and Florence. His train had reportedly derailed into a ditch, and only seconds later was struck by a second train, killing 42 and injuring 76. It was the fourth highest death toll in the history of Italian railways.

I thought about that. The guy was dead? He was alive before my journey, and now he's dead. The butterfly effect?

Did I cause his death?

That thought was too heavy to imagine. I pushed it aside—I had to. To dwell on it would only invite guilt and sorrow, and I was beginning to realize the darker side of this journey. Not all the changes I encountered would be for the better.

I leaned back in my seat, closed my eyes, and studied the color images of the victim's eyes on the screen of my mind. I examined the coins again, going over the details of the shepherd's crook and the raised letters minted on the surface. I could explain much of it in detail. I mean, after all, it turns out I am one of the world's leading experts on the Shroud of Turin. And I was shocked to learn that it was my own article that I was reading. How cool is that?

Something I had written in that article prompted me to reread one of the passages that explains Christ's crucifixion. I asked Martina to read me a passage in the Bible that depicted it. She paused for a moment and then responded:

I found this for you on the internet. It is from the Gospel of John, chapter 19, verses 16-18, New International Version: "Finally Pilate handed him over to them to be crucified. So the soldiers took charge of Jesus. Carrying his own cross, he went out to the place of the Skull (which in Aramaic is called Golgotha). There they crucified him, and with him two others—one on each side and Jesus in the middle."

"I was there."

Yes, you were, Michael. Is there anything else I can—

I whispered, "Stop," and the computer voice inside my head stopped talking. I turned to Ramona. "Rome, be honest. Do you think I was there?"

She glanced up from her novel. "Where, honey?"

"At the cross. Really there, I mean?"

Ramona frowned. "Are you doubting it now?"

"I'm having a hard time accepting it wasn't just a dream."

She closed her paperback and handed me a Kleenex so I could blow my nose. "Are you okay?"

I nodded. "So, I've been thinking about my two old friends, Jim and Rico. I mean, you do know them, right?"

"Yes," she said with a giggle. "I know Jim and Rico."

"If only I could share all this with them. I miss them both so much."

Ramona frowned curiously, then she smiled and offered an encouraging nod. "I have a feeling you'll see them both soon."

Where? I thought. *Heaven?* My eyes misted up. Ramona took my hand, offered a quiet prayer, and then squeezed it and reopened her novel—an old-style paperback. I thought about things for a few minutes, and then I closed my eyes and gave in to sleep. No dreams. No clouds. No A-bot—aka, Martina. Just sleep.

"Sweetheart," my wife said, shaking me awake. "Mike, we're about to land."

I didn't bother saying, already? I had been enjoying the miracle of deep sleep so well, that I had lost all track of time. The fact was, we had crossed the Atlantic in record time. The pilot announced it proudly over the intercom, before adding, "It has been a pleasure serving you today. Please fly with Delta again soon." I glanced at my wrist and asked Martina for the time. The screen lit up, reporting—06:53 (EST). Right on time.

"Cool," I whispered. "So cool."

The jet touched down delicately, lighting, and slowly lowering her nose to the runway. My body shifted forward and settled into an upright position as the plane decelerated to a coasting speed and taxied to the terminal. I waited along with the other passengers—I mean, some things will never change—and then followed Ramona and Simon off the jet and into RDU Terminal #2. Home.

We fetched our suitcases from the state-of-the-art luggage retrieval system built into the jetway. I shook my head, amazed by the compact flat units that rolled on single, rubber balls, like the new skateboards I'd seen back in East Beach. I was surprised by the way my suitcase balanced itself, rolling effortlessly behind me as we walked through the terminal.

I started feeling a little queasy. "I need to sit down," I said, grabbing my wife's arm.

"Can I get a wheelchair?" she murmured to no one.

Within a minute, we were sitting in an electric golf cart on our way to Ramona's car. The attendants helped me into the back seat of the vehicle, a Tesla Model Z with the standard self-driving feature. The black interior shone like polished leather. The heavy, rich, slightly musky scent of premium upholstery dominated the cabin. Ramona climbed in beside me. Simon got behind the wheel and touched a screen. A bank of computerized images lit up the dashboard. "A-bot," he said, "a message, please." He sat for a moment whispering to himself, and then said, "See you then." Then he turned and glanced at me. "Yo, dad, we need to make a stop on the way home."

CHAPTER THIRTY-THREE

Somewhere on Highway 70 between Raleigh, NC and Morehead City
Ramona's Tesla Model Z
Sunday, April 19—10:47 AM (EST)

The trip from Raleigh-Durham Airport to Morehead City took, as always, about three hours. It was a good trip overall, smooth and quiet, requiring only one rest stop at McDonald's along the way, putting us in Morehead City at 10:47 AM. Simon only touched the wheel twice, and that was in the drive-through. The vehicle's automatic GPS-guided steering system did the rest. Simon drove through town and took an unexpected left turn into East Beach just before the ICW bridge.

"Where are we going?" I said, curious that he hadn't gone straight across the bridge to Beaufort.

Simon said, "You'll see."

I shrugged. He took another left onto Main Street and then pulled the Tesla into the parking lot across the street from the old movie theater. I felt my eyes widen with surprise.

"Geez, what happened to this place?" I exclaimed, marveling at the clean sidewalks, the movie theater's colorful marquee, and the paved parking lot and alley that led to my gym. "It was a dump last time I saw it."

Simon rolled his eyes. "C'mon, dad."

"Ramona," I said, truly confused. "What's going on? Why are we here?"

"I think this might answer some questions for you," she responded.

"But, I really don't want to relive this place. There's too many bad memories."

"Come on," she urged. "You really need to see this."

As usual, I had no idea what to say. I climbed out of the car and walked slowly across the parking lot, breathing in air that no longer reeked of rubbish and empty wine bottles. I saw no homeless people leaning against the walls, no sign of gangs, and no cop cars idling at the curb. It was different—clean, refreshing, and entirely unrecognizable.

Ramona and Simon lingered a few paces behind, their quiet steps giving me the space I needed to navigate the terrain of my memories. I crossed the clean asphalt and turned down the narrow alley cutting beside the theater. Right there, in the quiet shadows of the brick walls, I stopped. My breath hitched in my throat as I stood frozen, staring at the exact coordinates where my life had almost ended.

"This is where it happened," I whispered, mentally replaying the moment.

Ramona and Simon joined me, waiting patiently for me as I relived the scene.

"I ran up those steps. Found Jim right there … just lying there—" I fought the emotional wave building in my chest and throat, but finally the tears burst forth. I wept like a child wounded deeply by life. I felt embarrassed, humbled, and so sad for all the brokenness in my life. "I'm sorry," I said, between spasmodic breaths. "God, I'm sorry."

I felt Ramona's arm around me.

Simon placed a hand on my shoulder. "It's all right, Dad. We're here."

I inhaled deeply to gather myself. I wiped my face of tears and breathed quietly for the next few moments until I could speak again.

"Myers stepped out of the shadows. Chrome revolver. I can still see it pointed at my face."

"Mike?" Ramona took a step back. "Corbin?"

I nodded. "He looked deranged. Insane."

"And that's what you remember? Corbin Myers shooting you?"

"That's all I remember. Next thing I knew I was in the ICU. They said I was comatose for days. Found out later Myers saved a bullet for himself." I pointed at the freshly swept sidewalk. "They found his body right there."

"Honey—" Ramona frowned, and took my arm. "I know this has been confusing for you. A terrible experience. But everything is not as it seems. Come on, we have something to show you."

Ramona started down the stairs. I hesitated and then followed slowly with Simon on my heels.

"Wait," I said, stopping and pointing at a new sign above the entrance. "That says c and m's. Where's the slaughterhouse sign?"

"Whatcha mean, dad?"

"Big Mike's Slaughterhouse. Where is it?"

"I don't know," Simon said, moving past me and pulling open the heavy steel door. "It's always been c and m's. Each of your surprises is old news to us. Why don't we go inside and see what else you find?"

By this point, I wasn't sure what to expect. I followed Simon inside the building and was immediately hit by the pleasant, sweet aroma of Gain-scented dryer sheets. I sniffed the air, puzzled. Gone were the manly aromas of dirty towels and sweat. I saw no reminders of the gritty, unwashed gym I once knew. Instead of the damp gloom of the old hallway, the air felt light and crisp, as if the very walls had been scrubbed clean of their history.

The sound of muffled cheering drew me down the hall toward the arena. I walked into the warehouse, shocked to find it no longer dimly lit by orange sodium-vapor lights—instead, the space shone brightly beneath banks of daylight-balanced LEDs. The octagon remained in its usual place, but it was now flanked by bleachers where a dozen spectators watched a fight in progress.

Most startling of all, the cage was gone. In place of the barbaric chain-link fencing, the mat was surrounded by a hazy blue shield—perfectly transparent, yet apparently impenetrable.

I watched with amazement as one of the fighters threw his opponent against the hazy wall; he bounced off as if repelled by an invisible forcefield and immediately continued to fight.

"What's that?" I said, elbowing Simon. "Where's the cage?"

"The fence?" Simon shrugged. "It's always been there."

I walked across the arena and stopped just short of the octagon, close enough to hear the grunts of the fighters grappling in the ring. The larger of the two men resembled Hulk Hogan, the other a bodybuilding nightclub bouncer with a tattooed scalp. The referee looked and moved like a Dole pineapple with legs. He glanced sideways and shouted, "Stop the fight!" Then he pointed at me and yelled, "Mike! Is that you?"

"Charlie K?"

The fighters stopped and turned my way. Charlie muttered something and the forcefield disappeared. He stepped out of the cage and trotted to the center of the arena. "Welcome back," he said, grabbing my hand and shaking it. "Dude, we thought you were a goner!"

"Guess God isn't finished with me yet."

"Well, I know EMS isn't. Dude, I've been riding with a new guy from Durham. Doesn't know a BVM from an IV catheter. I need you to hurry and get back."

"They tell me you're a supervisor now. When did this happen?"

"You lose your memory over there? About five years ago."

"Well, look who's back," another voice bellowed.

I looked up at the fighter lumbering toward me. Short and stumpy looking, with a Puerto Rican swag and enough rippling muscles to break a Brahma bull, he reminded me of an old friend I had said goodbye to months before. The sight of him made me gasp. I suddenly felt lightheaded. I thought I was seeing a ghost.

"Rico?"

"I thought I'd lost you, buddy."

"Rico," I repeated, trying to catch my breath. "What … I mean, how, where, what happened? Last time I saw you, you were dying!"

"Dying?" Rico wiped his eyes and said, "Bud, I thought I piledrove you a little too hard. Your brain's messed up worse than I thought."

"But what about the cancer?"

"Cancer?" Rico pointed at the octagon and laughed. "Only cancer I got's that lug-head in there waiting for me. New guy on the Knight Squad. Name's Claud. Get this, he claims to be descended from gladiators."

Gladiators?

I looked at the giant Italian with rock-like features a second time. He had all his fingers and no scars on his arms or face, but with blond hair, blue eyes, and the chiseled physique of a god, he looked like a clone of Claudius the Great. I had a sudden flashback to the great archway above the road leading to Golgotha. The last thing Claudius had said to me was, "We will meet again." I decided to keep that one to myself.

Charlie started talking, going on about my absence, and about all the trouble he'd had filling my shifts since I'd been gone, but his words trailed off as I pondered the sea of changes all around me. Another possibility entered my mind.

If Rico's still here, I'm still here, Charlie K is my supervisor, and an ancestor of Claudius the Great is standing in the ring right over there, then …

"Rico?" I said, my breath shallow. "What about Jim?"

"Stockbridge? Rico pulled off one of his sparring gloves and glanced at his wrist. A series of red LED numbers appeared—11:04. "I'd say he's at Moore Square preaching right about now. He never fights with us on Sundays. You know that."

I heard the scraping sound of a heavy steel door flying open. The front hallway flooded with sunlight as two shadows materialized in the glare. They stepped inside, and the door slammed shut behind them with a heavy, metallic ring that echoed through the arena. I watched them approach, their silhouettes growing larger and more defined as they drew closer. When they were about twenty yards away, my heart skipped a beat and I gasped.

It was a face I knew, yet it felt impossible in this new reality. Jim Stockbridge held out his hands, a wide grin breaking across his face, and said, "Hey, buddy. I heard you had quite an adventure."

Jim's name caught in my throat, a jagged lump of disbelief. I leaned over, my resolve finally fracturing, and broke into uncontrolled sobbing. The weight of the last few days—the confusion, the displacement, the sheer impossibility of it all—poured out of me.

I soon felt the presence of my friends closing in, a protective circle. I could feel the grounding weight of their hands on my shoulders as they offered quiet words of encouragement, anchoring me to a reality that finally felt like home.

"Jim?" I whispered. "You're alive."

"Why wouldn't I be?"

I opened my mouth to explain, but hesitated, choosing silence instead. My gaze shifted to the man beside Jim—a stranger with olive-toned skin and a cascade of black curls. His charcoal eyes held a quiet intensity, and his face seemed to radiate something beyond mere light. Though I had never seen him before, recognition struck me like a jolt of electricity from a wall outlet. He had to be the descendant of a healer I had met two thousand years ago. The son of another doctor I had encountered just days earlier. My breath caught in my throat.

"Luke?" I managed to say. "Luke Greco?"

"Is that a statement or a question?" Rico said.

"You're Loukas' son?"

"He's brain-damaged," Charlie added.

Rico released a loud, unrestrained burst of laughter. "Never should've dropped him on his head."

"Mike," Luke said. "You act like you don't know me, friend."

"I don't. I mean, I didn't, I just heard that you—"

"Mike," he said, "We've been working together for five years. Medic-seven, remember? And the Shroud?"

"The Shroud?"

They all gazed at me as if I had three heads. Luke took me by the shoulders and playfully shook me. "We have a new presentation called, What Killed the Man in the Shroud of Turin? We presented it last week at a conference in Florence, just before your accident. You don't remember that?"

"The guy that gave that lecture was named Grady. Patrick Grady."

Luke frowned. "You and I gave that keynote address, Mike."

I sighed. I could no longer speak.

"Whatever," Rico said, jumping in to add levity. "You two been down at Moore Square again preaching?"

"Yep." Jim put his arm around Luke's shoulder. "This guy is quite the evangelist."

"Lots of good gospel conversations and prayer," Luke added. "Speaking of which—" Luke placed his hand on my shoulder and bowed his head. "Lord Jesus," he said, boldly breaking into prayer. "Thank you for saving our good friend, Mike. Our brother in Christ. Our best friend for life." Rico prayed next, a prayer of thanksgiving and blessing. Jim thanked God for the gift of salvation and for bringing me home. And Charlie prayed that I'd be ready for work again soon so he could get me back on a truck. There was a moment of solemn silence, followed by a boisterous, concerted, "Amen!"

I opened my eyes and glanced around at the group—Jim, Rico, Charlie, and Luke. "Thank you, guys. For everything. It really is good to be home again."

"C'mon," Rico said, grabbing my arm. "Let's say hi to the group."

He introduced me around to the other guys at the gym. Claud shook my hand, but for the life of me, I couldn't remember him. But that made sense, didn't it? Everything changed when I went back in time—the butterfly effect. I thought of Claudius the Great and felt a tear well up in each eye. "One day," I said, gripping his outstretched hand. "I'll tell you a story about one of your forefathers. You've got great blood coursing through your veins, brother. Be proud."

The gym crowd gathered around and listened to an abbreviated version of my adventure, which I promised to finish later. Ramona and Simon walked in and said hello to everyone. It turns out they all know each other, too. Apparently, Ramona runs the place now.

After the crowd dissipated, two fighters climbed into the octagon and began a new sparring session. The spectators drew close to the electric blue-plasma fence and began to hoot and holler. I pulled Jim and Rico aside.

"This is too much," I said. "You both standing here." They stared at me, nodding patiently, probably not understanding, but pretending that they did. "I mean, I thought I'd lost you both."

There was an awkward pause before Rico replied, "Ramona said something about time travel?"

"Yeah," Jim added. "And a so-called butterfly effect? What's that all about?"

I glanced back and forth between my friends, as images popped in and out of my head. My mind broke under the weight of the memories. For a terrifying second, the smell of cordite filled the air, and I saw the crimson spray on the wall where Jim had fallen. Then the vision shifted, suffocating me with the sterile, sour scent of the hospice room where cancer had slowly hollowed out Rico's once-invincible body. The sudden adrenaline surge set my heart pounding like a trapped animal. I couldn't assimilate it—my body was reacting to a double funeral, while my eyes were staring at two living men.

But, no clouds appeared. There were no weird tastes, no colorful sounds—the seizures and synesthesia in me were apparently gone. I, too, had been changed—healed and set free by a man hanging on a cross. I took a deep breath to steady myself—another to slow down my heart. I felt amazed at the joy

I felt and the intense clarity of my mind as I stood there with my two best friends.

"Hey," I said, wiping a fresh set of tears from my eyes. "I've got so much to tell you guys."

"Well," Rico said, punching me in the arm. "Let's do it. How 'bout lunch at Sandy B's? It's your turn to buy, you know."

"Not today. I need to get home. It's been two-thousand years since I've seen the place."

"Right," Jim said, laughing out loud. "Grass will need to be cut."

"Hey!" I exclaimed, suddenly remembering my confusion at seeing a new sign hanging in front of the gym. "What happened to the Big Mike's sign? What's C and M's? "

A sudden voice sliced through the noise of the cheering crowd. "You forget me already, mate?"

I turned around to face a small Irishman with a crooked nose and sparkling green eyes. The once roughly crew-cut head had been shaved as slick as a cue ball, to match a freshly shaven face as pink as his arms. He wore creased khaki pants and a crisp black polo shirt with the logo of a penguin. He balled up his fists and assumed a fighting stance, but maintained a cordial grin that assured me it was all in jest. "You ready to brawl yet, Laddy?"

"Myers!"

The sudden appearance of my worst enemy caught me completely off-guard. My fists clenched as animal instinct took over, the heat of battle surging straight to my jaw. I stepped in to strike the man who had shot me, only to freeze. He didn't even flinch. There was a shattering calmness about him that completely derailed my momentum. No hostility, no panic—just an open, quiet curiosity.

I stared, paralyzed by the transformation of the man who had killed my friend Jim, and shot me. Corbin Myers' eyes, once wild with a terrifying, unpredictable fire, were soft. Grounded. Human. My breath caught in my throat as the violent urge evaporated from my muscles. I slowly lowered my hands, searching his gaze as the truth began to sink in. "You're different, too."

"What?" Myers said, staring at me, as if at a mirage. "Mike? Are you okay?"

"I, um … man, I don't know."

"Buddy," he said, laughing out loud. "I think they discharged you too soon."

"Myers, you shot Jim. You shot me. Then you turned the gun on yourself. But that can't be right."

"Mike, partner, old friend, I think you need a vacation."

"I don't know, man. I don't know anymore." I let out a breathless laugh, shook my head, and sighed. "Never mind. I mean, whatever. I mean, nothing makes sense to me anymore. Believe it or not, Corbin Myers," I said, grabbing him by the shoulders and shaking him, and then holding him at arm's length and gazing into his confused-looking face. "I don't really know you. But it is so nice to finally meet the real you!"

"Well, I have no idea what you're talking about, but thank you, partner. And it's good to have you back. We have a business to run."

I glanced at Jim and Rico for acknowledgement. They both nodded. "You mean this place? Wait a minute, the sign out front—c and m's fight club? That's—"

"You and me. Corbin and Mike's. It was your idea, chum."

"You know what," I said, with a deep, heavy sigh. "If I never witness another change in my life, it'll be too soon."

CHAPTER THIRTY-FOUR

Beaufort, North Carolina
Ramona's Tesla Model Z
Sunday, April 19—12:36 PM (EST)

It turns out Corbin Myers is a psychiatrist now. He has a history of schizophrenia—that hasn't changed—but he keeps it well controlled with medications and runs a successful business helping others find their way through mental illness. He and I started Big Mike's, well, um, make that C&M's, and have been close friends for years.

Rico has been healed of cancer by an experimental new drug developed by a pharmaceutical company in Greece, called—Loukas Industries. Who would've believed it? He's still a cop, fearless leader of the prestigious Knight Squad Anti-Gang Unit of the East Beach Police Department. And he's still the most powerful man I have ever met. Or is he? I pictured him in the ring with a guy named Crudelis. I wondered who would win that fight.

Charlie is my supervisor, and it only took a couple of weeks to realize I was actually a pretty good paramedic. For my first shift back, he threw me right into the fire, partnering me with Jim on Medic-7. Our very first tone was a cardiac arrest. Jim and I clicked immediately—no hesitation, just pure teamwork. We brought the guy back.

And Luke? What can I say about Luke? I liked the guy instantly. He's the spitting image of his great-great-great-whatever grandfather, a doctor named Loukas who, with my assistance, changed medical history with a few early inventions. And it turns out, Luke and I are the scheduled speakers at a world conference in Los Angeles next month—The Shroud of Turin, Matter Interpenetration and Image Formation Conclusions.

Would you believe we are the world's leading experts on the theory of image formation on the Shroud? It sounds absurd even saying it out loud. Yet, the physics of it—the precise math of radiation, cloth-to-body distance, and molecular degradation—is sitting in my head right now, as clear as my own name. Luke and I had done the research, compiled the data, and prepared the proofs, even though my hands couldn't remember writing a single line of it. I'm not sure exactly when or how I gained all this new knowledge about the Shroud. But then, I was there when they found it.

That truth anchored itself deep in my chest—the undeniable reality that God had sent me back through time to alter the course of history. Because of that miracle, my two best friends were alive. The man who had been my bitterest enemy was now my business partner. I had a new wife, a son, and a reputation as one of the world's leading experts on the Shroud of Turin—a distinction I shared with a brilliant new friend named Luke Greco. My old life was rapidly dissolving into a fading memory, replaced by a reality that was entirely, beautifully different.

The butterfly effect. Incredible.

I left the gym with my new family and had a quiet trip home. Simon made another wrong turn, making a left instead of right, toward the marshes of Crab Point instead of the Town of Beaufort.

"Where are we going now?" I said, not really sure I wanted to know.

"Home," Simon responded. "What do you mean?"

"Home's the other way, buddy. You're headed toward Crab Point."

"Dad, you confused, bro."

"Sweetheart," Ramona said, patting my knee. "Where do you think we live?"

I pictured our three-story home on our two-acre lot on the water in Beau Coast—the gated Beaufort community with its perfectly manicured Bermuda lawns, ancient live oaks, and private floating docks. I could almost see my Grady White 28-foot Coastal Explorer suspended in its boat lift, and my true pride and joy, the Bristol 38.8 sailboat I'd inherited from my dad, bobbing gently in the saltwater. Gloria and I had built a life there—we'd grilled, boated, and entertained, always planning to grow old in that slice of heaven. Yet the truth was finally taking hold. My old life wasn't coming back—it was just another lost dream drifting away in the wake of this new reality.

"Well—" I sighed. "I used to live at 223 Swan Court, but I have a feeling you're going to tell me I'm wrong."

"I wish," Simon said, with a grunt. "Sorry, but paramedics don't make that kinda money."

"Almost forgot," I said, with a dry chuckle. "So? Where exactly do we live?"

"Grandpa and grandma's old house."

"Next to the swamp?"

A flood of deep-seated memories rushed to the surface—flashbacks of happy times.

"I love that place! Some of my best memories are there. Grandpa's den always smelled like cedar planks. And grandma's kitchen was baked apple pies and fresh coffee. And the moment you stepped out back? Pure heaven—it was all oyster muck and salt air."

"That's it," Simon said. "Exactly."

"Grandpa was a shrimper," I said, the words spilling out before I could stop them. "I used to work the lines on the boat with him when I was a kid. He had this great little Boston Whaler runabout, too."

"We still got it, dad."

"Man, I spent hours on that thing when I was a boy. Me and my friends, Tommy and Herb, we'd putt around for hours with our cane poles, fishing for spots and flounder. Setting crab pots. So, then, we really do? We live in Grandpa's old house?"

"Sweetheart," Ramona said. "We've always lived here. We moved in when your grandparents died. We've been very happy here."

By early afternoon, we were finally home. Simon guided the car to the end of Shell Street, easing to a stop before a small white bungalow with its familiar red tin roof. I sat quietly for a moment, simply taking it in. It was just as I remembered—an unassuming, one-story cottage with clapboard plank siding and a sprawling front porch. Trails of Bermuda grass wove their way along both sides of the house, where bare earth met the reeds at the swamp's edge. The driveway remained unchanged, still layered with the crushed oyster shells I had once helped my grandfather spread as a child, leading straight to the modest one-car garage where he had kept his tools.

Simon lifted the garage door with an old-fashioned opener. My heart leapt with delight as my gaze landed on it—my canary yellow Dodge Challenger resting exactly where it belonged. "Thank you," I murmured. "I sure needed that."

Ramona led me inside, guiding me through the familiar space. The aroma of seasoned cedar filled my nostrils. The house felt snug. The low ceilings were a tight fit for a guy my size, and the carpet showed signs of age, begging for an update. But the kitchen appliances gleamed with a newness that gave the place a refreshed touch. The lighting made everything feel warm and inviting.

In the den, my eyes landed on the flat-screen TV mounted above the fireplace—an absolute marvel. A sleek pane of transparent glass, its display reminiscent of Greco's Screen, showcasing a striking digital image of a framed Caribbean landscape, with colors so vibrant I would have sworn I was in the BVIs. I sank into an unfamiliar chair, an old-fashioned leather recliner with a sturdy handle for propping up my feet.

"Hey, Simon," I said, settling in. "Where's the remote?"

"There's no remote. You can use A-bot. Hang on."

Simon turned on the screen, just by thinking it, I suppose. A second later the settings screen popped up. "Okay," he said. "Just say, A-bot, big screen, alpha hook-up."

I repeated what he had said, and immediately heard three soft, electronic beeps between my ears, followed by the familiar voice of my A-bot, saying:

Okay, Michael. You're all set. But remember, you changed my name to Martina, so from now on, you can call me that.

I chuckled and glanced at Simon. He shook his head and gave me a wink. "Welcome back to the future, dad."

After watching about 15 minutes of CNN and Fox News (still divided, still left v. right) Ramona led me out back to a small brick terrace adorned with climbing plants, and shaded by huge live oaks. It was a serene spot, perfect for enjoying the sea breeze and watching fishing boats come and go. I noticed a small wooden dock jutting out into the water between the reeds, where an 18-foot center-console boat floated alongside.

"That's grandpa's Whaler, right?"

"Grandma gave it to us when he died," Simon said. "We've done a lot of fishing in that thing."

"Are we still using cane poles?"

"Only occasionally, for kicks, when you bring out the shrimp and floating bobbers."

I chuckled. "I guess some things never change."

"So?" Ramona said, slipping her hand into mine. "What do you think, old man? Not too shabby?"

"Not too shabby." I inhaled a deep breath of the cool sea breeze. It smelled of oyster shells and muck, reminiscent of a pleasant childhood spent in the sound behind Morehead City. A smile came to my face. "I think I could learn to like this."

The three of us sat on the porch, deep in conversation for about thirty minutes. Simon spoke of his latest girlfriend, his job at the Beaufort boat docks, and his plan to enlist in the Marine Corps in the fall. Ramona filled me in on the gym, our friends, and the church we attended in town—my role as a deacon, and hers as the leader of the Wednesday night prayer team. There was so much to catch up on, but those first thirty minutes felt like the perfect beginning.

"You know," I said. "I still can't help but wonder if this wasn't all just a strange dream."

My wife smiled, and shrugged. "Oh," she said, handing me a padded, manila envelope. "I almost forgot. This arrived for you a couple of days ago. I think it's from Turin."

"Turin?"

It felt a little heavier than I had anticipated. The handwritten label was addressed to me, bearing a return address from Torino, Italy, and a priority postage stamp. The only person I initially associated with Turin was Greco, but then I remembered the others—Will Hendricks, the curator Dr. Gallo, and Nurse Martina. I held the envelope, staring at it with growing curiosity.

"What do you suppose this is?"

Ramona nudged me. "Well, open it, silly."

I opened the envelope and pulled out a handwritten note. I cleared my throat and began reading out loud:

"Mr. Peabody, I hope that you can find it in your heart to forgive me for the sin I have committed against you."

I glanced at Ramona, then shrugged and continued reading:

"I am returning two items that must be of great value to you. I am ashamed to admit that I took them after sedating you with midazolam while en route to the hospital. I have since realized the severity of my crime. Please understand that I am a struggling anesthetist with two children, no husband, and no other family. Life as a single working mother is almost impossible here. I saw in these items a way to finally provide for my children. Now I realize all I did was increase my guilt and sorrows.

"I also learned from you a most valuable lesson that has changed and saved my life. During the transport to Humanitas, you said something that made me pause. You said, 'Look at his face ... just look at his face and you will understand.' You were sedated at the time, so I'm not sure you were aware that you were speaking, but I knew what you meant. You meant, look at the Shroud. Look at the face of Jesus. Because of that, because of what you said, I have since given my life to Christ. And I plan to follow him for the rest of my life. And one day, I pray, you and I will meet again in heaven. Please accept my sincere apology for what I did to you, and do not hold a grudge against all Italians. Italians are good people. But, most of all, thank you! For leading me to the truth. For leading me to Jesus. Begging for your forgiveness."

"Oh, my word," Ramona exclaimed.

"It's signed, Paramedic Emma Esposito." I lowered the note and pictured Emma's face as she pushed the sedative into my IV. I remembered that she looked remorseful, as if she regretted something she was about to do. "Huh."

"Emma? Isn't she one of the paramedics who helped you?"

I nodded and tipped the envelope. With a heavy, metallic thud, a pristine chrome-and-silver Casio Tactical Rangeman G-Shock tumbled into my hand. I looked from the solar face to Ramona, completely blown away. "Are you kidding me? No way!"

Simon cocked his head, and said, "Isn't that a watch?"

"Best watch I ever had! I wondered what happened to this thing!"

"That thing's like a relic, bro. You've got an A-bot—you can't wear that."

"Watch me."

I slipped the Casio onto my wrist and locked the clasp. It felt heavy—a good, familiar kind of heavy. I suppose I hadn't realized just how much I'd missed it. But then, as I reached back in, my fingers caught on something else left inside the envelope. I pulled out a small, red-velvet pouch. Squeezing it, I could feel a metallic object hidden inside—round, flat, and instantly recognizable. I glanced up at Ramona, a sudden knot tightening in my stomach as I winced.

I hesitated, then slowly parted the pouch, my pulse quickening as I peered inside. A wave of dizziness overtook me—I could have fainted. My breathing stopped, suspended between awe and exhilaration. In that moment, certainty struck. I drew the small treasure from the bag and held it up to the light. Its surface shimmered—a crude, timeworn Roman coin minted with the unmistakable image of a shepherd's crook.

I gasped.

"Sweetheart?"

"Dad, didn't you say Peter gave you a coin?"

I nodded, too numb to speak.

"Oh, my!" Ramona drew a deep breath. "Michael? Michael, does that mean—"

I gasped, struggling to find my voice. Seconds passed before the words finally surfaced. "It means it wasn't a dream. I was really there."

I looked up at the ceiling, picturing the empty tomb, the burial cloth, and the moment Peter dropped the coin in my hand. Then my mind shifted to the cross, and the man hanging there by his pierced hands and feet. It's hard to wrap your head around someone having that much love—to just willingly give up his life for us like that. I could see his face in my mind, twisted in pain, and for a second, it felt like our eyes met. A sudden shiver ran straight down my spine.

"Crudelis was right," I whispered. "You *are* the Son of God."

"Mike," Ramona said. "Who is Crood-uh-liss?"

"Crudelis—" I closed my eyes and tried to picture the strong chiseled face of my enemy, and the fierceness with which he struck me when we first met on the street. "When I was in Jerusalem, I met a sadistic man. Hard. Tough. Very cruel. He was the Centurion in charge of the crucifixion." I paused for a moment to get my head straight. "At first, he was evil. My enemy.

He ruled with an iron fist—almost killed me in the garden. And for that, I hated him. But it was the way he laughed at him that made my blood boil."

"Michael?"

I could feel my throat tighten. I tasted salty tears as they ran down my cheeks to the corners of my mouth.

"He laughed when they drove the spikes into Jesus' wrists. He kicked him when he was down. He spat on him as he hung there. But when Jesus died, something changed. It was as if he suddenly realized his cruelty. He dropped to his knees at the foot of the cross and begged Jesus for forgiveness. 'Save me,' he said. 'I am a sinner.' And that was the moment I finally understood. Something deep inside, in my heart, told me what I had to do. I knelt beside him. I looked up at Jesus, and I asked him to forgive me. And together, this monster, this hardened killer and I … wept."

"Oh, Michael," Ramona cried, tears moistening her eyes. "That's beautiful."

"It was powerful."

"He saved you, dad."

"I'm not sure what that means, but I do feel changed. Different inside."

Ramona smiled. "Forgiven?"

"Yes—" I sighed. "I feel forgiven. But, also, confused. What do I do now? How do I start over? I've made so many mistakes, and hurt so many people."

"Honey—" Ramona grabbed my hand. "What's your heart telling you?"

I sighed and thought about it, and the name of a young medical resident surfaced, sharp and stinging. I could still see the way her face fell when I'd needlessly taunted her in front of the staff. How she had cried and run away from me. And the coldness I had felt toward her. I cringed at the realization that I had been her Crudelis—a cruel master of my small world. And like the historical Crudelis, my judgment had been as flawed as my character.

"First, I need to make things right with someone."

"Who?"

"Jenny Miller."

"Jenny Miller?"

"She's one of the new doctors at Regional. She was my resident, and I treated her like garbage."

"Michael, Jenny was never your resident—she's your doctor."

"My what?!"

"She's also Chief of Emergency Medicine, and Medical Director for East Beach EMS. And honey, you're not a doctor, anyway. Remember? You're a paramedic."

"That's what Greco tried to tell me."

"Well, he was right."

"I don't get it."

"You've always been a paramedic. Jenny isn't your student, honey, she's your boss."

I'd grown accustomed to the world shifting under my feet, but this one was a landslide. Jenny Miller? The mind-boggling truth didn't just hit me, it crushed me like a falling wall.

"Jenny Miller is my boss?"

I could only remember my old life, the arrogant physician who considered himself better than everyone else, always operating strictly for his own sake. So the realization that I wasn't a doctor after all, but a paramedic? Maybe justice had finally caught up with me—a man can only serve himself for so long.

I thought about what paramedics actually do—what my old friend Jim Stockbridge does every day—and suddenly, the North Carolina EMS protocols unspooled in my mind, stark and undeniable. The memory of running calls in the back of the rig with Jim emerged clear as crystal. I could smell the heavy exhaust of the diesel, feel the jarring hit of the potholes, and recall the exact flavor of queasiness that settles in when you're trying to start an IV or punch out a PCR on a moving truck.

I could feel it all. It wasn't just a memory—it was muscle memory.

"Rome," I said, turning and gazing into my wife's eyes. "I feel stuck, somewhere between my old life and my new one. What am I supposed to do?"

"Wait here—"

Ramona ducked inside the house and came back out a second later carrying a book. She slipped it into my hands—a worn, black, leather-bound Bible with fading gold edges. I looked down at the cover and caught sight of my own name stamped in gold at the bottom.

I stared at it, completely thrown. "This is mine?"

Ramona nodded. "You've had it as long as I've known you."

I opened the Bible and perused the pages, surprised to find yellow underlinings and small margin notes from cover to cover. It had clearly been well used over a period of many years. Suddenly, I felt a strange, deep yearning to turn to the Psalms—particularly Psalm 91. I read the first sentence silently, and then, with absolute clarity the next line surfaced in my mind. I quoted it aloud, as if I had known it for a lifetime. "I will say of the Lord, you are my refuge and my fortress—my God in whom I trust."

A sharp breath caught in my throat as I stared at Ramona. "How do I know this?"

"Michael, you have been reading that Bible since you were thirteen years old. You led me to Christ. Taught me how to read it."

"Me too," Simon said. "Dad, I'd be lost if not for you."

I lowered the Bible and shook my head. "I am so confused."

"Honey, we realize all of this is new to you. It will all come to you in time. Please remember, though, you won't have to walk through it alone. Simon and I will help you remember. And the Lord? He will teach you."

The weight of her words settled deep within me. He would teach me—of course he would. He was the Teacher, the one I had somehow always known as my Savior. In a world that had suddenly become completely unrecognizable, this single realization felt both inevitable and profound. It was the only thing in days that made perfect sense.

"Dad, there's something else," Simon said, startling me with the passion I saw in his eyes. "You need to tell your story. I mean, think about it—you're the only person in two thousand years who actually saw him on the cross. Do you even realize how insane of a gift that is?"

I inhaled deeply, as if it were my last. "I wouldn't know where to start."

Simon gestured with his hands, trying to piece it together. "Start with the Shroud. Tell 'em about Jerusalem—the people you met and what you saw happen to Jesus. I mean, Dad, what would He want you to say?"

I nodded slowly, contemplating the question—what would the Teacher want me to say? I felt the words forming in my chest, rising in my throat until they finally broke the surface. "I think He would want me to tell them the truth."

"And what is the truth?" Simon said, his face kind but hard.

I reflected on my journey—the faces I had encountered, the sorrow and suffering I had witnessed, and the way the Lord had used an ancient burial cloth to guide me to the cross. So much had changed, so many remarkable moments had unfolded. Yet, it was that singular, profound moment at the foot of the cross that made my heart pound—when I knelt beside Crudelis and vowed to follow Jesus Christ for the rest of my life. That was my moment of salvation. I looked at my son. Like mine, his eyes shimmered with unshed tears.

"Truth is, he loves us … so much he paid the ultimate price to save us."

I turned back toward the view behind my home, letting the vast stillness settle deep into my bones. Gone was the anger and arrogance and drive to succeed. There were no more dark clouds and seizures, nor the fear of grave, impending doom. I felt light and easy. At peace with myself and with God—finally at peace.

The air carried the faint, familiar scent of my childhood, yet the landscape had never looked quite this serene—a boundless, golden sea of reeds swaying gently before giving way to the sparkling green of the open water.

I rolled the ancient coin in my palm, awed by its incredible significance. A profound warmth swelled in my chest, replacing the ghosts of the past with a terrifying, beautiful certainty.

"To save me," I whispered to the wind. "Jesus saved me."

The End

www.ingramcontent.com/pod-product-compliance
Lightning Source LLC
Chambersburg PA
CBHW030515030826
49196CB00027B/139

* 9 7 8 1 9 6 5 6 4 9 1 5 2 *